Marion Lennox has written more than one hundred romances, and is published in over a hundred countries and thirty languages. Her multiple awards include the prestigious RITA® Award (twice), and the *RT Book Reviews* Career Achievement Award for 'a body of work which makes us laugh and teaches us about love'. Marion adores her family, her kayak, her dog—and lying on the beach with a book someone else has written. Heaven!

After writing more than eighty books for Mills & Boon, **Stella Bagwell** still finds it exciting to create new stories and bring her characters to life. She loves all things Western and has been married to her own real cowboy for forty-four years. Living on the south Texas coast, she also enjoys being outdoors and helping her husband care for the horses, cats and dog that call their small ranch home. The couple has one son, who teaches high school mathematics and is also an athletic director. Stella loves hearing from readers. They can contact her at stellabagwell@gmail.com.

ENGLISH LORD ON HER DOORSTEP

MARION LENNOX

THE LITTLE MAVERICK MATCHMAKER

STELLA BAGWELL

MILLS & BOON

First Published in Great Britain 2018
by Mills & Boon, an imprint of HarperCollinsPublishers,
1 London Bridge Street, London, SE1 9GF

English Lord on Her Doorstep © 2018 Marion Lennox
The Little Maverick Matchmaker © 2018 Harlequin Books S.A.

Special thanks and acknowledgement are given to Stella Bagwell for her contribution to the Montana Mavericks: The Lonelyhearts Ranch continuity.

ISBN: 978-0-263-26524-8

0918

MIX
Paper from
responsible sources
FSC™ C007454

FSC
www.fsc.org

This book is produced from independently certified FSC™
paper to ensure responsible forest management.

For more information visit: www.harpercollins.co.uk/green

Printed and bound in Spain
by CPI, Barcelona

ENGLISH LORD
ON HER
DOORSTEP

MARION LENNOX

To Olga and Olga.
With thanks for your friendship and your kindness,
and for your generosity in finding
my books so far away.

CHAPTER ONE

BRYN THOMAS MORGAN, Twelfth Baron Carlisle, Peer of the Realm, thought his week couldn't get worse. It could.

It said a lot for his state of mind—weary, horrified and disgusted—that while he searched in the rain and the dark to find the dog he'd just hit, his head was already rescheduling.

If the dog was dead, he'd take it to the local police station, explain how he'd hit it on a blind curve and let the locals look after their own.

His plane back to London was leaving in three hours and he had a two-hour drive in front of him. He had time to scrape a dead dog from the road and catch his flight.

But when he finally found the soggy heap of fur that had been thrown into the undergrowth, the dog was alive.

Despite being hit by an Italian supercar?

Twenty years ago, when he was a boy learning to drive the estate's four-by-four across the vast estates of Ballystone Hall, his father had told him never to swerve for an animal. 'You'll lose control,' he'd told him. 'Animals can usually judge distance and speed. If you swerve, they're more likely to be hit, not less, and there's a possibility you'll kill yourself, too.'

But this hadn't been a farm-vehicle-savvy calf, darting back to the herd, or a startled but nimble deer. This dog was a trudger: a dirty white, mid-sized mutt. It had been square in the centre of the country road, head down, looking almost as if a car coming around the bend would be doing it a favour by hitting it.

So of course Bryn had swerved, but the road was rain-washed and narrow. There hadn't been time or space to avoid it. Now it lay on the grass at the roadside, its hind leg bloody, its brown eyes a pool of pain and misery.

Bryn stooped over it and those eyes were saying, 'Kill me now.'

'You didn't think of taking pills,' Bryn said, but he said it gently. He liked dogs. He missed them.

But the dogs at home were currently being cared for by his mother and by the farm staff who valued them as they deserved. Not like this one. This dog looked as if it had been doing it tough for a while.

What to do?

He was trying to beat a storm that threatened to close the country down for a couple of days. A line-up of law-yers was waiting to meet him in London. He needed to get away from this mess and get back to Ballystone Hall, to the farm, to the cattle, to the work that filled his life. He also needed to finally accept the title he hated, and he still wasn't sure how to do that. The dreariness of the last months had hauled him close to the blackness he'd fought ever since…

No. Don't go there. Focus on getting on that flight.

But there was a dog. A bitch. Lying on the road. Bleed-ing.

It was a twenty-minute drive back to the last town. It was twenty-five minutes to the next.

It was eight o'clock at night.

The dog was looking at him as if she was expecting him to wield an axe.

'It's okay,' he told her, fondling the bedraggled ears. Forcing himself to think.

This was farming country, west of Melbourne. Where there were farms, there'd be a vet. He could ring ahead to warn he was coming, and pay whatever was needed to pass over the responsibility of taking care of her wounds and finding her owner.

But first he had to get her off the road. It was raining already and the distant rumbling of thunder threatened more.

The dog was bleeding. Blood was oozing rather than spurting, but it was enough to be worrying. He needed towels.

He was travelling light and a towel wasn't included in the sparse gear he carried. He was in Australia to try and distance his name from his uncle's financial mess. The debt collection agency was due to collect this car from the airport's valet parking tomorrow. It'd be a great look if they found it smeared with blood, he thought. That'd add even more drama to the mess that was his uncle's life.

'A pill would definitely have been easier,' he muttered to the dog, but he was already shrugging off his jacket, figuring how to edge it underneath so he could carry her. Then he headed back to the car to find a spare shirt to wrap the leg.

'Okay, dog, hopefully it's only your leg that's damaged,' he told her as he worked. 'I'll ring ahead to the next town and have the vet meet me. Let's get you safe and warm before the eye of this storm hits. I might need to break the odd speed limit but I can still catch my plane.'

Charlotte Foster—Charlie except when she was with clients—didn't like storms, though maybe that was putting it too lightly. In her neat little interior-design studio back in Melbourne, with solid town houses on either side, she could pull the blinds, put something loud on the sound system and pretend storms didn't happen. Here, though, she was in a dilapidated farmhouse with a rusty tin roof, she had no neighbours for miles and she was surrounded by dogs who were already edgy.

If Grandma were here she'd sneak into bed with her. How many times had she done that as a little girl? This place had been her refuge, her time out. Grandma had scooped her up every school holidays and brought her back here, surrounding her with dogs, chaos, love.

She sniffed.

Charlie wasn't a sniffer but she'd been sniffing for weeks now, and sometimes even more than sniffing.

Grandma…

There was a hole in her heart a mile wide.

The dogs, too, were acting as if the bottom had dropped from their world, as indeed it had. In the weeks she'd been here Charlie still hadn't figured what to do with them. They were rejects, collected over the years by Betty who hadn't been able to say no to anyone. To anything.

Charlie still didn't know what would happen to them. There was no way she could take six dogs back to her studio-cum-bedsit—seven if you counted Flossie, although she'd almost given up on Flossie.

Betty's note was still haunting her. That last night…she must have felt it coming. Pain in her chest? Breathlessness? Who knew? Whatever, instead of doing the sensible thing and calling an ambulance straight away, she'd sat down and written instructions for Charlie.

You know most of this but just to remind you of details.

Possum is a sort of fox terrier. Nine years old. Loves his black and white sock more than anything. There are spares in my bottom drawer in case of disaster.

Fred's a part-basset, part-vacuum-cleaner. He'll

eat anything on the basis he can bring it up later if it's not edible.

Don't let him near Possum's sock!

And so on.

But then, at the end…

Flossie's a sweetheart, but needy. You met her last time you came. She's only been with me for two months, dumped on the road near here. I need to keep her secure because any chance she gets she's off down the road, trying to find the low life who abandoned her.

Charlie had spent the last weeks caring for the dogs and other animals. Trying to figure a solution to the financial mess. Wanting to kill the scumbag who'd fleeced her grandma. Trying to block out the memory of her own stupidity, which meant she had no resources to help now. Her grief for the gentle Betty had been a constant ache throughout, but adding to it was the fact that when Betty had finally called the ambulance, the paramedics had left the gate open.

Somewhere out there was a lost dog called Flossie.

Charlie had enough on her plate with six dogs she needed to rehome. Flossie surely must be someone else's problem by now, but, still, she'd searched. She'd hoped. Betty would expect her to. Now, as the storm closed in, the thought of a lost Flossie was breaking her heart.

'You guys can all come into bed with me until it's over,' she told the dogs, who were getting more nervous as the sound of thunder increased.

Flossie… She'd be out there somewhere…

'I've looked,' she said out loud, defiantly, to a grandma who could no longer hear. To Betty, who she'd buried with grief and with love ten days ago. 'I've done all I can, Grandma. Now it's time for me to bury my head under my pillows and get through this storm without you.'

Yallinghup was the town ahead. It had a vet who was currently somewhere in a paddock with a cow in labour. He could hear the sound of wind in the background when she answered the phone. 'I can meet you in an hour or so,' she'd said brusquely. 'Probably. Depends when this lady delivers. I'll ring you back when we're done.'

Carlsbrook was the town behind. 'Dr Sanders is on leave,' the not so helpful message bank told him. 'In case of emergency please ring the veterinarian at Yallinghup.'

The dog was now lying on his passenger seat, looking up at him with huge, scared eyes.

Okay, next step…or maybe it should have been the first step. Find the owner. However, this wasn't exactly suburbia, with lots of houses to door-knock. This was farming country, with houses set back behind towering gum trees. He couldn't remember passing a house for the last couple of miles.

'But you must have come from somewhere,' he told the dog and fondled her ears again while he located her collar.

Flossie.

No more information. Great.

'Okay, next farmhouse,' he muttered and hit the ignition. 'Please let it be your owner, or at least someone who'll understand that I need to be gone.'

She really, really didn't like storms. She didn't like the dark.

She didn't like anything about this.

She should feel at home. She'd been coming here since she was a little girl, every school holidays, and she'd loved being here, helping Betty with the dogs, the chooks, the myriad animals Betty had housed and cared for.

She loved this place, but it was love of Betty that made her keep visiting, and it was that love that was making her stay now.

Three weeks ago Charlie had been finally starting to get over the mess her own life had become. She'd been scraping a living as an interior designer. That living had depended on her being at her studio to receive clients, but she couldn't be there now—because of Betty.

And Betty would never be here again. That was enough to make her feel desolate, even without thunderstorms. Now… There'd been five huge claps of thunder already and the rain was turning to a torrent, smashing against the tin roof so loudly it made her shudder. She needed to bolt for the bedroom and hunker down with the dogs.

But then…

Someone was knocking at the front door.

What the…?

Normally a knock at the front door would have meant an explosion of canine excitement but there was no excitement now. Charlie was in the farmhouse kitchen, and the dogs were lined up behind her, as if Charlie were all that stood between them and the end of the world.

Or the stranger at the door?

For there was someone there. What she'd assumed was lightning must have been car lights sweeping up the drive.

Who? Every local knew that Betty was dead. The funeral had seen almost the entire district turn out, but since then she'd been left alone. It was assumed she was here to put the place on the market and move back to the city.

She wasn't one of them.

So now… It was dark. It was scary.

Someone was knocking.

Weren't dogs supposed to protect?

'You guys come with me,' she muttered and grabbed Caesar and Dottie by the collars. Caesar was mostly wolf-hound. Dottie was mostly Dalmatian. They were both cowards but at least they were big, and surely that had to count for something?

She hauled them into the hall. The knocker sounded again over the rumble of more thunder.

She had a dog in each hand. Four more dogs were supposed to be lined up behind her. Or not. Three had retreated to the living room. She could see three tails sticking out from under the ancient settee. Only Mothball remained. Mothball was a Maltese-shih-tzu-something, a ball of white fluff, not much bigger than Charlie's hand, but what she lacked in size she made up for in heroics. She was bouncing around Caesar and Dottie as if to say, I'm here, too, guys. But Caesar and Dottie were straining back, wanting to add their tails to the settee pack.

Nothing doing.

'Who's there?' Charlie managed, thinking as she said it, Is an axe murderer going to identify himself?

'My name's Bryn Morgan.' The voice was deep, imperative, sure. 'I'm hoping you might be able to help me. I have an injured dog here and I hope you can tell me where I might find the owner. The name tag says Flossie.'

Flossie? She let her breath out in one long rush. Flossie!

'Please,' she said out loud, a prayer to herself, to Grandma, to anyone who might listen, and she opened the door to hope.

The house was two storeys of ramshackle. The veranda was wide and wobbly. Floorboards had creaked and sagged as he'd crossed it, and the line-up of saggy, baggy settees along its length added to its impression of something straight out of Ma and Pa Kettle. Or maybe the Addams family, Bryn thought ruefully, as a sheet of lightning seared the sky before he was plunged into darkness again.

And then the door opened.

Light flooded from the hallway within. Dogs surged forward, though not lunging, simply heading for a sniff and welcome—though there was a warning yip by an ankle-sized fluffball.

And behind them was a woman. Youngish. Late twenties? She was short, five feet four or so, with bright copper curls tumbling around a face devoid of make-up. She looked a bit pale. Her eyes were wide…frightened? She was wearing faded jeans and a huge crimson sweater. Bare feet.

She was looking straight past him.

'Flossie,' she said and her voice held all the hope in the world.

Thank you, he breathed to whoever it was who was looking after stranded and stressed gentry in this back-of-beyond place. To have lucked on the owner… He could hand her over and leave.

'You have Flossie?' she demanded, her voice choking. 'Where?'

'She's in my car,' he said, apologetically. 'I'm so sorry but I've hit her.'

'You've hit…' He heard the catch of dread. 'She's not dead?'

'She's not dead.' He said it strongly, needing to wipe that look of fear from her face. 'She's hurt her leg but I can't see any other injuries and her breathing seems okay. I'm hoping the wheel skimmed her leg and nothing else was injured. But the vet—'

'That's Hannah Tindall. Yallingup. I have her number.' She was already reaching for the phone in her back pocket. 'I'll take her straight—'

'Hannah's delivering a calf,' he told her. 'She should be through in about an hour. The vet at Carlsbrook's on leave.'

'You've already rung?' She took a breath and then another. 'Thank you. I…is she in your car?' She stepped towards him, past him, heading into the rain.

He was wet. She wasn't, and Flossie had already shown she was amenable to him carrying her. There was no reason for both of them to get soaked. He moved to block her.

'Find some towels,' he told her, gently now as if he was treating two shocked creatures instead of one. As maybe he was. 'Do you have a fire? She's wet and I think she needs to be warm.'

'I…yes. The kitchen… I have the range on…'

'Go grab towels and I'll bring her in,' he said and then hesitated. 'That is, if it's okay?' He looked past her into the hall. 'Do you have anyone to help?'

'I…' She took another deep breath and visibly regrouped. 'No, but it's okay. Of course it is. Please bring her in. Thank you so much.' Her voice broke a little. 'Oh, Flossie…'

She disappeared, almost running, into the back of the house, leaving the door wide and Bryn thought…what had he just asked her to do?

He wasn't thinking. The chaos of the last weeks had pretty much robbed him of logical thought.

He shouldn't have asked for access to the home of a solitary woman late at night. She'd run for towels and left him in the doorway, with total trust.

Trust. There was a word that had been lacking in his life for the last weeks. The days of interrogation, the sick sensation in his gut as he'd realised the extent of his uncle's dishonesty, the appalling feeling as he'd checked the local media…they'd made him feel as if he were smeared with the same smutty tar brush as his uncle. Yet here he was, in this woman's home, totally trusted. He should go give her a talk on trust and where it could lead—but she was trusting for a reason and he needed to honour it.

He headed back into the rain, which seemed to be increasing in intensity by the moment, gathered one injured pooch carefully in his arms and carried her inside.

The dog seemed limp, listless. Her bones were sticking out of her ribcage. If the woman hadn't been surrounded by visibly well-cared-for dogs he'd have suspected neglect but there was no neglect here. As he walked back into the hall she reappeared with her arms full of towels. She dropped them as she saw the dog in his arms—and burst into tears.

'Oh, Flossie…' She was sensible though, he thought. She didn't rush to hug. She came close and touched the dog behind her ear, a feather-touch. 'We thought we'd lost you. Oh, Grandma…' And then she hauled herself together, stooped and gathered the towels again and led the way into the kitchen.

It was a great kitchen. A farmhouse kitchen in the very best sense of the words. It was cosy and faded, with worn linoleum, an ancient wooden table and random wooden chairs with cheerful, non-matching cushions tied to each with frayed gingham bows. An ancient dresser took up almost the length of one wall and the opposite wall held the range and an extra electric oven—presumably for days when it was too hot to light the fire. The range was lit now, its gentle heat a welcome all on its own. A tatty, faded rug stood before the range and an ancient settee stood to one side. There were photographs stuck randomly to the remaining wall space, dogs, dogs and more dogs, plus the odd faded family shot. A guy in khaki took pride of place in the photograph display but the dog pictures were edging in, overlapping, as if the soldier's memory was being gradually overlaid by woofers.

Something was simmering on the stove. Something meaty and herby.

The whole effect was so comforting, so far from the bleakness of the last few days—so reminiscent of home?— he stopped dead in the doorway and had to take a moment to take it in. Which was used to good effect as the woman darted forward and hauled the settee closer to the fire.

'Put her down here. Oh, Flossie…'

And Flossie gave an almost imperceptible wiggle of her tail, as if she too recognised the kitchen for what it was. A sanctuary, a place almost out of this world. A time capsule where everything in it seemed safe.

He caught himself. Dog. Settee. He walked forward and settled her with care on the towels the woman laid out. Flossie's tail wagged again as her body felt the comfort of the settee and she looked adoringly up at the woman hovering beside her.

'Oh, Flossie…' the woman murmured again. 'What have you done to yourself?'

'I can't see anything obvious apart from the leg,' Bryn told her. 'I'm not sure if it's broken or not.' It was badly grazed, still sluggishly bleeding. 'I can't feel anything else but she hasn't moved.'

'It could be shock,' the girl said. 'And hunger. She's been missing for three weeks.'

'Three weeks!'

'I know.' She shook her head. Her fingers were running lightly over the dog's sides, watching for reaction. 'She's a stray, dumped here a couple of months back. People do that—toe-rags. They don't want an animal so they think, I know, we'll dump it outside a farm. And of course everyone knows Grandma takes strays in. So Flossie was dumped but she must still remember being thrown from the car. So off she went and I've looked so hard…'

The emotion he heard in her voice was for a stray dog she'd only known for weeks?

'That's your jacket underneath her,' she said, seeming to

notice the soft leather for the first time. 'Oh, heavens, it'll be ruined. I'll get it out for you... I don't know... Can I give you something towards cleaning?' She paused and seemed to regroup. 'Sorry. I'm not thinking clearly.' She took a deep breath. 'I'm Charlie Foster, by the way. Charlotte. You're... Bryn Morgan, did you say? I'm very pleased to meet you and I'm deeply thankful for your help, but I can manage now. I'll ring the vet as soon as she's available. Once Flossie's cleaned and fed, though, I'm hoping I might not need her. You've done...great. Thank you so much.'

She moved to edge the jacket out but he stopped her. 'Leave it.'

'You don't want your jacket?'

Um...not. Carrying a blood-soaked jacket back to the UK...it was a good one but not that good. 'It's fine,' he told her. 'Are you sure you're all right here? Your grandmother...'

'I'm fine.' She straightened and reached out and took his hand, shaking it with a firmness that told him this was a woman of decision. 'You've been fabulous, Mr Morgan, but there's nothing more you can do. I won't keep you any more.'

Great. He could step away, head back to the car. He could even make it to the airport in time.

'You're sure you'll be okay?'

'I don't think there's anything more you can do.' Which wasn't quite answering the question, but he agreed with her. The dog's tail was wagging, feebly but with every indication that warmth and food and medical care to her leg would see her recover. There was nothing more he could do, and he had a plane to catch.

'I'll see myself out, then.'

'Thank you so much.'

The hand clasping his... It was a clasp of friendship and gratitude and it made him feel...

Like he hadn't felt for a very long time. Not since he'd left home.

Maybe not even then.

He looked down at her, at her tumbled curls, at her face, devoid of make-up, flushed now with the warmth of the fire, her brown eyes direct and clear. She was smiling at him. She was half a head shorter than he was.

She made him feel...

He didn't have time to feel. He had a plane to catch.

'Good luck,' he told her, and on impulse he grabbed a pen lying on the table and wrote his name and email address on a pad that was clearly used for shopping lists. 'Will you let me know how things go? And if there are any veterinarian bills... I hit her. I'm more than happy to cover them.'

Something flashed over her face that might have been relief but was quickly squashed. 'It's okay. It wasn't your fault.'

'But you will let me know.' He took her hand again. It seemed strangely imperative that he didn't release it until he had her agreement. To head off and not hear anything seemed the pits.

'I will let you know,' she said and tugged her hand away and that was that.

He turned and headed back out into the night.

Why had it been so hard to tug her hand back?

It was the dark, she told herself. Plus the storm. Plus the fact that she had an injured dog on her hands and she wasn't as sure of treating her as she'd told the guy... Bryn.

Anyone would want company on such a night, she told herself, but there was a blatant, very female part of her that told her that what she was feeling was more than that.

The guy was gorgeous. More than gorgeous. He was tall, clean-shaven, dark hair, a ripped and tanned body, wearing good chinos and a quality shirt open at the throat. His voice had been lovely, deep, gravelly, English, with just a hint of an accent that might have been...something? Welsh, maybe. That'd fit with his name. Bryn. Nice name.

He'd been carrying her beloved Flossie with tenderness. There was enough in all those things to make her think... hormonal stuff, and he'd looked at her with such concern... He'd smiled, a lopsided smile that said it was sensible to leave but he didn't like leaving her alone.

The smile behind those dark, deep-set eyes was enough to make a girl's toes curl.

But men who made Charlie's toes curl had no place in her life. She'd been down that road, and never again. Besides, a woman had other things to do than stand here and feel her toes curl. Bryn was heading out of her life, and she had an injured dog to attend to.

But life had other plans.

She turned back and stooped over Flossie just as a vast sheet of lightning made the windows flash with almost supernatural light. There was a fearful crash, thunder and lightning hitting almost simultaneously. And then... extending into the night...something more. A splintering crash of timber.

There was a moment's pause, and then something crashed down, so hard the house shook, and her feet trembled under her. Every light went out. The dogs came flying from wherever they'd been and huddled in a terrified mass around her legs. She knelt and gathered as many of them into her arms as she could.

It must be a tree, she told herself. One of the giant red gums in the driveway must have come down. And then she thought... Bryn. Dear God, Bryn... He was out in that. Almost before the thought hit, she was on her feet, shoving the dogs aside, heading through the darkness to the outside door...

And just as she reached it, it swung open.

'Charlie?'

Light was flickering through the doorway, lighting his silhouette. A tree on fire? She couldn't see enough to make out his features, but she could see his form and she could hear.

'Bryn…' She backed away, almost in fright, and the dogs gathered again around her legs. She stooped to hug them again, more to give herself time to recover than to comfort them. For what she really wanted was to hug the man in the doorway. For an awful moment she'd had visions of him…

Don't go there. The vision had been so appalling it still had her shaking.

'I'm very sorry,' he said and he sounded it. 'But there's now a tree across the driveway.'

'Are you okay?' Her voice wasn't working right. 'You're not hurt?'

'Not a scratch.' He said it surely, strongly, as if he realised how scared she must have been. 'But I appear to be stuck. Unless there's another road out? I'm so sorry.'

For heaven's sake… He'd brought her dog home. He'd almost been killed by one of the trees she'd told her grandmother over and over were too close to the house. And *he* was apologising?

'There's no way out while it's pouring,' she told him. 'I…the paddocks will be flooding. And those trees…red gums…they're sometimes called widow makers.'

She caught a decent sight of him as the next flash of lightning lit the sky. He was wet, she noticed. He must have been wet before this. She'd been too caught up with Flossie to notice anything except how…

Um…she wasn't going there.

In fact she was having trouble going anywhere. She

was having trouble getting her thoughts to line up in any sort of order.

'Widow makers?' he queried, helpfully, and she struggled to pull herself together. She rose and faced him, or she faced the shadow of him. Every light was gone but the lightning was so continuous she could make him out.

'That's what they're called. The trees. River red gums. They're notorious. They drop branches, often on hot, windless days, when it's least expected. They look beautiful and shady and people camp under them.'

'Or park under them?'

'Yeah, and bang…'

'It's not exactly a hot, windless day.'

'No, but they're so tall they're the first thing that lightning strikes and Grandma won't…wouldn't…clear the ones near the house. Even the dead ones. She says they made nesting sites for parrots and possums. She says… She said…'

And then she stopped.

'Said,' Bryn said at last, very gently, and she flinched.

'I…yes. A heart attack, three weeks ago. That's why… that's why I'm here. These are Grandma's dogs.'

'So you are here alone.'

She shouldn't say it. It was really dark. He was nothing but a shadow in the doorway.

She should tell him she had a bevy of brawny men sleeping off a night at the pub upstairs.

She didn't.

'Yeah,' she said. 'And I'm not very good with storms.'

'Neither am I,' he told her. 'Do you have a lamp? Torches?'

'I…yes.' Of course she did. Or Grandma did. This was a solitary country house, with trees all around. Power outages were common, happening often when Charlie was visiting.

Not as scary as this one though.

She fumbled her way back into the kitchen, to the side-board, and produced a kerosene lamp. It was older even than Grandma, she thought. Lit, though, it produced a satisfactory light.

Bryn hadn't followed her into the kitchen. He'd stopped at the door, a darkened, watchful shadow.

Her fingers trembled as she lit the wick and re-laced the glass, and he saw.

'Charlie, I'm safe as houses,' he said gently. He thought about that for a moment and then he smiled, finally coming further into the room to inspect her handiwork. His voice gentled still further. 'I am safe,' he repeated. 'In fact, I'm even safer than houses that have red gums all around them. You think anything's likely to crash down on our heads? You think we should evacuate?'

She adjusted the wick until it stopped smoking, then turned back to the sideboard to find more. Grandma had half a dozen of these beauties, filled and ready to go.

The good thing about that was that she didn't have to look up. She could play with the lamps on the sideboard. She could speak without looking at him, which seemed... important. 'It seems...more dangerous to leave,' she managed. 'Even if there was a way out. And they say lightning doesn't strike twice in the same place.'

'There seem to be a lot of trees,' he said doubtfully. 'Do you think *same place* includes every tree less than twenty feet from the house?'

Oh, for heaven's sake... She swung around and glared. 'Mr Morgan, it seems...it seems you're stuck here for the night. I'm very grateful, and I'm not scared of you. But I am scared of storms. So while I'm happy to give you a bed for the night, supper, a place by the fire, it's predicated on you manning up and saying things like, "She'll be right," and, "What's a little lightning?" and, I don't know, "Singing in the rain" kind of stuff. So if you dare tell me there's a snowball's chance in a bushfire that another tree will come down and squash me, then you can step right out in the rain and take your chances. So what's it to be?' And she put her hands on her hips, jutted her chin and fixed him with such a look…

It was a look that even made him chuckle.

And imperceptibly his mood lightened. His night was messed up. More than his night. All he wanted was to be back at Ballystone, home with his dogs and his cattle, with this disaster behind him. He should be glowering himself.

Instead he found himself grinning at the red-headed firebrand in front of him, and searching for words to make him…what had she demanded? Man up?

'Don't take no notice of me, ma'am,' he drawled, still grinning, searching for a voice that might match the description. 'Yep, one of those tiddly little trees might fall but if it do, I'll be out there catching it with one hand and using it as kindling for your stove. You need more kindling? Maybe I could go out and haul in that tiddler that just fell.'

Their eyes locked. Her defiance gave way. A dimple appeared, right by the corner of her mouth, and the laughter he'd tried for was reflected in her eyes.

'What if I say yes?' she ventured, a tiny chuckle preceding her words.

'Your wish is my command,' he said nobly and then looked out to where he could see the ruins of the vast tree smouldering and sparking across the driveway. 'I might need a pair of heatproof gloves, though. That tree looks hot.'

And gloriously, she gave a full-on chuckle. It was a good laugh, an excellent laugh, and it produced a flash of insight. Looking at her, at the signs of strain around her eyes, at her pale face, he thought it'd been a while since this woman laughed.

It felt good…no, it felt excellent that he'd been able to make it happen.

'You want help with Flossie?' he asked, bringing reality back into the room, but the smile stayed behind her eyes as she answered.

'Yes, please. I would. Do you know much about dogs?'

'I've had dogs all my life.' He hesitated, still trying to keep that smile on her face. 'But is it manly to confess I faint at the sight of blood?'

'You carried her in. There's blood on your shirt.' It was an accusation.

'So I did,' he said, sounding astounded. 'And so there is, and I haven't fainted at all. Let's try this new world order out, then, shall we? Let's get your Flossie bandaged before my manliness fades before my very eyes. Okay, Nurse, I require more light, hot water, soap, um…'

'Bandages?'

'Of course, bandages,' he said and grinned and then looked down at Flossie, waiting patiently before the stove. 'And do you have a little dog food? A water bowl? I don't know how long it is since she's eaten but I'm guessing that may be the first priority.'

It was the first priority. She headed for the fridge to find some meat but her head wasn't entirely focussed on the first priority.

This man behind her was…beautiful.

CHAPTER TWO

ON CLOSE EXAMINATION Bryn decided Flossie's leg was probably not broken. She'd lost a lot of fur. An abrasion ran the full length from hip to paw but she was passive as Bryn cleaned, and when he tentatively tested the joint she barely whimpered.

She did, though, react with extraordinary speed when Charlie produced a little chopped chicken. And then a little more. She wolfed it down and lay back, limp again, but with her eyes fixed adoringly on Charlie. Her one true love.

'That's hardly fair,' Bryn objected. 'I get the messy part and you get the kudos.' He snipped off the bandage he'd been winding and looked at dog and girl. Charlie's nose was almost touching Flossie's. Her curls were tumbling over the dog's head. Flossie looked as if she hadn't seen a bath for months but Charlie seemed oblivious. Germs obviously weren't worthy of a mention.

'She could do with a wash,' he said and Charlie looked at him with the scorn he obviously deserved.

'You're suggesting we undo that nice white bandage, take her away from the fire and dump her in a tub.'

Flossie was looking at him, too, and the reproach in both their eyes...

Once again he had that urge to chuckle. Which felt good. Bryn Morgan hadn't chuckled in a long time.

He rubbed Flossie behind the ears. With the thunderstorm receding to a distant rumble, the complete doggy tribe was in the kitchen, nosing around with interest. A couple edged in for an ear-rub as well and suddenly he had a line-up.

'You can't pat one without patting all of them,' Charlie said serenely and once again he heard that chuckle.

It was a gorgeous chuckle. It made him…

Um, not. He had enough complications on his plate without going there. What was in front of him now?

He was sitting on faded kitchen linoleum before an ancient range, vintage kerosene lamps throwing out inefficient light but enough to show the raggle-taggle line-up of misbegotten mutts waiting to have their ears rubbed. While a woman watched on and smiled. While outside…

Um…outside. You could buy a house for the price of the car he'd been driving. How was he going to explain that one?

'I have a good, thick soup on the stove,' Charlie said, interrupting thoughts of irate bankruptcy trustees and debt collectors and car salesmen who still hardly believed in his innocence.

He focussed on the dogs instead. Would there be jealousy if he spent say one and a half minutes on Dog One and then two on Dog Two? He decided not to risk it and checked his watch. Charlie noticed and smiled.

'Do you have overnight gear in the car?' she asked. 'I could lend you an umbrella.'

That hauled him back to the practical. Overnight. Of course. He was genuinely stuck here. There were all sorts of problems he should be facing rather than how many seconds he'd been rubbing Dog One.

One of those was where his overnight gear was right now.

'You have a spare bed?' he asked, cautiously.

'I do. I'll put you at the back of the house to give you a

little peace because the dogs sleep with me. Except Possum. She usually sleeps by the back door. She's my guard dog but if there's any more lightning she'll be in with me. And Flossie will definitely be with me.'

'You'll sleep with Flossie?' She really was filthy.

'I'm sure it's good, clean dirt,' she said cheerfully. 'And I can't tell you how much I've worried about her. If I had half a kingdom I'd hand it to you right now.'

'Do you have a spare toothbrush instead?'

She blinked. 'Pardon?'

'I'm a bit averse to lightning,' he confessed. 'I'm happy for my overnight gear to stay where it is.' Wherever that was. Under one enormous tree.

He should tell her, he thought, but she was pale enough already and the knowledge that he'd been two seconds from climbing into the car and being pancaked was something she didn't need to hear about tonight.

He didn't want to think about it tonight.

'I do have a spare toothbrush,' she told him. 'I was at a conference in a gorgeous hotel…some time ago…' In another life. Moving on… 'The free toothbrush was so beautifully packaged I stuck it in my toilet bag. If you don't mind pink sparkle, it's yours.

'You'd give up pink sparkle for me?'

'I said you deserve half my kingdom,' she said and she was suddenly solemn. 'I mean it.'

'Then let's go with one toothbrush, one bowl of soup and a bed for the night,' he told her. 'I'll ask for nothing more.'

'Excellent,' she said and shifted across to help with the ear scratching. 'Soup and toothbrush and I don't know about you but I'm thinking bed's next on the agenda.'

Her arm brushed his and with the touch… Things changed.

The tension was suddenly almost palpable. Were both of them thinking the same?

'In your dreams,' she said, sounding breathless.

Of all the stupid… Were the tensions between them so obvious? And she caught it. 'I didn't mean…you know I didn't mean…' she stammered.

'I wasn't thinking,' he said, blankly, but he was lying.

'Yes, you were.'

'If I was, I shouldn't have.'

'I know nothing about you,' she said and then caught herself. 'But even if I did…'

'I'm a farmer from the UK,' he told her, feeling a sudden urge to explain himself. Get things on a solid basis. 'Thirty-five years old, here on family business. I'm heading back to London tomorrow.'

'It still doesn't mean I'm going to bed with you.'

'Of course it doesn't.' He managed a lopsided smile. What was it about the night that was making things so off kilter? 'Maybe electrical storms act like oysters,' he tried. 'But we're grown-ups now. We can handle it.'

'Yeah,' she said but sounded doubtful.

'So let's do introductions only,' he said, trying to sound firm. 'We'll get this on a solid basis. Not as a preamble to anything else. Just to clear the air.' More, he didn't want to make it complicated. Keep it simple, he told himself, and did. 'I've said I'm a farmer. I live a couple of miles from the Welsh border and I've been out here because my uncle's…'

That brought him up. How to explain Thomas? He couldn't. Not tonight. Hopefully not ever. He didn't even want to think of Thomas. 'My uncle's been living locally for a while,' he said at last. 'He's moved on, but I needed to deal with things he left behind. But it's done now. What about you?'

She looked at him doubtfully, as if she wasn't sure who he was and what on earth was happening. Which was pretty much how he was feeling. Tensions were zinging back and forth that had nothing to do with the lightning outside. Or maybe they did. Electricity did all sorts of weird things.

Like make him want…

Or not.

'I'm an interior designer,' she said at last. 'I had… I have my own business in Melbourne. But right now I'm baby-sitting seven dogs, two cows and fifteen chooks, trying to find them homes. Waiting for a miracle, which is not going to happen. Meanwhile, Mr Morgan, I have things to do, and not a single one of them involves thinking inappropriate thoughts about anyone, much less you. So you get these ears scratched and I'll get the soup on and we'll go from there.'

'And I'll be gone in the morning.'

'Of course you will,' she said briskly. 'Just as soon as I…' And then she faltered. 'I'm sorry. The tree…it'll take money to get that cleared.' But then her face cleared. 'It's okay though. As long as your car has decent clearance and the paddocks don't flood too badly, we can cut through a few strands of fencing and get you out across the pad-docks.'

Decent clearance…right.

'We'll worry about it in the morning,' he said and she sighed.

'That's my mantra.' She rose stiffly to her feet and looked down at him in the dim light. 'That's what I tell my-self every night…worry about it in the morning. Wouldn't it be wonderful if I didn't have to?'

The first storm front passed. The wind and thunder and lightning eased. Bryn slept solidly, in a decent bed, a hun-dred times better than the hard-as-nails motel bed he'd stayed in for the last few days. Carlsbrook was a one-pub, one-general-store town and why his uncle had set up base there…

But he knew why. Carlsbrook was a far cry from the resort-style lifestyle his uncle favoured but it was a district of smallholdings, of farmers proud of their cattle. It also had an aging population and sparse and difficult Internet connection, a district often cut off from the outside world.

It was a population ripe for his uncle's scumbag activities.

But tonight he hardly thought about his uncle. He slept deeply, in an ancient four-poster bed on the second floor, while the wind whirled around the ancient weatherboards and trees creaked and groaned. There was something about this house, this home… The dogs.

This woman…

It felt like home. It was a strange sensation. Home was a long way away, Ballystone Hall, hard on the Welsh border. It was a magnificent place to live, but he never slept well there. But here, in this bed with its tatty furnishings, he fell into a sleep that was almost dreamless.

He woke as the second storm front hit.

It hit with such force he felt the whole house shudder. The thunderclap was so loud, so long, that the shuddering was more than momentary, and the lightning that flashed across the sky made a mockery of the window drapes. It lit the whole house with an eerie light.

The second clap of thunder followed the first, even louder, even stronger.

And two seconds later a dog landed on his bed.

A second after that, five dogs followed.

He'd assumed they were sleeping with Charlie. They'd definitely abandoned ship though, or abandoned their mistress. The first one in, Stretch, was a sort of dachshund with a whiskery beard that said something had happened to impede an ancient pedigree lineage. He launched himself up onto the bed, and before Bryn could stop him he had his nose under the sheets, wriggling under the covers and heading down to Bryn's toes.

The next five dogs were all for following suit, but by then Bryn was prepared and had the sheet up to his neck.

And then the next lightning sheet lit the room and he looked at the door and Charlie was standing in the doorway holding a lamp. She was wearing a faded lacy nightgown and bare feet. Her hair was tousled as if she'd had a restless sleep. Her eyes were huge in her face and in her arms she carried Flossie. Whose eyes were also huge.

'I… I've been deserted,' she whispered. 'The dogs are scared.'

'And so are you?' He was trying not to smile. Dogs, woman, the whole situation… And a woman in a wispy nightgown with a lamp. But she did look truly scared.

'If it hits the house…'

'Have you seen the size of those trees outside? It'll hit those first.'

Maybe that was the wrong thing to say. Her face bleached even whiter. 'And the trees will hit the house.'

'Not on this side,' he said, struggling to think of the layout of the yard outside. His room backed onto the service yard out the back. The red gums were mostly at the front and the house was big. 'But it's really unlikely. I think the biggest has already been hit.'

'My bedroom's at the front.'

She stood there, her arms full of dog, and her face…

'Tell you what,' he said nobly. 'How about you sleep in here and I go sleep in your room?'

'N…no.'

'Charlie…'

'I don't like thunderstorms,' she whispered and there was an understatement. It was a big enough call that it had him throwing back the covers—shoving dogs aside in the process—and heading for the doorway. Heading for Charlie.

And when he got there, as soon as she was close, he realised the fear wasn't just on her face. She was trembling all over. The dog in her arms was trembling, too, and he realised why the dogs had abandoned Charlie en masse. They wanted a leader who wasn't terrified, and Charlie's face said she wanted exactly the same.

A pack leader. He could do this. It was kind of compulsory—that he moved to reassure. That he took the final steps and took her firmly into his arms.

And held.

Flossie was in there somewhere, sandwich squeezed, totally limp, totally passive. Bryn was wearing boxers and boxers only because his pjs were somewhere under a burning red gum. As he felt Flossie's rough coat against his bare skin he felt the dog trembling.

As Charlie was trembling.

He had Charlie around the waist. Her head was tucked into the crook of his neck as if she wanted to be close, closer.

He held her tight. His fingers splayed the width of her waist and his chin rested on her hair and he just…held.

And the feeling of home deepened, strengthened and something was happening…

Her hair was so thick, so soft, and it smelled of something citrusy, something gorgeous…

No, gorgeous was the adjective for the whole woman. For all of Charlie. That he be allowed to hold her…

She was totally still in his hold, yet not passive. She wanted to be held by him. There was a dog between them but he knew she wanted to be as close to him as she possibly could be.

Because she was scared. For no other reason. This was a frightened woman and he was comforting her.

But she was gorgeous.

There was that word again. It was as if the word itself had seeped into his head and was changing something inside him.

Gorgeous.

Another clap of thunder shook the house and he felt her flinch. If it was possible, dog and woman clung tighter.

From back in the bed there were six terrified whimpers.

What was a man to do?

'Come to bed, sweetheart,' he murmured into her hair. 'You and me and seven dogs. We'll ride out this mother of a storm together.'

'Together...' He felt the war within, the fear of the storm, the fear of the stranger.

'We can do this,' he said. 'One bed, one man and one woman might be a problem. One bed, one man and one woman and seven dogs... I doubt there's a problem at all.'

She slept and there were seven dogs between her body and his. There was one clap of thunder too much, though, and at some time in the night, even in her sleep, her primeval fears must have overridden every other consideration. She woke and she was spooned in a stranger's arms. Totally spooned. She had her back to him, his arms were around her and her body was curved into his chest. His face was against her hair. She could feel his breathing.

She could feel everything else.

He was wearing boxers.

He wasn't totally naked.

He might as well be.

Her nightgown was ancient lawn and flimsy, and she could feel his body against her. His chest was bare. His arms, muscled, strong, were holding her tight. Bare arms against bare arms. Skin against skin.

She could see chinks of sunlight through the drapes.

Flossie was lying at the end of the bed—she could feel her warm, welcome heaviness across her feet—but the rest of the pack had obviously taken off to check out the day. The storm was over.

She should tug away, out of this man's arms.

She'd wake him and he'd been so good…

It was more than that, though.

She really, really wanted to stay right where she was. For the moment the world had stopped. Here was peace. Here was sanctuary.

Here was… Bryn?

A man she'd known for what, twelve hours? Most of that had been spent sleeping. Oh, for heaven's sake… Get up, she told herself. Check on Flossie's leg. Go face the damage of the day.

But she didn't. She lay and let the insidious sweetness of the moment envelop her. She could lie here and imagine there were no problems. That Grandma wasn't dead. That she didn't have debts to her ears. That she didn't have to worry that she had no clue how to rehouse misfit dogs that she couldn't keep.

That she hadn't been betrayed by a low life herself, and that there seemed no one in the world who she could trust?

'Nice,' he murmured into her ear. 'You think if we stay here for long enough the rest of the world will disappear?'

So he was awake. And he had problems in his life, too? Well, didn't everyone? That made him…more human still.

Nice? No. Nice didn't begin to cut it. His body…if she didn't move soon…

And he got it almost the moment she did. 'Charlie, if we don't part I may well not be responsible for my actions,' he said and there was all the regret in the world in his voice. But she felt his body stir—where she most definitely didn't want his body to stir—and the fantasy had to end. As if in agreement, Flossie wriggled at the end of the bed and the day had to begin.

His arms released her. He shifted back. She struggled to sit up and it felt like the greatest grief…

Which was ridiculous. Her body was responding to the heightened emotions of the last weeks, she told herself. It had nothing to do with the body of the man pushing back the covers and rising to his feet…

Dear heaven, he was breath-taking.

Last night he'd said he was a farmer and his body confirmed it. He looked weathered, tanned, ripped, as if he spent his life heaving hay bales or shearing sheep or hauling cattle out of bogs or…whatever farmers did.

Which reminded her…

'There's probably stuff to do,' he said as if he'd read her thoughts. 'Dogs to let out? To feed? Other animals?'

'Cows to attend,' she told him. 'And chooks to feed. That is, if they've survived the night. But there's no need for you to stay. If the ground isn't too wet you can run your car over the back paddock. I can cut the wire and let you out to the road.'

'And leave you on your own to cope with the mess?'

'It's my mess. I've kept you long enough. Where were you headed last night? Melbourne?'

'I was,' he said, ruefully, reaching for his trousers. It was such a domestic thing to do. She was lying in bed while the man beside the bed was dressing. It was discombobulating. Weird. 'I was heading for the airport.'

'Then you've missed your plane?' She sat bolt upright and stared at him in horror. 'Because of Flossie? Oh, no.'

'There'll be other planes.'

'Will you forfeit your ticket? I can… I'll…' Yeah, right, pay for another airline ticket? With what?

'Charlie…' He must have heard the panic in her voice because he leaned over and put his hands on her shoulders. It was a gesture that was meant to steady her, ground her, and in some ways it did. In other ways she felt not the least bit grounded. What the feel of this man did to her...

'I hit your dog,' he said, softly but firmly. 'This is my responsibility.'

'Flossie should never have been out on the road.'

'How did she get out?' He flicked a glance down at Flossie, who was curled against Charlie's legs as if she never wanted to leave. Maybe he could see her point.

'When Grandma had the heart attack the paramedics left the gate open and Flossie disappeared. That was three weeks ago. I have no idea where she's been since then. I've hunted everywhere.'

'You weren't here when your grandmother died?'

'I was in Melbourne. I did make it to the hospital before she died. She wanted to know about all the animals. I told her they were fine. I told her... I'd look after them.'

'So what's happening to them now?'

'I'm finding homes for them,' she said, with more certainty than she felt. 'I'm trying to fix the farm up so I can put it on the market...' Her voice faltered at that. It wouldn't be her putting it on the market, she thought. It'd be the bank, trying to scrape back anything it could. 'But now...your plane...'

'It doesn't matter. For now it seems we need to feed animals, feed us and then take a look at the damage outside.'

'You don't need to stay.' The thought of him missing the plane because of her... How could she ever make it up to him?

'You mean you're not offering me breakfast?'

'Don't you want to...just leave?'

'Without breakfast? That was great soup last night but it didn't cling to the sides. I saw your fridge last night. You have eggs. Bread. Mushrooms...'

'But your plane...'

'There'll be another plane tonight.' If there was a seat available.

'To London. You're English?'

'Part English, part Welsh.' He'd sat on the bed and was pulling his boots on, and once more that impression of domesticity intensified. 'Where I live is border country.'

'Your farm…'

'My farm's in England. Just. Right, what's first? Will the dogs be downstairs waiting to be let out?'

'Grandma has a doggie door. She closed it when she had Flossie but since Flossie left…'

'I doubt if Flossie's thinking of leaving,' he said gently and leaned over Charlie to pat her.

And as if to deny his words Flossie struggled to her feet—well, three of her feet—and staggered across the bed towards him.

He scooped her into his arms and held her, smiling down at her.

'I'm thinking this girl's great,' he told Charlie. 'I suspect we don't even need the vet. But I also suspect there'll be a need for a nature call.'

'The yard outside the kitchen's enclosed,' Charlie told him. 'I'll be down in a moment. You won't let her out, will you?'

'I'll stay with her the whole time,' he said and then his smile turned to Charlie, a smile that almost had her heart doing back flips. Where did a man ever learn to smile like that?

'Take your time getting dressed, Charlie,' he said gently. 'I suspect you could do with a morning's break from responsibility. I'll check your charges and the damage outside.' He stooped and touched her face, a mere brush of finger against cheek. Why did that make her feel…as if she didn't know how she was feeling? 'You need help,' he told her. 'A morning might be all I can give, then I'll give it willingly.'

* * *

She took him at his word. She stood under the shower and tried to allow the hot water to calm her.

It sort of did. For some reason the appalling mess of the last weeks had receded. Someone was helping. What was more, she was trusting him. He was presently feeding the cows, collecting eggs and letting the hens out for the day, doing everything a farmer would know how to do.

But why was she trusting? How did she know who he was? Had the mess her grandmother had got herself into taught her nothing?

Oh, for heaven's sake, what was he going to do? Steal her eggs and run? There was little else left in the place to steal.

Everything was sold. All that was left was the value-less. A sad little cow and her bag-of-bones calf. Chooks that were almost past laying. Seven assorted dogs.

Her grandmother's jewellery box was empty. The shelves had long been stripped of anything saleable. Even the gorgeous old lounge suite, faded but beautiful, had been carted off to the auction rooms.

For the last few weeks Charlie had been consumed by an anger so deep, so vast it had threatened to overwhelm her. She hadn't been able to put it aside for a moment.

But now, with the hot water streaming over her naked body, her anger had been overlaid. She was suddenly thinking of a guy called Bryn with a lazy smile and gentle hands.

A man who'd held her in sleep.

A man who was getting on a plane tonight and she'd never see again.

Which was why she was getting out of the shower right now because standing under the hot water fantasising about the man was dangerous indeed—and besides, she was missing out on being…with him.

Or not. It was only because she needed to cook breakfast, she told herself as she tried to rub sense into herself with the threadbare towel. She had things to do. Sensible things.

She wasn't hurrying because Bryn was downstairs.

Liar.

Breakfast seemed top of the agenda but there was a problem. She came downstairs just as Bryn came through the kitchen door from outside, and she could read *problem* on his face.

'What?' she said with trepidation. 'Flossie…'

'Flossie's fine,' he said hurriedly. 'She's hopping on three legs but she lined up for her kibble with the rest of them. She even put a bit of pressure on her pad when she thought she was being beaten to the feed bowls.'

'You've fed them.'

'Yes, ma'am.' There was that smile again. 'I hope that's okay with you. I assumed that industrial drum of kibble by the back door was for them.'

'I'm not reduced to eating kibble myself,' she joked but it didn't come out as she'd meant it to. It came out sounding needy. But Bryn's smile had faded. He looked preoccupied. 'There's something else?'

'You have a cow in a bog,' he told her. 'The creek's a quagmire but she's obviously tried to reach it. I have no idea how she's worked herself into such a mess. Luckily her calf had the sense not to join her. The calf was standing on the bank making her displeasure at her mother's idiocy known to the world, but that's made things worse. The cow's desperate to reach her and has dug herself deeper. I've put the calf in the shed, so now we have one stuck cow to deal with. Do you have a tractor?'

'Um…no.'

'A neighbour with a tractor?'

She gazed out of the window at the debris scattered across the paddocks. Last night's storm had been appalling. Every local farmer would be out assessing damage to their own properties. Besides, Jock next door had been scathing of Grandma's cow and calf.

'Not even the knacker's 'll want them,' he'd told her when she'd tentatively asked if he could take them on. 'You can't take 'em back to your city apartment? The best thing to do is take 'em down to the back of the gully and shoot 'em. Tell you what,' he'd said in a spirit of neighbourliness because this was at Grandma's funeral and he was trying to be helpful. 'I'll do it for you if you like.'

She didn't like, and now…to ask if he'd abandon assessing damage on his place and spend the morning saving a cow…

Bryn was waiting for an answer. Did she have neighbours who'd help?

'No,' she said a bit too abruptly and got a sharp look in return.

'They're not helpful?'

'They'll be busy. And they don't think much of Cordelia.'

'Cordelia?'

'Cordelia,' she repeated. 'Her calf's Violet. And don't ask. I have no idea how Grandma chose names.'

'Then I guess Cordelia needs to be dug out,' he said as if it was no big deal. He sounded almost cheerful. 'I might need some help. Can you show me where your spades are kept? And I'll need rope and planking…'

I might need some help…

See her gobsmacked.

Did he know how sweet those words sounded? For the last three weeks they'd been thrashing themselves around her head. *I might need some help…* She did need help. And now this man was assuming a bogged cow—*her* bogged cow—was his responsibility and he was asking for her help.

Did he know how close she was to bursting into tears on his chest?

Oh, my.

'But coffee first and toast,' he told her. 'She's in trouble but she's not going anywhere. If she was dumb enough to try and get to the creek to drink when all she had to do overnight was open her mouth and swallow, then she can wait until we fuel up. Toast and coffee and let's go.'

Charlie wasn't a farmer. Actually, neither was her grandmother. This place represented the remnants of the family farm, but Grandma had never been interested in farming. After her husband had died she'd sold off most of the land and committed herself to caring for injured wildlife. As she'd grown older she'd confined herself to dogs and chooks. Every now and then she'd let the neighbour bring his cows in to keep the grass down, but she'd spent the rest of her life collecting strays.

Six months ago she'd found a cow wandering along the road at dusk, a hazard to traffic, obviously neglected. Three weeks later it had given birth, much to Grandma's delight. Cow and calf were rangy, weird-looking bovines with no proven ancestry. No one had wanted them—except Grandma.

Charlie should have locked them in the sheds for the night. The truth was she didn't know how. How to make a cow go where it didn't want?

Bryn had, though. He'd driven the calf into the shed and Charlie was impressed.

Now they just had to deal with Cordelia.

Uh oh. Charlie walked down to the creek with Bryn and her heart sank.

Cordelia was obviously a cow accustomed to hard

times. She'd sunk to her haunches in mud and was gazing down at the mire in deep despondency, as if thinking: If this is the way to go, then so be it.

'Grandma has troughs near the shed,' Charlie said as they gazed at the cow together. She was wearing jeans and wellingtons and carting a couple of spades. Bryn was wearing his gorgeous city shoes and the trousers and shirt he'd had on last night. He was carrying four lengths of planking and rope. She was trying not to be…aware of him. Very aware.

It wasn't working.

'I even left the shed door open,' Charlie told him indignantly, pushing aside inappropriate thoughts with difficulty. 'I went out in the rain especially but did she want to go in? No! And how do you get a cow to go where she doesn't want to go?'

'With a decent dog?' Bryn said and grinned down at the pack following them. They'd left Flossie sleeping by the stove, but the rest were bounding around them, joyous in the sunshine and the sense of doing. Cattle dogs? Not a one of them.

'You show me how and I'll train them,' Charlie told him.

He checked them for a moment, grin still in place. Possum, a sort of fox terrier. Fred, part basset, part…lots of things. Caesar, a wolfhound who trembled behind the back of the pack as if to say, Protect me, guys. Dottie, a Dalmatian so old her dots were faded to grey. Then there was Mothball, the fluffball, and Stretch, a sort of sausage dog whose tummy actually touched the ground when he ran. And Flossie back at the house.

'I can't imagine,' he said faintly.

'Don't you laugh at my dogs.'

'I wouldn't dare.' But still he grinned and she managed a smile back.

It really was a great morning. The sun was on her face.

Her stomach was full of toast and coffee. She was still warmed with the memory of being held in this man's arms...

Whoa.

'Tell me where to dig,' she managed, a bit too fast, a bit...breathlessly.

'I'll do the digging.'

'You have to be kidding. In those clothes?'

'I already asked... You don't appear to have wellingtons in my size. Besides, that's what water's for. Washing.'

'Bryn...'

'What's the choice?' he asked.

And there wasn't one. Unless she went next door and borrowed a rifle.

No, there wasn't one.

'Right then,' Bryn said and laid down his planking and took the two spades from her shoulder. He laid one down on the ground. 'It's up to me.'

She picked it back up and glowered. 'It's up to us.'

'Right, ma'am,' he said and grinned again, looking ruefully down at his city shoes. 'You know, I should be bored out of my mind in a plane right now. How can I possibly regret my change of plan?'

It took skill, strength and patience to dig a cow out of a bog. Firstly there was the imperative of keeping the cow calm. Struggling would make her sink deeper and that was where Charlie came in.

'You've been feeding her for the last weeks?' Bryn asked and when she agreed he set her task.

'Right. You're the cow whisperer. You squat by her head, block as much of me as you can and tell her all about the hay bales back in the shed.'

'I want to dig.'

'We can't always get what we want,' Bryn said, unperturbed.

Charlie thought, Yeah, tell me about it.

So she stooped as ordered and tried to do the cow-whispering thing but the cow wasn't having a bar of it.

'It's as if she thinks we're trying to dig her out to turn her into sausages,' she said indignantly as Cordelia did a bit more thrashing and Bryn nodded.

'Some cows are bred for intelligence. Obviously not this one. Okay,' he conceded. 'Let's go for fast. Grab a spade and help.'

Excellent. She dug, ankle deep in mud, shovelling the squishy mud from in front of the cow.

'We need to get deep enough to lay planking so she can haul herself up,' Bryn told her. 'But if you're getting blisters…'

'I'm not getting blisters.' She wasn't, but she was aware that as shovellers went she came a very poor second to the man beside her. He looked as if he'd shovelled a thousand cows out of bogs in his lifetime. His spade work was steady, methodical, effective, and he could load his shovel with twice as much sludge as she could.

He really was a farmer.

She was so lucky to have him here this morning. What good fairy had decreed he be the one to hit Flossie…and bring her home…and stay…?

Even hitting Flossie… Flossie must have been wandering for weeks. Sure, she'd been hit by a car, but this morning she was putting weight on her back leg, and if she still looked good when they got back to the house Charlie might not even have to pay for vet bills.

Magic.

Well, sort of magic. There were lots of things about her situation that weren't magic, but right now, steadily shovelling, she could put the worries of the world aside and soak in the moment.

Soak was right. Her gum boots weren't exactly effective. She was wet and filthy. And Bryn… Somewhere under the mud were his feet. They'd put the planks under their feet as they dug but it didn't help much. The mud was insidious.

He didn't appear to notice. A farmer born and bred.

'So your cows,' she said cautiously—she really would like to know more about him. 'Intelligent, are they?'

'You have to believe it,' he told her. 'Mensa candidates all.'

'Right.'

'You think I'm joking? My top ladies… I can call them by name.'

'How many ladies do you have?'

'Enough to keep me busy,' he said enigmatically and that smile returned again. 'More than you. It's hard to make a living with two cows. So how about you? Can you make a living interior designing from here?'

'No,' she said shortly. 'I need to get back to Melbourne. Just as soon as I find homes for all these guys.'

He paused and looked at Cordelia, who'd finally stopped struggling and now appeared to be bored. Then he glanced back at the assorted dog pack, gambolling in the sunshine. Misbegotten? Maybe that was too strong a word for it, but these dogs hadn't been chosen for their cute appeal.

'And what happens if you don't find them homes?' he asked, gently now because maybe he knew there were nerves he was touching.

'I have no idea,' she snapped. 'I can't see them in a one-bedroom studio in Melbourne. Even if I could, I suspect my landlord would take a dim view.'

'Especially of Cordelia,' he agreed. 'Though we could wash her and spruce her up a bit. Maybe tie a few interior-design ribbons on her horns and set her up as a conversation piece.'

She didn't smile, she just kept on digging as the grey descended again. What were her options? They were down to practically zero.

Maybe it would have been a kindness to invite her neighbour over with his rifle.

'So tell me,' she said, desperate to change the subject. She was digging again, concentrating fiercely. 'Why are you in Australia? What put you on the road outside Grandma's place last night? I know you were heading for the plane but why were you here in the first place?'

'Family business.' That was curt. The smile had gone from his eyes.

'You said…your uncle? A death?' she queried, and she thought she shouldn't go there but anything to distract her from the thoughts of rifles and long-term outcomes.

'Not a death.' He paused in his digging. 'Let's shift these planks back a bit. I'm thinking if we take a bit out from where we are now we can slope the planks down to her. She could possibly struggle out now but she'd have nowhere to go.'

They messed around a bit, shifting planks, doing busy work while Bryn's face stayed grim.

There was stuff going on in this guy's life, too. Rifle kind of stuff?

'It's okay,' he said at last. 'No, it wasn't a death, though it could have been. My uncle's been in trouble. I've done all I can to help.'

'Financial trouble?'

'You could say that.'

'There aren't many farmers around here who aren't,' she said, sympathetically. 'The last drought—'

'He's not a farmer,' he said, curtly, cutting the conversation with a tone that said it was going no further. He had his planks adjusted and dug silently for a while. Charlie had paused. Not because her hands hurt, although her hands actually did hurt, but because Bryn was digging carefully now, forming a slope, and she needed to figure what was happening. He was making what was essentially a ramp.

And he didn't want to talk about his uncle.

Fair enough. It wasn't her business. And besides, they were getting to the pointy end of this rescue business.

Bryn stepped back and surveyed his handiwork. Cordelia looked up at them with bovine lack of interest, as if the ramp Bryn was making had nothing to do with her. Talk about dumb…

'Maybe she's cold,' he said, generously.

'Maybe she's thick,' Charlie responded. 'If I was her I'd see the ramp and be hauling myself up.'

'It's lucky she's not. She might sink again. Let's get these planks in position so she has something solid to grip.'

'And then you'll make her move how?'

'Pull,' he said solidly. 'One thing I've learned in thirty-five years of farm life is how to get dumb beasts to do what you need them to do. The only exception is my stupid uncle.'

And then there was silence as he roped the cow, as he checked the planks again, as he put Charlie at the far end of the rope and took a grip himself. It was seemingly a tug of war, with Cordelia on one team and Charlie and Bryn on the other.

But it felt okay, Charlie thought, as she gripped the rope in two hands and prepared to pull. For Bryn was behind her.

She was…a team.

'Count of three, pull,' Bryn ordered. 'One, two, three…'

And they pulled. Cordelia gave a vast, indignant bellow as if she'd decided she was quite comfortable in the mud and wouldn't mind staying there. But their grip was relentless, and finally she gave into the strain around her neck—and a leg squelched up from the mud and onto the planking.

'Harder,' Bryn said from behind her and she gave one last heave—and Cordelia was up on the planks, heaving herself forward, then staring wildly towards the barn where the calf was bellowing. And two seconds later they were being shoved off the planks as a desperate, mud-coated cow was off and galloping towards her calf.

Charlie tumbled backwards. Bryn wheeled and caught her but overbalanced himself. Quick as lightning Bryn rolled sideways, lifting her high and rolling until she was off the mud and onto grass.

She was choking on laughter, lit with triumph. Bryn was holding her. The sun was on her face, but her face was coated with mud.

As was Bryn's. He was laughing, too, his dark eyes twinkling down at her. They were a muddy tumble of triumphant bodies and it seemed entirely appropriate that Bryn's arms stayed around her and held her, that laughter enveloped them, that Charlie twisted in his arms so she could see his face, so she could share his laughter.

And somehow, someway, for some ridiculous reason, it seemed entirely appropriate that Bryn should place his mud-smeared hands on either side of her mud-smeared face—and that he should kiss her.

A kiss… Here… Now… Of all the inappropriate things to do.

But it wasn't inappropriate.

Why?

Was this the culmination of weeks of shock, of grief, of stress, of hopelessness and, finally last night, of fear?

And sleeping in this man's arms?

Or was it simply wanting him?

For she wanted him and there was no doubting it. As

her mouth met his, it was as if every nerve ending knew where it wanted to be centred and it was right here.

His kiss started tender, started as a question, but that question was answered with a definite yes. Her kiss back was the response he needed. The kiss turned strong, commanding, even possessive, and that was fine. No, it was more than fine, because right now she wanted to be… possessed? Maybe. For the last weeks she'd been spinning out of control, in some sort of crazy, non-predictable vortex. But right now her world had stilled, had centred, and it was centred on this man.

On this moment.

On the heat of his mouth.

She felt as if she were melting. The strength of him, the sureness…

He was a farmer and he felt like it, a man of the land, a man who knew how to get a frightened cow from a bog, a man who knew what a woman wanted.

She wanted him.

Which was crazy.

They were lying full length on the lush, storm-wet spring grass. The morning sun had little strength in it yet but she wasn't cold. Bryn was her heat source. He was her centre. He felt, he tasted, he held, like a man who could lift her out of the misery of the last few weeks.

In truth, he already had.

He was a stranger and he had a plane to catch back to England. This moment must be transient. But she was holding his face in her hands to deepen the kiss, holding as if she had the right to keep holding. She could forget everything else in the joy and the triumph of this moment—and who could blame her?

The kiss deepened and deepened again. If they'd been in the comfort of a bedroom instead of a soggy piece of turf, with water soaking fast through their clothes, then who knew what would have happened?

Or if Bryn hadn't had control because Charlie surely didn't...

But he did and, after a glorious few minutes of blocking out the world, the cold and wet finally permeated. Sense prevailed, and finally, reluctantly, they drew apart.

To laughter of course, because that was what this man seemed all about.

'Well,' he said. 'That was quite a morning. Is that the way you always thank your farm hands for services rendered?'

If they look—and feel—like you, she wanted to say. But she didn't say anything. She couldn't. She wanted this moment to stretch on for ever.

But Bryn was rising, holding out his hands, tugging her up after him. She rose a little too fast, so she was tugged close, breast against chest, and when he put her back a little she wanted to protest.

But he was being sensible and so must she.

'We need to check Cordelia,' he said and there was a reluctance in his voice that told her that maybe he was feeling the same as she was. As if the last thing she wanted was to move away from this spot and check a muddy cow. 'We need to let her into the shed to join her calf. And then we need to dry off.'

Sensible. Right.

'I hope you have a change of clothes in the car,' she said and was proud of how steady her voice sounded.

'Cow first. We're not going to all that trouble to have her die of hypothermia. Let's get her in the shed with... what did you call her calf?'

'Violet.'

'Of course. How could I have forgotten Violet?' He smiled down at her, and with the back of his hand he traced a line down her muddy cheek. And it was quite possibly the sexiest, most amazing sensation she'd ever experienced. Every nerve in her body seemed to swerve, point, arrow itself to his touch. She wanted...she wanted...

Oh, for heaven's sake, she was a grown woman, and no matter what she wanted, she couldn't *have*. She had a cow to dry. Reality to face.

'Right,' she said, and with enormous difficulty she turned away and started trudging towards the outbuildings. Cordelia had already reached them and was bellowing her indignation at not being able to reach her calf. On the other side of the door Violet was bellowing in response. Charlie's problems slammed back.

What on earth could she do with two cows?

She was going to dry them, that was what, and then she'd do what came next, one step after another, for as long as she could. While this guy left and headed back to the UK. While the world turned as it always did, without noticing that one tiny speck seemed to have fallen off.

Now she was being melodramatic. She needed to get a grip. She squelched doggedly on but her foot landed on the edge of a wombat burrow and she slipped.

Bryn's hand came out and caught her and held, fast. And she let her hand stay.

Of course she did.

She needed to face reality—but not quite yet.

CHAPTER THREE

IT SEEMED BRYN knew exactly how to clean a filthy cow, which was just as well because Charlie had no clue. She'd have fussed about hot water—which wasn't exactly possible in a tumbledown barn, and Cordelia wasn't exactly small enough to take into the house and pop into the bath.

But Bryn simply hosed the worst of the mud from her—'Left on it'll cake and leave her cold.' And then found a bunch of rags. He handed some to Charlie and took more himself.

'We rub,' he told her. 'It'll warm us up as well as Cordelia. She is cold. We dry her, we feed her well and then we keep her in the shed with her calf until we're sure she's recovered. If we leave her like this she may well go down, and if she drops it'll be hard to get her up again. We've dodged one vet visit with Flossie. Let's not risk another.'

So despite her wanting to head into the house and a warm bath herself, she stood on the opposite side of a cow to Bryn and she rubbed and rubbed, and Bryn rubbed and rubbed…and it was more of the same, she thought. He… this whole situation…*this man*…made something happen to her body…to her mind?

Bryn's words kept playing in her head. *We. We* dry her. *We* feed her well.

We was a magical word. It made her feel shivery but not from cold.

How long since she'd been part of *we*?

The calf was nudging around them, heading for Cordelia's teats, backing out and checking them out and then darting under again. She was a strange-looking calf, still a bit bony from a malnourished start, but nosey and pushy and…fun? She had one huge white eye in an otherwise black face, which made her look like some sort of bovine pirate. She kept trying to shove Bryn out of the way as she tried to access her mother's teats and Bryn did his best to accommodate—but Violet was still pushy. She kept popping up from the teats to check on Charlie, and the sight of her pirate eye under Bryn's arm made Charlie want to chuckle.

Bryn was so good. His affection for the calf seemed immediate. He obviously loved animals.

The sight of him was doing something to Charlie that she didn't understand. Right now she didn't want to understand. She just wanted it not to end. She was still wet but the rubbing not only warmed her, but was somehow… mesmeric?

Bryn was talking in soothing tones to Cordelia. Cow talk? In Welsh?

'You're thinking she understands?' she asked.

'All cows know Welsh. It's international cow language.'

It was a very silly answer but she liked it. She went back to rubbing, insensibly happy at the ridiculousness of it.

'So why the trouble?' Bryn asked, gently, and it was like being pulled back into the real world but this was Bryn asking. He was leaving soon and somehow it didn't seem wrong that he should ask. But still, she didn't want to emerge from her happy place.

'Trouble?'

'I can see it on your face,' he said. The laughter had gone, but the gentleness remained. 'Trouble apart from your grandma's death.'

'I…'

'You don't need to tell me if you don't want.'

'I guess.' She shrugged and rubbed for a bit more and then thought, *Why not?*

'It's just… This is Grandma's farmlet, but it's mortgaged. Heavily mortgaged, for more than it's worth. There's no money. The bank's repossessing. They've given me another month, which considering the size of the debt is good of them, but after that, I need to be gone.'

'And you live in Melbourne.'

'I'm supposed to live in Melbourne, but if you can tell me what I should do with seven decrepit dogs, a dumb cow and calf, and chooks that are way past point of lay…'

'There are animal refuges.'

'There are,' she told him. 'And I've talked to them and they've told me frankly what chances my dogs, Grandma's dogs, have. The people running them are fantastic but they run on the smell of an oily rag and right now they're in trouble. The government's just made puppy farming illegal, with huge penalties. All the dodgy backyard operators are dumping their breeding stock before the new penalties come in, and there are so many dogs needing rehoming they can't cope. They've said they'll keep Grandma's dogs for a month and do their best to find them homes but they're not hopeful. None of my…none of Grandma's dogs are what you'd call cute. So after a month…'

She paused and rubbed Cordelia a bit more and struggled to continue. Forcing herself to think of the other animals. 'And a cow and calf like this? Scrawny, mixed breed, neither dairy nor beef? I might be able to find a place for the chooks, but the cows and the dogs…' She shook her head. 'Somewhere up there Grandma's breaking her heart and so am I.'

'Hey,' he said and her hand, which had been rubbing

with a fierceness that was almost desperate, was suddenly grasped and held. 'There are solutions. There must be.'

'You tell me what they are, then,' she said and tugged her hand away because a woman could only indulge in fantasy for so long and the time for fantasy was over. 'Are we done here? Let's go find your gear from the car, get cleaned up and get ourselves ready to face the day.' And then she shook her head. 'Or not. There's no need for you to face anything. I'll cut a hole in the fencing along the dry part of the boundary and you'll be right to go.'

'I won't be,' he said, almost apologetically.

'What?'

'The tree that came down last night,' he told her. 'It came down on my car.'

She stared at him in horror. 'On your car?'

'Right across the top. I haven't checked closely but from where I was standing when the tree came down…well, she won't be driveable.'

'But I thought…' Her heart almost seemed to stop as she thought of the implications. 'Your car… That tree… You could have been in it!'

'So I could,' he said, equitably. 'But I wasn't, which is why I'm doing the Pollyanna thing this morning. The sun's out, I'm not squashed, and there has to be a solution for all things.'

'I need to see,' she said, appalled, and he took her rags from her and gave Cordelia a farewell pat.

'Okay,' he warned. 'But it won't be pretty.'

It wasn't pretty.

So much had happened this morning that she hadn't even checked out the front of the house. She'd taken Bryn's word that the driveway was blocked and then been…distracted. They left the sheds, rounded the house and she stopped dead.

Dead. That pretty much described the massive gum

that had crashed right across the driveway. In fact it had been dead for the last couple of years, killed by drought, or simply by old age. It had been the biggest tree on the property, a giant that even alive had been far too close to the house for comfort.

But there was no way Grandma would have cut down such a thing, and seeing it now, split, shattered, still smouldering at the stump, Charlie felt her eyes fill. She remembered it as a magic, living thing.

When she was eight years old her grandfather had fitted a rope ladder to the lowest branch. It had been a messy year. Her parents had been going through a vitriolic divorce and Charlie had been sent to Grandma and Pa's, 'to get her out of the way'.

Blessedly Grandma had decided that was exactly what Charlie needed. A place of her own. She'd been provided with armloads of comics, the kind her mother would never let her near. The first fork of the tree formed almost an armchair. Charlie had lugged cushions up there, hauled the rope ladder after her and pretended for a blessed while that the world didn't exist.

And now…

'A friend, was it?' Bryn asked and she looked at him in astonishment. What sort of guy guessed a tree could be a friend?

She shook her head, too emotional to speak, then gave her face an angry swipe. So much emotion. She needed to move on, letting the bank have what was left of this tree as well as what was left of this place. And the dogs and cows…

Did banks take dogs and cows?

And somewhere under this mess were the remains of Bryn's car. It had been squashed on her land while he'd been returning her dog who'd been wandering untended.

Could he sue? Of course he could.

How could you sue someone who'd been sucked dry?

Trying to fight off the wash of something dangerously close to hysterics, she edged towards the vast mound of splintered tree. The deluge of rain that had followed had stopped the whole thing being burned. There was still ancient foliage on the dead wood, the remains of vast branches with millions of leaves.

The car was on the other side of the trunk. She could just see. It was yellow. A branch had smashed down over the front but the body was still in...

In shape?

In the shape of a bright yellow, once stunning, Italian supercar.

Here.

She stepped back as if she, too, had been burned.

She'd seen this car, before her grandmother died. She'd driven from Melbourne for the weekend, and arrived as the guy had been leaving, a man in his sixties, smooth, urbane, wearing a suit that had screamed money. He'd given her a smile that had made her edgy—or maybe she'd already been edgy, what with a supercar parked in Grandma's yard.

'Good morning, Miss Foster. I'm Thomas Carlisle. You're earlier than we expected. Your grandmother told me you were coming today. Sadly I can't stay and talk, but do let me tell you what a wonderful woman your grandmother is. Clever, intuitive, forward thinking. It's been a pleasure doing business with her.'

And he'd gripped her hand, warmly, strongly, as if he'd had a right to hold her—and then he'd slid into his horrid yellow car and slimed out of her life. Out of her grandmother's life.

Leaving catastrophe.

'I've just invested a little money,' her grandmother had told her, defensive already. 'It's a solid investment and he's such an intelligent man. And he's a baron, Charlie—

a proper baron. You're supposed to address him as Lord Carlisle, but he says "call me Thomas". He has a stately home and everything.

'He doesn't boast about it, though. I wish he could have stayed to talk to you but of course he's so busy. He has a brochure up in the general store and everyone's talking about it. Look.' She'd handed Charlie a glossy, gold-embossed pamphlet. 'See what I'm now part of.'

'Straws,' she said now, faintly, the sour taste of that conversation rushing back.

And Bryn, standing beside her, got it.

'You met my uncle, then?'

So she was right.

'Your uncle…' She whirled on him, fury threatening to choke her. 'That scumbag is your uncle? You're in that scheme that robbed half this neighbourhood of their savings, that made Grandma…that caused her…that…'

She could no longer get words out. She turned back and stared at the remains of one ridiculous supercar and all she felt was fury that the stump hadn't burned far enough to reach it. 'Get off my property,' she managed. 'I don't care that your car is wrecked. I don't care how you manage it. Get off this land now or I'll ring the police and have you carted away. Come to think of it I should ring them anyway. Your uncle…'

'Charlie, he's nothing to do with me.'

'No? Family business, isn't that what you said? *Your* family. So where is he now? He was supposed to have committed suicide, only the police say it was faked. They said he's probably in Brazil or somewhere, but wherever he is he'll be poncing round being Lord Whatever He Calls Himself This Week, selling these useless straws and talking old people into investing in his phony, cruel schemes.'

And then she paused. 'Or maybe he's still here. Is that why you're here? To help him get away? Whatever it is, I want nothing to do with it. Nothing to do with you. I don't care if you're covered in mud, Bryn Morgan or whoever you are. I've done with lying and cheating and I'm not as trusting as Grandma. I'm not even going to thank you for saving Cordelia. Or Flossie. Get off my land—or the bank's land—and get off now.'

And she turned and headed for the house at a run.

As Lord Carlisle of Ballystone Hall, Bryn led a privileged life. From the moment his grandfather had crumpled, had turned to him in shattered dependence, he'd decided the only thing he could do was to care for the vast estate, to pass it on—to whoever—with pride. He'd worked hard, hands on, doing what he loved. The lands had improved. The lot of the tenant farmers had improved, and the Ballystone stud cattle were starting to be known the world over.

Regardless, one thing Bryn didn't have to worry about was his creature comforts. There had always been a hot bath at the end of the day, excellent food, staff to see to details.

Staff was what he needed now. Help to get out of this mess.

He was filthy. His jacket was somewhere inside the house, blood-stained, abandoned after carrying Flossie in last night. He'd been wearing a light shirt, trousers and shoes, which had been enough while working hard with Cordelia but now... The sun wasn't strong enough to stop the cold. He was wet, muddy...no, make that filthy, and he was cold.

The farmhouse behind him looked firmly locked. He could still feel the echoes of the slam of the front door.

He raked his hair and a thick wedge of mud came away on his hand. Digging cows out of bogs was a filthy business.

He needed his phone. It had been in his jacket pocket but

he'd taken it out when he'd used the jacket to carry Flossie. It'd be lying on the passenger seat of the car.

He had a change of clothes in the car.

If he could reach the car he could get his clothes, get his phone, wash down in the shed and ring for assistance. He could even ring the police, and get the stolid local sergeant to explain to Charlie that he wasn't the scumbag she thought he was.

If she'd listen.

He wanted her to listen.

Why?

And strangely, tangentially, he was suddenly thinking...

No! The last thing he needed right now was emotional entanglement. Actually, the last thing he needed *ever* was emotional entanglement. The thought of loving someone else...

Just no.

But why was he thinking of that now? It didn't make sense, but he was.

When he was nineteen years old he'd lost his father, his uncle, his cousin and his twin sister, in the one appalling tragedy. The grief he'd felt that day was enough to last him a lifetime. During the ensuing years he'd tried dating— of course he had—but the moment he felt himself getting close that fear closed in. He held himself to himself.

But he hadn't held himself to himself last night or this morning. He'd held Charlie as if he cared.

He did care.

Why?

Because it was time out of frame, he told himself. These last few weeks, dragged into his uncle's sordid mess, away from home, away from anything that seemed solid, his normal defences weren't working. They'd be working soon enough. He knew that. But while they weren't...

'Pull back,' he told himself. 'Let yourself help, let yourself be a friend, but no more than that.'

'She doesn't want to be a friend. She thinks you're as bad as your uncle.' He was talking out loud.

'That makes it easier. She has no need of emotional connection and neither do you. What's happened last night and this morning was an aberration. Move on.'

So finally he shoved the thought of Charlie's anger away as best he could—and the emotions that went with it—and tackled what lay in front of him.

The tangle of smashed branches prevented any access to the car. A vast branch was blocking the passenger side. A smaller one lay across the driver's door, and one had slammed right across the engine.

He glanced back at the house. As he did, the curtains of the front window were hauled shut.

No help there. Not that he blamed her. What his uncle had done was horrific.

He'd thought Thomas only victimised farmers with Hereford herds. If he'd guessed her grandmother was a victim he would have explained earlier, but it was too late now.

But knowing what she was thinking...

Don't go there.

He needed to stop thinking of Charlie and focus.

Clothes. Phone. Car.

He thought back to the shed, where Cordelia and Violet were presumably still recovering. While he'd been rubbing, he'd noticed an ancient scythe; like the ones tenant farmers had used to harvest crops a hundred years ago. He liked old tools.

He'd also noticed old saws. He didn't like them so much.

He looked again at the tree and he thought longingly of the well-maintained chainsaws in the vast outbuildings at Ballystone.

Beggars can't be choosers. When in Rome do as the Romans do. A bad workman always blames his tools.

Yeah, how many other platitudes could he think of? he wondered as he trudged back towards the shed. He'd obviously have plenty of time to think of them.

He was sawing his way into his car.

She shouldn't look. She was showered and warm and the doors were firmly locked and she should be over it, but she was still shaking with anger and she was still furiously aware that That Man was still on her property.

The bank's property.

She should call the police. They'd want to know he was here. She'd almost done her own citizen's arrest. He was stuck.

She was upstairs in Grandma's big front bedroom, edging the drapes aside just slightly so she could look.

He'd stripped off his shirt, or maybe it had ripped while he'd fought his way through the tangle of smashed wood. He was bare to the waist. He was sawing methodically, back and forth, long, even strokes.

The tools hadn't been used since Pa had died, almost ten years ago. She knew the saw would be rusty.

Excellent, she thought savagely. He'd have his work cut out for him. Even if it took him the whole day, that was a token recompense for all the pain his relation had inflicted on this community. On Grandma.

On her.

She headed back downstairs and fished in the bureau for the glossy brochure Grandma had shown her. It was a magnificent production, with a picture of a stunning Hereford bull on the front, a beast even Charlie could recognise as something special. In the background was what looked like a little like a castle, ringed by mountains.

Once in a lifetime opportunity to gain access to sperm straws from the herd of Lord Carlisle of Bally-stone Hall.

The brochure followed with a string of stunning comments from the UK's most respected farming magazines.

'What Lord Carlisle has done has produced an advance in breed quality never before seen in this country...'

There were links to articles astounded at what this breed was achieving.

And then the offer...

Straws of semen for sale under strict conditions. These straws are sold with conditions that each progeny will make a return to the company. If you don't wish to purchase semen, you have this once in a lifetime chance to invest in this amazing breed.

Apparently Lord Carlisle had no desire to make more money himself but having set up his breeding herd at home he wished to see it expand into 'the colonies'.

There was sworn proof of testing, of stunning results from careful breeding. There were photographs of semen straws with the coat of arms of the Carlisles discreetly embossed on the outer wrapping. The straws had numbered certification of authenticity.

Included was a description of genetic markers to identify progeny and protect 'copyright', and enough science to make her eyes water.

There was enough promise of profit to make Grandma hand over what money she had and then head to the bank to borrow more. To a greedy bank manager in a small community who'd been dazzled himself.

It was all so stupid. So farcical. A decent Internet search could have exposed the scam before it began. But this was a depressed farming community, where drought and failing profits had eaten away its foundations. The young had mostly left, for the city and for secure jobs. What was left was a core of elderly farmers, struggling to make ends meet, struggling to keep their land. They'd been clinging to hope, and hope was vulnerable. This man had targeted them well.

By the time Charlie had realised what was going on, the whole thing had been exposed. There'd been no need for Charlie to do any sleuthing—the police had done it for her. The real Lord Carlisle was said to keep himself to himself, an old man, almost a hermit, and in ill health.

The man calling himself Thomas Carlisle had obviously taken advantage, creating his own fraudulent online presence. Certification, paperwork, sperm containers, had all been stolen. Signatures had been forged. With no authority, he'd sold empty promises. Lies. Heartbreak.

The real Lord Carlisle had been contacted and was said to be appalled.

She headed to the Internet now and skimmed the recent media reports of the scam. Thomas Carlisle, real name Thomas Morgan... She hadn't even registered the name.

He was Bryn's uncle. Bryn was driving his uncle's car. He'd come to help a man who'd ruined lives.

Charlie sat at the kitchen table, her fingers seemingly paralysed on the keyboard. She was weeping.

These last months...the desperate call from Grandma... 'They're taking my land, love. The house... They're saying by the end of the week...'

She'd come down straight away, into a mess. She'd transferred what had been left of her own funds as a stop gap because she hadn't been able to see any other way of halting the bailiffs. She'd headed back to Melbourne to see lawyers…

And then the heart attack, the loss, the grief…

This man's uncle.

She'd kissed him.

Yeah, she'd been as naïve as Grandma.

She thought of him now, sawing with a rusty blade, trying to get into a car that must have cost far more than the value of this farm.

'I should ring every farmer in the neighbourhood and let them come to watch,' she said out loud, but she knew she wouldn't. Because the damage had been done, and maybe she understood now the way her grandmother had been conned.

'Because he smiles,' she muttered. 'And that smile… If his uncle was like him…'

She sniffed and sniffed again and then headed to the kitchen to cuddle Flossie, who was looking much perkier than last night. The bandage around her leg was still in place, looking almost professional. She thought of Bryn, of his tenderness as he'd cared.

'It's all a deceit,' she muttered as the rest of the dogs mustered in for a cuddle as well. 'How stupid am I? As stupid as Grandma, or stupider. He can saw out there for a month, I'm not going near.'

He'd been sawing for an hour when a truck pulled in from the road outside. There'd been a few cars pass, but the thought of flagging anyone down for help was daunting. But the rickety truck slowed as it passed, then did a U-turn and came into the yard.

An elderly farmer climbed out and stared at the mess in bemusement.

'What the…? You okay, mate? Charlie? She's okay?'

'She's in the house,' Bryn told him. 'She's fine. My car got squashed last night with all my gear in it.' He straightened and wiped away sweat. 'I don't suppose you have a chainsaw I could borrow?'

And then the guy saw the car and Bryn saw his face change.

How many people in this district had been conned?

'You're...'

'I'm nothing to do with him,' Bryn said wearily. 'I'm just returning the car to the...'

'He's his nephew! He came to help him!'

She must have been watching. Charlie's head appeared at the top-floor window. She yelled and the guy backed away as if Bryn smelled. Which, considering the mud and the sweat, wasn't surprising.

'What the...? You okay?' the farmer yelled up to Charlie. 'What's this low life doing here?'

'I'm fine,' Charlie yelled back. 'He's getting a taste of summary justice. Leave him to it.'

'He might be here for a few days,' the farmer yelled back and then he grinned. 'Couldn't happen to a better piece of... Yeah, I won't say it. Got a mess on my own place, love, but if you're sure you're okay...'

'Thanks,' Charlie yelled back. 'But I'm okay. Let's all mind our own business. This guy's nothing to do with us.'

She slammed the window shut, the truck did a fast reverse and Bryn was left alone again.

He sawed on.

In a way, the hard work helped. For the last week he'd been stuck in a dingy motel room or in the interrogation room at the police station, fielding questions from police, from accountants, from lawyers, trying to sort his way through a financial nightmare. His own lawyers had flown out in the end, and the mess was sorted as much as it could be, but the week had left its mark. He'd felt dirty even before he'd arrived here, and Charlie's contempt was making it worse.

What else could he do?

Years ago his family had abandoned the idea of compensating for Thomas's crimes. What Thomas had stolen, gambled, conned in his lifetime was enough to destroy everything they'd worked for and more. This scam had been a small one in the scheme of things, and it spoke of desperation. Thomas loved all things European. For him to spend months holed up in such an out of the way place, conning little people... He'd have hated it. And now he'd be in some even more distant country, conning more?

What could Bryn do about it?

Nothing, he conceded. The Ballystone Hall website, used only as a tool for marketing his cattle, was now plastered with warnings of this scam. It was hurting his own finances. People were now questioning the integrity of the Ballystone herd—with good reason. The last weeks had cost him a fortune. The idea of compensating every victim...

'You can't do it,' his lawyers had advised and they'd advised strongly. 'Your grandfather accepted it and you need to accept it, too. If you do it once you'll be admitting familial obligation, and you'll have every one of your uncle's victims from the last thirty years suing you.'

So he had to wear it, and it made him feel ill. Yesterday all he'd wanted was to get home and put this behind him. He couldn't bear to face the victims of Thomas's deceit.

He was facing Charlie.

Or not facing her. She was locked inside the house, hating him, hurting because of what his toe-rag uncle had done.

If Thomas were here now...

He wasn't. There wasn't a thing Bryn could do about

his uncle. He had to put all his faith in international policing and hope that one day justice would catch up with him.

Meanwhile, could he help Charlie? Pay her out? He could do that without getting emotionally involved.

But the lawyers' warnings rang in his ears. 'One payout and you're liable for millions. Don't even think about it. Most countries have victims of crime compensation. We're sorry, my lord, but you'll just have to wear it.'

He was wearing it now.

All he could do was saw, and heave away dead timber, and feel…as if it wasn't even close to being near enough.

He was still on her land.

Three hours later he was still sawing, and Charlie needed to take the dogs for a walk, check the chooks and make sure Cordelia was doing okay. And get out of the house.

She couldn't sit in the kitchen and rage for the rest of the day. Or for the rest of the week. Or until the bailiffs came and repossessed Grandma's farm.

He'd sawed for a full morning. Maybe that was enough. What she most wanted was to get rid of him and the way he was going…her neighbour had said a few days. She wanted him gone now.

She looked out again at the mass of timber. He didn't seem to be making inroads. There was still a mess around the car.

Needs must, she thought, sighing. She had to let the guy off the hook.

How?

His phone must be in the car. Otherwise he'd have rung for help by now. If she lent him her phone he could ring for a tow truck, for a woodcutter who was handy with a chainsaw—for a hire car? He'd have to pay—she had nothing to pay with—but that was his call. But she bleakly, finally accepted that she needed to approach him, maybe find the numbers, offer her phone, wait until he'd made the calls.

'Okay, Charlie, suck it up,' she told herself. 'Go lend the toe-rag your phone and give him the right numbers. Anything to get rid of him.'

But it took courage to walk out of the front door.

After her post cow-digging shower, instead of putting on another pair of ancient jeans she'd gone a bit formal. As a defence? Who knew? But for some reason it made her feel a smidge more in control. She'd pulled on black trousers and a crisp white shirt and she'd twisted her hair into a neat knot. Now that decision seemed sensible. She was a career woman, and she knew how to handle conmen.

Or maybe not, but she surely knew not to do anything like kiss them. Idiots kissed conmen and she wasn't playing the idiot one moment longer.

Go and get rid of him. Fast.

CHAPTER FOUR

SHE LEFT THE dogs inside. If she let them out they'd be bouncing around her, joyful to be out and doing, and she didn't want their joy undermining her disdain. Bryn was at the far side of the bulk of the tree. She stalked around, fighting for courage. Keeping her disdainful face on.

And then she stopped.

He wasn't sawing into the car, or, if he was, he was doing it the long way.

What she hadn't realised from the glimpses she'd dared from upstairs was that he was working in from the far reaches of the driveway, unblocking the route to the house. He was forming a mountain of twigs and dead-leaf litter, stacking it well past the driveway. Anything that could be used as firewood he was stacking closer—where it could be loaded onto a trailer to be taken to a woodshed? He was clearing her drive as he worked.

Why?

He surely wasn't intending to drive his over-the-top sports car out. Even from here she could see it was damaged past repair.

Did he think she'd drive him?

That didn't make sense. He was giving himself hours of extra work, when surely the best option was to simply reach his car, reach his phone and call a cab.

She stared in stupefaction and, as if he sensed her presence, he looked up, saw her and stopped sawing.

'What are you doing?' she asked stupidly, and, even more stupidly, here came his smile again. In the face of all he and his appalling uncle had done, how he had the effrontery to smile...

To kiss her...

Do not think of that kiss.

'I'm sawing,' he said helpfully, and went back to sawing.

She stood and watched. He sawed as if the ancient, rusty saw he was using was brand new, built for the job. His strokes were long and steady, with no hesitation, no catching. Charlie had tried to use a saw before, and she knew it was hard with well-cared-for tools. To saw like this, with a rusty blade...

He'd said he was a farmer. Maybe it wasn't all lies.

But most of it was. She glanced again at the squashed car and thought of the damage, the pain. She hardened her heart.

'You don't need to clear the driveway,' she said, and was proud of how cold she sounded. 'There's no way you'll be driving out. There's a local cab company in Carlsbrook. If you pay enough they'll take you to the airport. There's a guy who lives a couple of miles from here, a woodcutter. I've checked. He has more than enough work after last night to keep him busy for months but if you pay him enough he'll cut a path through to your car.'

He stopped sawing again and straightened, watching her.

'And where does that leave you?'

'That's not your business. I want you off my land.'

'Will he clear your driveway?'

'Eventually.' If she paid him. *With what?*

Don't go there.

'"Eventually" isn't good enough,' he said and went back to sawing.

'You can't clear it by hand,' she said, stunned, but he didn't pause as he answered.

'I'm thinking the bulk of it'll be done by this evening. By then I'll have reached my car. I'll retrieve my phone—and my gear with a change of clothes—and I'll do my own organising to get me out of here. And you'll be left with a clear driveway. So thank you for the offer, Miss Foster, but I don't need it.'

She was feeling…a bit dizzy. This man was a toe-rag. Why wasn't he acting like one?

Because charm was his middle name? She was beginning to realise just how her grandmother had been conned.

She was looking for the con now. She wasn't clever enough to find it but she knew it'd be there.

'I don't want you on my land any more,' she said, and it came out petty. Like a kid saying, 'I'm taking my bat and going home.'

He straightened again then, and set the saw aside. Once again she was caught by the sight of him. Naked to the waist, every inch of him toned, muscled, hard…

Was he really a farmer?

The way he handled that saw…

Do not let yourself be conned!

She walked forward, proffering the phone, holding it out as if she were handing over something distasteful to someone who was even more distasteful. As if she'd need disinfectant when she was done.

He smiled but his smile was rueful and he shook his head.

'I'm not taking more from you, Charlie.'

And what was there in that to make her blink? To make her eyes suddenly well so she had to fight back stupid, unwanted emotion.

Do not trust.

'Go inside and ring the police at Carlsbrook,' he said, just as gently. 'Ask to speak to Sergeant Marlow. I've been working with him for the last few days, trying to clear up what I can of this mess.'

'Of...your uncle's mess.'

'Yes.' He was looking straight at her, his gaze on hers, serious, steady.

Steady. It was a strong word but it resonated. In all this mess, he seemed somehow...solid.

Right. Grandma had thought that. Grandma had lost everything.

'Thomas Carlisle is an alias,' he told her, confirming what she'd just learned. 'He's really Thomas Morgan. My uncle. Once upon a time he was part of my family but that was a long time ago. He was wild as a youth, he was in trouble with the law before he turned twenty and he's gone from bad to worse. He broke my grandmother's heart. My grandfather died recently still despairing of him.'

'So you knew...'

'We've known for years that Thomas is a slime ball. We didn't know of this particular con until the police contacted us.'

His voice was deep. Even. Steady.

There was that word again.

'He's stolen from us,' Bryn said. 'From my family. From me. From everyone he touches.'

'He wasn't a Baron. A Lord.' She should have researched it herself, she thought wildly. She'd been so caught up in her personal distress.

'No.'

'And you... You really are a farmer?'

He held out his hands then, large, capable, worn. Hands that had carried Flossie in last night. Hands that had dug

Cordelia out of the mud. Hands that had sawed for three hours without blistering.

'Farming's my life,' he said simply. 'I'm only here—'

'To rescue your uncle.' She said it flatly because it was the truth and she had to cling to it. Families didn't discard members. They stood together against the world.

Like she and Grandma. Going down together.

'I came because they told me Thomas was dead.'

That hauled her out of her introspection. It was a blank statement, bald, and it held her.

'Dead…'

'If you've indeed been conned by Thomas, you'll know he set this up with so much skill he might have got away with it.' His voice was suddenly tired. 'You might not know that he's conned people before. There are lawsuits against him at home and in half a dozen other countries. This was a small-time scam compared to the others, mostly I imagine because there are any number of law agencies looking for him. Now he's running out of options.'

Still he hadn't moved. They were thirty feet apart, a mile of distrust between them, and the bleakness in Bryn's voice seemed to make the distance greater.

'It seems, to give him time to get out of the country, he parked the car above the cliffs overlooking Deadman's Reach by the river north of Carlsbrook,' he said wearily. 'What a name, by the way—it's almost designed to live up to its reputation. He left a note saying he was tired of running, that he regretted his life of lies, that he was done. He left one shoe artistically at the cliff edge, and tossed another to land on a ledge below. He made scuff marks at the cliff edge and his briefcase wide open, so we could assume the wind had blown things away. He left the car, which he'd only leased. Leased with fraudulent papers. So I had a call…'

'You had a call?' She was struggling to take this in.

'I'm...' His voice faltered and something washed over his face—a shadow of pain? It was an impression only though, fleeting and gone before he continued. 'I'm pretty much his only relative. My father died some years ago and my grandfather recently. I couldn't ask my mother to come to Australia to prove her brother-in-law hadn't actually committed suicide but had taken off on yet another false passport to somewhere he could start conning people all over again.'

'You knew he wasn't dead?'

'I guessed. Once I was here I was sure.'

'That's what the police are saying,' she whispered. 'That it was fake. But you... You said you're here to help him.'

'I didn't say that. I've done as much as I can to undo the damage he's done but helping Thomas... If you knew how much I wanted to...' He paused and gazed around him, at her land, or the land that the bank now owned. 'No. Fury gets me nowhere.'

She shook her head, trying to rid herself of confusion. This man... Why should she trust him?

'The car...' she managed, looking at the wreck of the over-the-top sports car, and he sighed and even managed a wry smile.

'Yeah, that's my call.'

'Your call?'

'He used my name to lease it,' he said wearily, almost apologetically. 'That's another reason I had to come. I told you he's stolen from me. He came to my home...a while back and stole identity papers. Plus the rest. The car's the tip of the iceberg. It's...it *was* to be collected by the dealership in Melbourne.' He looked at it ruefully. 'It was hard enough to explain I wasn't responsible for the debt before it was squashed. Now...'

'You're responsible for that?' It was unbelievable. But suddenly...she did believe him.

Why? His uncle had been a consummate con artist. This man, with his blazing good looks, his smile… He was so far out of her realm…

Or he had been. But maybe Thomas *had* stolen from him, too, and she'd made him battle a fallen tree the whole morning and he'd saved Flossie and he'd saved Cordelia and…and…

She felt about two inches tall.

She could choose not to believe him. That'd be easier.

'If you need to keep thinking of me as a scumbag, go right ahead,' he said and, for heaven's sake, it was as if he'd read her mind.

'I don't get it,' she said, and she knew she was sounding desperate. 'How can I believe you're a farmer when you swan around in such a car? They cost…'

'I know exactly how much this one cost,' he said and named a figure that made her almost do a double take. And then, stupidly, the smile returned. 'But you know, life's not all mud. Sometimes a man needs to stop and smell the roses.'

'I don't know what you mean?'

'The police collected me at the airport and brought me here,' he told her. 'They put me up in the Carlsbrook Motel, which leaves a lot to be desired in the comfort department. I've spent days being grilled like a criminal. I had the distinct impression I'm lucky not to be behind bars myself and only the fact that I'd voluntarily flown out here gave them pause. Thomas has put my signature on a power of paperwork, and he's done it well. When they finally stopped suspecting me, I was still facing a mass of legalities. Finally I was cleared to go home but the police weren't offering to take me back to the airport. However, this car needed to be taken back to Melbourne. And what a car!' His smile became a grin then, suddenly pure mischief. 'So I thought…'

'You thought you'd just…'

'Have fun,' he said, but he said it quite gently. 'Because I've learned from hard experience that you can let grey overwhelm you, or you can catch at slivers of light.' He paused and watched her for a moment. 'I suspect there've been very few slivers of light in your life lately,' he said. 'Just how badly did Thomas hurt you?'

'You don't know details?'

'I don't know individual cons,' he said apologetically. 'The police seemed to think it was none of my business. They've cited privacy provisions, and, to be honest, I couldn't face knowing the details of every farmer he's hurt. He's done this before, Charlie. I can't undo—'

'Of course you can't,' she said hurriedly. What was he thinking, that she expected him to pay back every cent his toe-rag uncle had stolen? No one could do that.

'So tell me what's happened to you,' he said.

'You don't need to know,' she muttered and scuffed her foot on the gravel of the driveway, and Bryn set his saw down and walked around the fallen tree until he was in front of her. Right in front.

He put his hands on her shoulders and gripped, hard. She'd been staring down at her shoe, at the groove she was making in the gravel. She couldn't look up.

'Charlie…'

'Don't.'

'Please, will you tell me?' he said. 'I need to know.'

'Like the police said, it's not your business.'

'It just got personal. Charlie…'

'Okay, he took everything,' she said and the desperation was back in her voice. She couldn't stop it. 'He came in here because this looks like a farmhouse but of course it's only twenty acres because Grandma sold off the rest of the farm when Pa died. She did that so she could feed her waifs and strays. So she only had one cow and one calf and even Thomas had to concede she couldn't use one of his semen straws on such small, scrawny cows. But that didn't stop him explaining what a fantastic scheme it was. He told her what she was doing was marvellous and he wanted to help, so he'd offer her a once in a lifetime opportunity…'

'Hell.'

'It was hell,' she whispered. 'Because she still had an overdraft facility that's been sitting there from the time this was a working farm and the bank manager at Carlsbrook is lazy and has never checked. No one even queried when she withdrew a sum that I can't bear to…' She shook her head. 'No matter. It's done.'

'Oh, Charlie.'

'Yeah, and it seems Grandma wasn't the only local with stupid overdraft limits. Head office put the heat on the local bank manager and suddenly Grandma was in so much trouble. I managed to cover enough for her not to be evicted straight away but it was never going to be enough to keep her here. So she was appalled and grief stricken and then she had a heart attack.'

She shoved back then, away from his hold, anger and grief overwhelming her. 'And then she died,' she managed. 'So that's that. And I'm sorry. I'm sorry about your uncle and I'm sorry about Grandma and the dogs and the cows and my business but I'm darned if I can see a silver lining anywhere.'

'Then why don't we make one?'

She'd been close to tears. Very close. She could feel her whole body trembling but Bryn's unexpected response brought her up short.

'What…?'

'It seems to me that we've both had a few tough weeks,' he said. 'So what should we do about it?'

'I…' She blinked. 'I have no…there's nothing…'

'Nothing silver lining-ish?'

'Lining-ish?'

'I'm from the old country,' he told her. 'I suspect we have a far more extensive vocabulary than you colonials.'

She didn't doubt it. That voice… It did things to her.

Do not go down that road.

'If you're relenting on making me walk off the property, I might grant myself a break from wood-chopping,' he was saying. 'But it's no use heading back into the house and sitting over a cup of tea playing who's the most miserable.' His voice softened. 'I concede, by the way. You are by a long shot. I've just been messed around by my uncle. You've lost your grandma.'

'You've missed your plane.'

'I have at that. But I've decided, right this minute, that it doesn't matter.'

'Of course it matters. I can call a cab. There'll be another flight tonight.' And then she paused in horror. 'But you didn't turn up. They'll charge you for another fare. Oh, my…'

'I've already thought of that,' he said, suddenly smug. 'Travel insurance. I'm a man prepared, and accidents are covered, which pretty much takes care of a car squashed by a lightning strike. So that's my flights covered. Though I'm doubting they'll cover the car.'

'What will you do?'

'Not panic,' he said firmly. 'Because panic does nothing. Instead I'll ring the collection agency and remind them that they did agree to me driving it back to Melbourne. Via email. They were relieved at the offer because it meant they didn't need to send their people to retrieve it. So my people can talk to their people while I focus on the important things in life. Like silver linings.'

'Your people?' she queried.

'Lawyers.' He hesitated. 'Where are your people?' he asked.

'I don't…'

'Your mum. Your dad. Your boyfriends, girlfriends, neighbours…'

'You saw one neighbour…'

'For two minutes and then he was off. Leaving you with a mess and someone he thought was low life. Just how alone are you, Charlie Foster?'

'I have the dogs.'

'Right.' He was surveying her thoughtfully. 'The dogs. And chooks and cows. They need to be included in our silver lining.'

'I don't know what you mean?'

'Meaning what, right now, would make you happy?'

'A home for the dogs?'

'You don't want to keep them?'

'How can I? I have a studio in Melbourne.' For which the rent was overdue already.

'Okay, too hard for today,' he said, still watching her face. 'What we need is something immediate.' He stood and gazed around, at the undulating hills, at the vast gums in the distance. It was a perfect rain-washed morning.

'It's a morning for doing,' he said.

'You've already been doing. You need to catch a cab.'

'I could,' he agreed. 'Leaving you with a squashed sports car, a driveway full of dead tree and other problems so assorted I can't begin to understand. But I've decided that walking away isn't the action of a hero and I've always wanted to be a hero.' Then, at the look on her face, he grinned. 'Come on, Charlie. You've been had by Thomas, but for every villain there has to be a hero. Ask any decent movie-maker. I know I should have donned a cape, called on my superpowers and cleared this tree in an instant, but you'll just have to settle for what you can get. And what you've got is my decision not to go home and leave you in this mess.'

'There's no need…'

'There is a need,' he said and he reached out, lifting her chin so her gaze was forced to meet his. 'It's Saturday and even superheroes need weekends. So how about we take the weekend as our silver lining and let the world break in again on Monday? What about it, Charlie Foster?'

'I don't…what are you suggesting?' She was reaching the point where she was too flummoxed to answer.

He gazed around again, and then focussed on the now massive heap of dead-leaf litter and mess he'd hauled away from the stump itself. The sun had been up for hours now and the rain-soaked mess had steamed itself dry. There was not a breath of wind. It was as if the storm last night had been a figment of their imagination.

'Bonfire,' he said in the tones of a small boy, suddenly fired with excitement. 'This lot would burn like firecrackers. We might need to phone your local fire brigade to warn them but…there's no rule against it, is there?'

'I…no…' At this time of the year half the locals were burning off to make undergrowth safe for the summer bushfire season.

'There you go, then. And we could have baked potatoes for lunch. Or maybe make that dinner. It might take a while to burn down to hot coals.'

'You want to stay for dinner?' She was having trouble making her voice work.

He'd been surveying the leaf litter but now he turned back to her, his eyes holding hers, warm, reassuring—and so, so compelling. She could see why Grandma had fallen for Thomas' charms.

She was wiser. Of course she was. Oh, but this smile…

'Let me stay,' he told her. 'Charlie, I want to help. I want to finish clearing this mess. I want to get the car off your land. I want to make sure Flossie's okay and that Cordelia's recovered from this morning's adventures. More, I want to see if there's any other way I can help.'

'Thomas was…only your uncle,' she managed. 'And he's hurt you, too. You don't need…'

'But I want to, Charlie,' he told her. 'So you have a man before you asking to be a superhero.' His grin widened at that. 'I'll admit I might be lacking in the Lycra department, but are you a woman intending to say no?'

That grin…that smile…

It was too much. The strains of the last few weeks were almost overwhelming but right now…

A superhero minus Lycra? She was close to laughter but also close to tears. Hysteria was edging back. But Bryn was weaving a spell with his smile. Offering her a silver lining?

Or just a bonfire.

It might be…fun.

Where had that word been lately? she thought. And where would it be in the future?

Take it now.

Bryn was watching, waiting for her decision.

'I don't have any potatoes,' she said, because right now the only imperative seemed to be the truth.

'That little blue car behind the house…is that yours?'

'I…yes.' She'd have to sell it, but she wouldn't go there now.

'Then let's do what you offered to do last night. Cut the fence in the top paddock and break out. Let's head into town and stock up on provisions and then come back and start our weekend. Potatoes on me,' he said grandly.

The thought of her car was put aside. This man was buying her potatoes? What an offer. She was forced to chuckle.

'Isn't your wallet in the car?'

'My wallet's in my back pocket, a little soggy but intact. There's the difference between me and superheroes in Lycra. How many of them have back pockets?'

She choked but struggled to stay with…sense. 'Your wallet has enough for potatoes?'

'Even for a bottle of wine.' His smile widened and it was as if the sun had come out. But the sun was already out, she thought wildly. She was delusional. She was becoming mesmerised by this man's gentleness, his smile, his…

Trustworthiness?

Don't go there. There was no reason at all for her to trust, she told herself. He was asking nothing except to be allowed to buy potatoes and wine and make a truly excellent bonfire.

Somehow she forced herself to pause, making herself examine the offer from all angles. She didn't trust. She couldn't.

But she did want time out. A bonfire. And wine.

And this man for a weekend?

Oh, for heaven's sake…

But the thought wouldn't go away and the grey had suddenly lifted from her world. It'd descend again soon enough, she thought, but for now…

'Okay, let's go chop holes in fences,' she said, a trifle breathlessly, and his smile gentled. Changed…

'Excellent. Very excellent decision, Charlie *bach*.'

And then, before she could begin to guess what he intended, he took her face in his hands. He tugged her forward and he kissed her.

It was a feather-kiss, no more, a mere brush of his mouth against hers. It had none of the passion of this morning. It was no promise, no hint at foreplay, no indication of anything to come. It was simply a kiss of tenderness, a contract sealed between two who might become friends. A mark of darkness past, with silver lining to come.

He pulled away and he was smiling again.

'Do you have anything in the house I could wear?' he asked, almost apologetically. 'I'm not exactly presentable. I could send you into town on your own but it doesn't seem a very superhero sort of thing to do.'

She *could* go on her own. It'd be sensible.

But suddenly Charlie wasn't being sensible. She was being the very opposite of sensible. That kiss…

She had nothing left to lose, she thought, and the kiss had fired a warmth in her that she hadn't felt for far too long.

Ever?

But enough of introspection. There seemed magic all around, and suddenly she was taking it. She had her very own superhero for the weekend and there was no way a woman would leave a superhero behind while she went grocery shopping.

She thought of him carting her groceries out to the car and suddenly she was almost blushing. Oh, for heaven's sake…

'There might be stuff of Grandpa's,' she said slowly. 'Grandma never threw things out.'

'Excellent,' he said and he took her hand. 'Okay, Charlie. Find me something to wear and let's have fun.'

And who could resist? Not Charlie.

The world was grey but for this weekend, the world was…hers?

What had he done?

He'd promised to stay for the weekend.

He'd kissed her again! Why?

His defences were right down, smashed by shock, betrayal and the bleakness of the last weeks. Somehow he'd have to build them again.

But he glanced at Charlie, at her face, at the beginning of a tremulous smile. He felt her hand in his.

Defences would have to wait until Monday.

CHAPTER FIVE

HE DIDN'T JUST buy potatoes. Once in the general store at
Carlsbrook, Bryn suddenly became...someone who'd drive
an Italian supercar?

Not exactly, Charlie thought, as she followed the trolley propelled by this man on a mission. He was wearing
his own pants because nothing of Grandpa's had come
close to fitting. They were liberally mud-spattered. One
of Grandpa's sweaters had stretched beyond recognition
over the years, and was now large enough to encompass
his broad shoulders. It was faded and there were moth
holes in the sleeves. His shoes were so filthy she couldn't
see where mud ended and leather began.

He looked like a down-at-heel farmer, who hadn't bothered to change into his going-to-town best before leaving
the farm.

But despite his clothes he didn't look like a down-at-heel
farmer. Sure, he was wearing what looked like mucking-
out-the-pigsty gear. Yes, he looked weathered, his eyes
crinkled in the way of farmers the world over, men who
spent too long in the sun and wind and rain. Yes, the hands
holding the trolley were farmer's hands, big, worn, capable...

But the way he held himself... He was tall, tanned and
ripped, and despite his clothes he'd had the girls at the
checkout a-twitter from the moment he'd walked in.

And as Charlie headed for the potatoes, he turned stubborn and headed for the delicatessen section.

'First things first,' he decreed. 'Entrée. What sort of cheeses does this place stock?'

Good ones. There were a couple of top-notch cheese producers in the valley and the supermarket stocked them for passing trade. Not for locals. No farmer around here could ever afford them.

But it seemed Bryn could. 'Excellent,' Bryn decreed and bought six large wedges.

'Six!' Charlie's eyebrows hit her hairline. 'We can't eat six.'

'You're talking to a man who's spent the morning being a lumberjack. Watch me.'

She watched in stupefaction as he proceeded to load the trolley with enough food to feed a small army—an army with very specific and expensive dietary requirements. And part of her was joyful.

Ever since that first panicked call from her grandmother and the transfer of every cent she possessed, she'd been pretty much living on homemade soup and pasta. Now Bryn was loading up steak. Sausages. Lamb chops. Bacon. Butter. Nuts and crisps. A frozen apple pie. Cream. Beer. Wine. Even champagne. Oh, for heaven's sake...

'There must be caviar around here somewhere,' she muttered as he tossed in vacuum packs of smoked salmon.

'Really? Shall I ask?' Bryn turned to the girls at the checkout counter. 'Miss Foster's looking for caviar. Are we in the right aisle?'

She choked. The girls at the registers looked at her and looked at Bryn and decided the question was too hard to answer. Instead they giggled.

'Just how long are you intending to stay?' she asked faintly as a cabbage landed in the trolley on top of the champagne. A cabbage?

'As long as it takes,' he said enigmatically. 'Baked potatoes… We need tinfoil and sour cream and bacon and coleslaw but I have a feeling one cabbage is not the total coleslaw ingredient list. Suggestions?'

She stared at the pile in the trolley. 'You're planning to stay…how long?'

'Our bonfire won't be coals until tonight and I haven't eaten since breakfast. The steak's for our very late lunch.'

'The salmon…'

'Snacks,' he said enigmatically. 'Lumberjacks get hungry. No caviar? That's a shame. Does your hardware section run to saws?' he asked the girls. 'Big ones?'

'Bryn, you can't…'

'I can.' He stopped then and turned to face her. They were in the middle of the vegetable aisle, surrounded by cabbages. A couple of middle-aged women were watching with unabashed curiosity, as were the girls on the register, but he didn't appear to notice. His attention was all on her.

'You're too alone,' he said, loudly enough for anyone—everyone—to hear. 'There's not a lot I can do to repair the damage Thomas has created but what I can repair I will. I don't have the money to compensate every victim of every scam but on a personal level… I wish to leave you enough wood to keep you warm for as long as you have here. I wish to clear your driveway. I wish to help you find homes for all your grandma's assorted dogs and cows and chooks. And most of all… Charlie, I want to make you smile. Thomas robbed you of your grandma and a whole lot more. I don't have to be back in the UK for a few more days. Let me do this.'

And then he held up his hands in a gesture of surrender, as if acknowledging there was more that could be read into what he was saying and he wished to back off.

'And, Charlie, it's potatoes and salmon and coleslaw

only—as long as I can discover how to make coleslaw. Nothing else. I'm not here to press unwanted advances...'

'What does that mean?' one of the checkout girls demanded of the other.

'Means he doesn't want to sleep with her,' the second girl said. 'Pity. If he asked me...'

'I can give you a great coleslaw recipe,' one of the shopping ladies volunteered, and smiled at Charlie. 'Charlotte, you go for it. You know your grandma would have wanted you to.'

'He's Thomas Carlisle's nephew,' Charlie said helplessly. 'He's admitted it. Thomas Carlisle. The guy who called himself Lord Carlisle. He stole from all of us. Why should I trust him?'

There was silence at that while Bryn was assessed. Clearly Grandpa's ancient sweater didn't fit with the remembered Thomas and his sleaze and his car and his lies. And then one of the checkout girls spoke up. 'I know about this guy.'

Everyone turned to her. Or maybe not Bryn, but Charlie wasn't looking at Bryn. She was trying very hard not to look at Bryn.

'I mean...' The girl seemed embarrassed with the attention and her friend had to elbow her in the ribs before she could continue. 'I mean...you know my dad's a cop? He said the creep's nephew has been here. They thought he was in the scheme too, but he came all the way from the UK to say he wasn't. This guy must be him. And he's gorgeous, miss,' she said in a hurry. And then she subsided as her previous pale complexion transformed to bright pink blush.

'You might be interested in the special on fancy coffee in aisle two, this week only,' her friend ventured, manfully trying to deflect attention from her friend's blushes. 'Just saying. If you're getting fancy stuff you'll need good coffee. And we do have saws. Any hardware you want. Anything else?'

'Dog food,' Bryn said, seemingly not the least perturbed. 'If you can point us to dog bones…'

'I'll show you,' one of the shoppers said warmly. 'And then I'll give you my coleslaw recipe. Oh, Charlotte, we were so worried about you.'

You still should be, Charlie thought wildly. I'm in such trouble.

The next few hours seemed to pass in a blur. They drove home and Bryn cooked them both steak for a late lunch. Steak—and he'd even bought enough for the dogs! Then Bryn headed back to the tree.

'Let's get ourselves a really big pile and light it at dusk,' he said. 'Do we need to notify your fire authorities that the mother and father of a burn is about to happen? Can you do that?'

Charlie did what she needed to do, then went out to help.

She had six dogs bouncing around her and she carried Flossie in her basket. Bryn had checked her leg and was happy enough to go without vet's advice. By now Charlie was trusting enough of his farming and animal experience to take his word.

'I'm thinking she might even be up to a bath tonight,' Bryn had told her as he'd reapplied the bandage. 'If we're gentle.'

We?

The word seemed to be seeping around her heart, on one level comforting, inviting, even seductive…

On another level, deeply scary.

Of all the things she didn't need in her life right now it was another man complicating things.

Except he wasn't complicating things. He'd saved her dog. He'd bought her enough food to last for a week and he was sawing his way to a clear driveway, free of charge. He was being a friend, so the least she could do was stop quibbling and go help.

As she walked down the driveway, loaded with dog, he didn't look up. He'd stripped off to the waist again. He was halfway through sawing a massive limb. His movements were rhythmic, even hypnotic—and that was how she felt. Hypnotised. By a beautiful body?

She couldn't afford to be hypnotised by anything—or anyone. But the day was gorgeous, the sun was on her face, the dogs were happy—even Flossie was wagging her tail. She had something to focus on other than the relentless worry and grieving that had been her life for the last few weeks. Or longer…

And she had someone to do it with. Someone like Bryn.

Don't think about Bryn. Do what he's doing: focus on the job at hand.

Yeah, right. A girl could work and look at the same time. A girl could work and feel.

A girl would be nuts not to.

He had company. Charlie.

Bryn was working with an excellent saw, and it made a difference. It should be making rhythm easy to maintain.

It wasn't. He was distracted.

Charlie had set Flossie's basket under a nearby tree, positioning it so she could poke her head into the sun if she wanted, or curl back into her basket into the shade.

She was a dog who'd run away. The gate was wide open now but she wasn't even looking at the gate. She was snoozing. Her fellow dogs were frolicking around her. They were occasionally stopping by to give her a conspiratorial sniff, but Bryn was sure there were no break-out conspiracies happening.

Why would there be? He glanced again at Charlie and his saw faltered as if it'd caught a knot in the wood.

It hadn't. The falter had been his call entirely.

Charlie was collecting armloads of fallen branches, small stuff, carrying it out into the midst of the paddock, the place he'd decreed would make a great bonfire setting.

She was dressed in old jeans, a faded windcheater and wellingtons. Gum boots, he'd been told when he'd bought some from the general store. Charlie's grandpa's feet had been just a bit smaller than his so he'd splurged.

'You can't spend all of this,' Charlie had expostulated and he'd thought of how little gum boots cost and how little Charlie's debt would be in the scheme of things. He'd wanted to write a cheque right there. Only his lawyer's stern decree had stopped him.

'One payment and you admit liability. This is a no-fault situation unless you do anything stupid.'

They'd probably think chopping up dead trees on one of the victim's farms would classify as stupid.

It didn't feel stupid. It felt good.

Charlie's copper curls were tied back with scarlet ribbon into a…a what? A ponytail? It bounced as she walked.

She was whistling, a happy, tuneless little whistle. It was a good sound. No, it was a great sound. The dogs were bouncing around her and he thought, She's making them happy.

And then he thought of her last night, of her fear, and he knew things hadn't been happy for a long time.

Even before his scumbag uncle had made things worse?

Maybe he was imagining things, but he didn't think so. Something about Charlie mirrored Flossie's misery—something spoke of long-term weariness, almost defeat.

He shouldn't be staying on. He'd pretty much forced himself on her but there was something…something…

About the way her ponytail bounced?

It wasn't just that. Surely it wasn't. There were plenty of attractive women back home and he was sure lots of them had ponytails. One hint to his mother and he'd have a bevy of ponytails lined up for his inspection. She was desperate for him to move on but he wasn't interested. Since the tragedy on the estate, he'd steered clear of any serious relationship. Love hurt. Ponytails could keep their distance.

But this one…

It wasn't guilt that was keeping him here, he conceded. Even though this scam of Thomas's was a bit different in that it had directly involved him, he was pretty much over feeling guilt about his appalling uncle. 'That man was born evil,' his mother had told him. 'I have no idea why. He was born into such a lovely family but your father says he was born wanting to hurt people. He's given your grandparents such grief. Do what you need to protect the title and put him out of your mind.'

He did. He had.

So why was he still here? Why not just arrange someone to pay to do what he was doing?

Because a bouncy ponytail was whistling across the paddock towards him. She saw him looking and paused and smiled, and that smile…

It was enough to make a man almost break the saw on the next knot.

It might even be enough to break through the fear he had of relationships.

Um…not. But it was enough to make him think: There are things in this woman's past, and I need to find out what.

At dusk they lit their bonfire and it was pretty much the most spectacular bonfire Charlie had ever seen. The evening was warm and still. The mountain of dead leaves caught and blazed, sending sparks sky-high and radiating scorching heat. Bryn had lit the base and stepped back.

And stepped back again. And stepped back again and again and again.

Until he reached the spot where Charlie had set up a picnic rug—actually two picnic rugs because there were seven dogs who thought rugs beside bonfires were meant to share.

'It'll be an hour before we have enough embers to bake potatoes,' Charlie said, offering a bottle from a capacious basket. 'Want a beer?'

'And crisps and cheese and biscuits,' he agreed and flopped down beside her.

He'd pulled on her grandpa's sweater again. Some time during the afternoon he'd finally managed to access the car. He now had his own stuff, but he'd only brought business gear, plus a cashmere sweater for the plane—and this wasn't the night for cashmere sweaters.

He was filthy. It had been a day of hard physical work, and it felt…excellent.

He poured wine for her and a beer for himself and sat beside her and looked at the fire and felt…

As if this were home?

There was a crazy thought. Home was on the far side of the world. Home wasn't here.

This woman was here.

This woman who he'd met less than twenty-four hours before.

'Tell me about you,' he said, not for something to say but because he suddenly very much wanted to know. Needed to know?

'I'm hungry,' she said and loaded a cracker with Camembert and popped it into her mouth. There followed a couple of silent minutes while the Camembert was given due reverence and then she smiled. 'Now I'm not quite so hungry. But I do need more. Is that Stilton? Wow!'

'There's possibly more to you than the fact that you're hungry and you like cheese,' he ventured and she smiled.

'I like sausages and baked potatoes, too. And wine.'

'A woman of depth. But—'

'Tell me about you first,' she said, hurriedly.

Yep, he thought, that's a woman thing. A learned thing. Ask a guy to talk about himself and the conversation's pretty much taken care of.

So what to tell her? How much?

He sat and loaded his own cracker and drank some beer and thought of home, of the vast estates, of the title, of the responsibilities that went with it.

But he didn't want it. Okay, the land, the cattle, the estate, they were things he loved, but the title should never have come to him. Baron Carlisle of Ballystone Hall... Lord Carlisle... His grandfather's death had made it all slam back. He'd had the title for a mere two months, but its inheritance had made the whole tragedy of the past slam back.

And now... Charlie had been scammed by a title. How to tell Charlie that was who he was? If she'd done a thorough search of his uncle's background she might have discovered that Morgan was the family name of Baron Carlisle, but she obviously hadn't searched that far.

Did she really want to know?

She was scoffing cheese, savouring every mouthful. She had dogs draped over her legs. The firelight was playing with her hair, making the copper curls glint. This was time out of frame for both of them.

To announce his title...he couldn't bear to. He could tell the truth without it—as he'd like to live the rest of his life without it.

'Okay, potted history,' he told her. 'I'm a farmer. My family's run beef cattle for generations. I love farming. It's in my blood—it's who I am. I'm thirty-five years old and still single, much to my mother's disgust but that's the way I like it.'

'You prefer your own company?'

And there was another decision.

He paused and thought about all the flip answers he could give. None seemed appropriate.

What was it about this setting, this time, this woman…? He rarely spoke of the tragedy that underpinned his life. He couldn't tell her about the title but the rest, with Charlie it seemed right.

'There was…an appalling accident when I was nineteen,' he told her, softly, almost tentatively. Exposing a wound that could never heal? 'I guess it's taught me that solitary is best.'

'Oh, Bryn,' she said softly. 'You want to tell me about it?'

Did he? Somehow it seemed he had to.

'I was away at university,' he said, talking into the stillness. Staring at nothing in particular. 'My sister was studying, too, but she'd come home for the weekend. Like many farming families, my grandfather, my uncle—my dad's older brother, not the one who scammed you—my dad, and my cousin Alan were sharing the farm, the land, the work. Our farm's large. Normally it's more than enough to support two families—plus my grandfather—but right then we were struggling. It was summer, there'd been a drought, and the huge underground water tank we used for house water had finally emptied. Just as it did, a massive storm came in from the north, with the authorities predicting a huge dump of rain. So my father and uncle decided to work in a hurry and clean it. They used a petrol-driven pressure pump.'

'Oh, Bryn, no…'

She got it, he thought. How many people would? But

then, she had the advantage of knowing a tragedy had happened. His family had had no such warning.

Bryn had been interested in how things worked since birth. The rest of his family, not so much. It had become a standing joke. By the time he was ten years old it was standard practice… 'The tractor's stalled. Go get Bryn.'

But he'd been away at a house party with university friends. It had been Sunday morning, and there had been no one to tell them that their plan was dumb.

More than dumb.

Tragic.

'The fumes made them pass out,' he said, trying to keep bleakness from his voice. 'They would have died quickly as the fumes would have built and built.'

'Oh, Bryn…'

'There's more.' He closed his eyes, trying to block the scenario. The nightmare.

Say it like it was.

'Sunday lunch,' he managed. 'They didn't come home. My mother, my grandfather, my cousin and my sister…they were all waiting. So Alan and Louisa—my cousin and my sister—went looking. They saw my dad from the top—my uncle was further along the tank. We guess they assumed my uncle had already gone for help so they rushed down the ladder but by then the fumes had built up so much…' He shook his head. 'I guess…the only thing…the only thing that helps is that it would have been fast.'

He stopped. Was there no way he could ever shake off the grief, the guilt that he hadn't been there, the aching loss of so much of his family? Knowing he never could. 'I don't think you ever get over something like that,' he said at last and it was all he could say.

'Oh, Bryn, I'm so sorry.'

'It's okay,' he said brusquely, even though it wasn't. Even though it could never be okay. He shrugged. 'So there you have it. My uncle and my aunt divorced early so there's only Mum and me. We don't live in grief all the time but it's always with us.'

'She lives with you?'

'Um…not.' He smiled then, laughter unexpectedly resurfacing at the thought of his eccentric mother. After years of dreariness she'd found ways of distracting herself from a grief-ridden past.

'There's a scary word I'm sure exists for cases like mine,' he said, 'and it's called matricide. Mum is…well, matchmaking's probably too small a word for it. When she hits me at breakfast with a list of potential brides, she's in danger of being choked on her toast. And she likes…pink. She lives in the d— in a cottage next to the main house now, where she can pink to her heart's content and we get on much better. She doesn't hit me with brides until lunch time and by then I've had coffee and can handle it. I listen politely and then head back to the cows.'

There was a long silence. Charlie seemed to be taking it in, internalising. After so many reactions, so many years of hearing so many platitudes, so many appalled reactions, he found himself grateful.

'So your scamming uncle?' she asked after a while, quietly, and he was grateful. Past tragedy wasn't to be dwelt on.

'The uncle who died was my dad's elder brother,' he told her. 'The Thomas who scammed you was younger. Apparently he was a wild child, a wilder young man and eventually he turned criminal. We've seen him on and off over the years but only when he was after more money. He broke my grandparents' hearts. This last scam…' He shook his head. 'It's unforgivable. I'm so sorry.'

'It's not you,' she whispered and her hand slid silently into his.

And that felt…amazing. It was a simple gesture, a momentary act of empathy and why it made him feel…

He didn't understand how it made him feel. He disengaged because he didn't need sympathy, but loss of her hand felt like another grief.

'Enough of me,' he said, almost roughly. 'Fair's fair, Charlie Foster. Tell me about you.'

'There's little to tell.'

That was a deliberate deflection. She wasn't used to talking about herself, he thought.

'You said you're an interior designer.'

'You wouldn't think so, to look at me.' She looked ruefully down at her grubby, dog-hair-covered self. 'But I am. Tell me about your house. What's the décor of your farm? Modern? Shabby chic? Don't tell me, I'm guessing authentic provincial?'

He smiled, thinking of home, of so many generations of taste flung together in so many weird ways. But he wasn't letting her off the hook.

'You,' he said firmly. 'So you went to university?'

'I did,' she conceded. 'What did you study?'

Honestly, this was like blood from a stone. 'I started an engineering degree with a bit of commerce on the side. I decided if I was to be a farmer I was to be a canny one. So who sent you to university?'

'I guess… Grandma.'

'Your parents?'

'They're not on the scene. Mum's an anthropologist. Dad's a professor of anthropology, which is how they met. He's in the US now, on his third wife, with seven children that I know of. I don't hear from him. My mum's currently in Brazil, still bitter over what she sees as Dad's betrayal. She sends me a card at Christmas.'

'That's tough.'

'Not so tough,' she said. 'Dad's family had money,

though I gather Dad's share's dried up now. I'm guessing one paternity suit too many. But when I was young there was enough money to send me to the best boarding schools. I spent the holidays here with Grandma and Pa. I loved art, so Grandma and I sat down and thought about careers where I could use art to make a living. Grandma was…sensible then.'

'Not sensible for the last few years?'

'Increasingly dippy since Pa died. This place has never been very profitable and she was lonely and bored so she sold most of the land to set up an animal shelter. That meant she had a nice cache your uncle could steal—and of course the bank manager hadn't updated her overdraft limits after she sold the farm, so on paper it looked like it was still there as security.'

She was still steering around herself, he thought, pushing away the personal. So ask it straight out. 'Charlie, am I right or was there trouble even before your grandmother got herself in so much debt?'

'I was worried about her. She was getting older, frail…'

'Charlie…' He reached out and touched her face, the faintest of touches. Interrupting her words. Hauling her back to the personal.

'There was trouble in your world before,' he said and she flinched.

'How did you…?'

'I don't know. But I can sense…shadows.'

'Money hassles can do that to you.'

'So there were money problems before?'

She chewed her bottom lip. He refilled her wine glass and watched as the firelight flickered over the trouble on her face.

She wasn't used to sharing, he thought.

Why did it seem so important that she did share?

Why was it so important that she trusted him?

He sat and waited. The dogs were settled, content to lie on their rug and enjoy the warmth from the fire, the proximity of humans. Tonight even Flossie seemed content.

The silence deepened. He wouldn't press, he decided. He knew, deep down, that Charlie wasn't accustomed to talking about herself.

Her childhood must have been solitary. He thought of his own. His mum and dad had always been there for him, and he and Louisa had been loved. They'd had the run of the lands. The tenant farmers' kids had been their friends—were still his friends. His grandfather, his uncle, his cousin, had always been there for him. Home was a haven.

He looked around at the land Charlie must have thought was her home. It now belonged to the bank. Her grandmother was dead. She must feel...untethered?

That was how he'd feel if he lost Ballystone, he thought, and it didn't matter that Charlie's loss was twenty acres and if Bryn lost Ballystone it'd be thousands of acres. He knew deep down it'd feel the same.

'I was married,' Charlie said across his thoughts.

That was a shock. The words were blunt, harsh, and he wasn't sure where to take them.

'Do you want to tell me about it?' he asked, thinking he needed to back off. But he didn't want to.

'Not much.'

He nodded, and scratched the ear of a black and white fox terrier who appeared to be missing an ear. Possum. By now Bryn had learned all their names. It seemed Possum was called Possum because he was obsessed with the species. Any faint rustle and he was onto it. His lack of ear was evidence that the brush-tail possums around here were bigger than he was, and far more vicious.

'He was like your uncle,' Charlie said and her voice was little more than a whisper.

Like Thomas. Uh oh. But he didn't respond. Shut up, he thought. She'll tell you if she wants.

'How was I to know?' she said, flatly now, staring at the fire and not at him. 'I met Graham as I was getting started as an interior designer. He was older than me and gorgeous. He had a name in the business, and he was loving, totally attentive—and he loved my work. It was so flattering but what I didn't realise—what I was too stupid to see—was that he was marrying a workhorse. That's what he needed and that's what he got. He brought me into the business and I worked my butt off.'

'Oh, Charlie…'

'I was dumb,' she whispered. 'Young, naïve, stupid. I met him as I finished my course and he was trying to set up a glitzy interior-design studio for the rich and famous. What I didn't see was that I was simply cheap labour. I guess…he must have loved me at some level, but the bottom line was that he didn't have to pay a wife. He loved being the frontman, the guy out there wooing the clients. The hard work of sifting through fabric swatches trying to find a match, endless phone calls to suppliers, trying to juggle finances…not at all. But he expanded the business and I was too young and too stupid to object. You should have seen our premises—you have no idea how swank. Of course all of it was on borrowed money but I was so busy trying to keep clients happy I didn't realise what a house of cards it was. Then it started to get nasty and suddenly he was gone, with a wealthy client, with homes here, in New York, in Hawaii. Leaving me with debts up to my ears.'

'Like my uncle,' he said softly. 'The moral compass of a newt.'

'Never trust people with Italian supercars?' she whispered. 'I'll add expensive watches to that list. Titles and mansions and promises and lies… I'd just managed to haul myself out of the mess he landed me in when Grandma landed me in another. And now…' She looked bleakly at the dogs. 'Now it's not just money. These guys… I can't bear to think about it.' She sighed and almost visibly braced. 'But that's enough of bleak. Is this fire died down enough to bury spuds?

'Can we scrape some coals out a bit so we can cook the sausages? I'm still hungry. Come on, Bryn Morgan. Let's get on with our silver lining.'

So they did.

For the rest of the night there was no talk of lies, of cheating, of debt. No talk of the past. They ate. They lay on their backs on the picnic rug and watched the stars appear. Bryn had thought the stars back home were bright but these were amazing. Or maybe it wasn't the stars that were amazing.

Charlie was pointing out the Southern Cross, the Big Dipper, Orion's Belt, the Pointers, and he listened to her soft voice. He watched her hand gently pat Flossie's head— Flossie had somehow edged onto their blanket and her big, soft head was nestled in the crook of Charlie's arm…

The night was still and warm. The fire had died to a mass of embers, every now and then spitting a spray of sparks into the night, sparks that looked as if they merged with the stars. There was still heat from the fire, but it was a gentle heat.

They'd buried their spuds and then dug them up and eaten them and Bryn couldn't remember when anything had tasted so good.

Was it just that the past few weeks had been so bleak, filled with lawyers, police, investigators, the knowledge that his name had been used to con small people, people like Charlie…?

But Charlie wasn't small. She was warm and curvaceous and kind, and her hand was stroking Flossie and…

And this time it was his hand reaching out and taking hers. So both their hands were resting loosely on the dog's soft fur.

Charlie's hand stilled.

She could pull away. There was no pressure.

He would put no pressure on this woman.

What was he thinking? Where were his thoughts taking him?

He knew exactly where his thoughts were taking him. Or where they already were, and they'd been there from the moment he'd walked into this farmhouse and seen her, scared, defiant, brave. How many women would open their doors to strangers on such a night? And she'd been so joyous when it was Flossie, a misbegotten mutt that only someone like Charlie could love.

Someone like Charlie.

How much debt was she in? How much trouble?

She had a good career, though. She could walk away, leave these animals to refuges, wipe her debts with bankruptcy, take a paid job.

It was unthinkable.

He could help. Surely?

And then out of nowhere, the thought, and even as the thought flashed through his mind it was in his mouth, spoken, out loud. A wish.

'Charlie…'

'Mmm…?' It was a sleepy murmur. The day of hard physical work, then good food, good wine, warmth and peace was doing its work. Was that why she was leaving her hand under his?

Or was the link as important, as strong, as meaningful, as it was to him?

That was a crazy thing to think. How could it be making sense—but suddenly it did, and the words were there. Spoken.

'Charlie, I want you to come home with me.'

CHAPTER SIX

THE NIGHT STILLED.

Neither of them spoke. There seemed to be no words.

Charlie's hand still lay under his but it had stiffened. No longer was it loose, warm, trusting. It was as if she was waiting for…what? The axe to fall?

This woman had been betrayed, he thought. By her absentee parents, by her husband, by his uncle. She didn't trust. And how could she trust? What he was proposing was crazy.

It was crazy for him, too. He didn't do relationships. So why did what he was feeling now seem so different? As if the rules he'd held rigidly to for so long no longer applied?

'What…what are you saying?' she whispered at last and finally she drew her hand away.

He wanted it back. The link seemed more than important while he tried to sort what he needed to say.

What he'd asked had been a spur of the moment thought, an idea only, but this woman didn't need speculation. She needed facts, something solid she could trust. Trust was something he could offer but who knew if it'd be accepted?

He had to give her space. The linking of their hands was a pressure she didn't need, and maybe it formed an emotion he needed to back away from.

Facts. Right.

He thought of what he could tell her—he should tell

her—who he was, the extent of his fortune, the power he wielded back home. And he thought of her words... *'Titles and mansions and promises and lies...'* She didn't need that. More, she couldn't trust it. What he needed to offer was something solid, with no embellishments. Something to take away the shadows, not add more.

She was still fixedly watching the stars. Thinking who knew what? He had an image suddenly in his head of a fawn he'd once found, separated from its mother. Trapped in briars. Watching him approach without moving, but with every fearful sense tuned to what was coming.

He'd managed to free it so it could run back to where it belonged. He needed to do the same here, but he didn't want Charlie to run. Whatever he offered had to be non-threatening.

'Charlie, I told you I'm a farmer,' he said and waited until he got a slight nod. It wasn't a committal to anything other than she'd listen, but it was enough.

'My land's been in my family for generations,' he told her. 'It's good land—no, it's great land—and it's prosperous. I'm what some would call a warm man.'

'A warm man...'

'Wealthy, if you will.'

'You've had to pay to come here,' she said cautiously. 'And lawyers...'

'Believe it or not, it hasn't dented my income.'

She was still staring at the stars, her body rigid. She couldn't trust, he thought, and his heart twisted. This woman...she seemed so alone.

'I could pay your debts,' he told her and he watched the rigidity increase, the way her face closed and he knew there was more than one reason why he couldn't go down that road. But he repeated the sensible one. 'My lawyers tell me, however, that if I pay one lot of Thomas's debts then I set a precedent. It'd mean I could be accepting liability for them all and no one's wealthy enough to cover Thomas's scams. But what I can do…' His hand touched hers again. 'What I'm free to do is be a friend. I can offer you a holiday in the UK on my farm. I can afford your fares easily. You could come…for two weeks maybe? I'm not sure of your work commitments. You could come for however long you can manage. But here's the thing. I'm also in a position to take your menagerie with me.'

'My…menagerie…'

He was thinking fast. How to make this offer seem… not ridiculous.

'I'm not sure about the hens,' he confessed. 'Charlie, could you bear to leave the hens behind?'

'There's a place that'll take the hens,' she managed, bemused, humouring the lunatic? 'A friend of Grandma's. A place that houses ex-battery hens, a lady who's passionate about chook care. For a donation…'

He smiled at that, liking that he'd crossed the first hurdle and made her listen. 'I doubt a donation to poultry welfare would count as legal precedent for settling Thomas's debts.' He couldn't resist. He touched her nose. Lightly. Just to see if he could make her smile back.

She didn't. She was still rigid.

'It's crazy,' she whispered. 'Seven dogs. Two cows…'

'Charlie, my farm's big enough for two cows to spend the rest of their days grazing to their hearts' content. I can put them with the rest of my herd, taking them out only when the bull has access. They'll cost me nothing but a little extra feed in winter. I suspect there's quarantine, but Cordelia's coped with being stuck in mud. Quarantine with her baby beside her should be no big deal.'

'You're crazy. It'd cost—'

'Shut up about the cost,' he said firmly. 'I've said I can afford it. You need to trust me on that, Charlie.'

Trust? She didn't. How could he expect her to? She

turned and looked at him and then turned back to star watching. 'You're being…it's nuts.'

'No, it's fun.' He touched her nose again, willing her to lighten. 'Fun for you and security for the dogs.'

'I don't get it.'

'I have two plans here,' he said, unbelievably firmly for a man whose plans were building as he spoke. 'Number one is a holiday—a real holiday—for one Charlie Foster. Number two is finding homes for seven needy dogs, good homes, personally inspected and approved by that same Charlie.'

'You really are nuts.'

'I might be,' he agreed and thought suddenly of his mother's reaction when seven dogs were unloaded from quarantine crates at Ballystone. The thought made him smile. His mother would have kittens—and then she'd put the almost frightening power of aristocracy and her love of animals to the fore.

'Charlie, you haven't met my mother, and you need to,' he told her. 'She's crazier than I am about animals. The one thing our nation is known for is dottiness about dogs. I'm thinking Mum could organise a heartrending piece in our local paper, outlying Thomas's infamy. That'll get the locals in. Thomas might be a villain but he's *our* villain and the locals follow his infamy with morbid curiosity. We could add a picture of each of your dogs, saying that Thomas has robbed them of their happy ever after. If we add a lump-in-your-throat description of their backgrounds to go with them I'm guessing we'll have queues wanting to adopt. And my plan is…you and my mum can have fun vetting each potential owner personally while you have a break. Fun, Charlie *bach*. How does that sound?'

'It won't… We can't…'

'We can,' he said, and enough of star watching. He took her hands and tugged, forcibly so Flossie slipped sideways and Charlie was lying on her side facing him, with Flossie sandwich-squeezed between them.

'It will work,' he said strongly. 'My mother will love doing this. I'll love doing this. I'm promising good homes, Charlie, I swear.' He hesitated, knowing this plan had to be solid. 'And if we don't find them good homes, our farm is big enough to house them all.'

'Seven…you'd go nuts.'

'What's a dog or seven on a place as big as ours? The place is already impregnated with generations of dog hair.' He grinned. 'Who knows? They might even become cow dogs.'

'In your dreams.'

'Maybe, but it'd be fun watching them try.'

'You're nuts,' she said, dazed. 'The whole concept's nuts. But even if it wasn't…the dogs… I mean, that'd be great but… I don't need to come. Bryn, the cost…'

'I can easily afford it. I promise that, too. What's more, Charlie, you'll have a return ticket in your hand before you leave. No tricks. I'm offering you a break from everything you've been facing here. A holiday on a farm that's just as beautiful as this one, but different in so many ways. Have you ever been to the UK?'

'I…no.'

'There you go, then. I have plenty of room to put you up. By the way, even though I'm sure my adoption plan will work I'm thinking of keeping Flossie myself. I don't see why my neighbours should get all the joy. And trust… Charlie, my mother's house is two minutes' walk from mine and if you don't want to stay with me then she'll love to have you. Or if you're really unsure, you can stay at a B&B in the local village. No pressure. So go on, Charlie, just say yes.'

She stared at him, incredulous. 'This is…'

'Sensible. Fun, too. More silver lining.'

'But why are you doing it? You don't need to feel guilty for what your uncle did.'

'I don't. I'm doing this because I want to. Yes, I feel bad about the way Thomas treated you, and that you've been having such a bad time even before his scam, but I'm doing this because it sounds fun. Charlie, if you stay miserable then you've been robbed of far more than money and pride. Don't let the toe-rag win.'

He hesitated, then motioned to the pile of stacked wood on the far side of the driveway, all that was left now of the towering gum. 'When lightning hit that tree I was within a hair's breadth of being pancaked, but if I'd been pancaked I would have been pancaked in an Italian supercar. That's because at the end of this dreary week, when the sensible course would have been to drive back to Melbourne with my lawyers, I thought dammit! This car was leased in my name and how many chances would I ever have to drive such a beast?' He hesitated again and then forged on. 'I guess…that's what my sister's death taught me. That tomorrow mightn't come. So… How many chances will I ever have to take seven dogs and two cows and one Charlie back to my estate and find them all homes?'

'Estate…'

'Every man's home is a castle,' he said grandly.

'You're not finding me a home.'

'Don't mess with my fantasy.' He grinned. 'Or it might not be fantasy. I could ask Mum to put you in the newspaper, too. One fabulous interior designer, slightly dog-stained but very, very beautiful…'

'Don't…'

'Okay, we'll cut the beautiful. The picture will be worth a thousand words.'

'My home's here. I mean…in Melbourne.'

'Of course it is,' he said, gently now, his smile fading.

'I know that. But for the next few weeks… Seeing a bit of England. Finding the perfect home for seven dogs…'

'It's crazy to go all the way to England to find homes for seven dogs.'

'Crazy but fun. Wouldn't it be fun, Charlie?'

She was looking at him as if he were a sandwich short of a picnic. 'But to say you'll keep them all…'

'That's a fall-back position but it's still no big deal. My mother will love them and so will I.'

'She sounds…'

'Fun.' He was repeating the word but it seemed important. 'Despite her shadows, she's incorrigible. Charlie, come home with me and meet her.'

'But…'

'No buts. Just come.'

She stared at him in the moonlight, totally bemused. 'You're crazy,' she said at last.

'Granted.' His smile came back. 'But what's the alternative? Are you committed to work as soon as you leave this place?'

'I…no. I need…to find a new apartment. So much…'

'Right,' he said, moving on. 'What's a couple more weeks, then? And what's the alternative, Charlie *bach*?'

'What…? Charlie *bach*? You called me that before. What does it mean?'

'Charlie dear.'

'You're kidding. Don't call me that.'

'Why not?'

'Because it makes me feel…it makes me feel like I don't want to feel.'

She was looking straight at him, her eyes wide in the moonlight. There was a long silence. Things were changing. Massive things.

He didn't do relationships. He didn't.

This though…the way she made him feel…

'Does it make you feel like you'd like to be kissed?' he asked, and it felt as if the world had stopped and was waiting for her answer.

She closed her eyes and he watched as she took a deep breath and then another. The world held its breath.

Something changed in her face. Twisted. Cracked.

Something in the whole night changed.

And finally she answered. One word.

'Yes.'

Yes. One word to change the world? For this night, it was the only word he needed.

He took her face between his hands and drew her gently, slowly, infinitely tenderly towards him.

He smiled down into her face, drawing out the moment, because something inside him told him this was important. This seemed precious, fragile, something that mustn't be rushed.

'Charlie, you realise this can't be like our kiss in the bog after rescuing Cordelia?' he said softly. 'That was an adrenalin rush, great but unplanned and you didn't know me. This time, you need to trust. So… Are you sure, Charlotte Foster?'

He'd had to ask. This was her home, he was an uninvited guest and she was alone and he wouldn't, he couldn't press. But trust… It was a huge ask.

But her answer was ready.

'I'm sure,' she whispered and she opened her eyes and smiled. 'You kiss me or I kiss you,' she whispered. 'Either way, Bryn Morgan, let's do it.'

He'd kissed women before. Of course he had. His mother had had potential brides lined up from the moment he'd hit his teens. Maybe even earlier.

But he was thirty-five years old and he'd never felt a kiss like this.

It felt right.

It felt as if his heart was being given right then and there.

The warmth, the heat, the wanting…

She moulded to him, with Flossie squashed somewhere between. It wasn't Flossie's heartbeat he was feeling, though. It was all Charlie's, and it felt as if their heartbeats merged in that moment.

Becoming one?

It didn't make sense. Nothing made sense, but right now who was trying for sense? Every nerve ending was focussed on one kiss. There was no yesterday, no tomorrow, no thought of anything beyond this moment, because right now, right at this moment, his world was changing.

Bryn Morgan, Lord Carlisle, Baron of Ballystone Hall, had always considered Ballystone was his home.

It wasn't.

His home was suddenly…here.

What was she doing? She didn't trust. She couldn't.

Okay, she didn't, but for now her world was on hold. She could stop trusting again in the morning. For now all that mattered was that Bryn was holding her. The fears, the distress, the weariness had disappeared. She wanted nothing but this man.

The kiss filled something deep inside, an aching void she scarcely knew she had. To draw away was impossible. It'd be like drawing away from life itself.

She felt herself melt into him and her body reacted with joy.

It was dangerous. She'd been down this road.

No, she hadn't, her body told her. She'd never felt like this. And what danger was there in melting? She was a grown woman. She'd take this one night…

So when he put her away from him, just a little, when

he smiled down at her, his eyes dark with passion, with tenderness, with desire, when he said, 'Charlie, if we're to stop, we need to stop now. I want you more…'

'You can't want me more than I want you,' she said simply and put her hands on his face and drew him back to her. He'd take her to his bed, she thought, or her bed, although seven dogs might mess with even the most passionate lovemaking. And then a thought. 'Bryn, we don't have…'

'I believe I do,' he said, and his voice was different, husky, as if he wasn't so sure of himself. But the smile was still there, and the tenderness and…the need. 'I've sawed the car free and also freed my toiletries. Charlie, I'm thirty-five years old and single. My bag's ever hopeful.' He touched her lips. 'But this isn't hopeful. This is… different. Charlie, are you sure?'

And there was only one answer. This wasn't a dream because she already knew it would happen, and her body was reacting with joy.

Trust didn't matter, she decided, at least it didn't matter for now. Trust was for tomorrow. Tonight was for a man and a woman and nothing else.

'Yes, Bryn, I'm sure,' she whispered, and tonight started right now.

She woke in the small hours, when dawn was drifting in through the open window. She lay in Bryn's arms and she felt…loved.

It was illusory, she thought. It had to be illusory because she was a big girl now and she knew how the world worked. Trust was what you did before the world fell apart.

But her world had already fallen apart, so what the heck? She could lie here cradled in this man's arms, skin against skin, feeling loved, protected, desired.

She could let herself pretend.

And when he stirred and woke and smiled sleepily at her, with passion already kindling behind that gorgeous smile, when he said: 'So what do you think, Charlie love? Will you trust me enough to come home with me? With your dogs and your cows and...you?'

When he smiled at her in such a way, she thought how could trusting hurt her any further? A couple of weeks with Bryn in England? Letting him in some way compensate for his uncle's scam? He didn't need to. The plan seemed crazy, but if he could afford it, what did she have to lose?

She could lose her heart, a small voice whispered, but she blocked it out. Which was really hard to do when he was smiling at her in such a way...

It's just for two weeks, she told herself, striving desperately for sensible. She'd be simply giving herself time out and in the process giving Grandma's animals their only chance of good homes.

And what was her alternative? She was facing eviction from her studio. She needed to find a job, pick up the pieces of her life, but two weeks wouldn't make a difference.

And if a part of her...a really big part...was saying two weeks' time out, time away from here, time exploring his farm, time seeing the real Bryn...

Well, that was a dangerous thing to think. That scared her, but at her heart she knew she wasn't sensible at all. A sliver of light had entered her bleak world.

The sliver was hope.

But he was waiting for an answer. Waiting to smile at her again. Waiting to take her back into his arms and show her...how joy felt.

So what was a woman to say?

Will you trust me enough to come home with me?

'Yes,' she whispered as she sank back into his arms. 'Yes, I believe I will.'

* * *

He was taking Charlie home for two weeks.

Two weeks only.

There was a part of him, a huge part, that was hoping it'd be for more.

But one step at a time, he told himself over the next few days. She didn't trust and why should she? There was the whole thing about his title. He should tell her now, but he knew instinctively that it'd be asking too much to put that on her. Not now. Once she found out… Well, the airfare was flexible. If she hated what he was—as he still hated it—she could always return, or use her ticket to see a little more of England. She'd see her animals safe. They could both move on.

What was it about her that made him feel bleak at the thought?

He thought of his mother. She'd reacted with almost ludicrous excitement when he'd told her he was bringing Charlie for two weeks.

'It's only for a holiday, Mum. Thomas has cheated her and we can help. She needs to see her animals resettled.'

'But you like her?'

'Of course…'

And that was enough for Alice, carried away in extravagant hope.

Hope *was* extravagant, he thought. How could two weeks change something so deeply embedded into him, the fact that he walked alone?

But a part of him was questioning already, before his mother even asked the question.

Had his wall of loneliness already been breached?

There were formalities to be sorted before Charlie, seven dogs and two cows could travel. The bank was due to take possession of the farm in about three and a half weeks.

She could leave then. Bryn, though, had to leave earlier. There were legalities from Thomas's scam that needed to be cleared and he needed to be home to do it.

But he did manage to spend four more days with her, and those days seemed to change him. Those days had him thinking the nightmare of his past might be something he could finally put away. It was too soon to say— of course it was—but each day he spent with her his life seemed lighter.

They worked side by side, sorting the detritus of her grandma's belongings, clearing the remainder of the mess of the tree, cooking, laughing, loving. And as the days wore on, the more taking her back to the UK seemed the most important thing he'd ever worked for.

And yet, he couldn't tell her how important it was. He knew her trust was fragile. This woman had been betrayed. Even as they made love he could see the questions. When would this end?

When he told her he was the Lord Carlisle of the glossy brochures? When he finally revealed the title he loathed? He wasn't courageous enough—or stupid enough—to reveal that yet. He could only hope that when she reached Ballystone, she'd see for herself that Thomas's lie was his reality. That underneath the title and the wealth, he was simply a farmer she could trust.

For now he had to focus on practicalities.

Practicalities revealed problems. It seemed dogs could only be imported as pets, with a limit of four dogs per person. After a call to his lawyers it seemed easier to declare they were his dogs and his mother's, that he and his mother had bought them from Charlie and wished to import them to their new home. Charlie would simply be escorting them. That declaration involved more trust, and it seemed a major step when Charlie agreed.

There was another hitch. He was faced with a form declaring he and his mother had no intention of selling or disposing of the dogs. After reflection, there seemed no problem. He had many tenant farmers, and it'd take little organising to find them good homes on the estate. As a last resort, the dog pack at the Hall would simply expand.

He couldn't talk to Charlie about that, either. Telling her about his tenant farmers meant she'd have to know about his title. The prospect kept drumming through his head. How would she react?

As if it didn't matter, he told himself, but it was a plea inside his head. Please let her not care about titles. Yes, it'd be a shock when she reached Ballystone, but surely once there she'd see the estate for what it was, big, a bit ramshackle, a bit overwhelming but underneath…home? And even if she reacted with disgust, she'd have her return ticket. She'd have her holiday and her animals would be safe.

He had to shut up and hope. He wasn't risking her pulling back now, because every morning he knew he wanted her more. Leaving her, hoping she'd follow, was almost more than he could bear.

And it seemed she felt the same. 'I can't bear you to go,' she whispered on that last morning. 'This seems like a fantasy. I'll wake to reality.'

'You'll wake in England, with seven dogs, two cows and me. If that's reality…is that so bad?'

'Something will happen. You won't be there. You'll turn to dust?' She managed a slightly shame-faced smile. 'I know. You're real and you've been wonderful and, Bryn, despite everything that's happened, this has been one of the best weeks of my life. But happiness doesn't last.'

'Yes, it does,' he said resolutely. 'It must.'

'When your family died…'

'Mum and I both thought our world had ended,' he told her. 'And so it had. It was the end of that world. But here

I am, lying with a woman called Charlie in my arms and I'm thinking…a whole new world is ours for the taking. You want to join me in this brave new world, my Charlie?'

'It's only for two weeks,' she whispered, still fearful. 'It's…just a holiday.'

'So it is.'

'But I still can't believe it's real. Bryn… Just hold me for a while before you go. Let me have a few more moments believing this will happen.'

He held her and hoped she believed.

He wasn't sure that either of them did.

CHAPTER SEVEN

HE LEFT, AND what followed was three long weeks of waiting. They video-called and he worried as he saw her face, etched with the strain of packing, doubt that she was doing the right thing. Finally, though, she was in the air and he was driving to London to collect her.

The dogs were arriving on a later plane. The logistics of transporting seven dogs had been a nightmare. His mother was officially importing three dogs and Bryn was importing four. 'Tell me why I'm adopting three dogs?' his mother had asked faintly, and she'd watched in bemusement as he'd made a hash of trying to explain. She was confused? He felt the same.

But it *was* happening. The dogs would arrive three days later. That'd give Charlie time to find her feet.

Or get cold feet and turn and run before they even left Australia?

The finalising of dog flights had been Charlie's doing. He wondered if there really had been no room on her flight, or if the delay had been deliberate. Was she giving herself time to check him out first—was he who he said he was? Was his offer real?

She couldn't completely trust, he thought, not where her grandmother's animals were concerned.

For her to trust…

Maybe he should have told her…

But it was too late now. He was in the arrival hall, watching as each passenger emerged from the customs hall. The place was packed with excited relatives and friends. There were balloons, flowers, emotion…

He hadn't brought flowers or balloons, but emotion was there in plenty. That she'd trust to come all this way…

And then she was there, standing uncertainly in the doorway, in her standard uniform of jeans but in a new, fresh windcheater. She was dragging a battered roller suit-case behind her. Her curls were tousled and her eyes were shadowed.

She looked battered herself, he thought. Thinner. The last weeks had been tough and once again he felt the tug of remorse that he hadn't been able to stay and help her pack.

He watched her for a moment more, soaking up the sight of her, her presence, the almost primeval surge of joy that said his woman was here. His woman? Surely it was too soon, but that was how it felt as he edged his way through the sea of balloons and flowers and hugging rela-tives. Finally she saw him and her face broke into a smile he thought he'd remember all his life. Relief was there in spades, but there was more. There was deep, abiding trust and it worked both ways. As he reached her and gathered her into his arms he truly felt that he'd come home.

The moments from alighting from the plane, going through Immigration, waiting for the baggage carousel to do its in-terminable thing, had been some of the longest of Char-lie's life. During the flight itself she'd felt almost numb. The last weeks had been filled with legalities, practicali-ties, emotion. She'd packed up the farm, putting the things she most treasured into storage. She'd done the same with her studio in Melbourne. She couldn't afford to keep it.

Everything she possessed was now in a tiny storage

shed or in the suitcase she carried—or in quarantine in Melbourne waiting to catch a following plane.

How much trust did she have in this man waiting for her? When she'd boarded the jet in Melbourne she was so tired she could hardly think. She'd dozed her way to London, but when she'd landed, when the seat-belt light went off and her feet were walking, taking her closer to where Bryn had promised to be, the sense of panic was almost overwhelming.

What was she doing, trusting this man to do what he'd said he'd do? Was she mad? She should turn around, get back on the plane and go home now.

But he'd offered her animals a home. She'd seen the paperwork. Their transport had been paid in full. And for her…this was just a holiday, she told herself. It was simply a part of his generosity. A two-week break on his farm.

But deep down, she knew it was so much more. She knew he wanted her.

Why?

What was the catch?

Stop it, she told herself as panic started again. He's just a farmer, solid, a guy who has enough money to make a wonderful, generous gesture. He's a guy who couldn't resist driving his sleazy uncle's supercar but, still, he's a guy with no frills. A guy with a smile to die for.

A man whose body made her melt.

But as she was waved through Customs, her feet seemed to be moving all by themselves. She was in some crazy dream. She'd been sucked in by that smile, that tenderness, that care, and who knew what lay in front of her?

'He's a farmer,' she whispered to herself. 'A farmer like Grandpa. He has a toe-rag uncle who's conned him like he conned everyone else but otherwise he's solid. Sensible. Kind.'

The doors slid open to reveal the sea of waiting faces, the balloons, the crowds waiting for their loved ones.

And then, across the sea of heads, she saw…a smile. A smile that said it was okay, no, more than okay. A smile that said that solid, sensible and kind didn't begin to describe this man.

A smile that said Bryn was here, waiting to welcome her home.

Home? That was a crazy thing to think, because this was only a holiday. In two weeks she'd go back to Australia, find herself a job, another place to live and get on with her life.

But Bryn was coming towards her, cutting through the crowd with ease. He was wearing what she guessed many farmers wore when they came to town—decent chinos, an open-necked, gingham shirt and a casual oilskin jacket. His smile creased his weather-worn face and lit his eyes.

He was walking toward her, a big man with quiet authority. He was smiling and thanking as people moved aside to let him through, but he had eyes only for her. The people moving might think his smile was for them but she knew…

And maybe the crowd knew too, because eyes were turning to her, to see where this man was moving. Were they sensing romance? Sensing a happy ending?

It was no such thing, she thought breathlessly, but then he reached her and his arms caught her and swung her high. He smiled up into her face, his eyes loving, laughing, joyous.

And then he tugged her back down and into him. His mouth met hers and the crowd around them burst into spontaneous applause.

But Charlie didn't hear. All that mattered was that Bryn was holding her. She was in his arms and, dumb or not, the sensation was totally consuming.

Charlie Foster had come home.

* * *

What followed was a gorgeous, peaceful drive back to the farm.

They were in his battered farm vehicle. 'Sorry, love, Mum has a meeting with the church ladies in the next town. She says she's very happy you're here, Charlotte Foster, and she sends a big welcome, but you're not seventy and you don't have arthritis so that means you get this and she gets the padded leather sedan.'

It made her chuckle. It made Bryn's mother seem… less scary. 'I need to warn you, she'll be matchmaking like mad. You'll have to wear it, I'm afraid. Like I've had to wear it all my life.'

She chuckled again. Bryn's mum didn't seem a threat. The morning was gorgeous and she was sitting by Bryn's side taking in a world she'd never seen.

His farm was almost on the Welsh border, he'd told her, three hours' drive away. That was fine by her. By Australian standards it was close and the vehicle felt good. It smelled strongly of dog and other things, indescribable farming stuff. There was a box of businesslike tools in the back and the duco was liberally mud spattered.

'I should have got it cleaned for you,' Bryn told her but she shook her head.

'I like it the way it is. It smells…like Grandpa's truck. It smells normal.'

'And you the interior decorator.' He smiled across at her. 'I'm shocked. I hoped you might make a few suggestions while you're here about sprucing things up. For instance, this. Interior suggestions?'

'You mean…the car?' she asked cautiously and he grinned.

'I do mean the car. Let's start small. If you do a good job here I might let you into my shed by the end of your stay.'

'You'd let me decorate your shed? Isn't that sacrosanct?'

'Yes, but it's messy.' There were, in fact, many sheds, but he'd had one heated for use when he was mending things. Or pondering mending things. Guy's stuff, he thought and he grinned.

'You don't really want me in your shed,' she said and it was an accusation.

'Not until you've proved your mettle. Okay, the car... suggestions.'

She gazed around her at the battered vehicle that looked as if it had been used for years doing tough farm stuff. She couldn't think of a single thing she wanted to improve.

Like its owner. There was not a thing she wanted to improve there, either.

But he was waiting, smiling, daring her to suggest.

'Okay,' she said, bending her mind to the challenge. 'The first thing we need...you carry livestock in this car, right?'

'Right,' he said cautiously. Dogs all the time. The occasional calf.

'Okay, then pests are going to be a problem. I suggest a fly sticker.'

'A fly sticker?'

'A cute little yellow sticker that hangs from your visor and catches any bug that dares enter. Then I'm thinking dream catchers to match. Very tasteful.' She gazed around at the dog-hair-covered interior—he'd obviously made an effort to brush her seat clean but nothing was going to get rid of the evidence of years of dog occupancy. 'Then there's the dog hair,' she said happily. 'If you can't beat it, join it. I'm recommending faux-fur seat covers. I can order online if you like, maybe rainbow to match the dream catchers? Or faux leopard skin? That's practical. The dog hair will disappear so you'll never notice. You'll need two sets so you can toss one set in the wash if things get really messy.'

'You're...very kind,' he said faintly.

'Don't mention it. And then outside…' She stared thoughtfully into the distance, formulating plans. 'I know. We could transform it into an *oonce* car. How cool would that be? Driving over the farm ooncing like anything.'

'Um… Ooncing?'

'I've only seen a couple, in Melbourne on the nightclub strip late at night, but they're amazing. You need a powerful sound system, by which I mean head-blowing-off powerful, and rainbow-coloured strobe lights underneath that can be synced with the music.' Then, at the look on his face, she chuckled and relented. 'You think that's over the top? You may be right. Let's make it uni-coloured. Purple seat covers? Purple dream catchers? We can find strobe lights that make the entire underside of the car flash purple. The cows will love it. Imagine coming home late at night, across the fields, with your *oonce* car…'

'Why is it called *oonce*?' he asked faintly.

'Because that's what it feels like—*oonce, oonce, oonce*—like a heartbeat. It stays with you for weeks.'

'I can…no, I can't imagine…'

'And then your shed,' she said happily. 'Ooh, Bryn, I can't wait to get my hands on it. I think I'm going to enjoy myself.'

'Great.'

'You do trust me?' she said and twisted so she was looking directly at him. 'After all, I've trusted you to come all the way to England. The least you can do is let me convert a wee car.'

'If you really want to.'

There was a moment's silence at that. 'Really?'

'Really.'

'You'd let me?'

'Charlie, I trust you.' He searched for the biggest commitment a man could make. 'Even with my shed. Such is my trust.'

Wow, Charlie thought, and she sank back onto her seat and gazed ahead in stupefaction.

Trust…

This man…

Where was this going? She had no idea.

It scared her but there was something building inside, a warmth, a strength, a surety.

It wasn't to be trusted, she told herself, but there was that word again.

Trust.

And then they slowed and Bryn took a right-hand turn from the highway. The roadside sign said Ballystone Hall. And then, before she could respond, he turned again, through grand stone pillars and onto a private road.

Ballystone Hall.

The name was like a slam to the side of her head.

The brochure.

This was the seat of the Barons Carlisle and it was also the home of the magnificent Ballystone Hereford Stud. It was the place Thomas had used for his scam. Photographs of this Hall, this property, even the cattle she could see grazing in the distance, had been plastered over the glossy literature used to cheat and to swindle.

The Hall loomed ahead, a vast pile of grey-white stone, three storeys high, surrounded by sprawling lawns. There were acres of paddocks…no, fields…stretching away to mountains in the west. It looked as if it had been here for centuries, settled, magnificent, grand.

A stately home.

Ballystone Hall.

'Where…why are we here?' she stammered.

'Because we're home.'

To say she was stunned was an understatement. There were no words for how she was feeling.

She'd been looking forward to a comfortable farmhouse,

solid, yes, substantial even, as he'd told her money wasn't a problem. But this…

'Stop,' she whispered, struggling to get the word out.

Bryn nodded as if he'd expected this response. He came to a halt in the middle of the driveway.

Driveway?

Massive oaks formed a grand avenue, sweeping up to the Hall in the distance. It'd take ten minutes to walk the length of the driveway alone.

'Is this…?' She could barely get the words out. 'Is this where you live?'

'It is,' he said gently and then before she could get the next question out, before she could even begin to form the sentence, he answered it for her.

'I'm Bryn Morgan,' he told her. 'Charlie, I know I should have told you earlier but to be honest… I thought if you knew you might not come. So I am Bryn Morgan but I'm also a baron. Since my grandfather's death I'm Lord Carlisle of Ballystone Hall.'

The words were doing her head in. Thomas… Fraud… Ballystone Hall…

'Thomas…your uncle…he said he was Lord Carlisle.'

'Thomas was Thomas Morgan. He was my grandfather's third son. My father was second in line, so when he and his elder brother and my cousin were killed I became the heir. Morgans have held the Carlisle title for generations.'

'But… Lord Carlisle's in his nineties,' she managed. 'It says so on the internet.'

'I suspect the site you saw hadn't been updated, or you looked before he died. My grandfather only died three months ago. His death was probably hastened by the shock he felt at Thomas's scam. He was the Eleventh Baron Carlisle. I'm the Twelfth.'

'I-I have no idea of what's going on,' she stammered,

staring out at the intimidating driveway. 'Bryn, you're scaring me.'

'The last thing I want to do is scare you.' He was watching her as a cat watched a mouse, she thought, even as she acknowledged her thoughts were verging on the hysterical. But that was what it felt like, that he was watching for what her next move might be.

There were lies everywhere. When would she ever learn?

'I haven't lied to you,' he said and that scared her even more. Could he read her mind? 'I thought…if I threw the title at you back in Australia…well, it still seems unreal to me and I wasn't sure how I could make it real for you. But I'm a farmer called Bryn Morgan, Charlie. Nothing's changed.'

'You're kidding.' She waved wildly in the direction of the Hall. 'How do I know anything's real? You've probably just rented this for the weekend. Or this is some sort of blow-up stately home you've hired from a theme park?'

'Why would I do that?'

'I have no idea, but nothing's making sense.' Her thoughts were swinging wildly but suddenly they focussed. 'The dogs,' she gasped. 'They're already kennelled in the transit holds. They'll be here in three days. I have to stop them coming.'

'Why would you want to stop them coming?'

'Because they can't come here.' She was staring at the Hall as if it were some sort of monster. That was what it felt like, she thought. It was as if the building itself were mocking her.

The last few weeks she'd felt the burgeoning of faith in this man, the slivers of light that said here was something, someone solid… But who was he? An hereditary baron. Lord Carlisle of Ballystone Hall. It sounded like a hero in a romance novel. He should be wearing breeches and cravat and riding boots, with valet in attendance.

She took a deep breath and made a valiant effort to be rational.

'So you own this place,' she said and was proud of the way her voice sounded.

'I do.' He was sounding cautious, as if not sure where to jump. That made two of them.

'And you're saying… You're Lord Carlisle.'

'I am.'

'But you call yourself Bryn Morgan.'

'I am Bryn Morgan.'

'Thomas called himself Carlisle—Thomas Carlisle.'

'Thomas is Thomas Morgan. He *is* my uncle. He used the name Carlisle to evade police, and also to make the use of the title seem more plausible.'

His answers seemed to be wafting over her head, an irrelevance. She was staring at the great house and remembering the glossy brochure with photographs of exactly what was before her now. Pictures of a historic mansion at the end of an avenue that was truly breathtaking.

The promise of money, money and more money.

'This *must* be part of his scam,' she whispered. 'The Ballystone Stud Herefords. Known the world over. What did he tell Grandma? A lifetime opportunity. Step right in, suckers, and let me bleed you dry.'

'Charlie…'

But she didn't want to hear. She'd been stupid to come. Stupid as she'd been stupid before. 'Just take me to the nearest railway station,' she said wearily. 'Or let me out here and I'll hitch but I'm going home.'

'What, now?' He had the audacity to sound bemused.

'Of course now.' The words were practically a shout and they reverberated through the vehicle with such intensity it shocked her.

There was a moment of silence while both of them seemed to take stock. But Charlie wasn't taking stock. She was concentrating on breathing.

Paper bags were good for panic attacks, she thought. Where was a paper bag when she needed one?

'I think,' Bryn said at last into the silence, 'that maybe you're overreacting.'

Overreacting? She looked again at the opulence of the place in front of her and thought underreacting was a better description. 'This place was used to con Grandma out of her life savings,' she muttered. 'And me. Can you blame me for not wanting anything to do with it?'

'Yes, this place was used,' he agreed. 'As my grandfather's title was used.' For the first time she heard a trace of uncertainty in his voice. 'Charlie, if I'd told you we were coming here, would you have come?'

And there was only one answer to that. 'No.'

'And that's partly why I couldn't tell you,' he said softly. 'Because it seemed desperately important that you come.'

He reached for her hand but she pulled away, as if the touch might burn.

For weeks now, ever since she'd learned the true extent of Grandma's tragedy, she'd felt trapped. The sensation now was more of the same. A lot more.

She was stuck in his car. She was forced to listen.

'Charlie, I needed you to come,' Bryn was saying. 'Back in Australia this place would have seemed a dream to you, or, more likely, a nightmare. I knew you'd see it as part of the fraud. But I need you to see it as it really is. It's just…home.'

'You have to be kidding. How can this be home?'

'Believe it or not, it is,' he told her and his smile returned. It was a gentle smile, though. She was reminded suddenly of the way he'd treated Flossie that first night. An injured creature… Was that how he saw her?

'I only use one wing of this place,' he told her. 'I moved in to keep Grandpa company. Mum lives in the dower house.'

'The dower house!'

'Believe it or not, we have one,' he said. 'That's what I'm asking you to believe.'

'You've lived here for ever?'

'Yes.'

'But the scam…'

'Can I tell you about it?'

She glared. She crossed her arms across her breast and concentrated on glaring. 'Yes,' she snapped and a rueful smile lit his eyes. But then he started talking and the smile died.

'My uncle Thomas was, well, wild is maybe too kind a word for it,' he told her. 'Even when he was small he hated the farm. His life's been a constant of gambling, cheating, lying, living far above his means. My grandfather's always been more than generous but he's squandered everything he's been given. We haven't seen him for years. But last year he came to visit. He'd heard Grandpa was failing and wanted to see him. We let him stay because how could we not? But he badgered Grandpa for more money. There'd be money in Grandpa's will but he wanted it then. It seems he was in trouble with money-lenders—which might be the reason he ended up in Australia. But by then Grandpa was confused, too ill to respond, and I ended up hauling him bodily out of the bedroom. He spent the night abusing me, he got drunk on Grandpa's best whisky and then he passed out.

'The next morning he still seemed asleep so I left him to go check on the cattle. When I came back he was gone. It wasn't until the police contacted us that we realised he'd rifled the office, stealing empty semen packs, literature, the things we'd ordered in bulk when the herd started being recognised. He'd been careful to only steal enough so we wouldn't notice.'

'But...' She was still having trouble getting her voice to work. 'It doesn't...it doesn't matter. You told me lies.' She was holding desperately to her indignation. It seemed the only thing she had to cling to.

'I told no lies,' he said strongly. 'Not one. I'm a farmer, Charlie, first and foremost. I have boots and wellies and battered rain hats in the mud room. I have sheds full of farm gear, calving equipment, everything I need to make this place work.'

'But you're a baron.'

'You think I like that?' Unexpected anger blazed, his eyes darkening to almost black. 'You think I want it? My uncle was always supposed to inherit, and my cousin after him. Next in line was my father. And they all died and I was left. Even then there was my grandfather, the real Lord Carlisle. He's the only person I can think of when I think of the title. He was a kindly, gentle man, bereft from his losses, and while his death was expected it's still left me gutted. So, yes, Charlie, I'm a baron, but it took four deaths of people I loved for me to become one. So if you think that's an occasion for joy, for shouting to the roof-tops that I'm the new Lord Carlisle—'

He broke off, seemingly drained, but still searching for words. 'And then there was my uncle Thomas,' he said wearily. 'He took my family's legacy and he smirched it. So the title...who wants it? Not me. You ask why I didn't tell you? Yes, I thought it might stop you coming but, at a deeper level, it's not who I am. If that's who you thought me, I'd be pulling you here on false pretences.'

She thought about that, or she tried to think. The muddle in her head couldn't be untangled.

His grief...

Don't go there. She had enough of her own to handle.

'So first you say if you told me I might not have come, and now you say I might have come *because* you're a baron?' she managed. He might be angry but she was angry too. And confused. He had his reasons, but he had deceived…

And she was in so much trouble. His smile, his explanation, the way he made her heart seem to twist.

But she couldn't be sucked in. Not again. This was so foreign to her, so crazy, so…unreal.

It *was* unreal, she thought, staring again along the avenue towards the Hall. Sure, this man told a good story and it might even be true, but to trust him… If she let herself be driven down this avenue, if the great doors opened and closed behind her…

The feeling of being trapped was almost overwhelming.

She wasn't being reasonable—she knew she wasn't—but the betrayals of the past were all around her. Her parents. The smooth-talking liar who'd been her husband. Thomas…

'Bryn, I need to go home.' Somehow she steadied, and for a moment she felt a flash of pride that she'd managed to set the hysteria aside. 'I'm sorry.' She took a deep breath and turned to him, facing him square on. 'You…you've been wonderful. Crazily wonderful. You've done such a lot for me and you're offering to do more. What you've just said… I'm sorry but I can't be part of it.' She took a deep breath and struggled to explain further, for he deserved an explanation. She had to believe him enough to try.

'Bryn, my husband walked out on me two years ago,' she told him. 'Our marriage was never good but at least I trusted him. I was a fool. Then Grandma…she was good at trusting as well. Even my mum… She trusted my dad and his betrayal drove her out of the country. She's hardly been back.'

'You're still saying I'm like that?' The anger was still in his voice and she flinched. But she had to keep trying. She had to make him see.

'No, Bryn, I'm not.' She was trying to get it right in her own mind. 'But I don't know you. This...' She waved towards the Hall, and out over the land to the distant hills. 'This has been a shock but I think I needed that shock. Because I was about to jump again.'

'Into trusting.'

'Into loving,' she whispered. 'And that's the scariest of all.'

There was a long pause. A very long pause.

'You think you might love me?' he asked at last. It wasn't spoken like a lover. Anger still resonated.

'I can't.'

'Can't doesn't mean you don't.'

'Can't means I have to pull back. Bryn, it's too soon, too crazy, too unreal. I've been out of control for too long and sitting here staring at your gorgeous house, thinking of your life, even your trauma, I'm thinking here I go again, jumping into trust... Bryn, please, I need to go home. The animals aren't due to fly out until tomorrow. I can cancel their flights. Please don't stop me. I need to do it.'

'What will you do with the dogs?' Anger had been replaced with weariness.

'I have no idea,' she said honestly. 'But the worst-case scenario is the refuges and at least there they'll be treated with kindness until...'

'Until they're put down. You'd do that to them?'

'How do I know what'll happen to them here?' she demanded, confusion almost overwhelming. 'For all I know they'll be used here as... I don't know...fox bait?'

'As if such a thing was possible. Even if it was... Do you really think I'd let that happen?' Anger blazed, full force.

She was being unreasonable, unfair. She knew she was, but she was past explaining.

'No.' She fought for control again, for reason. 'Of course…of course I don't. But I can't…'

'Trust.'

'That's right,' she said wearily. 'I'm sorry. But please take me to the nearest transport back to the airport. I'll repay you for the flights. When I can.'

'There's no need.'

'There is a need.' She closed her eyes, aware of a wash of fatigue so great it terrified her. Was she being stupid? Maybe she was, but there was nothing she could do about it. 'Bryn, please.'

'There's nothing I can say?'

'Nothing.'

There was silence for a long time. She felt his frustration. More, she felt his anger. Because she couldn't trust?

It couldn't matter, she thought. She had to find her feet again. Somehow.

And Bryn knew it. He swore, very softly, and then he turned on the engine.

'Okay, Charlie,' he said bleakly. 'Let's get you back to the airport.'

And then he paused. A car was pulling up behind them. A big white sedan, glistening in the morning sun.

It had turned into the avenue a bit too fast and skidded to a halt as the driver realised the way was blocked. The driver's door flew open and a woman emerged, little, buxom, dressed in an electric-blue frock, a startling pink jacket and heels that were far too high. Her silver white curls, piled into a messy knot, were embellished with streaks of the same electric blue as her frock and she came running towards the car with a beam a mile wide.

'Oh, help,' Bryn said.

'Help?'

'If you thought you were trapped before,' Bryn muttered, 'heaven help you now, but you're about to meet my mother.'

'Charlie!'

Normally when Bryn met his mother after an absence his reaction was to flinch. And then brace.

His mother was, to say the least, full-on.

Those meeting her for the first time might have said Alice Morgan was eccentric and maybe she was. Her eccentricity, however, was a shield. He knew it. The loss of her husband and her daughter had almost destroyed her but somehow she carried on. She faced the day with a beam a mile high, and her warmth and generosity were legion. So instead of bracing right now, Bryn climbed out of the vehicle to deflect her from diving right in to hug Charlie. And as he did he found himself hoping...

When all else fails, bring in the big guns.

His mother.

'Is she here?' She tugged back from him and peered into the car's interior. And saw Charlie. 'Charlotte...' Her beam turned full on as she headed for the passenger side of the vehicle.

Charlie emerged to meet her, looking stunned.

What had he done to her?

Alice was enveloping as much as she could into an embrace. Charlie wasn't big but his mother was tiny. Bryn came from a family of big men, and they'd been the ones to pass on their genes. His mother's genes of little, blonde and bubbly were all hers.

'Dear girl... He wouldn't let me ring you,' Alice was saying. 'I wanted to, to tell you how welcome you were, but Bryn said it'd be pressure on you to come and it wasn't fair. A two-week holiday? How wonderful. And he did pass my message on about the dogs? That they're so welcome? And so are you. You did know that, didn't you?'

'I…yes, I did.' Charlie was still being hugged but Alice had pulled back a little and looked at her critically.

'Oh, my dear, you look exhausted. Those awful aeroplanes. I went on one once. Ugh.'

'You flew to Edinburgh for Great Aunt Edith's eightieth,' Bryn said mildly. 'You were in the air for an hour.

'Totally discombobulating,' Alice agreed. 'I had jet lag for weeks. What you need is a nice bath and some tea and then a sleep. Bryn hoped you might be staying at the Hall but honestly, dear, it's a cavern. You could fit a family into every bedroom. The dower house is much cosier. I think the peony room. I've just had new curtains hung—isn't that lucky?'

'Mum, Charlie's not staying,' Bryn said and that brought silence.

Alice paused and her eyes did a thorough search. On the surface Alice Morgan might appear to be bubble and fluff but underneath there was piercing intelligence. She was looking at Charlie now and Bryn knew she'd be seeing the exhaustion, but beyond that… The shock. The fear.

'Oh, my dear, what's happening?' She wheeled about to face Bryn. Accusing. 'She's scared. Charlotte's scared. Why?'

He held up his hands in defence. His mother was all accusation. 'I just… I might not have told her how big the Hall was.'

'Or that he was a baron,' Charlie whispered. She gestured helplessly at the amazing avenue and the miles of lush farmland stretching to the mountains beyond. 'Or any of this. I thought… I thought he was a farmer.'

'And so he is a farmer,' Alice said roundly. 'A foolish one, though. Bryn… Are you mad? The first time I saw it I almost had a palsy stroke. Come and meet my family, your father told me, and we ended up here. For high tea. With a butler, even! Thank heaven we don't do that any more but this place is still enough to scare a girl out of her senses.' She turned back to Charlie. 'You have to grant that my son's heart's in the right place, though. It always has been. When he rang and said we were adopting seven dogs—'

'But you're not adopting,' Charlie said helplessly. 'He said…you were organising homes…'

'I guess we are,' Alice told her. 'Homes here. Did he show you the paper we had to sign that said we had no intention of getting rid of them? That's the immigration rules. We need to bring them in as personal pets. I had to sign too, because there's restrictions on numbers. Not that I mind. The dogs here have a very good time and…' she waved an inclusive hand '…we appear to have enough room. But enough. Why is Bryn saying you're going home?'

'Because I don't trust him,' she said wildly. 'All of this…' And she wheeled on him. 'The dogs…advertising…you said…'

'It was what I thought,' Bryn said apologetically. 'It was only when I downloaded the formal papers I realised. But it doesn't matter, Charlie. We have many tenant farmers who may wish to take on a dog with such a story and if they don't, then, as Mum says, we have plenty of room.'

'You didn't tell me.'

'And he should have.' Alice put her hands on her hips and glared. 'Why didn't you?'

'I wanted Charlie to come,' he said simply. 'Charlie, I couldn't risk you not coming.'

'It was so important?' his mother demanded.

There was a pause. He met Charlie's look full on. She was looking bewildered, angry…so many emotions. He wanted to gather her and hold her but the time for that wasn't now.

The anger he'd been feeling had faded. There was only Charlie and there was time only for a simple truth.

'It was so important,' he said gently. 'It was the most important thing I've ever wanted in my life. That you come.'

She was so confused.

Where did she take it from here?

In a romance novel this should have been the happy ending. If she took one step forward she knew she'd be enfolded in his arms, cherished, held...

Held.

There was the rub. Held?

How could she risk being held?

Her heart said it wasn't a risk at all, but her heart had betrayed her before, as her mother's heart had betrayed her, as had Grandma's heart. Trust was such a fragile thing and the consequences of it failing were enormous.

He'd lied to get her here. Or...okay, he hadn't lied but he might as well have. He'd deceived by omission. Leaving out the bits that'd scare her.

She was so bewildered, so tired, so...

'Let her be, Bryn.' Alice edged between Charlie and Bryn, doing her best to block out Charlie's view of Bryn— hard given that Bryn was over six feet tall and Alice was barely five. In heels. But she was insisting that Charlie's focus had to be on her. 'You need to leave everything aside,' she said. 'Everything that Thomas has done to you and everything that my son has said or not said, or done or not done. Bottom line? Bryn tells me that seven dogs are booked to arrive here in three days' time and two cows a little time after. Yes or no? Bryn?'

'Yes,' Bryn told her.

Alice nodded. 'There you go. I've seen the documenta-
tion. Charlie, do you believe that's happening?'

'I…yes.' She was having trouble getting her voice to
work.

'That's a start,' Alice said. 'So right now you don't need
to trust any further. Here's the suggestion. Forget my son
for a while.'

'Forget…

'He has plenty to do without bothering you,' Alice told
her. 'For the next few days, come and stay with me, in the
dower house. Bryn can leave you alone. He can spend a
bit of time reflecting on his folly and think about what
he's going to do about it, but that's up to him. What I suggest you do now is rest. A long, hot bath, Charlotte, and
don't tell me you don't want one. I can see it from here.
Aeroplanes are horrible and Bryn says you'll have been
exhausted before you left. Then you can spend a few days
pottering around the estate, doing a lot more resting. In
three days we'll receive the dogs. Bryn will collect them
from the airport and get the paperwork sorted.'

'I will,' Bryn said helpfully from behind his mother.

Charlie thought, Is that laughter back in his voice? She
cast him a suspicious glance but he was back to being bland
again. And…concerned.

The concern seemed such a part of him. An intrinsic
part of who he was.

Dared she trust it?

'Just do it,' he said now, gently. 'Charlie, let my mother
take over for a while. You don't need to trust. You just
need to take your bath and potter and let events unfold.'

'I can stay in a B&B,' she said, feeling foolish.

'You can,' Bryn said and that smile was definitely back
in his eyes. 'That's a step better than going all the way
back to Australia. But Mum has a guest bathroom to die
for and she's aching for a guest. Isn't that right, Mum?'

'Why would you stay in a B&B when you can stay with me?' Alice demanded and tucked her arm through Charlie's. 'Go away, Bryn, and herd some cows or dig a post hole or something to vent a little spleen.'

'I don't need to vent some spleen.'

'Yes, you do, dear,' she told him. 'I can tell. Go away and let me talk Charlie into taking advantage of my truly sumptuous bathroom.'

She gave in. Of course she did. Demanding to return to Australia on the next plane was an overreaction. She'd stay until the dogs arrived.

She lay in the Baroness's over-the-top opulent bathtub, with bubbles floating around her, surrounded by a sea of pink bathroom décor, and she still thought returning to Australia was sensible.

There was so much she didn't understand. This place. This man…

Bryn. The man who'd awakened a sliver of trust, who she'd thought…

Yeah, she wasn't going down that path.

She sank further into the bubbles and thought of what she'd seen so far. The dower house was a manor in miniature and it was pink as far as the eye could see. Pink carpets, pink settees, great bowls of fresh flowers, mostly pink. Chandeliers, glittering, reflecting the pink.

There were pink cupids on the ceiling she was gazing up at.

It should be enough to make the interior designer part of her bolt in horror, but it was so over the top it was fabulous. It was a fine line to admire such over-the-top pinkness, Charlie thought, and she wasn't sure whether she was brave enough to cross it.

She wasn't sure she was brave enough…for anything.

Where was Bryn now?

In the Hall? Surrounded by servants? Preparing luxury dog kennels for seven soon-to-be indulged dogs?

That was a crazy thought. It should make her smile but she didn't feel like smiling. She was so far out of her depth.

And he'd been angry. Was he still angry?

Forget it. Just do what comes next, she told herself, swiping bubbles from her nose. A week here max, to see the dogs settled, then home.

Where was home?

Oh, for heaven's sake… She had friends. She planned to couch surf while she found a paying job. She had clients who'd surely…possibly…return to her?

But first she had to get away from here.

Get away from Bryn?

'Don't think about Bryn,' she said out loud, but the words seemed to mock her.

Bryn Morgan.

Lord Carlisle.

She did need to go home.

This wasn't what he'd planned. He'd got her here, he had her on his land—and she was staying with his mother.

How had that happened?

He was a baron. Didn't that give him any rights? In the olden days a Peer of the realm could surely insist his wench meekly came at his bidding.

His wench? The thought made him grimace. Charlie was anything but. She was her own woman, a woman he didn't know enough but wanted to know more.

Heaven knew he'd exposed enough of himself to her now.

He was sitting in the Hall's vast kitchen, eating eggs and bacon and fried bread straight from the pan, feeding the odd crust to the collie at his feet. His father had given him Sadie as a pup. Bryn had been fifteen. The now ancient dog was now lying over his feet, oozing devotion. She was normally a comfort, but he couldn't find comfort now.

He should have told Charlie.

If he had she would have rejected him sooner. And now…he'd let his anger hold sway and he knew he'd frightened her.

'Dammit, Sadie, what would you do next?' he demanded and Sadie wagged her tail and looked hopeful.

Have another rasher of bacon, her look implied, and Bryn sighed and obliged. And thought of Charlie.

Another rasher of bacon?

If only it were that easy.

CHAPTER EIGHT

WHAT FOLLOWED FOR Charlie were three days in a sort of limbo. She slept fitfully. She walked Alice's Labradors for miles, exploring a countryside so different from the one she'd come from.

'There's an old copper mine with uncapped shafts on the western boundary,' Alice warned. 'The rest of the property's yours to roam, though. Neighbouring farmers are all Bryn's tenants, so tell them you're our guest and you'll be made welcome.'

She didn't tell anyone anything. She avoided everyone. As much as she could without appearing rude she even avoided Alice. Alice was friendly, open, aching to talk, but Charlie didn't want to talk.

She especially didn't want to talk to Bryn—and he didn't seem to want to talk to her.

Each morning he turned up to his mother's kitchen for breakfast in what seemed to be a long-standing tradition and he was…nice to her. But he was respectful of her boundaries.

She tried to respect his. She was here to settle her dogs and her cows, and then she'd go home. She shouldn't ask questions.

But three days was a long time to hold back questions. 'Why don't you live in the Hall?' she finally asked

Alice. Yes, she was being careful of boundaries but surely it wouldn't hurt to ask.

'Bryn doesn't like pink,' Alice said darkly.

Bryn had just left, striding off to do whatever peers of the realm did all day. Charlie was watching him as he negotiated the path through his mother's overcrowded—and very pink—rose garden and thought he looked anything but a peer of the realm. He looked like a farmer, in faded, stained moleskins, a khaki shirt with sleeves rolled to show muscled arms, his hair already tousled from working before breakfast, doing…what she was trying not to think he was doing. Being an ordinary farmer?

He wasn't. He was something that scared her.

'It wasn't just my love of pink,' Alice said and Charlie realised she'd been silent too long after her question and Alice had been watching her watching Bryn. Maybe she hadn't closed her face enough. Maybe something of what she was feeling was showing.

Except she didn't actually know what she was feeling.

'Sorry?' she said, feeling confused, and Alice poured herself another cup of tea from a pot with pink roses all over it and prepared to expand. But with another cautious look at Charlie. It was as if she was measuring what she wanted to say against what she saw on Charlie's face.

'After the tragedy I was…in trouble,' she said softly. 'And so was Bryn. We'd lost so much. My father-in-law, brother-in-law and nephew had been living in the big house and we'd been living here, so suddenly there were two houses between three people. Bryn came home from university and threw himself into the breeding program. I grieved and did hardly anything but eventually I thought I'd redecorate. In pink.'

'Pink,' Charlie said faintly.

'I know it's over the top but I was desperate for a project,' Alice admitted. 'And I may have lost a little perspective. In the end Bryn said it was either pink or him, but, to be honest, we were both so grief stricken we were feeding each other. Seeing Bryn's grief made me sad and vice versa. Meanwhile Bryn's grandfather was like a ghost in that mausoleum of the Hall. It was the same between us. My father-in-law could hardly bear to look at me and I was no help to either of them. So Bryn moved over there. I knew it was awful. It was as if he was abandoning any chance he had of ever forgetting, of ever having fun, but there seemed no choice. He's done everything in his power to help his grandfather and I love him for it but I regret so much...'

Her voice trailed off. Bryn was striding into the distance with his ancient collie by his side. Charlie watched him go and thought of him as a teenager, hauled shockingly from university, trying to cope with his mother's and his grandfather's grief as well as his own.

'He's gone for the morning and then he's off to collect the dogs,' Alice said and Charlie realised that she was being watched. Alice was back to being brisk, practical and bossy. 'So now...wouldn't you like to see the Hall? You're an interior decorator and I'd love your opinion. Sooner or later Bryn will to have to put resources into the Hall, and, I'll admit, pink may not be the way to go. Though it's tempting. Come and tell me what you think.'

She hadn't been in the Hall. She didn't want to. She was almost...afraid to?

It was Bryn's home and there seemed all sorts of reasons she should stay away. The agreement was that she'd see the dogs settled and then she'd leave—without getting any more involved than she was now.

But Alice was rising, taking dishes to the sink, brisk and efficient.

'It's nonsense that you leave without seeing the Hall,' she told her. 'Two minutes while I redo my lipstick and let's go.'

So like it or not, she got the grand tour of the Hall, and at the end of it she was starting to see why Alice was veering towards pink. A one-solution-fitted-all approach seemed the only way to go when the prospect was so daunting. It was a vast mausoleum of a place, a three-storey rabbit warren with almost three hundred years of history.

Most of the rooms were dust-sheeted. 'We've never been brave enough to do more than peek under them,' Alice told her and Charlie peeked and saw a household frozen in time. Faded grandeur, mouse-chewed furnishings, great windows with massive, frayed drapes rotted with years of too much sunlight from the south-facing windows, or mould on the north-window drapes. There was one massive bedroom that looked ready to sleep in—the bed was made up and a fire laid in the grate, but it seemed that wasn't used either.

'That's where Bryn's grandfather slept,' Alice told her. 'When Bryn inherited the title I told him he should take it over. It's where every baron has slept since the Hall was built and I keep it ready. He has to accept it one day, but the idea of taking on that role... Alone...' She shook her head as if shaking off a weight and then kept going, towing Charlie from room to room until she felt her head spinning.

'This is crazy. How many bedrooms?'

'Fifteen,' Alice told her. 'Though I may have miscounted. The servants' rooms make it more. They're upstairs and horrid. I'd never put a servant in there. Not that we have servants any more. We have a lovely lady from the village who comes and cleans but Bryn said live-in servants make him nervous. We do have staff working with us on the land, of course. But come and see the living rooms.'

Living rooms! They were faded, ancient, never stepped in. Vast reception rooms, a ballroom, a great hall set up as a massive dining room, a library to take her breath away… This was true aristocracy stuff.

She was right to run, Charlie thought, as she wandered from room to room. That Bryn could possibly want her to stay…share…

The thought was crazy.

And then Alice led her into the kitchen and that gave her pause.

The kitchen was also vast but it was a used room. An enormous Aga took pride of place, radiating gentle heat. The floor was stone, worn with generations of use. The ceiling had wooden beams that seemed to match the enormous table running almost the length of the room.

Bryn obviously used this as his office and his living room. A computer sat at one end of the table, with a pile of bookwork. More bookwork lay on a beautiful old desk beside the dresser. A worn dog bed lay before the fire and the south sunlight shimmered through casement windows that looked feet deep. There was an ancient club lounge to one side, liberally covered with dog hair, and a small television on the top of the dresser. It was warm, comforting…great.

The place reeked of history, of centuries of good food and friendship, of warmth, of laughter…

Of home?

'We should put a false floor over these horrid stones,' Alice said. 'Linoleum would be so much easier on the feet.'

'Did she tell you she brought home samples of floor coverings?' And Bryn was there, standing in the doorway, smiling at his mother with fondness as well as exasperation. Seemingly unaware that Charlie had stilled in shock. 'And they were all…well, guess.'

Guess? When her heart was hammering in her chest? But some things were too obvious for words.

'Pink?' she managed, and there was that smile again…

'So, Charlie, what would you do with my kitchen?' he demanded, smiling straight at her. 'You're an interior designer. Pink linoleum?'

She had to collect herself. She had to ignore that smile and make herself breathe. 'Sorry, Alice, it'd be a crime,' she managed and she even managed to smile back at Bryn. 'The floor has to stay as it is. Most of this kitchen has to stay as it is. It's fabulous.'

'One in the eye to you, Mum,' Bryn said cheerfully and then he paused. 'Most?' he queried.

'I'd be tempted to sand back those beams,' she told him. 'You don't want to lose that fabulous patina of age but they were obviously put up rough. To be honest…a few hundred years of grease and spider webs… It could be improved.'

Bryn gazed up at the beams towering above their heads. 'I've never really looked,' he said thoughtfully. 'Spiders, eh? You'd destroy a three-hundred-year-old ecosystem just to make the place look pretty?'

'This place isn't meant to be pretty,' she retorted. 'But if you mean would I consider stopping the result of three hundred years of spider-breeding falling into my porridge, yes, I would.'

'We could lime-wash them pink,' Alice said happily and then as both Bryn and Charlie turned to look at her she giggled and held up her hands in surrender. 'I know. I'm letting go of my pink…slowly. It was there when I needed it but I'm moving on. Bryn, I haven't shown her the cellars or the outhouses yet but I'll leave them to you. Or your bedroom! He sleeps where the butler's supposed to sleep,' she told Charlie. 'Honestly, you can see what I'm up against.' She smiled at Charlie, a warm, deep smile that had meaning behind it, a meaning Charlie couldn't quite fathom—or didn't want to fathom. 'Meanwhile I have roses to deadhead. Bryn, I leave her to you.'

She bustled to the door, and then she paused and skewered her son with a look that mothers used the world over. Mostly parents used that look when they'd reached last resort. 'Clean your room or else…'

This direction was simpler.

'Make her stay,' she said and then she was gone.

Make her stay.

It was as simple and as complicated as that, Bryn thought.

It had nearly killed him to leave her be for the last few days, to know she was so close and yet so far.

Why hadn't he told her the facts from the start?

Because it wouldn't have made a difference, he thought. Or maybe it would. Maybe it would have stopped her coming here in the first place.

She was here to provide for the security of her grandmother's animals. That was all. She'd make sure he'd do what he'd promised and then she'd leave.

To go home to what? Debts up to her ears? He didn't need to be told the chances of her accepting more help from him were zero.

And further contact? The chances of that were zero as well.

'You want a job as an interior designer?' he ventured. 'This place is at your disposal.'

'But you've apparently already knocked back your mother's very kind offer.'

'I did at that.' He tried to smile, to make her smile back. It didn't come off. 'Charlie, stay.'

She tilted her chin and met his gaze. 'Why would I?'

'Because I want you to.'

'I don't understand why you would.'

'I'm sure you do,' he said gently. 'But I think you're afraid.'

'I'm careful. I need to be.'

'Of course you are. So accept this as a working proposition. Stay with Mum—she'll love it. Then work your way through this mausoleum and figure how we can make it a paying proposition.'

'You want to make this place pay?'

'It's too big for one man,' he said. 'Even if that man finds a wife, has a family, ends up with a dozen kids and even more dogs. My thought is that we could make part of it a luxury farm retreat. It's big enough for guests to be completely separate. It could be…fun.'

'Fun…'

'For…both of us? I'm guessing that's what's been missing in your life for a long time, Charlie *bach*.'

He was watching her face, watching for a reaction, and a reaction wasn't coming. Her expression was closed, wary, as if waiting for a trap.

He'd been around creatures enough to know that coming closer would be a disaster. He had to stay back, even though that edge of anger was making its presence known again. Why couldn't she trust?

'Wouldn't it be fun, though?' he said. 'To rip off the dust sheets, to uncover history, to work out what we could keep, what guests could use, what we ourselves should treasure.'

'We…' She said it as a whisper and he heard the fear. What the…?

'Mum and I,' he said, trying not to snap, and then as the fear didn't fade he decided to say it straight out. He'd shut up once and it had backfired. He had to be honest.

'Charlie, I'm about to say it like it is,' he said and he dug his hands deep into the pockets. What he was about to say should be said with a woman in his arms, but if he tried that he knew she'd run. 'I think I'm in love with you.

I think you're the woman I want to spend the rest of my life with but you're looking at me like I have a loaded gun and I don't get it.'

'I'm sorry,' she whispered. 'But…love? We've known each other for how long?'

'For little more than a month. So yes, it's crazy, but you know what's even crazier? I felt this way from about two hours after I'd met you. So that's being honest, Charlie, and now I need you to be honest back. Is it possible that you feel the same way?'

'I can't!' She sounded panicked.

'You can't or you don't?'

'L-look at this place,' she stammered. 'You're a baron. Lord Carlisle of Ballystone Hall. You own everything as far as the eye can see. If we got together… Okay, if we married… Baroness Carlisle? Lady Carlisle? How ridiculous is that?'

'It's just a title.'

'Which you didn't tell me about. How could I ever…?'

'Trust me? You did when you thought I was just a farmer. That's all I am, Charlie. The rest is an accident of birth. If I was born with a gammy leg would you still trust me?'

'I…of course… I mean…'

'Then what's the difference? I was born into a family with a title.'

'You didn't tell me.'

'Because I was still struggling with it myself. I still am. But it's surface. Something I'm stuck with. I hate that you're judging me for it.'

Silence. The ancient grandfather clock in the corner started its sonorous boom. One, two…all the way to ten. While Charlie watched him.

Oh, for heaven's sake, he thought. The rile of anger grew. He was exposing all here, and did she even get how hard it was to say it? But maybe what he was feeling wasn't anger. Maybe it was pain. Whatever, the clock reached its tenth gong and he was done.

'I can't force trust,' he said, and he could hear his own frustration. 'And I won't force anything. All I'm saying is that there's work here for you. You could stay, draw up plans for the Hall, think about what you'd like to see done—I trust you, you see, not to lumber me with pink. And we could take our time to see how things progress. Maybe they will and maybe they won't but you could trust enough to give it a try.'

'Bryn...'

'I've said enough,' he said roughly, not bothering to disguise the anger now. He glanced—unnecessarily—at his watch. 'I need to go,' he said. 'I have things to do before I collect the dogs. Isn't it lucky there's no room in the car for you? You'd be stuck with me for hours. You and me and seven dogs. You never know what I'd try on.'

'I don't...not trust you.'

'That's a lie,' he said brusquely. 'No matter. I'll bring the dogs back here and I'll care for them. Because I said I would, Charlie. You believed me that far at least. The rest...it doesn't matter. Or it can't matter. Leave it.'

Except it did matter.

She felt about three inches tall. Or maybe not even that much.

She should be driving to the airport to collect her dogs. *Her dogs.* He was doing this for her. He'd gone to enormous trouble and expense. The least she could do was trust him.

The problem was, though, that she didn't trust herself.

He could have sent one of the men to collect them. There was a small army attached to this estate, mostly tenant farmers who helped out with Bryn's herd, but also a farm manager and extra hands at need. She'd walked the estate and talked to enough people to know the lines blurred, between tenant, boss, neighbour and…friend.

Bryn was admired. Loved even. His crazy mother was adored.

So why couldn't she throw her hat into the ring?

Because she was afraid?

Or…because there was no way a woman like her deserved a guy like him?

Was that the crux?

Left alone, she wandered through the vast rooms of the mansion and thought of what she could do if she was given free rein. The tiny upstairs servant quarters would make ideal bathrooms. The grand rooms below could incorporate discreet staircases. A couple of the rooms at the end were big enough to put in the tiny lifts she'd read about, so those rooms could be fitted for the elderly or those with a disability. Guests would flock to stay in such a home.

She looked out of the windows at the rolling hills, turning to mountains in the background. At the sleek cattle grazing in the morning sun. At the tiny historic village down the road, at the tenants' houses, beautifully maintained.

This place was fabulous.

Bryn was offering her a place here.

She had no right…

He wanted her.

But for how long?

'So take a risk,' she told herself. 'You can trust again.'

It didn't work like that, though. Trust had to come from the heart, and it didn't operate on command.

She took a last glance around at the fabulous Hall, at a project that could keep her happy for years. She thought of Bryn. He was a man who could keep her happy…for ever?

Or not.

She knew she was a coward. She couldn't help it though. She wanted…to keep her heart safe.

She was going home.

CHAPTER NINE

To SAY SEVEN DOGS were excited to arrive at Ballystone Hall was an understatement. They'd been crated separately for the flight, then confined in the car.

Bryn opened the rear doors and the dogs leapt out in one unruly heap. The doors of the dower house were flung open. Charlie stood there beside his mother—and then Charlie was suddenly no longer standing. She raced through the garden path as the dogs raced towards her. She held out her arms and then she was on the ground, buried by a mass of hysterical, barking, joyous fur.

How many women would do this? Bryn thought. She'd sacrificed her business to try and get her grandmother out of trouble. She'd refused to send the dogs—and the cows—to refuges where they'd almost certainly eventually be put down. She'd travelled half a world to see them safely settled—she'd even had to trust him.

He was figuring it out by now, just what a big deal trust was. He'd done a bit of…sleuthing? His lawyers had hired investigators to try and find Thomas' whereabouts. It hadn't seemed too big a deal—hardly even intrusive—to have them check on the ex-husband of Charlotte Foster.

'The guy seems almost as big a slime ball as your uncle,' his lawyer had told him yesterday. 'He's currently got bankruptcy proceedings against him and there's a paternity suit in progress. It seems like your Charlotte's one of a line.'

Your Charlotte. He thought of those words now as he watched her tumble with the dogs, holding as many as she could, laughing…weeping?

Yeah, weeping but there wasn't a thing he could do about it because he wasn't allowed near.

Because she'd been taught not to trust by experts, and who was he to undo years of distrust?

If she could love…

She certainly could, he thought, watching the mass of dogs, the laughter, the tears, the flying fur. He felt anger, frustration…love.

'She had a shower this morning,' his mother said. 'What a waste.' She was walking down the path to join him, watching the tumbling mass in approval. The Ballystone dogs were watching on the sidelines. They were clearly ready to check these new arrivals but even they seemed to know that what was happening between Charlie and her dogs was special. 'Are you going to introduce us?'

He could do that, mostly because it didn't require him taking his eyes off the tumbling, hugging Charlie. It even gave him time out from the aching hunger around his heart.

'Possum's the fox terrier,' he told her. 'She's missing an ear and she minds. When you greet her she'll put up a paw as if to hide it. Like she's embarrassed. Fred's part basset, part who knows what? His name should be Hoover because that's what he does. Hoovers everything up on the understanding that if it's not edible he can bring it up later. Flossie's the white scraggy mutt—part poodle, part a million other varieties. She's the one I hit, but as far as we can tell she's suffering no long-term consequences. The wolfhound's Caesar. He shakes when he's frightened and he's often frightened. Dottie's the Dalmatian. Her teats are hanging so low because she was used for puppy farming and then dumped when she'd outlived sequential pregnancies. Mothball's the Maltese fuzzball—you try and hurt Charlie—or even hug her—and you'll need to contend with Mothball. And finally there's Stretch... He's the one on top of Charlie now. A sausage dog. A vegetarian. He loves lentils but don't give them to him. His wind could clear the great hall.'

His voice trailed off. He was watching the mass of girl and dog.

His mother was watching him.

'You love her, don't you?' she whispered.

He didn't turn. The question hung.

'I was talking about the dogs,' he said at last.

'Surface talk,' she said dismissively. 'You love Charlie.'

'Yes,' he said simply because there was nothing else to say.

'But she's going home.'

He shrugged. 'Wherever home is. She has no money, no job, nothing. Here... I could offer...' He shrugged. 'It doesn't matter. She has to go her own way.'

'You could follow.'

'What, and leave you with the dogs?'

'For such a cause, yes. I'd even let them share my pink living room.'

'Greater love hath no parent,' he said and smiled and hugged her but his eyes were still on Charlie.

How could he make her trust?

He had no idea.

'Well, we're all eating in the great hall tonight,' Alice said, breezily cheerful again. 'We have seven new residents and we need to celebrate. Charlie, wiggle your way out of that tangle. Bryn, take the dogs and Charlie and show them their new home. I'm about to organise a feast.'

'Please, don't go to any trouble,' Charlie managed, emerging from dogs.

'No trouble at all,' Alice said, poking her son hard. 'It's Bryn who has to conquer...trouble?'

By dinner time the dogs were exhausted and happy to settle by the great fire in the massive dining room while their associated humans ate dinner.

Charlie was also exhausted but it wasn't physical exhaustion. Bryn had taken the dogs—and her—for a long exploratory walk over the estate. He'd been quiet for most of the time, peaceful even, strolling as if there were no undercurrents at all. He'd spoken only briefly, pointing out a cluster of heifer calves with obvious pride, showing her the field Cordelia and Violet would call home, showing her an ancient stone wall, which rumour had it had Roman foundations, talking of the problems with an old mining site on his west border and what the environmental people were doing now...

It was a gorgeous day and Bryn hadn't seemed to notice her silence. He'd simply been a good host, describing his land. He'd thrown sticks for the dogs, laughed at their antics. They were crazy happy to be out of confinement and he seemed content, too. He seemed...as if he was enjoying life.

For Charlie, though... Every moment brought a build-up of tension.

Why can't I relax? she asked herself. Why can't I just enjoy?

Why can't I treat this man simply as a friend?

Or more to the point... Why can't I let myself treat this man as more than a friend?

She was being stupid. A coward. She knew she was, but there wasn't a thing she could do about it. She'd dug her hands deep in her pockets and left them there, as if she suspected that if they escaped she might find her hand in Bryn's and how disastrous would that be?

Stupid, stupid, stupid, but by the time they'd walked the estate and she'd come home…no, not home…by the time they'd come back to the dower house…and Bryn had left her to clean up for dinner she was emotionally exhausted. Then, sitting at the vast dining-room table covered with peonies and sweet peas and roses, all in silver vases that must be worth a fortune, with the dogs by the fire, with Alice beaming and with Bryn watching her with that same gentle, understanding smile… By that time she was so tired she wanted to weep. Her defences were taking every ounce of self-control. The emotional barrier she'd built was impenetrable, to be defended at all times—but at what cost?

Alice had pulled in the big guns for the night. 'We do this for special,' she told Charlie happily. 'In the old days the family had chefs, undercooks, kitchen maids, butler, manservants, the works. Now I have a lady from the village and a couple of girls who pop in at need. I have no idea what all the servants did.'

'They catered to our every whim,' Bryn told her. 'But we can't think up enough whims to keep them employed.'

But Charlie wasn't thinking about whims. She was thinking of Alice's words. We do this for special. What was special about this night?

It was the night to mark…the end? The dogs were here and happy. She could go home.

The food, the setting, were magnificent. Charlie should have loved it. Instead she toyed with the food, trying to dredge up an appetite she'd completely lost.

The dogs seemed to be peaceful here already. Could she go home tomorrow?

'I enquired about flights while I was at the airport,' Bryn said, cutting across her thoughts. 'There are empty seats on a flight on Tuesday. Unless you want to stay until Cordelia and Violet…'

'I don't,' she said, too fast, and got a grave look for

her pains. She caught herself. 'I'm sorry. That sounds… ungracious. But I do need to go home.'

'What will you do there?' Alice asked and Charlie thought Bryn wouldn't ask that. He'd guess how much it hurt.

'I have friends I can stay with until I find my feet,' she said, trying to sound more certain than she was. But she did have friends. She would be okay. 'There are always desperate calls for interior designers from socialites who want impressive party venues,' she told them. 'I have friends in the industry who'll give me casual work until I can organise myself again.'

'You'd rather organise parties than stay here and oversee the development of the Hall?' Alice asked in astonishment. 'I know…' She held up her hands to ward off Bryn's protest. He didn't want her pressured, but Alice had no such qualms. 'I understand Bryn not liking pink is an issue, but there are other colours.' She turned dreamy. 'Maybe we could have a marine theme. That might work being so far from the sea. A beachside holiday when there's no beach. A challenge… We could use something like Neptune's Retreat as the formal name and put Ballystone Hall in small letters underneath. We'd need to install a pool, though. With one of those wave makers?'

She was off and running and Charlie looked at Bryn and Bryn looked at Charlie and their lips twitched. More. There was laughter in both their eyes, but the laughter faded almost as soon as it appeared.

There was regret. Loss?

The home phone rang.

Saved by the bell, Charlie thought as Bryn sighed and rose, but she didn't know what she was being saved from. Seeing the pain in Bryn's eyes? Reflecting her own pain?

'This is where we need a butler,' Bryn growled. The ladies who'd helped in the kitchen had gone home, so Lord

Carlisle had to head out of the room and answer his own phone. He was trailed by all the dogs.

They heard him talking, briefly, urgently, and then he was back.

'The team reclaiming the mining site either didn't seal the fence properly when they left tonight or someone's been messing around up there looking at what they're doing,' he said brusquely. He looked only at Alice—as if Charlie were already gone? As if that final gaze had been a goodbye? 'Ewan Grady's cattle have broken through and so have some of ours. There are exposed shafts up there. We need to get them out before we lose any.'

'Ewan's one of our tenant farmers,' Alice told Charlie. 'I think I told you. The mine…they're uncapping the shafts to make more permanent repairs but at the moment they're exposed and dangerous. Bryn, do you want help?'

'Ewan and his son are there already,' Bryn told her. 'We don't want anyone up there who doesn't know the place backward.' And then finally he did look at Charlie. His face was grim. Because of his cows? Or because of her? 'Goodnight, Charlie,' he said brusquely. 'Sleep well.'

And he was gone.

Charlie was left looking at Alice. Who looked at her… with understanding.

Alice…

This woman had watched her husband leave to clean a water tank and he hadn't come back. And her daughter, too…

'He knows what he's doing,' Alice said soundly. 'Don't worry.'

'How can you ever stop worrying?'

'You have to trust,' Alice said gently. 'Otherwise you'll go mad.'

Alice started clearing but there wasn't much to clear. Charlie walked out to the massive front doors, opened them and watched the tail lights of the Land Rover. She watched them until they disappeared into the distance.

There was nothing she could do. She'd be no help up there.

If she stayed here…if she trusted…could she learn?

She closed her eyes and then Alice was there, touching her arm.

'Come and help me wash up,' she said gently. 'And don't look like that, sweetheart. Or if you do…think about what you can do about it.'

'I can't…'

'I think you probably can.'

She steered her back inside and closed the big doors after her. The dogs milled around their legs, excitement over. Heading back to the fire.

And Charlie stopped dead. Checked. Rechecked. And finally said it aloud.

'Alice…where's Flossie?'

Once upon a time Flossie's devotion had been absolute. That devotion had been repaid by dumping, by abandonment. Since then Flossie had learned new people, new devotion, but the last few days had been confusing to say the least. New country, new dogs, new faces…

Flossie had stood with the other dogs by Charlie's side but she'd seen tail lights retreating into the distance. She knew what that meant.

She'd started to run.

Alice and Charlie spent useless minutes searching the house, searching the yard, calling. 'She must have followed the car,' Charlie said at last. 'I had the door open. For a moment… I wasn't looking.' She felt dreadful but still…following the car would be okay. Surely? The mine wasn't so far that Flossie couldn't catch up, and the men would see her.

Bryn would rescue her yet again.

But she couldn't count on it. She wouldn't count on it.

'Can we go?' she asked, but Alice was already reaching for her jacket, grabbing a couple of pairs of wellies.

'Of course,' she said briskly. 'Bryn won't want Flossie up there while he's trying to herd the cows. Come on, sweetheart, let's go stop your dog being helpful.'

By the time Bryn reached the mine, Ewan and his son had already herded most of the cows to safety. A couple of younger cows were dodging them, though, maybe enjoying the excitement. Part of the fence was down, knocked by the cows?

Bryn turned to Ewan's son, a lad of about eighteen. 'Can you head back to the farm and get some decent rope so we can pull this fence back together?' Ewan's car was parked at the far side of the mine. 'Skirt right round,' Bryn said brusquely. 'No one falls down a shaft on my watch.'

He and Ewan returned to cornering, backing the two reluctant cows, working with torches, taking care at each step.

Flossie couldn't run as fast as the car but she kept it in her sights. By the time she reached the mine, though, the vehicle was parked, its lights off. There were men moving through the shadows with torches. There were cows.

This was unfamiliar. None of the voices seemed right.

And then, on the far side of the tailings, another vehicle... Tail lights.

It started steadily down the hill.

Flossie stared desperately across the tailings and knew what she had to do.

She didn't go around the tailings, though. She cut straight across. And halfway across…a shaft.

'What the hell…?'

The scream cut the night. It wasn't human, it was a high-pitched yelp, followed by the sound of shale falling. Something heavy falling with it.

A dog.

He and Ewan stilled and stared at each other.

'One of your dogs?' Ewan said, his eyes reflecting Bryn's horror. 'It must've followed…'

'Flossie,' Bryn said bleakly, instinctively guessing what had happened. They had the two young cows backed against the remainder of the fence. Their work was almost done. 'You get these two out and I'll check.'

He hardly needed to check, though. He picked his way carefully across the tailings, towards the shaft where the howl had come from.

He'd been through these tailings yesterday, checking on the work, worrying about the open shafts and kids who wanted a bit of adventure. He'd rung the head of the team doing the work. 'I want those shafts covered, now.'

It hadn't happened.

The shaft where the noise had come from was probably the deepest.

Flossie…

Alice barrelled her beautiful sedan up the hill towards the tailings and Charlie was out of the door almost before the car stopped. Bryn's Land Rover was in front of them. A stout, squat figure Charlie didn't recognise was driving two cows forward. He made an urgent motion for them to stay back.

Charlie did as ordered, but it almost killed her to stay still while the cows were encouraged past the parked cars to join the herd further down the hill. Finally, with its members intact, the herd started moving placidly away. They were free to talk.

'This is Ewan,' Alice told Charlie. 'A neighbouring farmer. Ewan, have you seen…?'

'The dog? Is that what you're looking for?'

'Yes,' Charlie said thankfully. 'Is she here?'

'In a matter of speaking,' Ewan told her. 'There's a dog just fallen down a shaft. His Lordship's checking on her now. You ladies stay by the car. I need to find out what he's doing.'

Only of course they didn't stay by the car. Alice had torches in the trunk, a mother of a torch and a smaller one with a brilliant beam. 'We often find stock on the road,' Alice said, and the fluffy pink Baroness was suddenly a brisk and efficient farmer. 'We're used to dealing. Watch your feet, Charlie.' She tossed her a pair of wellies. 'You fall and Bryn will have my hide. You will not fall down a shaft.'

A shaft… Flossie…

Alice knew this land but was still ultra-cautious, picking her way between heaps of loose dirt. Charlie followed, feeling ill.

'They've made a right mess,' Alice said grimly over her shoulder. 'The shafts have been capped for over a hundred years. Our strategy was to fence it off more securely and reforest, until nature does the rest, but the conservation people said no, the capping has to be done properly. They've removed trees and dug out the old caps. Maybe they're right long term, but, oh, Charlie, some of these shafts…'

For the first time Charlie heard her voice falter. Alice had lost a husband and a daughter, Charlie thought. She was crossing loose tailings in the dark, heading towards her son who was…

Where?

Right over a shaft. Lying flat on his stomach so he could point his torch down. For an awful moment Charlie thought he was lying on loose shale but then she saw he'd hauled timber up to make himself a solid base. There were lanterns set up beside him. Ewan and Bryn were both farmers. They'd be used to calvings at night, caring for stock. They were equipped, competent.

Safe? Not so much.

Bryn heard them come. He rolled sideways to talk as they approached. The ground was damp and mud had clung. He was filthy.

His face was grim under the dirt.

'She's down there. Hell, Charlie, I'm so sorry.'

That made her feel how small? Of all the things, that his first thought was to apologise to her…

'I let her out,' she told him. She was walking towards him but Alice clutched her arm and Ewan made an involuntary step to ward her off.

'Land's not stable any closer,' Ewan muttered, casting a worried look at Bryn. 'His Lordship shouldn't be there.'

But from below came a faint whimper, of fear and of pain.

Flossie…

'How…how deep?'

'Deep,' Bryn said grimly. 'But it goes deeper. She seems wedged on a ledge about twenty feet down. I can see her. She's lying still. If she moves, though…'

He stopped and Charlie saw a wash of anguish cross his face.

'I'll ring Davey and tell him to bring the gun.' It was Ewan, speaking softly but matter-of-factly behind them. He was a farmer, facing facts.

Dear God.

'Isn't there…? I could…' She wasn't even sure what

she'd intended to say. Ring a rescue service, a fire department, what? If this were a child, maybe there'd be men and women prepared to risk their lives, she thought, but it *would* be risking lives. The shale was crumbly. These were ancient tailings and there'd been rain. Who knew what the state of the shaft would be?

A gun. A blast downward. A fast end.

Flossie.

The failures of the last few weeks—or maybe even the last years—were all around her. She'd brought the dogs over here. She'd set this tragedy up.

She couldn't help it. Her knees crumpled and she buckled and clutched her stomach.

'No gun,' Bryn snapped, cutting through her anguish. 'Charlie, don't look like that. I'm going down. Ewan, ring Davey and tell him to collect the climbing gear from the Hall. It's in the last stall of the stables. Tell him to wake John. He taught me to abseil as a lad. He's too old to do this now, but he'll make sure the gear's right and he'll supervise. Tell him to bring a couple more of the men. I'll need strength to haul us up. Mum, can you ring the Carlisle vet—have her on standby? Get her out here if she will. Charlie, there are planks over the pile of rubble near the Land Rover. Haul them over to make a solid base around the top of the shaft, working from where you are and slowly into me. We'll set up a line across the top of the shaft and rig torches facing down so I can see. Let's move, people. Go.'

'You can't!' She was aghast, but Bryn was already facing down again, assessing what he could see, focussing on what lay ahead. Alice stooped to kneel beside her, hugging her close, and she turned to her. 'Alice... Flossie... she's a dog. I can't ask...'

'You don't have to ask,' Alice told her.

Charlie thought wildly, this woman has lost so much,

and here was her son, threatening to climb into an ancient shaft, threatening more grief? But…

'Bryn's not stupid,' Alice said and her voice was assured, with hardly a hint of the fear she must be feeling. 'He knows what he's doing, love,' she said. 'He wouldn't try this if he didn't think he'd succeed. I trust him and I think you should, too.'

Trust, Charlie thought wildly. How could she trust? He'd kill himself. Of all the—

'Charlie, don't make this a big deal.' Bryn's voice cut across her thoughts. He'd rolled again so he could face her across the tailings. 'I can see the sides of the shaft and they're looking stable. We can plank the top and run ropes from far back where we have solid ground. Flossie seems to have the sense not to struggle. If this was stupid I wouldn't be doing it. And Charlie…you might have let her out but this is not your call. Flossie officially belongs to me. She's my dog on my land. My decision. Tell her, Mum.'

And Alice even managed a smile. 'This is Bryn Morgan,' she said, a trace of laughter in her voice. 'He's Twelfth Baron Carlisle of Ballystone Hall, and what he says goes. We're mere minions, my dear. All we can do is trust.'

There was that word again. Was she kidding? Trust… How could she do that?

It seemed she had no choice.

Suddenly they had a team. Tenant farmers, workers at the Hall, the vet from the local village. They'd been summoned by Lord Carlisle but there was not a hint of resentment. Nor was there a murmur that what he was doing was stupid.

His lordship's dog was down the shaft. *His* dog. That was the story. Lord Carlisle was doing what he must to recover his own, and as Charlie worked she had a weird, almost ghostly sensation of centuries past, of the Barons

Carlisle of Ballystone Hall through the ages expecting their wishes to be fulfilled.

There was respect here, though, and there was the trust that Bryn had asked from her. Respect and trust weren't things that could be inherited.

There was also concern. He was putting himself in harm's way and they cared.

As she cared?

How could anyone care as much as she did?

Bryn had given her a task and she was pathetically grateful. Instead of standing by, watching in fear, she was lugging timbers, working from far back, making the ground as stable as she could. As more people arrived they helped, and she was part of a team.

Bryn was organising ropes, working with Ewan and John. John was a grizzled guy in his seventies. She'd been introduced to him a couple of days earlier, Bryn's farm manager, a man of few words but reeking of common sense. His presence reassured her—a bit.

Not so much to stop the fear.

Alice was hauling timbers, too. They'd been dressed for dinner. Charlie had been wearing soft grey trousers and a turquoise blouse. Alice had been wearing a pale pink dress, beautifully tailored.

They were both now wearing a liberal coating of mud. Neither of them cared. They were working side by side, grimly intent and Charlie knew that, despite her reassuring façade, Alice's fear was the same as hers.

Halfway through manoeuvring a plank into place she felt the fear hit in full force, a fear so great it immobilised her. She closed her eyes and went to say something, but Alice was beside her, firm and sure. Guessing what she was about to say out loud.

'Don't say it,' she said urgently. 'He won't listen.' And then, softly, speaking only to her, 'Charlie, this isn't all about the dog. He needs to get Flossie out of this shaft for himself. And for me.' She hesitated a moment and then added. 'And for you.'

'Alice, he can't.'

'He has to,' Alice said grimly. 'Ever since the tragedy... He blames himself for that day. He'd bought the petrol pump and shown his dad how to use it. He never...we never dreamed his father would use it underground.' She shook her head, as if shaking off a nightmare. 'Enough. That's past but now... Bryn struggles. He needs to learn to trust himself again.'

Bryn? Needing trust? The concept felt like turning the world on its head. She pushed it back, focussing on the closer thought. 'How can you bear it?' she whispered. 'If you lose him...'

'I won't lose him,' Alice retorted. And suddenly the grip on her shoulders tightened. 'But you...will you lose him? He's yours if you want him, Charlie Foster, but it takes courage.' She hesitated and glanced over to where Bryn was edging towards the shaft. 'It takes trust from both of you. Over and over again. You love and you love and you love and...'

Enough. Her voice broke. She let Charlie go and swiped angry tears from her face. 'You just do,' she said. 'Bryn's trusting us to keep this ground stable so are we going to stay here quibbling or are we going to cart more timber?'

And there was only one response.

They carted more timber.

Was he a complete idiot, risking his life for a dog?

This wasn't a dog, though. This was Flossie. Charlie's dog. Would he do it for his own?

Yes, he would, he conceded, as he tightened his harness, letting John check and recheck. He'd do it because he loved Sadie. And his mother's dogs? Okay, they were useless but he loved them, too. And come to think of it…unless a dog was a stray…but then even if it was a stray… Could he point a gun when there was a real possibility of rescue?

He couldn't and that was something to remember. It was something to focus on other than the vision of the gaping shaft, the crumbling walls, oozing water, totally unstable.

They were rigging a rope ladder so he had something to keep his feet on, because finding footholds in shale walls reeked of stupidity and he wasn't stupid. Or not completely stupid. The plan was for two groups to lower him, one group controlling the ladder, the other the harness.

Every movement he made would be controlled from above. All he could do was trust. But these were people he'd known all his life. His mother. His people.

Charlie?

He glanced across at her anguished face. For a moment, their gazes met and held.

Locked.

A silent promise.

'I will come back to you,' his gaze said and he was sure she got it. And his next thought was an almost a primeval response to her look of anguish. 'I will come back and claim.'

How feudal was that? Feudal and sexist and totally inappropriate, he thought. Just lucky he didn't say it out loud. But then… Had she sensed what he was thinking? The way her lips curved… Was that a smile?

Maybe he wouldn't have to claim his feudal rights, he thought. Maybe the maiden would come willingly.

It was a good thought. No, it was a great thought, inappropriate or not. It was a thought to carry him over the lip of the shaft and into the blackness of the void below.

It was the longest wait of Charlie's life. The team holding the ropes worked by inches. They were acutely aware of the crumbling structure of the shaft, that one false move, one solid bump if Bryn swung and hit the sides, could cave the whole thing in. They worked in almost total silence. Apart from the curt orders of the two in charge of ladder and harness, and the muffled words from the man being lowered, there was nothing.

They were dropping the ladder, the harness, the man, in measured steps. The two in charge set a beat to work to. One, two, down, one, two, down. Every downbeat meant the ropes were eked out a couple of inches at a time.

It was infinitely, agonisingly slow. For those in the background it was killingly slow.

Charlie was clutching Alice and Alice was clutching Charlie. Who knew what Alice was thinking? All Charlie knew was that they were almost conjoined, linked by their love of the man being lowered down the shaft.

Love. There was a huge concept.

Or maybe it wasn't. How many songs were there in the world about love? How many forms did love take?

The first flurry of romantic love? The hormonal rush that blinded to a lover's flaws? The love she'd thought she'd had for the man she'd once so disastrously married?

Or this, she thought, the idea embedding and growing as time stretched on? A love that was deep and abiding. A love that transcended romantic.

A love that said trust was bone deep.

She stood and watched Ewan, lying at the top of the shaft, pointing his torch downward, directing operations. Both teams were well back, lowering their ropes secured with planking. Only the ropes inching downward denoted anything was below.

Her whole world was below. It was a man descending into the blackness to save a dog that, whatever he said, wasn't his. Flossie was her dog.

But it didn't matter. She knew at some deep, instinctive level that he'd be doing the same if it weren't her dog. She looked at the people around her, the tenant farmers, the workers from the Hall, even his mother, and she saw fear but she also saw total trust.

This man was…their man. Their trust and their love was absolute.

And what she was feeling right now bought into that. It was nothing to do with fear, she thought. It was so much more. It was as if something had washed through and left her completely, irreversibly changed.

'Bryn,' she whispered and it was so much more than a word.

It was a vow.

And then there was a sharp, muffled command from below. Both teams stilled and the whole world seemed to hold its breath. The silence went on and on. No one moved. No one spoke.

And then, finally…

'Up.' The single syllable was almost a grunt, as if a truly Herculean effort was being made. It was enough to start the teams again. Once again though, they worked with agonising slowness. There was just as much risk raising as in lowering, maybe more, because if he was carrying Flossie there'd be more weight.

She didn't know if he was carrying Flossie. The teams would know because of the change in weight but Bryn was wasting no words, no effort, in reporting.

And Charlie wasn't asking. She was no longer thinking of Flossie.

Bryn. Her love. Her man.

And finally he was nearing the top. There were curt orders from Ewan, because he still wasn't safe. Dragging him over the edge could make things collapse. But Ewan and John were lying full length on the planking, grasping with a strength she couldn't imagine. A limp bundle of fur was being passed up, seized, dragged backward.

She should rush forward. Flossie was her dog. Flossie was what this was all about. But other hands were taking Flossie. The vet was here, giving orders, carrying Flossie away from the shaft so she could see the damage.

But Charlie's gaze was still locked on the shaft. On Bryn. On the final few inches.

He was being hauled upward, his arms grabbed, tugged backward to safety. He was standing. John and Ewan were half holding, half hugging, their grimed faces a mix of triumph and relief.

He was safe. He was standing on firm ground, looking around. Seeing his mother, giving her a faint smile. And then…seeing her.

Looking. Just looking.

And that look… The promise in that gaze… With it, the loneliness and distrust inside her cracked and then shattered—and then disappeared as if it had never been.

She smiled. It was a crazy, tear-filled smile, a smile she'd never known she possessed but it was his, all his.

And finally she walked forward, through the mud, across the planking, to take the man she loved into her arms.

It was the moment when Charlie Foster gave her heart for ever.

Flossie was headed for a night at the veterinary clinic. It was miraculous that she'd survived, but her injuries were a little more serious than when she'd had her encounter with the car. Her leg was broken this time, and she had myriad grazes. 'She'll be okay,' the vet told them. 'But a bit of sedation and some IV fluids will help her recover faster.'

They thanked everyone. Charlie hugged everyone. It

was hard to hug when she was being hugged herself but from the moment he'd surfaced, Bryn had his arm around her. He seemed to need the contact.

That was fine by her. Contact… Body against body. Bryn.

He was by her side. He was safe.

Bryn.

Alice's sedan proved no match for mud stirred by the vehicles of those arriving to help. It had to be abandoned to be collected in the morning so they drove home together. They drove in near silence—the emotions they were all feeling left little room for words. Bryn pulled up outside the dower house, helped his mother from the car, hugged her hard and then turned to Charlie.

'There's room in my bed tonight,' he said simply and Alice smiled as if she'd expected those exact words. She kissed Charlie and then slipped through her front door and closed it behind her.

So Charlie came on home with him because…that was how it felt. Suddenly this vast mausoleum of a Hall was… home.

Because Bryn was there.

They showered, still almost in silence. Together. It felt right. It hardly even felt sexy. Bryn's body showed the marks of rope burn, scratches where Flossie had struggled, grazes. Charlie helped him clean them, loving every mark.

'Love,' Bryn said softly as the final graze gave up its mud. And he tugged her into his arms, snagged towels and carried her up the grand staircase to the vast bedroom, to the four-poster bed that the Barons Carlisle of Ballystone Hall had slept in for generations.

'Because it's time we took our place where we belong,' he told her.

He lowered her onto the sheets and she smiled and smiled. And then she claimed her man.

* * *

Her man. That was what it felt like, she thought as she woke in the soft dawn light. She was spooned in his arms; the warmth enveloping her was something she'd never felt before…

'I'm in love,' she whispered into the dawn, and the arms holding her tightened.

'I hope so,' Bryn growled. 'If not we're in trouble because this is your home. Now and for ever.'

Now and for ever. She let the words drift.

They were just words.

They were the most important words she'd ever heard.

But some things had to be said. This man had done nothing but give, while she…

'Bryn, I didn't trust you,' she whispered. 'I'm so sorry.'

He turned her then, gently, so their faces were inches apart on the great down pillows. 'Life's taught you not to trust,' he told her.

'Life's kicked you around, too.' She hesitated but it had to be said. There was room for nothing but honesty now. 'And death. So much tragedy…how can you still love?'

'I was lucky,' he said simply. 'Those I loved gave me so much love in return.' He leaned forward that last couple of inches and kissed her, tenderly, with all the love in the world. 'You get love, you give love,' he said softly. 'It seems to me, Charlie *bach*, that it's been lacking in your life. There was only your grandparents to love you. Now though… You have seven dogs, and a couple of cows arriving some time soon. You have Alice, who's already crazy about you. And you have me. So that's, let me see, eleven known love donors. With that much love coming your way, my Charlie, do you have enough to send some back my way?'

And there was only one answer to that. She tugged him

into her and kissed and then there was no room for words for a very long time.

They slept again and when they woke…

'I know I should do this properly,' Bryn said sleepily, holding her close. 'Fancy restaurant, orchestra, ring cunningly hidden in the chocolate soufflé…but if you feel we can get by without the soufflé… Charlie, will you marry me?'

Would she marry him? Would she wake beside him for the rest of their lives? Would she trust this man with her heart, with her love, with her future?

How could he ask such a question? The answer was all around them, an aura so strong surely he could see it. There was love in this room. Love and laughter and dogs and maybe kids and maybe even grandkids and wonder and hope and trials and joy.

Marriage… The joining together of two people who loved each other to the exclusion of all others.

Two people who trusted each other for life.

He was asking for an answer. He really didn't know? She saw the trace of uncertainty in his eyes, the trace of doubt behind his eyes and she couldn't bear it. She smiled and she smiled and her fingers touched his lips, his face. It was a battered face this morning, scratched and bruised.

She loved it. She loved him.

The question hung. Charlie, will you marry me?

'How can you doubt it?' she whispered. 'Bryn, you've trusted me from the start but me…it's taken me a while but I'm there now, with all my heart. Will I marry you? Yes, my love, I will.'

They loved again and then they slept, and woke when the sun was high and Alice was calling up the stairs.

'Hey, you two, don't you believe in answering the

phone? I phoned the landline and your mobile phone. Nothing.'

'I turned my phone off,' Bryn whispered to Charlie. 'You want to pretend we're not here?'

There were dogs scratching at the door. Alice was still below stairs, obviously respecting their privacy—a bit—but by the sound of her voice she was full of import and Charlie wouldn't put it past her to power up the stairs and burst right in.

'My phone must have got wet down the shaft last night,' Bryn called out. 'Mum, can you take the dogs? Charlie and I are...busy.'

'Busy!'

'We're also engaged,' he called and Charlie almost choked at the thought of Alice's face downstairs. But it seemed Alice was made of too stern a stuff to be distracted by a little thing like an engagement.

'About time,' she retorted. 'But I have news.'

'News?'

'Thomas has been arrested in Thailand,' she told them. 'And we have an extradition treaty with Thailand. End of scams, Bryn. He's coming home to face trial.'

'Excellent,' Bryn murmured and Charlie heard a gasp of what was surely indignation from below stairs.

'Is that all you can say? Bryn, don't you care?'

'It's good that he's stopped from scamming,' Bryn said, tugging Charlie close again. 'But for the rest... Nope, don't care.'

'Bryn...'

'I have other things to care about than my sordid uncle,' Bryn said, smiling at Charlie. And such a smile... 'I have many things to care about, the loveliest being in my arms right now. So, Mum, if you don't mind...would you be good enough to take the dogs for a walk so I can get back to my caring?'

There was another gasp from downstairs and then a choke of laughter. But then…ever the mother. 'You're not holding her against her will, are you, Bryn? Charlie, are you okay?'

'I'm fine,' Charlie called back, choking on laughter. Choking on happiness. Choking on love. 'I'm absolutely fine.'

'We're both fine, Mum,' Bryn called. 'And we intend being fine for the rest of our lives so if it's okay with you… fine starts now.'

CHAPTER TEN

THE WEDDING OF Bryn Thomas Morgan, Twelfth Baron Carlisle of Ballystone Hall, was a great occasion, bruited not only in the neighbourhood but in the society pages across Britain. Since the tragedy, given the Eleventh Baron's age and distress, the media had left this family alone, but now they woke to the fact that one of its most eligible aristocrats was about to wed. Journalists and photographers thus descended as a pack, expecting…pomp?

They didn't get pomp.

By rights the wedding should have been held in the family chapel, or in the little village church, but this was a celebration the like of which the district hadn't seen… for ever? The shared joy of Flossie's rescue seemed to have embedded Charlie in the hearts of the district—they'd seen her lugging timber—they'd seen her distress and her joy at the happy ending. They'd also seen the way the Baron had come straight to her, the way he'd held her. This was a happy ending beyond happy endings. The joy between Charlotte Foster and Lord Carlisle was thus deemed to be a fine thing and it was something to be shared.

The wedding was therefore held outside, on the lawns of Ballystone Hall. A massive marquee was set up—decorated mostly in pink because Alice was in charge of decorations and both Charlie and Bryn thought, Why not pink? They were so happy, why shouldn't Alice be, too? So as the music swelled, as the time approached, Bryn stood with John by his side, under an arch of pink roses.

Waiting for his bride.

But first came the dogs because the dogs had brought them together and dogs would be part of their lives for ever. There were ten dogs, each walked by their own attendant.

First, Bryn's Sadie walked by Ewan.

Then Alice's two dogs, walking on either side of Ewan's wife, the lady who *did* for Alice. Eilwen was beaming and beaming and it seemed almost as if the dogs were beaming as well.

And then came the Australian contingent. They were led by the six people who'd offered them forever homes, four tenant farmers, the local postmistress, and the head of the conservation team. He'd come to the Hall the day after the shaft drama with apologies and gone home with Stretch, the sausage dog. Stretch was now in charge of making shafts safe, or at least supervising the team doing it. For bureaucratic reasons the two dogs now living away from Ballystone were deemed borrowed, not given, but that was okay. It meant they still had to visit and all six dogs had owners who loved them.

Happy ending all round?

Absolutely, for here was another happy ending. Flossie was walking by herself. She was carrying a limp, but maybe a limp wasn't a bad price to pay for her happy ever after. For the Hall was her forever home now. They could leave the doors, the gates open all they wanted. There was no way she'd leave.

And Bryn had trained her for her role today. She was carrying a ring box around her neck. Flossie. Ring bearer.

She reached Bryn's side and sat as he'd taught her. He put a hand down to pat her head but Bryn wasn't looking at Flossie.

He was looking at his bride.

For Charlie was walking steadily towards him. Alice was by her side, her sole attendant, the woman she'd chosen to 'give her away'. Alice, beaming and beaming. In glorious pink.

But he wasn't looking at his mother, either.

He was looking at Charlie.

She was wearing a rainbow.

'You can wear white.' He'd heard Alice discussing it with her. 'Yes, it's your second marriage but no one cares. But I know where we can order you the most beautiful pink gown...'

He would have even married her in pink, he thought, the smile in his heart growing by the moment. But he didn't have to marry her in pink., because this was Charlie and Charlie had blossomed. Charlie had opened, unfurled, trusted and...loved. One colour would never be enough for this woman.

For Charlie was her own woman. She knew what she wanted. The dress she was wearing was simple but wonderful, a wafting creation of rainbow silk. It had tiny capped sleeves, caught in under her breast and then swirling out, a cloud of rainbow colour. She'd let her curls fall free. A cluster of rosebuds nestled in her curls and she was wearing diamond eardrops that had been in his family for generations.

'What if I lose them?' she'd protested.

'I'll buy you more,' he'd promised. 'But they're just things, Charlie *bach*. Lose them or not, it doesn't matter. All that matters is you.'

So she did wear them, because they fitted the outfit perfectly. They were just...what she wanted?

Except they weren't what she wanted. He knew that now. This was Charlie, and even if she'd worn nothing in her ears, it wouldn't have mattered. She wanted him.

And Bryn? He wanted Charlie, with all his heart. He

wanted her smile. He wanted to wake every morning with her beside him. He wanted his Charlie to love him for ever, and magically she wanted it just as much as he did.

She was reaching him now, pausing for just a moment to pat Flossie because Flossie was being extraordinarily good and a woman had to give a dog her due. But her smile didn't leave Bryn.

'Hey,' she whispered and they might as well have been alone.

'Hey, yourself,' he whispered back and it was too much. She was so achingly beautiful. Before the crowd, before all these people, he lifted her and swirled her so her dress flared out in a riotous circle of colour. The guests and the media went wild. Then he used the time while the vicar waited for the crowd to settle to kiss her as he needed to kiss her. As he intended to kiss—and be kissed—for the rest of his life.

'Hey,' he said again, as finally they broke apart, as finally reality broke in. 'You want to get married?'

And she looked up at him, mistily, through tears, this man she loved with all her heart. This man she'd trust for ever. This man… Her man.

'I think I already am married,' she whispered back and finally they turned to face the patiently waiting vicar. 'That's the way I feel. But let's say I do.'

So they did.

For the rest of their lives.

* * * * *

THE LITTLE
MAVERICK
MATCHMAKER

STELLA BAGWELL

To my late brother, Lloyd Henry Cook.
I miss you so much.

Chapter One

"Wow! Look at all the people, Dad! This is gonna be super fun!"

Stifling a groan, Drew Strickland pulled his gaze away from the large crowd milling about on the grassy lawn of the Rust Creek Falls park to glance down at his seven-year-old son, Dillon. The child's brown hair was already mussed despite the careful combing Drew had given it before they'd left home, plus the tail of his plaid cotton shirt was pulled loose from the back of his jeans. However, it wasn't the boy's disheveled appearance that concerned Drew. It was the mischievous twinkle in Dillon's brown eyes that worried him the most.

Like his late mother, Dillon didn't possess a shy bone in his body, and Drew had the uneasy feeling that before this back-to-school picnic ended, his son was going to do a bit too much talking. Mostly about things he shouldn't be talking about.

"It does look like plenty of folks are here today," Drew replied to his son's excited comment, while silently wishing he could think of one good reason to grab Dillon's hand and hightail the both of them away from the gathering. But that would hardly be fair to his son. Nor would leaving give Drew the chance to be a dad for one day, at least. And being a real, hands-on dad to Dillon was one of the main reasons his parents had pushed him to move to this little mountain town. It had been their way of forcing Drew to take on the full responsibility of Dillon's care.

"That's gonna make everything better!" Dillon grabbed a tight hold on his father's hand and tugged him toward the crowd. "Come on, Dad. I want you to meet my new friends."

Drew and Dillon had only moved to Rust Creek Falls a month ago, yet already his son had made fast friends with many of his second-grade classmates and most of the adults who called Strickland's Boarding House their home. As for Drew, he had a few relatives in the small Montana town, but no one he could actually call a close friend. But then, a doctor, especially an OB-GYN, didn't have much time to socialize.

Who was he trying to kid? Drew wondered. He'd never been a people person. Even when Evelyn had been alive, he'd always been more than happy to stand in the background and let her do most of the talking.

But Evelyn wasn't at his side anymore, he thought grimly. She never would be. And now it was up to him to step forward and be the kind of father that Dillon needed and deserved. Even if that meant mixing and mingling with total strangers.

Father and son had barely moved more than ten feet into the gathering when two young boys and a girl, all of them Dillon's age, came racing up to them.

"Hi, Dillon!" the three children shouted in unison.

Grinning broadly, Dillon gave his friends a wave, then proudly began introductions.

"Dad, these are my best buddies." He pointed to a towheaded boy with a face full of freckles and then to the other boy with black hair that looked as though it was just starting to grow out from a summer buzz cut. "This is Oliver and Owen. And that's Rory," he added, pointing to the lone female.

Even though Rory was wearing jeans and a T-shirt like her male counterparts, the plastic tiara crowning her long blond hair was an all-girl fashion statement.

Drew smiled a greeting at the trio. "Hi, guys. It's nice to meet some of Dillon's friends."

The boy named Oliver immediately spoke up, "Dillon says you're a hero. 'Cause you're a doctor. Is that right?"

A hero? Far from it, Drew wanted to say. If he'd been anything close to a hero, his wife would be walking around this park with her son, rather than Drew. But to hear that Dillon had put him on such a pedestal filled him with gratification, even if it was undeserved.

"I am a doctor," Drew answered simply.

Owen looked properly impressed. "Gee, can you sew up cuts and fix a broken arm?"

"Of course he can, silly!" Rory chided her friend. "Any ole doctor can do that."

"My dad can fix anybody that's sick," Dillon boasted proudly.

"Dillon," Drew gently admonished. "You're stretching things a bit."

"Well, almost anybody," the boy amended.

Deciding that was enough medical talk, Oliver said to Dillon, "Wanta come with us? We're gonna go gather some pinecones."

"What for?" Dillon asked.

The black-haired boy rolled his eyes. "To throw at the dorky first graders, what else?"

Drew was about to tell his son he wasn't about to throw pinecones at any child, much less one younger than him, when Dillon suddenly said, "Naw, I'm going to stay with my dad, so I can show him around. He doesn't know many people yet and I do."

"Okay. See ya later, Dillon," Rory called as the three kids turned and ambled away.

"Dillon, this deal with the pinecones, I—"

"Oh, that was nothing, Dad. Oliver wants to act like he's a tough guy, but he ain't."

"He isn't," Drew corrected his son's grammar.

"That's right. Oliver is just a big mouth. He wouldn't hurt a flea even if it was biting him."

Drew let out a heavy breath. At thirty-three, it had been many years since he'd been a boy of Dillon's age. And even then he hadn't been surrounded by a group of friends. He'd spent most of his time on the back of a horse, helping his father and brothers work their ranch near Thunder Canyon, a town just several hundred miles from Rust Creek Falls.

"I'm glad to hear it," Drew told his son, then glanced at his watch. "Are you hungry? I'm sure there are some tables of food around here somewhere."

"Oh, no, Dad! We don't want to eat yet. Let's walk around and look at the girls."

Girls? He hadn't noticed his son talking about girls. But that was probably Drew's own fault. Before they'd moved to Rust Creek Falls a month ago, Drew hadn't spent the kind of time a real father should spend with his son. For the past six years, since Evelyn's death, Drew had been content to let his parents Jerry and Barbara deal with raising Dillon. But now, the move away from Thunder Canyon had forced Drew to become a hands-on father and he was beginning to see the task wasn't easy.

"Look at the girls?" Drew asked drily. "Are you thinking you'd like to have a girlfriend?"

Dillon's impish grin grew sly as he tugged on his father's hand. "I have to find the right one first, Dad. Let's go!"

Finding it easier not to argue the point, Drew went along with his son. With any luck, he thought, he'd run into someone from the clinic and strike up a conversation that would divert Dillon from his matchmaking game. Yet as father and son moved deeper into the crowd, Drew failed to spot one adult he knew well enough to greet, much less engage in a chat.

Realizing Dillon was yanking on his arm, Drew looked down to see the boy pointing toward two women standing in a group of people gathered in the shade of an evergreen.

"Oh, look at that one, Dad. She's really pretty. And the one next to her with the red hair is, too. Don't you think she'd make a great girlfriend?"

Totally bemused by his son's suggestions, Drew glanced at the two women who'd caught his son's eye. He vaguely recognized the one with long dark hair as Paige Traub and the redhead standing next to her as Marina Dalton. Both were elementary teachers at his son's school.

"They're both very pretty, Dillon. But both of those ladies are already happily married."

Dillon tilted his head to one side as he cast his father

a dubious look. "Don't you want to be happily married, too, Daddy?"

Feeling as though he'd been sucker punched, Drew was forced to look away and draw a deep breath. Being only twelve months old when his mother had died, Dillon had no memories of her. He couldn't know how much she'd loved her baby. He couldn't remember how her hands had gently held and soothed him. Or how her soft voice had sung to him. No. Dillon couldn't remember anything about the woman who'd given him life. But Drew hadn't forgotten. If anything, he'd clung to her memory, while deep inside, the resentment of losing her festered like a sore that could never heal.

Bending down to his son's level, Drew gently tried to explain. "Look, Dillon, your dad has already been happily married to your mother."

Dillon's little features wrinkled up in a frustrated frown. "But what about *now*, Dad? You're not married now!"

Straightening to his full height, Drew let out another long sigh. God help him get through this day, he prayed. "Dillon, I understand that most of your friends have married mommies and daddies. But those daddies are different. They're not like me."

Dillon's bottom lip thrust forward. "But you could be like them," he argued. "If you wanted to!"

His patience wearing thin, Drew ushered his son forward. "That's enough of that. Come along and we'll get something to eat."

For the next few minutes, Drew managed to keep Dillon's attention on a plate of sandwiches and chips. But as soon as the food disappeared, Dillon was anxious to return to his quest of finding a girlfriend for his father.

Thankfully, Drew spotted his cousin Claire Wyatt on the opposite side of the milling crowd. She worked as a cook at Strickland's Boarding House and was married to Levi, who managed a furniture store in Kalispell. Since their daughter, Bekka, was only four years old and not yet ready for kindergarten, Drew wasn't sure what Claire was doing here at the school picnic. He supposed she'd taken the opportunity to visit with friends. At the moment she was in a conversation with an older couple he'd seen a few times in the boardinghouse.

"There's Claire," Drew said, in an effort to divert Dillon's attention. "Let's go talk with her."

"Aw, Dad, don't be a fuddy-duddy. We talk to Claire all the time when we're home," he reasoned. Then, like a bird dog that had spotted a flock of quail, the child suddenly went on alert. "Look at that lady over there by the punch bowl, Dad! She's pretty, huh?"

Drew was about to warn Dillon that if he didn't quit this nonsense right now, the two of them were going to leave. But before he could get the words out of his mouth, Dillon yanked on his hand and pointed straight at the woman.

Drew glanced in the direction of his son's finger to see a tall young woman with a blond braid hanging over one shoulder and a pair of long, long legs encased in close-fitting blue jeans. He had to admit Dillon had good taste. She was definitely pretty. But Drew wasn't interested in women. Pretty or otherwise.

He was about to turn his attention back to Dillon when she suddenly looked up and caught the two of them ogling her. Even with a few feet of ground separating them, Drew could see a blush sting her cheeks before she quickly turned her back to them.

Oh Lord, she'd probably already sized him up as some sort of creep, Drew thought.

"Dillon, it's not polite to point. I don't want to see your finger pointing at anyone again. Hear me?"

It wasn't often that Drew scolded his son over anything. But to be honest he wasn't around long enough to do much scolding, or otherwise. These past four weeks, since they'd moved to Rust Creek Falls, had been the first time Drew had parented Dillon without his parents or grandparents to back him up. From this little outing today, it was clear he had plenty to learn about corralling a seven-year-old boy with the energy of three kids.

"Okay, Dad. I won't point," Dillon promised. "But let's go talk to *her*. She looks nice!"

Drew was about to warn his son that just because she looked nice didn't mean she'd be receptive to meeting strangers. But the words never made it past his lips. Dillon began to tug him forward, and deciding it was easier to go along than to make a scene, Drew reluctantly followed his son.

By the time they reached the woman by the punch bowl, she'd turned back around and Drew could see she was eyeing the both of them with wry speculation.

"Hi! I'm Dillon Strickland," Dillon boldly introduced. "This is my dad. His name is Drew Strickland."

Her gaze traveled from Dillon to Drew, then back to the child, before a wide smile spread across her face.

"Well, hello, Dillon and Drew," she said warmly. "I'm Josselyn Weaver."

She shook Dillon's hand and then turned to Drew. "I'm the new school librarian at Rust Creek Falls Elementary," she informed him.

Drew extended his hand, and for a moment their

palms touched and her small delicate fingers wrapped around his. He wasn't sure why the brief contact registered in his brain, but it did. And he couldn't let go of her hand fast enough.

"Nice to meet you, Miss Weaver," Drew politely replied. "Dillon is in the second grade this year and new to town. So I thought it would be good for him to attend the picnic today and see some of his teachers and friends."

"For sure," Josselyn said with another broad smile for Dillon. "Do you like to read, Dillon?"

Drew was shocked to see his son was already completely charmed by the new librarian. His mouth had fallen open, while twinkling stars were lighting up his brown eyes.

"Oh, yeah!" he exclaimed. "I love to read. Well, I mean—I do if I can't play video games or watch TV. I have lots and lots of books, though."

Drew cast a skeptical glance at his son. As best as he could remember, the shelves on the walls in Dillon's bedroom might be holding two or three children's books and a few comics. If Dillon was reading other things while Drew was working at the clinic, he didn't know about it.

"My son does read," Drew told her, "but I think the 'lots and lots' is stretching it a bit."

Josselyn laughed and Drew decided the sound was like the happy ring of sleigh bells on a snowy morning. He wished he could hear it again.

"That's okay," she assured him. "The fact that he reads even one book is encouraging. And it's my job to find stories that make children want to read more."

"I read the funnies in the newspaper with my gramps," Dillon spoke up. "He says I'm a good reader."

"Well now, that's great to hear," she told him. "Then I'll be seeing you whenever you visit the library."

"Oh, you bet! You'll be seeing me plenty." He grinned at Josselyn, then looked proudly up at Drew. "My dad helps women get babies."

It was a good thing Drew wasn't drinking punch. Otherwise, he would have spewed a mouthful all over the woman.

Josselyn Weaver turned a bemused look on Drew and for no reason at all, he found himself studying the green color of her eyes. Like a first leaf in spring, he decided. "Uh—pardon my son. He means that I...deliver babies. I'm a doctor. An OB-GYN."

Her gaze carefully slipped over his face, as though she was trying to decide for herself if he was actually a doctor. A woman's doctor, at that.

"I see. Do you work here in Rust Creek Falls?"

"For now. I'm here on a temporary basis. The clinic is expecting another doctor to join the staff after the first of the year. He's away right now. Doing Peace Corps work."

"And you're filling in until he gets here. That's nice."

She might call it nice, but for Drew this whole move to Rust Creek Falls had been an upheaval. He'd never been a person who cared for change. Thunder Canyon, where he'd been born and raised, where he'd lived with Evelyn and worked at the local clinic, was home to him. It was where he felt comfortable and hidden from the rest of the world. But this cheerful woman didn't need to hear about his gloomy thoughts.

"I hope that my being here is helping the community," he said, then glanced down at Dillon. The boy was closely watching the exchange between his dad and Josselyn Weaver. Drew could only imagine what was going on in the fertile imagination of his son's mind. "And Dillon is enjoying the change."

"That's good. I don't imagine he's had any trouble making friends."

"No. He's never been remotely close to being shy."

Dillon's gaze vacillated between the two adults before he finally settled his attention on Josselyn.

"Are you married?" the boy asked bluntly.

The woman's cheeks turned beet red and it was all Drew could do to keep from groaning out loud.

"I'm so sorry, Miss Weaver. My son definitely needs more lessons in manners. You see, he, uh, is on a search to find his dad a girlfriend," Drew attempted to explain.

"No! Not a girlfriend," Dillon immediately corrected. "I'm gonna find him a wife!"

The sound of conversations were all around them and throughout the crowd were spates of laughter, along with shouts and squeals from playing children. Yet the short space between Drew and Josselyn Weaver felt thick with silence.

"Oh. Well, that's a serious search," she said, her dubious gaze landing on Drew's face.

Mortified at the whole situation, Drew grabbed Dillon by the hand. "Uh—we have to be going. It's been nice meeting you, Miss Weaver."

Before she could say more, Drew quickly urged his son away from the pretty librarian.

Dillon instantly complained, "Dad, why are you leaving Miss Weaver? She was really nice! And pretty, too! And she liked talking to us. I could tell!"

His expression grim, Drew stared straight ahead as he hurried his son through the crowd. "I think we've done enough picnicking for one day, son. We're going home."

"Why are we going home?" Dillon stubbornly demanded. "We haven't talked to everybody yet."

"We didn't come to the picnic to talk to *everybody*," Drew said, trying to keep the thread of anger in his voice from unraveling completely. "And we certainly didn't come to pick out girlfriends or wives, or any such thing as that."

"Aw, Dad, you're messing up bad," Dillon grumbled. "You're letting a good one get away."

The comment had Drew glancing down at his son. What could a seven-year-old boy know about women? *Apparently quite a bit*, Drew thought. Josselyn Weaver was beautiful and intelligent and sweet. The kind of woman a man searched for in a lifelong mate. But Drew wasn't searching for a mate. Short- or long-term. And the quicker Dillon got that through his head, the better.

"We're not on a fishing trip, Dillon."

"That's right," Dillon said sullenly. "Gramps takes me fishing. Not you."

Gramps. Yes, in one short month Dillon and his great-grandfather had formed a strong bond between them. And Drew was glad Old Gene had taken such an interest in Dillon. He was pleased that his son had found a solid male figure to connect with while they were here in Rust Creek Falls. Yet Drew couldn't help but be envious of the close connection. It was something he'd never had with his son. And to make matters worse, Drew had no one to blame for the distance between them except himself.

A stronger man wouldn't have allowed the death of his wife to cripple him to the point that he needed help just making it through the day, much less taking care of a baby. A man of deeper character would have never buried himself in his work and allowed his son to be raised by others.

Drew didn't know whether moving to this little mountain town had opened his eyes or if the fact that Dillon seemed to be growing up at a rapid rate was making him look at his life differently. But either way, Drew realized he wanted to make a change. One that would bring him closer to his son.

Chapter Two

That evening on Sunshine Farm in her cozy little cabin, Josselyn sat cross-legged on the couch and stared blankly at the TV perched in one corner of the living room. After a very long day at the town picnic, she'd thought she would unwind by watching one of her favorite programs, but so far her mind refused to latch onto the plot. The characters could've been speaking in a foreign language for the past thirty minutes and she would've never noticed.

Josselyn aimed the remote at the TV and pressed the off button. She was wasting her time, she thought. Ever since the school picnic had ended and she'd driven home, she hadn't been able to think about anything except Drew Strickland and his adorable son.

When the two of them had first approached her, she'd guessed the mother had been somewhere in the crowd visiting with friends. But then Dillon had made that comment about finding his father a wife and blown her assumption to pieces.

So where was Dillon's mother? she wondered for the umpteenth time. Even if the boy's parents were divorced, the mother should've found the fortitude to put her differences with her ex aside and attended the school picnic with her son.

With a sigh of frustration, she tossed aside the remote and left the couch. *Darn it!* Why couldn't she quit thinking about the dad and son?

Probably because the dad was drop-dead delicious, she thought as she gazed out the window at the shadowy patch of lawn in front of her cabin. Even now, hours after their impromptu meeting at the park, his image was still burned in her brain. Tall, long-legged and lean, Drew Strickland was a genuine Doctor Dreamy. Dark brown hair, cut in a short, ruffled style, had framed a face dominated by brown eyes and a pair of firm lips that were bracketed by the most gorgeous dimples she'd ever seen on a man.

The doctor ought to be carrying a warning hazard to all women who came within ten feet of him, she thought with a wistful sigh. And if that wasn't bad enough, his son had been so cute and endearing she'd wanted to snatch him up in a tight bear hug.

So Dr. Drew Strickland has enough sex appeal to rob a woman of her breath. And his son is the kind of kid that touches the very middle of your heart. That doesn't mean you have any business thinking about them. They're both heart trouble walking on two legs. You need to forget them and get on with your life.

Yes, getting on with her life was the very reason she'd moved to Rust Creek Falls in the first place, Josselyn reminded herself. She hadn't studied long and hard to acquire a master's in library science just to get herself mixed up with a lost cause. One that would end up dealing her far more misery than happiness.

A few weeks ago, Josselyn had been living in Laramie, Wyoming, in an apartment not far from her parents, Velma and Walt Weaver. Her two older brothers, Lloyd and Cameron, both worked on a prominent cattle ranch outside the city, while her younger sister, Patti, was still living with their parents as she finished up her last year of college. The Weavers had always been a tight-knit group, and none of them except for her mother had understood Josselyn's need to move and start a life away from the place where she'd been born and raised. If her father and siblings had it their way, she'd still be there, making the same rounds with the same group of people she'd known since kindergarten.

Earning her diploma had opened a whole new world to Josselyn, where fresh faces and exciting opportunities waited around each corner. Ignoring her family's argument to remain near Laramie, she'd begun searching for jobs in neighboring Montana. Once she'd landed the library position at Rust Creek Falls Elementary, she'd turned her focus to finding a place to live. Somewhere far away from concrete and busy streets.

The moment she'd spotted an article somewhere about Sunshine Farm located near Rust Creek Falls, she'd been instantly intrigued. The piece had been about Amy Wainwright and how the woman had visited the farm to attend the wedding of a friend and eventually ended up finding her own true love, prompting the journalist to dub the farm the Lonelyhearts Ranch.

The story of Amy's happy ending had perfectly fit Josselyn's sunny attitude about life. Sunshine Farm was a place where loving couples chose to take their wedding vows, plus it had a guesthouse for folks who wanted to forget the past and make a fresh start. Josselyn wasn't running from a heartbreaking past. Nor was she planning a wedding for herself. She didn't even have a boyfriend, much less a fiancé. All the same, Sunshine Farm, or the Lonelyhearts Ranch, whichever name a person chose to call it, was the perfect home for her.

Thoughtfully, she turned away from the window and plucked up a white shawl from the back of a chair. After being in a crowd of people all afternoon, the quietness of her cabin should have been soothing. Instead, it was allowing her to think far too much.

With the shawl wrapped around her shoulders to ward off the evening chill, she went outside and walked across a grassy slope, past a big yellow barn and on toward the main house of Sunshine Farm.

A porch light illuminated a door at the back of the house. After rapping her knuckles lightly on the door frame, Josselyn let herself in and found Eva Stockton at the counter putting a snack of homemade cookies and mugs of coffee onto a wooden tray.

The room was warm and Josselyn caught the faint, lingering scents of grilled beef and green peppers. With Eva cooking hearty meals every night for her husband, Luke, it came as no surprise that the kitchen was one of the first rooms the man had remodeled in the old farmhouse.

"Oh, hi, Josselyn," the pretty blonde said cheerfully. "You're just in time to join us in the living room. The cookies are chocolate chip with macadamia nuts. They're rather good, even if I did make them."

Since Eva worked at Daisy's Donut Shop in town and was considered one of the best cooks around, Josselyn had no doubt the cookies were scrumptious. "Please don't tempt me, Eva. A person can't eat just one of your desserts. And I stuffed myself at the school picnic today."

"Well, if you'd like coffee just help yourself," Eva offered.

"Actually, I thought I'd check in on Mikayla," Josselyn said. "Is she in her room?"

"I think so. And I'm sure she'll be glad to see you. With little Hazel still in NICU, she can't help but be a bit mopey."

Josselyn gave Eva an understanding nod. "Having a premature baby can't be easy. I'll take her some coffee and see if I can cheer her up a bit."

Picking up the tray, Eva shot her a grateful smile as she started out of the kitchen. "I knew the first moment I met you that you were going to be a perfect boarder here at Sunshine Farm."

Josselyn laughed lightly. "How could you have known that?"

"Something about the kind twinkle in your eyes," she tossed over her shoulder.

With Eva gone, Josselyn helped herself to the coffee. Once she'd placed two mugs on a tray, she decided to add a couple of cookies, just in case Mikayla might be hungry for a treat.

Carefully, she carried the lot upstairs and knocked on the door to Mikayla Brown's room. After a moment, the door swung open and Josselyn gave the other woman a cheerful smile.

"Room service," she announced. "Coffee and cookies. Want some company?"

With a lopsided smile, the pretty brunette gestured for Josselyn to enter the room. "You're too sweet. How did you guess I needed a pick-me-up?"

Josselyn put on her cheeriest smile and hoped it would rub off on her friend. "I didn't. I'm really just being self-ish. I needed a little company."

She carried the tray over to the far wall of the room, where a rocking chair and a stuffed armchair sat at an angle to each other in front of a tall-paned window. Situated between the chairs, a low wooden table held a small old-fashioned lamp with a glass globe.

Josselyn placed the tray next to the lamp. When she straightened, Mikayla was there to give her a brief hug.

"Thank you for coming," she said, her voice cracking slightly. "I only got home from the hospital an hour ago and I'm already wishing I was back there. I need something to take my mind off Hazel."

"Then we both needed company," Josselyn said. "Which chair do you want?"

"I'll take the armchair," Mikayla told her. "Being in the rocker makes my arms ache to hold my baby. I've decided I'm not going to sit in it until she comes home from the hospital."

Josselyn eased into the wooden rocking chair with a red cushion tied to the seat. "I understand why you want to stay at the hospital to be near your baby, but you do need to rest, Mikayla. You need to recuperate, too, so you'll be feeling your best whenever Hazel does get to come home."

"That's what the nurses keep telling me. That I need to give my body a chance to bounce back from giving birth. But it's very hard to leave my daughter. Even long enough to get a night's sleep."

Josselyn could hear the desperate longing in Mikayla's voice, and though she didn't yet know what it was like to have a child of her own, she could very well imagine how torn her friend was feeling.

"Do you have any idea when Hazel might be released from the hospital?" Josselyn asked.

Taking a seat in the armchair, Mikayla took one of the mugs and a cookie from the tray. "Thank God, she's doing really well. Her doctor says she might get to come home at the beginning of next week. I'm afraid if I start counting the days I'll jinx things. But I'm so excited."

Mikayla had come to Sunshine Farm seven months pregnant and single, after she'd discovered the father of her child having sex with his paralegal right in his office. However, since then, Mikayla's life had taken several drastic turns. Only last month, she'd met wealthy businessman Jensen Jones and the two had fallen in love. Then unexpectedly she'd gone into premature labor.

Josselyn picked up the remaining coffee mug and took a cautious sip. "That's wonderful news, Mikayla. And it sounds like we'll be hearing wedding bells pretty soon, too."

Mikayla sighed. "As soon as we can have Hazel safely with us at the ceremony. Jensen and I are waiting to see how things go with the baby before we set a definite date for our wedding. But we're hoping we don't have to wait too long. For now, he's searching high and low for the perfect house for the three of us to move into." Her smile full of love, she added, "Jensen wants me and our baby to have the best."

"Of course he does. And I'm so happy for you, Mikayla. You and Jensen and little Hazel are going to have a wonderful life together. And you certainly deserve it."

"Well, things were going pretty awful there for a while," she admitted, then, smiling wistfully, she glanced toward the lace-covered window. "But coming here to Sunshine Farm has changed all that. I'm beginning to see why folks are starting to call it the Lonelyhearts Ranch. Something about people finding love in Rust Creek Falls has spilled over onto this place." She slanted Josselyn a sly glance. "So are you going to be next on the wedding planner's list?"

Josselyn laughed. "Really, Mikayla. You know I haven't even been on a date since I moved here. Well, maybe one if you count the lunch I had with the sixth-grade history teacher."

"By the way, you never mentioned how things went that day."

Josselyn shook her head. "I wish I could say the guy made my heart flutter. Instead, I struggled to keep from yawning. Raymond is nice enough, but he's about as dull as the paint on my little car. And that's pretty dull."

Mikayla chuckled. "Never fear. You're working in Rust Creek Falls now—where love is in the air, or the water, or something. I'm positive that you're going to meet a handsome guy that will sweep you off your feet before you ever realize what's happening."

Josselyn sipped her coffee while the image of Drew Strickland paraded through her mind. "I'm not really hunting for a man to love, Mikayla. If it happens, that would be nice. But I'm not sitting around pining over the fact that I'm twenty-five and still single." She looked thoughtfully over at her friend. "Actually, I did meet a really cute guy today. At the school picnic."

Her interest piqued, Mikayla leaned forward in the chair. "Oh, now this is the kind of news I want to hear. Tell me. Is he someone new in town?"

"That's the impression I got. He said he was here on a

temporary basis. I haven't seen him around Rust Creek Falls before today. And believe me, Mikayla, he's the type that a woman doesn't forget. But I was thinking you might know something about the man."

Mikayla's brown eyes widened. "Me? How would I know? I've not exactly been a social butterfly since I moved here."

"He's an obstetrician," Josselyn explained. "Dr. Drew Strickland. I thought you might have seen him around the clinic."

A clever smile suddenly spread across Mikayla's face. "I've seen Dr. Strickland more than you can imagine. He was the doctor who attended me that night I went into premature labor."

The information shouldn't have surprised her. Rust Creek Falls was a small place. It wasn't like there was an abundance of obstetricians around. "You mean he delivered baby Hazel?"

Mikayla nodded. "I have to admit he's a terrific doctor. Very caring, serious and thorough. Although, his bedside manner could be a bit better."

"Grumpy, huh?"

"No. Actually, he was very kind. It's just that he keeps his conversations to the minimum and as best as I remember, he never cracked a smile. But to be fair, he wasn't exactly dealing with an easy situation when he delivered Hazel."

Somehow Mikayla's observation about the man didn't surprise Josselyn. Drew Strickland had seemed only too eager to let his son do all the talking. Until the boy had started chattering about finding his dad a wife. Then the man had seemed to be totally embarrassed and even a bit angry. Why he'd reacted in such a way Josselyn could only guess.

"No," Josselyn agreed. "I don't suppose either of you had reason to smile during that stressful situation."

"So what was Dr. Strickland doing at the back-to-school picnic?" Mikayla asked. "Or did you actually talk to the man?"

"We talked. Briefly. After his son walked up and introduced himself and his father."

It was Mikayla's turn to look surprised. "The doctor has a son?"

Josselyn nodded. "He's seven and in the second grade. And cute as a button, I might add."

"Eva told me a little about his family," Mikayla replied. "But she didn't mention a son. And I haven't heard anyone around the clinic mention Dr. Strickland having a child."

"Hmm. That's odd. You would think one of the nurses would have said something," Josselyn mused aloud. "Do you know anything else about the man? I keep wondering about the boy's mother. She wasn't with them."

Mikayla broke off a piece of cookie and popped it into her mouth. Once she'd chewed and swallowed, she said, "Could be the woman was at the picnic—talking to someone else at the time."

Josselyn shook her head. "That's possible. Except that Dillon let it slip that he's trying to find his dad a wife."

"Awww. Poor little tyke. He must be wanting a mother something fierce."

Just thinking about the eager way little Dillon had been gazing up at Josselyn sent a pang right through her heart. There had been a real look of longing on the child's face. One that she hadn't understood completely until this moment.

"I think you must be right, Mikayla. Maybe...maybe he doesn't have a mother at all."

"Sounds to me like the good doctor is either divorced or widowed."

Widowed. Drew had looked to be in his thirties. At that age, she'd not considered the possibility that he might have lost his wife. But that could definitely explain the lost look she'd noticed in his eyes.

"If you're wondering about Dr. Strickland's marital status then you must be interested in the man," Mikayla remarked.

Clutching her mug with both hands, Josselyn stared into the brown liquid while a blush crept into her cheeks.

"I guess you could say I'm a little interested," she admitted with a sheepish grin. "After all, the guy is definitely dreamy looking. His son is such a sweet boy—he must be a good dad. Wouldn't you think?"

"I've heard nothing but raves about his services as a physician, but as for his private life, I wouldn't know. Maybe you should find that out for yourself," Mikayla suggested impishly.

Josselyn sighed. "I doubt I'll ever run into Dr. Strickland again. Besides, it was obvious he wasn't the least bit interested in me."

"Hmm. How could you tell?"

Josselyn let out a cynical grunt. "As soon as his son mentioned the word *wife*, he couldn't get away from me fast enough. And since I never spotted the two of them again, I assume Dr. Strickland must have left the park and taken his son home."

"I wouldn't take his sudden disappearance personally," Mikayla told her. "The man was probably embarrassed that his son said such a thing to you."

"Now that you mention it, his face did turn a little red," Josselyn murmured.

"Well, just in case you might actually be interested, I do know that he lives at Strickland's Boarding House. Old Gene and Melba are his grandparents."

"Oh. I hadn't made the connection to the boardinghouse," Josselyn said. "Do you know if he has any other relatives around Rust Creek Falls?"

"Three cousins, all of them sisters. Claire, Tessa and Hadley. Claire is married to Levi Wyatt and I believe they have a little girl, Bekka. She goes to the day care here in town. Claire cooks for the boardinghouse. Tessa is a graphic designer. She's married to Carson Drake and they have twins. Hadley is a veterinarian who's married to Eli Dalton. As far as I know they don't have any children yet."

"Hmm. I wonder about his parents or if he has siblings." She felt her cheeks growing even hotter as Mikayla continued to study her closely. "Forget I said that. Something is wrong with me tonight, Mikayla. I'm saying and thinking things that are completely off the wall. Maybe I need something to eat to get my brain back on track."

Laughing softly, Mikayla gestured to the other cookie still lying on the tray. "A little sugar should make you forget all about the sexy doctor."

Josselyn reached for the cookie, but as she bit into the scrumptious treat, she had an uneasy feeling that it was going to be a long time before she managed to push Drew Strickland and his son out of her mind.

Chapter Three

Early Monday morning while he waited for Dillon to dress for school, Drew sat at the kitchen table in the boardinghouse, eating the last of his breakfast of toast, bacon and dark black coffee.

Most of the other boarders chose to take their meals in the dining room of the old four-story house, but Drew liked his privacy. Gossiping back and forth across the table wasn't his thing. And to make matters even more uncomfortable, as soon as the tenants had learned he was a doctor, he was constantly approached for free medical advice.

Dillon, on the other hand, relished sitting around the big dining table and listening in on the conversations. It was no wonder the boy was seven years old going on fifteen, Drew thought wryly. And he could only imagine what Josselyn Weaver had thought when Dillon had blurted out that bit about finding his dad a wife. A full day had passed since the picnic, but the memory of the incident still left Drew smarting.

That afternoon, throughout the short walk from the park back to the boardinghouse, Drew had tried to lecture his son on the right and wrong things to say to a lady. And though Dillon had attempted to show a little remorse at his behavior, it was obvious to Drew that his son wasn't a bit sorry for all his bold talk.

"Do I hear a sigh over there? Is something wrong with your breakfast?"

Drew glanced over at his cousin Claire, who was busy flipping pancakes on an industrial-sized grill.

"No. Everything tastes great, as usual. Thanks, Claire."

"Well, you sound like something is wrong. Work getting you down?"

"I love my work. I'm even busier than I thought I would be here in this little town."

The pretty brunette slipped the browned pancakes onto a warmed plate. "Guess Rust Creek Falls does feel tiny to you after living in Thunder Canyon," she commented. "You must be missing your parents and your brothers."

Drew had to admit he'd missed his parents an awful lot when he'd first arrived here in Rust Creek Falls. He hadn't realized just how much he'd depended on them to keep Dillon corralled until he'd been forced to take on the job by himself. As for his brothers, all four were younger than Drew. Billy and LJ were both ranchers like their father, while Benjamin was a doctor. Trey managed the horse stables at Thunder Canyon Resort. All of them worked long hours, which made it difficult for the brothers to spend much time together.

"I do miss my family," Drew replied. "To tell you the truth, Claire, I didn't think I was going to like living in Rust Creek Falls. But the town and the people have grown on me."

"That's good. From what I see, Dillon has fallen in love with the place. You might have a hard time getting him to move back to Thunder Canyon."

"I suppose I should be happy that Dillon's gotten so close to his great-grandfather. At least he's not sitting around crying to go home."

Claire walked over to where he was sitting and looked down at him. "I hear something else in your voice, Drew. Do you resent the fact that Dillon has grown so close to Old Gene?"

Tossing his napkin onto his empty plate, he picked up his coffee cup. "No. I might be a little envious, but I don't resent it. I suppose what you're hearing in my voice is a father wondering if he's raising his son right."

An understanding smile on her face, Claire walked back over to the stove. "There isn't a parent alive who doesn't have doubts about being a good mom or dad. Where Bekka is concerned, I question myself every day."

That was just normal parenting, Drew thought ruefully. Claire had always been a full-time, hands-on mother. Whereas he'd basically turned his twelve-month-old son over to his parents and asked them to care for the baby. At the time, he'd felt it was the only thing for him to do. Losing Evelyn had jerked the ground from beneath his feet. He could barely function or take care of himself, much less a baby who needed endless attention. Not to mention that every time he'd looked at Dillon's little face, he'd been consumed with loss and self-blame over his wife's senseless death.

"You don't understand, Claire. When Evelyn died— well, I was a pretty worthless human being."

She frowned at him. "That's an awful thing to say

about yourself, Drew. You were in shock. Anybody in your shoes would've been. Evelyn's car accident was something that rarely happens. A tree toppling onto her car as she drove little Dillon to day care—it was freakish. Nothing about it made sense. I'm sure it will never make sense to you."

Drew bit back a sigh. He didn't like talking about Evelyn's accident. Didn't like remembering that it had been his turn to drive Dillon to day care that morning. Instead, Evelyn had offered to do it for him and as a result she'd lost her life. It was a fact that would always haunt him and, though six long years had passed, Drew was still living the nightmare.

"No. It doesn't make sense," he agreed. "To be honest, I'm still damned angry about the senselessness of it all. And I'm angry at myself for not realizing that those early years of my son's life were the very time I needed to form a bond with him. Not now—six years later."

Claire cast him a gentle glance. "You're a good father, Drew. You just don't realize it yet."

He rose and carried his dirty plate and cup over to a big double sink.

"Something I do realize, Claire, is that you're a good cousin," he told her, doing his best to give her a smile. "Now I'd better get upstairs to see what's keeping Dillon. Don't let Grandma work you too hard today."

Claire laughed. "I'll take a break while she's not looking."

Later that morning, Josselyn was putting a stack of returned books back on their proper shelves when a group of second-grade students trooped into the library. The normally quiet room instantly came to life with the sound of tapping feet and voices that were several decibels above hushed.

"Hi, Miss Weaver. Remember me?"

Turning, she was more than surprised to see little Dillon Strickland grinning up at her. Since school had started over a week ago, this was the first time she'd seen the boy in the library.

Smiling back at him, she said, "Sure I remember you. You're Dillon Strickland."

His brown eyes sparkled and Josselyn couldn't help thinking how the boy's features resembled his father's.

"And my dad is Drew. Remember him?"

That was something she hadn't been able to forget, Josselyn thought wryly. Throughout the weekend, the man and his son had drifted in and out of her thoughts.

"Yes, I remember. Your dad is Dr. Strickland," she said, and, deciding it was time to get on with school matters, left it at that. "I'm happy to see you in the library, Dillon. I believe this is your first visit since school started."

His eyes wide, he glanced around the rows of bookshelves, and as Josselyn studied the expression on his face, she got the impression he was seeing the library for the very first time.

He swiped at the dark hair hanging near one eye. "Uh—yeah. I've already read all my books at home. So I wanted to get some more. Reading is fun. Real fun."

Josselyn smiled to herself. "I'm glad you think so. What kind of books were you looking for today? Maybe I can help you find something."

"Oh, I like all kinds." With a look of bemusement, he peered up and down the aisle. "Do you have books about fish? I like fishing. Me and my grandpa go to the river and catch trout."

Grandpa. Mikayla had mentioned that Old Gene and Melba Strickland were Drew's grandparents. Could this child be referring to Old Gene, or did Drew or his ex-wife have parents living in or around Rust Creek Falls?

Josselyn was telling herself that Drew Strickland's private life was none of her business when Dillon suddenly interrupted her thoughts.

"I should have said great-grandpa." He spoke again. "My grandpa Jerry doesn't live here. He lives in Thunder Canyon with Grandma. Old Gene lives here."

"Old Gene is your great-grandpa?"

Another wide smile dimpled Dillon's cheeks. "Yeah. But I call him Gramps. Bet you know him, don't you? Everybody knows Old Gene. He has lots of friends."

"No. I've heard of him, but I've never had the opportunity to meet him," she said, trying to follow his conversation while a girl with brown braids stood a few steps away, waving frantically to attract Josselyn's attention. "Now we'd better see about finding you a fishing book. Follow me, Dillon, and I'll show you."

"Miss Weaver, I need help, too!" the young girl wailed.

"I'll be right back, Chrissy," she assured her. "You might want to look at the new-arrival section until it's your turn."

Clearly disappointed, the girl gave Dillon a glare before she stomped off in the opposite direction.

"Chrissy needs to learn her manners," Dillon muttered.

Josselyn certainly agreed, especially since it wasn't

the first time the girl had tried to push her way to the front of the line.

"Or maybe she don't understand," Dillon said with a shrug of one shoulder. "Maybe she don't have a mother. Like me."

The boy's empathetic remark made Josselyn desperately want to stop in the middle of the aisle and hug him tight. It also had her mind whirling with even more questions about Drew Strickland. But now wasn't the time or place to talk to the boy about personal matters. And even if they had been somewhere other than school, Josselyn certainly wasn't about to pump the child for information.

"Well, I wouldn't worry about it, Dillon. She'll get her turn. Right now, let's find you a fishing book. Maybe one with a grandpa in it. How would that be?"

He grinned up at her. "Oh, that would be super! I'll read every word, Miss Weaver."

"Looks like school is rubbing off on little Dillon," Melba commented, as she eased her frame into an armchair.

Drew lowered the medical journal he'd been reading to look at his grandmother, who'd finally found the time to sit down. Since he and Dillon had come to live at the boardinghouse, he'd learned one thing. His grandparents were always busy and appeared to have the energy of a pair of teenagers. Where they found such get-up-and-go Drew could only wonder.

"What are you talking about?" Drew asked her.

The gray-haired woman inclined her head to a spot on the opposite side of the sitting room. Drew glanced over his shoulder to see Dillon cozied up to his great-grandfather. The boy was holding an open book in his lap and appeared to be reading the story to Old Gene.

"I never noticed Dillon liking books before. Did he do a lot of reading back in Thunder Canyon?" Melba asked.

Drew should've been encouraged to see his son take an interest in reading. Books opened up a whole new world to a child and generally made them better students. Yet he couldn't deny that it hurt to see Dillon happily reading to his great-grandfather. Drew had been here in his grandparents' living room for the past half hour, but instead of sitting on the couch, close to his father, Dillon had chosen to ignore him.

The move from Thunder Canyon to Rust Creek Falls was supposed to have drawn Drew and Dillon closer together. At least, that's what Drew's parents had believed. Jerry and Barbara had certainly used that particular argument to persuade their son to take the temporary job at the clinic. But as far as Drew could see, his parents had been wrong. The move had actually pushed Dillon closer to his gramps.

"I think reading is something new for Dillon," Drew said to Melba, while telling himself he was being childish to resent his son's relationship with Old Gene. The two of them were good for each other and that was the most important thing.

Melba pulled a piece of knitting from a sewing basket sitting next to her chair. "That's good. Maybe he'll decide he wants to be a doctor someday. Like his dad and uncle Ben."

A cynical grunt erupted from Drew. Dillon never talked about wanting to become a doctor, or even be like his father. "I seriously doubt Dillon will want to go into the medical field, Grandma. He thinks being a horseman like his uncle Trey or a rancher like his grandpa Jerry would be more fun."

Focused on her knitting stitches, Melba smiled knowingly. "Nothing wrong with that. Most little boys like the idea of being outdoors and living the rough, tough life of a cowboy. But give him a few years. He might set his sights on something altogether different. Like a businessman or a lawyer."

During the first year of Dillon's life, Evelyn had often talked about their son's future and the dreams she had for him. She'd always summed up her wishes in one word. *Happy.* That was the main thing she'd wanted for Dillon. To live a full and happy life. Since her death, Drew had fallen short in the dad department. But he was determined to change. To make certain Evelyn's vision of their son's future came true.

"Sometimes I wonder, Grandma, if becoming a doctor was the wrong path for me. I was raised a rancher—a cowboy. Things might have been better if I'd never left that life."

Frowning, Melba lowered her knitting and studied him over the rim of her reading glasses. "How could you think such a thing, Drew? You studied so long and hard. Babies are a family's hopes and dreams and you help them come true by seeing those new little lives safely enter the world. It's an admirable profession."

Along with all consuming, Drew thought ruefully. Even now, as he sat quietly here in his grandparents' living room, his evening could change in a split second with an emergency call. Babies didn't wait for a convenient time to arrive.

"Yes, but I might still—"

He stopped abruptly and Melba's keen eyes were once

again studying him closely. "Might what? Still have Evelyn? Is that what you were going to say?"

Drew silently cursed, knowing the perceptive woman was going to hound him until she got an answer.

Claire had started in on him this morning and now his grandmother this evening. Both women ought to know he didn't want to talk about his late wife. Anyone in his family should understand that just speaking her name was like swallowing shards of broken glass. Yet they had to bring up the whole tragedy, as if talking about it was going to make all the pain and loss go away. Damn it, why couldn't they see that nothing was going to make things better for him?

Releasing a heavy breath, he closed the journal and laid it aside. "Something like that."

Melba's lips thinned to a disapproving line. "You're thinking like a fool, Drew."

He couldn't help but bristle at her unkindly observation. "Am I? Well, it was an emergency medical call that sent me to work instead of taking my son to day care. It was my job that put Evelyn in that car. If I'd been working on Dad's ranch, the accident would've never happened."

"You think so, huh? Well, I don't." She leveled a pointed gaze at him. "Things in our life happen for a reason, Drew. Until you realize that and accept it, you're never going to be happy."

Happy. That was a condition Drew never expected to experience again, he thought bitterly. His happiness had died beneath that oak tree.

He was trying to gather the words for a reply when a buzzer sounded, alerting his grandparents that someone was at the office at the back of the boardinghouse.

Frowning, Melba glanced at the clock on the wall. "Now, who could that be at this hour? All the boarders are paid up."

"Could be a new tenant, Ma." Old Gene spoke from his spot on the window seat.

Sighing, Melba laid her knitting aside and rose from the comfortable armchair. "I'll go see."

"I'll go with you," her husband said.

She started out of the room. "No need for that. We have a vacancy. I'll take care of the registry."

"Just the same, I'm going with you," Old Gene insisted, as he left his seat next to Dillon and joined her at the door.

"But, Gramps, I haven't finished the story yet!" Dillon complained.

Old Gene cocked a bushy eyebrow at his great-grandson. "You read the rest of it to your dad."

Dillon scowled. "But he don't like fishin'!"

"He might if you give him a chance," Old Gene said as he followed his wife out the door.

Dillon stared sulkily at the floor, a reaction that surprised Drew. It wasn't like his son to be crabby.

"Bring your book over here, son," Drew invited.

His bottom lip pushed petulantly forward, Dillon snapped the book shut. "I don't want to read anymore," he muttered.

Drew contained a weary sigh. "Okay. But come here anyway. I want to talk to you."

Dillon jammed the book beneath his arm and walked over to the couch. "Am I in trouble?"

Was he really so miserable of a father that Dillon thought the only time his father wanted to talk to him was when he needed to be disciplined? The idea was one more heavy weight on Drew's shoulders.

"No." He patted the cushion next to him. "Do you think you've done something wrong?"

Dillon climbed onto the couch and scooted backward until his athletic shoes were dangling off the edge of the seat.

"No," he mumbled. "But I guess I wasn't talking very nice to Gramps just now."

"Well, you could have been more understanding," Drew gently agreed. "Gramps has work he has to do."

Dillon's lips twisted into a smirk. "Not like you, Dad. You work all the time."

He might as well have been kicking him in the shins, Drew thought. It wouldn't have been any more painful.

"I'm not working now," Drew said pointedly. "So show me your book."

Relenting, Dillon placed the book flat on his lap. "See. It's about a boy who catches a great big fish, but nobody will believe him."

"Why not? Doesn't he show the fish to everyone?"

Dillon shook his head. "He can't. While the boy wasn't looking, a raccoon snuck up and stole the fish. Nobody believes that, either."

"Sounds like this guy has a big problem."

Dillon's chin bobbed up and down. "He's pretty sad right now. I hope he gets happy by the end of the book."

"I do, too. Being sad isn't any fun." Drew gestured toward the book. "Did you get the book at school or does it belong to the little boy who lives downstairs with his mother?"

Frowning, Dillon glanced up at him. "You mean Robbie? No. He can't read very good. He's got something wrong with his eyes and he sees things funny."

From the few times Drew had spotted the little boy around the boardinghouse, he would guess him to be about the same age as Dillon and extremely shy. Most of the time he'd remained half-hidden behind his mother, a thin, harried-looking young woman. "How do you know this?"

"'Cause Robbie told me so. He has to take extra lessons to read better."

Leave it to Dillon to know more about their neighbors than him, Drew thought. His son did get around.

"I got the book about fishin' at the library at school. Miss Weaver helped me pick it out."

Miss Weaver. Drew had pretty much pushed the brief meeting with the woman out of his thoughts. At least, that's what he'd been telling himself. But the images of her gentle smile and soft green eyes were still dancing through his mind, reminding him that he was a long way from forgetting.

"Miss Weaver—the lady we met at the picnic," Drew stated more than questioned.

Dillon's sulky demeanor suddenly vanished with a bright smile. "That's right. The really pretty one! She's super nice, Dad. And she knows all about books."

Drew started to explain that Miss Weaver knew all about books because that was her job, but he quickly nixed that thought before he spoke. Dillon was a child. Hard facts weren't what he needed to hear.

"I'm glad she was so helpful. Uh…you didn't say anything about me to her, did you?"

Dillon's smile faded, but didn't quite disappear. "No.

There was too many kids around. Besides, I figure she was thinking about you anyway."

Over the years, Drew had learned to expect the unexpected from Dillon, but this was one time his son's remark took him aback. "Why would you have that idea, Dillon? The woman doesn't even know me."

"Sure, she does. She met me and you at the park. So when she seen me in the library, that made her think of you. It's simple, Dad."

Simple. There was nothing uncomplicated about this quest of Dillon's to find his father a wife. And what had gotten into his son, anyway? Even though Dillon's mother was gone, the boy still had plenty of mothering from Drew's mom and grandmother. It wasn't like he'd grown up in an all-male household and was starved for maternal attention.

"Well, simple or not," Drew told him, "I don't want you going around talking about finding me a wife. Not to strange women. Not to anyone. Can you promise me that?"

As Drew watched his son's mouth fall open, he expected to hear a loud protest. Instead, Dillon said, "Okay, Dad. I promise."

Drew patted his knee. "Good, boy. Now, about this fishing book. You know, what you told Gramps about me not liking to fish was wrong."

Dillon's face was a picture of surprise. "It was? I never seen you go fishing before."

"Well, it has been a while," Drew conceded. About eight years, he thought ruefully. "I used to take your mother fishing back in Thunder Canyon. There was a big stream on the family ranch with lots of trout. And after we caught a bunch, we took them home and had a fish dinner."

"Golly, that sounds like fun. Why don't you do that now, Dad?"

Yes, why didn't he?

Because Evelyn is gone. Because going without her wouldn't be the same. You've used that excuse for the past six years of your life, Drew. When are you going to throw it away and start enjoying these precious years with your son, instead of clinging to a memory?

Torn by the reproachful voice in his head, Drew stared at the window on the opposite side of the room. Oh how he wished he could open the paned glass and let all the painful memories in his heart fly away. Never to torment him again.

"Dad? Why don't you go fishing now?"

Dillon's repeated question pulled Drew out of his wistful reverie and as he looked down at his son, he did his best to ignore the guilt pressing down on his shoulders.

"I'll tell you what, Dillon, if you'll finish reading your book to me, I'll promise to take you fishing."

Dillon eyed him skeptically. "You really will take me? You're not going to say you have to work?"

Dear God, he had a long ways to go to prove himself as a father, Drew thought. "I'm not just saying it." To underscore his words, Drew made an x across his heart. "I really promise."

"Okay, Dad! We got a deal!"

Dillon raised his hand for a high five and as Drew gently slapped his palm against his son's, a small sense of triumph rushed through him.

* * *

By the time Friday arrived, Josselyn decided that where little Dillon Strickland was concerned, something was amiss. So far the boy had visited the library every day this week, at times during periods when he should have been on the playground running and playing with his friends.

Not wanting to get the boy in trouble, Josselyn hadn't spoken to his teachers about his unusual behavior. After all, fretting over a child's visits to the library sounded ridiculous. Even to Josselyn. But Dillon was checking out more books than a normal child his age could read in a month. And each time she questioned him about the books, he evaded answering by steering the conversation back to the fishing story.

Clearly he'd read that book. He even talked about how he was going to be like the hero and catch the biggest fish in Rust Creek Falls. But she'd make a bet that the other books had never been opened.

Josselyn stared at the small sticky note lying on her desk. The telephone number scratched across it was the contact number Drew Strickland had provided to the school.

She glanced at the large clock hanging on a far wall of the library room. The man was a doctor. She didn't like the idea of interrupting his work. But it was nearing the lunch hour. Hopefully he'd already dealt with most of the morning patients.

Drawing in a bracing breath, Josselyn punched in the numbers, and as the ring sounded in her ear, she wondered why her heart was beating a mile a minute. This was nothing but a school-parent call and Drew Strickland was little more than a stranger.

"Dr. Strickland here."

As soon as the rich, male voice came back at her, Josselyn's pent-up breath rushed out of her.

"Hello, Doctor. This is Josselyn Weaver, the librarian at Rust Creek Falls Elementary. We met at the school picnic."

After a short pause, he said, "Yes, I remember. How are you, Miss Weaver?"

A physician would be asking about her well-being, she thought. "I'm good, thank you. I—uh—apologize for calling you at work. Do you have a minute or two? I promise this won't take long."

"You've called at the right time. My nurse is having lunch, so I have a short break. Is there something I can do for you?"

Her mouth suddenly turned as dry as Death Valley in mid-July. "Actually, I'm calling about your son, Dillon. I've been seeing quite a bit of him in the library."

"That's encouraging. Maybe he'll develop a love of reading."

For no sensible reason at all, she was suddenly picturing the shape of Drew Strickland's strong lips and the deep dimples carved into his cheeks. Just the thought of kissing him was enough to make her breath catch in her throat.

"Yes. I'm hoping that happens, too."

He must have heard something amiss in her voice because he suddenly asked, "Are you calling because Dillon has been acting unruly? If so, I'm not surprised. I'm fairly sure he's not yet learned that a library is a place for silence."

In other words, Dr. Strickland hadn't visited a library with his son before, she concluded. But that wasn't all that unusual. Some men's reading habits never went beyond the newspaper or an occasional magazine.

She said, "Students are taught the rules of etiquette by their teachers before they visit the library. Besides, Dillon hasn't been unruly. He's—well, he's coming in every day and checking out an unreasonable amount of books. When I questioned him, he says he's reading all of them. Is that what you're seeing at home?"

This time there was a long pause before he answered.

"I'm not exactly sure. I'm in and out of the boardinghouse so much answering emergency calls. Dillon could be reading when I'm not around."

Which could be most of the time. She was beginning to get the picture now. Apparently Dillon needed more than a mother. He needed his father's undivided time and attention. But she wasn't about to point that out to the man. His idea of proper parenting was his business. Not hers.

"Oh. I see."

Silent seconds passed before he spoke again. "Tell me, Miss Weaver, do you think my son has a problem?"

She wasn't certain about Dillon's problem, but she realized she had one of her own. He was tall, dark haired and sexy enough to curl a woman's toes. Just the sound of his deep male voice was making her skin prickle with awareness.

"I'm not sure. I just know he's spending an inordinate amount of time in the library."

"This deduction is coming from a librarian?"

Josselyn bristled. No matter if the man was a walking dream, she didn't deserve or appreciate his sarcasm. "Yes. And you can do what you like with the information. As a part of the school staff, I thought you should be alerted to your son's behavior. Thank you for your time, Dr. Strickland. Goodbye."

She hung up the phone, then, realizing she was shaking, rose and walked over to a window that overlooked the school playground. Except for a few yellow cottonwood leaves rolling across the dormant lawn, the area was quiet. But as soon as lunch was over, the area would be full of children, most of them laughing and playing. Would Dillon be among them? Or would he choose, as he had yesterday, to come into the library and talk to her, rather than play with his friends?

Josselyn hadn't bothered telling Dr. Drew Strickland that bit of information. Not when he'd seemed to be dismissing her concern about Dillon as much ado about nothing.

Maybe she doesn't have a mother. Like me.

The boy's remark was still haunting Josselyn. Almost as much as the sad shadows she'd spotted in Drew Strickland's gorgeous brown eyes.

Chapter Four

Monday afternoon, thirty minutes before it was time to pick up Dillon from school, Drew was kindly escorted to the library by a teacher's aide.

"No need to knock," the dark-haired woman told him. "Miss Weaver is still here. She never leaves until long after the last bell rings."

"Thanks."

The woman went on her way and, taking a deep breath, Drew opened the door and stepped inside the world where his son had been spending an inordinate amount of time. Or so Miss Weaver had said.

Throughout the weekend, he'd thought about her call. The words she'd said and the way she'd said them had stuck in him like thorns of a briar branch. His son wasn't getting the attention he needed at home. At least, not the right kind. She'd not uttered those exact words, but the tone in her voice had been clear, and that bothered Drew. Bothered the hell right out of him.

At first glance, he spotted a large oak desk situated close to a window. At the moment it was empty, and as he walked slowly toward it, he glanced between the tall shelves jammed with books. The aide had said Miss Weaver was still here, but the long room was as silent as a tomb.

And then he heard faint footsteps moving across the hardwood floor. Pausing, he turned toward the sound and waited for her to appear from the maze of bookshelves. When he did finally catch sight of her, his breath caught in his throat.

Miss Weaver had looked fresh and young and pretty at the picnic. Today she appeared totally different. From the bright red skirt that hugged her hips to the white blouse tucked in at her slender waist, she looked all-woman.

"Oh," she said, as she looked up to see him standing at the end of the aisle. "I thought I'd heard footsteps. I expected to find one of the students."

Drew waited for her to walk to him. All the while his gaze was taking in all sorts of little things about her. Like the fuchsia color on her lips, the black high heels on her feet and the way her blond hair curled against her shoulders. No wonder his son was spending so much time in here, Drew thought. Dillon probably saw this woman as some sort of enchanting princess.

"One of the aides escorted me here to the library," he told her. "I...uh, hope I'm not here at a bad time. I thought I might talk to you for a few minutes before school lets out and I have to pick up Dillon."

He could tell by the way she was sizing him up that she was surprised to see him. He could've told her he was just as surprised to find himself here.

"Of course," she said. "Would you like to have a seat?"

"I would. Thanks."

He followed her over to the front of the desk and eased onto one of two heavy wooden chairs angled to one side. He was expecting her to take a seat in the executive chair behind the desk, but instead she sat directly across from him.

Drew tried not to notice as she crossed her long legs and adjusted the hem of her skirt. But he did notice, and the fact irritated him. His job required him to look at the female anatomy all day long. He saw all shapes and sizes of women, ranging in age from the very young to the very old. The only thing that ever caught his attention was when he spotted a health problem. Otherwise, he was totally indifferent. So why was the sight of Josselyn Weaver's legs making him think about things he thought he'd forgotten years ago?

Clearing his throat, he said, "I've been thinking about our phone conversation, and I realize I wasn't exactly helpful. I'd had a rough morning at the clinic and my mind was, well, a bit distracted."

"That's understandable. We all get like that from time to time."

Not like him, Drew thought. For the past six years, he'd tried to function as a normal person while half of his mind was thinking about Evelyn, missing her and cursing the accident that had taken her away. It hadn't been easy. It still wasn't.

"You're being kind and I don't deserve that."

She studied him with an odd look and Drew was glad she didn't ask him to explain the comment that had slipped out of him as though it had a will of its own.

"Dr. Strickland, I'm sorry if my call alarmed you. That wasn't my intention. All in all, I'd say Dillon is a bright, intelligent, well-rounded boy. And I enjoy having him in the library immensely. It's just that he's going a bit overboard with the books and the time he spends here. Some days he ignores his lunch recess and spends the break time in here with me. He really ought to be out running and playing with the other children. I've tried to encourage him to do just that, but he seems to want to talk."

Dreading what she might possibly say next, Drew invited, "Please call me Drew. And as for Dillon, I had no idea this was going on, Miss Weaver. Uh—what does my son want to talk about?"

The smile on her face could only be described as sunny, and in spite of himself, the sight of it lifted Drew's spirits.

"Nothing strange. The kind of stuff that little boys are usually interested in. He talks about going fishing with his great-grandfather. And he mentions living on a ranch back in Thunder Canyon and riding horses with his other grandfather. Is that true? Or is that just a child's wishes?"

"No. All of that is true. We moved here from Thunder Canyon a few weeks ago."

"Oh, I'm sorry, I was a bit confused. The other day in the park you mentioned your son was new to town, but I just assumed you'd moved here a few months ago, not a few weeks."

He shrugged. "It would've been better for me and Dillon if we could have made the move a bit earlier— so that he would've had more time settling into his new surroundings before school started. But it takes lots of situating and planning for a doctor to leave his practice in the care of another physician. The first week of August was the earliest I could manage."

"Yes, I can see where your job would make a move

challenging," she replied. "So this Thunder Canyon that Dillon speaks of, is it in Montana, too?"

He nodded. "South of Bozeman. My parents own a ranch a few miles out of Thunder Canyon. Dillon stayed with them while I worked at the medical clinic there. Mom and Dad are like his second parents."

"So he did ride horses and feed cows and all that kind of thing?"

"Yes. As soon as Dillon was old enough, my dad let him tag along to do the chores. He's taught him a lot about ranching."

Her smile deepened as she openly studied him. "And what about you? Were you ever a cowboy?"

About a hundred years ago. Or that's the way it felt to Drew. So much had happened in his life since he'd left the ranch and headed out to get his medical training. "I was born into that life and was raised helping my father work the land and the livestock. I know as much about that vocation as I do doctoring."

"Hmm. You've surprised me."

"Why?"

"You look like a doctor. Not a cowboy. And I should know. I have two brothers who work on a ranch outside Laramie, Wyoming."

So she had brothers. What about sisters and parents? More important, what about a special man? Drew was shocked at how much he wanted to ask her about her personal life.

He said, "Well, like the old adage goes, you can't judge a book by its cover."

Laughing softly, she gestured to the rows of shelves filled with books. "Yes, that I should definitely know."

As he recalled from their brief meeting in the park,

the sound of her laugh was easy and pleasant. Drew realized it would be nice to hear it again. And again. But he was intruding on this woman's time and the bell was about to ring. Dillon would be waiting at the car.

Drew rose from the chair and Josselyn joined him.

"Well, perhaps Dillon is missing the ranch," he said, carefully steering the conversation back to his son. "Although he hasn't indicated that to me."

"Now that I've learned you've only been here in Rust Creek Falls a *very* short time, I understand Dillon's behavior a bit better. Everything is new to him and his daily routine has changed. He'll settle in soon."

Drew wasn't so sure his son's behavior had anything to do with their move from Thunder Canyon to Rust Creek Falls. He figured it had everything to do with the boy's wish to find his father a wife. But Drew wasn't about to bring up that awkward subject to this woman. Once was more than enough. And thank God, she'd seemed to have forgotten Dillon's outburst in the park.

"I hope you're right." He reached to shake her hand, but the moment she placed her hand in his, his initial intention was instantly forgotten. Instead, he simply held on to her fingers and relished the way their soft warmth wrapped around his. "Thank you, Miss Weaver, for your time and your patience with my son."

"Please, call me Josselyn."

Her gaze connected with his and Drew felt a strange jolt to his senses. Peering into her green eyes was like walking into a cool, grassy meadow. "All right, Josselyn. And hopefully this obsession Dillon has with the library will ease soon."

"Oh, believe me, Drew, I want Dillon to continue to come to the library and for books to be a part of his life.

Don't worry. I have a feeling Dillon is going to find a happy medium."

Clearing his throat, Drew forced himself to drop his hold on her hand. "That's my wish, too."

"Uh, before you go," she said, "I'd like to invite you to a parents' reading club meeting for the students. It will be held here in the library at seven this Thursday night. I'll be talking about ways to get children interested in books and some of the new editions we plan to add to the school library this year. I realize your time is limited, but I hope if you're free, you'll think about attending."

Oh, he'd be thinking about it, all right, Drew thought. Thinking about seeing her again. Damn it.

"I'll see what I can do." He glanced at his watch just as the bell rang. "Thanks again. I'd better go catch up with Dillon."

As he hurried out of the library, he had the uncomfortable feeling that Josselyn was staring after him.

By a quarter past seven on Thursday night, Josselyn had decided that Drew wasn't coming to the meeting. Which surprised her somewhat. When he'd shown up unexpectedly in the library to talk to her about Dillon, he'd seemed genuinely interested in making sure his son remained on the right track at school and at home. But maybe she'd read too much into that one exchange with the man. Especially when she'd been having all sorts of problems trying to concentrate on Dillon's behavior rather than his father's sexy presence.

The man was a doctor. He could be dealing with a patient tonight. Considering all the pregnant women she'd seen around town, he probably stayed busy delivering babies. Since she'd moved to Rust Creek Falls, she'd been told stories about Homer Gilmore spiking the wedding punch a couple years back, which resulted in the town's baby boom nine months later. But as far as Josselyn could see, love and babies continued to be a hot commodity in the mountain community. Even without the aid of spiked punch.

Standing near a table set up with coffee, hot chocolate and punch, Josselyn was scanning the crowd when she saw the door to the library swing inward. The moment Drew stepped through the opening, her pulse leaped into a rapid flutter.

She wanted to walk across the crowded space and give him a personal greeting, but quickly decided against giving the locals anything to gossip about. Anyway, he was no different than any other parent here tonight. Maybe if she kept repeating that fact to herself, she'd eventually be convinced.

Over the rim of her coffee cup, she watched him make his way through the group of people. A few spoke to him in passing, while one woman actually grabbed him by the arm and pulled him aside. Judging by the impatient frown on his face, Josselyn decided the middle-aged woman was probably using the impromptu meeting to get free medical advice.

Deciding it wouldn't hurt to help him make a quick escape, Josselyn tossed her cup in a trash basket and made her way over to him.

"Hello, Dr. Strickland," she greeted. "I'm happy to see you could make it tonight."

He excused himself from the woman and turned to Josselyn with a smile of relief. "Hello, Miss Weaver. I apologize for being a little late. Things were hectic at the boardinghouse and for a while I wasn't sure my grand-parents were going to be able to watch Dillon. Thank-fully things quieted down."

"Well, after all the trouble you've gone to to get here, I hope you're not too bored with the meeting. Anyone who wishes to express his or her views or ask questions is encouraged to do so. I'm not much of a speaker, but I am passionate about coming up with ways to get chil-dren to read. So I'm hoping this meeting will generate some helpful ideas."

For the first time since she'd met the man, a faint smile crossed his face.

"I think your passion has rubbed off on Dillon. When I left the boardinghouse, he was actually reading a book to his great-grandfather. And it wasn't the same fishing story."

"That's encouraging news," she told him, then, real-izing a few of the people in the crowd were looking in her direction, she glanced at the clock on the wall. "I'd better get things rolling before the guests get restless."

Drew couldn't believe he was using these few pre-cious hours away from work to sit through a meeting about books and kids. The day had been especially stressful, with one patient developing toxemia, another suffering an early miscarriage and a third threatening to go into premature labor. He'd been forced to send the first two patients to the hospital in Kalispell, while the third he'd put on medication and bed rest. That had only been a portion of the morning. The rest of the day had been jammed with patients and endless interruptions.

To say he needed some quiet time was an understate-ment. But ever since Drew had talked to Josselyn Weaver three days ago, she'd been traipsing through the back of his mind, reminding him that he was not only a father, but also a red-blooded male. If he really wanted to be honest with himself, he'd admit that he was sitting here on a plastic chair in the middle of a crowd of strangers simply because he'd wanted to see Josselyn again.

And it was definitely worth it, he thought, as he watched her move away from an easel displaying a montage of colorful book jackets. She was wearing a pale pink sweater dress that clung to her slender curves, while her thick blond hair was pulled into a braided chignon at the back of her head. A single strand of pearls circled the base of her throat and matched the simple pearl drops hanging from her ears. She looked elegant and sexy at the same time, and Drew wondered why now, after all this time, this particular woman was pricking his interest. It wasn't like he was searching for a wife, or even a lover. In fact, he seriously doubted he'd ever be capable of loving another woman in his lifetime.

So why was Drew wasting his time in a school library when he could be home with his feet up?

"Thank you all for coming tonight. And please feel free to contact me with any ideas or questions you might have about the library, or your child's reading habits."

Josselyn's closing words penetrated his wandering thoughts and he looked around to see most of the crowd had left their seats and were migrating toward the exit. Drew waited until the last stragglers had spoken to Josselyn and departed the library before he left his seat and walked to where she was busy clearing her desk.

"Nice meeting, Josselyn."

Glancing around, she smiled at him. "Thanks. At least

I didn't see anyone sleeping. Just a few yawns now and then," she added jokingly.

He gestured to the books she'd stacked to one side of the desk. "May I help you with those? Or putting away the chairs?"

She straightened away from the desk and Drew found himself looking directly into her face. Had she really looked this pretty the last time he'd seen her? That day in the park he'd felt like he'd been gawking at her, but apparently he'd barely skimmed her features. Otherwise, he would have noticed how her skin had an iridescent glow and her eyes sparkled with life.

"Thanks, but I'll deal with the books in the morning," she told him. "And the janitors will take care of the refreshment table and chairs."

"Then you're finished for the evening?" he asked, surprising her and himself with the question.

"All finished," she replied. "Was there something else you needed to discuss with me?"

Drew felt like a complete idiot as a wave of heat swept over his face. "Nothing specific. I—uh—wondered if you might want to join me for a cup of coffee. Daisy's Donut Shop is keeping later hours these days. It might still be open."

She considered his invitation only for a moment. "It would be nice to unwind for a few minutes before I head home," she said, then smiled. "Thanks for asking, Drew."

A ridiculous spurt of joy shot through him. "The pleasure is all mine," he murmured. "My car is parked right outside. I'll drive you back here when we're finished."

"Sounds good. Let me get my handbag and jacket and I'll be ready to go."

* * *

Short minutes later, at a small table in one corner of the only bakery in town, Josselyn sliced her fork into a piece of pecan pie and lifted it to her lips.

"Mmm. No one bakes desserts like Eva Stockton," she said after she'd swallowed the bite. "It's a good thing she does most of her pastry cooking here at Daisy's Donut Shop instead of home on Sunshine Farm. I'd be weighing fifty pounds heavier in no time."

"Sunshine Farm," Drew repeated thoughtfully. "I've heard that name mentioned around the clinic. Someone said it's the old Stockton place. Is that right?"

"You are right," she answered. Then she asked, "Are you acquainted with the family?"

He nodded. "I'm acquainted with most of the long-standing families of Rust Creek Falls. Some of the Stricklands have lived here for many years, so this town has always been like a second home to me. In fact, my four brothers and I attended Luke Stockton's bachelor party."

She said, "Since I've moved to the area, I've learned to be cautious about what I say. Everyone seems to be related or, at the very least, friends. As for Sunshine Farm, some folks around here are beginning to call it the Lonelyhearts Ranch because of all the people who seem to find love there."

"Is that where you live?" he asked.

Sitting across from Dr. Drew Strickland, enjoying pie and coffee, was the last thing Josselyn had expected to be doing tonight after the library meeting. She still couldn't quite believe he'd invited her, or why he'd bothered. With his good looks and social standing as a doctor, he couldn't be desperate for female company. And for all she knew, he might have a sweetheart back in Thunder Canyon. Someone who was helping him get over his lost love.

"Yes. I live in one of the cabins," she told him.

"I haven't driven out that way in years," he admitted. "I guess I'd forgotten about the place having cabins."

She nodded. "From what I've been told, the Stockton boys were helping their dad build them at the time the parents were killed in that horrible car accident. But I'm sure you know all about that."

His face paled noticeably and then his gaze dropped to the cup he was clutching with both hands. "Yes. It was tragic. Even more so because it split up the family by forcing the siblings to go to separate homes. But then, tragedies tend to tear people apart."

There was no mistaking the grim bitterness in his voice, and Josselyn decided that at one time or another this man must have experienced his own private hell. Had he lost Dillon's mother to an accident? She was beginning to think so. And though she desperately wanted to ask, she tamped down the urge. It was far too soon for such a personal question.

"Or bring them closer together," she suggested on a more positive note. "The Stocktons are continuing to do repair and remodeling work around Sunshine Farm. Especially on the cabins. There are seven cabins in all. Although not all are rented because of the ongoing construction. They also rent out a few rooms in the big farmhouse. Actually, a patient of yours, Mikayla Brown, lives in one of them. That is, she'll be living there until Jensen Jones finds a house for the three of them—which I'm sure will be sooner rather than later."

He looked up and she was relieved to see the color had returned to his face.

"I'm happy to say things worked out well for Ms. Brown and her newborn. I was told her baby was released from the hospital a couple of days ago. Everyone on staff at the clinic was glad to hear it."

Josselyn's smile took on a wistful quality. "I've already met the baby and she's gorgeous. She named her Hazel."

He didn't say anything, and as she lifted her coffee cup, she noticed he was regarding her with a thoughtful eye.

After a moment, he said, "You say that like you wish you had children of your own."

She sipped the coffee, then placed the cup back onto the table. The man's job was delivering babies. That was the only reason he was asking the question, she silently reasoned. Not because he was *that* interested in her personal life. "I do want children. When the time is right. And the perfect man comes along."

A wry smile slanted his lips. "I didn't know such a thing existed."

Heat rushed to her cheeks and she laughed, hoping the sound would divert his attention. "Well, I should've said the perfect man for me."

He continued to study her closely. "So you're saying you haven't found him yet?"

His question caused her pulse to pick up its pace. "No. I dated a few men back in Laramie, but none seriously. For a long time I was mainly focused on my education. You see, acquiring my degree took a while. I had a scholarship and grants to help with expenses, but college doesn't come cheap. My parents are hardworking, but not wealthy. I had to work part-time while I took classes."

"Same here. I received a few small scholarships, but they weren't enough to see me through years of med school. I worked at odd jobs to help with the cost."

And what about Dillon's mother? When had she come into the picture and where was she now? The questions were burning Josselyn's tongue, but she kept them to herself. This was the first, and probably the last, time she'd be on an outing with this man. She didn't want to ruin it by prying. Even though it hadn't seemed to put him off from asking her whether she had a special man, she thought.

"So you're from Laramie," he said after a moment. "I've been to Cheyenne, but never to Laramie. Did you always live there?"

She nodded. "Born and raised there. Dad is a lineman for a local electric company. He's worked at that for close to thirty years. And Mom is a practical nurse at one of the city's hospitals."

He settled comfortably back in the wooden chair and Josselyn couldn't help but notice the wide breadth of his shoulders and the way the fabric of his shirt stretched taut against his muscled chest. In spite of his having an indoor job, he looked very strong and fit. Which made her wonder if he visited the gym or hiked some of the nearby mountain trails. Whatever he did for exercise appeared to be keeping him in top physical condition, she decided.

"My folks have always been ranchers," he told her. "I have four brothers. Trey, Benjamin, LJ and Billy."

Seeing he'd decided to share a little personal information, she decided to follow suit. "Lloyd and Cameron, my two older brothers, are ranch hands. And I have a younger sister who's still at home finishing her college. Her name is Patricia, but we all call her Patti. We all have our little spats from time to time, but we're actually a very close family."

"Sounds like us Stricklands. So why did you want to move away from your parents and siblings? No job openings around Laramie for a librarian?"

"There were a few positions open. One in particular my family wanted me to accept. The job would've paid more than my position here at Rust Creek Elementary. But it was for a private library and I wanted to use my education to work with children. Anyway, I've always been considered the adventurous one of the Weavers. I like seeing different things and meeting new people. And I've definitely done that since I've moved to Rust Creek Falls."

"Do you like it here?"

She sipped her coffee. "Very much. There's something about this little town that digs in and takes a hold of a person's heart. It certainly has mine. So you're here only on a temporary basis?"

He nodded. "For as long as the clinic needs me," he explained. "Frankly, I wasn't too keen on making the move. But my parents suggested the change might be good for Dillon—and for me. Plus, the clinic here in town desperately needed another OB-GYN. And I was in a position to help."

"I see."

"You do? Well, I can see that leaving the familiar was easy for you, but it's different for me. I have to consider Dillon's needs. And I thought—"

When he didn't finish, she ventured a question. "The move might be difficult for him?"

A grimace turned down the corners of his lips while his grip on the thick coffee cup grew knuckle white. The negative reactions told Josselyn this move to Rust Creek Falls had been much more of an upheaval for Drew than it had been for his young son.

"To be honest, it had been years since I'd been away from Thunder Canyon for any length of time. Not since my wife died. I wasn't sure I could handle Dillon on my own. In Thunder Canyon my parents had always been there to back me up when I needed help with him."

Since my wife died. Just hearing him say the words and the strained tone of his voice made her heart ache for him. "Oh, I see. I mean—I understand better now. I'm so sorry about your loss, Drew."

His eyes narrowed with disbelief. "What didn't you understand, exactly?"

She shook her head. "Dillon said he didn't have a mother, but I thought he meant she lived somewhere else. Dear God, it's no wonder he—"

She broke off awkwardly and his lips took on a wry slant.

"He what? Is hunting a wife for his father?"

"Something like that. He definitely gravitates toward female company. I've noticed he's pretty tight buddies with Rory at school."

"Yes, I've already heard quite a bit about Rory. Especially how well she can throw a baseball." Shrugging, he picked up his fork and sliced off a piece of his apple pie. "I've been trying to understand why Dillon has decided he wants a mother at this time in his life. You see, he doesn't even know what having a mother is like. Evelyn died when he was only twelve months old. It's not like he can remember. Or miss what he's never had."

Josselyn struggled to hide her surprise. Dillon was seven years old so that meant Drew had been a widow for six long years. Was that because he still loved his wife? Or was it because he had no interest in having another one? The idea hit her hard. Which was a ridiculous reaction. She was having coffee with the man. Not planning a future with him.

"Well, this whole thing could have something to do with your move here to Rust Creek Falls. Could be some of Dillon's new friends are talking about their mothers and he wants to be like them," she said in an effort to ease his concerns. "I figure he'll grow out of this. But what about you?"

His fork paused in midair. "Me? What do you mean?"

Recognizing her lungs had quit working, she forced in a long breath. "I mean you've been single for a long time now. Is that how you want your future to be—living your life all alone?"

"What we want and what we're handed in life are two different things. Clearly, it was meant for me to be single. Otherwise, Evelyn would still be alive."

She'd known a few mulish men, but she couldn't recall any of them being like Drew. He was looking at the future through a dark, narrow tunnel.

"People do get married again," she suggested. "After they've passed through a period of grief."

His nostrils flared as though her remark was insulting. As Josselyn studied his brooding expression, she decided she wasn't about to apologize. If she had to carefully weigh every word she spoke to this man for fear of offending him, then he wouldn't be worth the bother.

"I'm not some people," he said bluntly. "And I've already had one wife. I don't want another one."

Oh my. He was so full of bitterness, she could practically see it oozing out of him. And just when she was beginning to like him, she thought sadly.

"Well, I'm sure when Dillon gets older, he'll understand why you didn't give him a stepmother." To soften her words, she forced a cheery smile to her face. "Who knows, your son might even be glad that you didn't. Children can change their mind on a whim. Like cornflakes for breakfast one morning and French toast the next."

He arched a brow at her. "What would you know about kids? Besides helping them with books?"

She let out a soft laugh. "I happen to have been a child once—a few years ago."

To her relief a faint smile crossed his face.

"At one time I must've been Dillon's age," he said. "But that was so long ago. So much has happened in my life since then that it's hard to remember those carefree days."

Not bothering to worry about what he might think, she reached across the table and placed her hand over his.

"Would you mind telling me what happened to your wife?"

His brown eyes suddenly filled with shadows and for a moment she thought he was going to tell her to mind her own business. But then his gaze fell to where her hand was lying across his. He stared at the connection as though having a female touching him was something highly unusual.

"She was driving Dillon to day care early one morning. When she stopped at a stop sign, a huge oak tree on the corner of the intersection toppled over onto the front of her car. She was killed instantly. Dillon was in the back seat and escaped the incident without a scratch."

Her head swung back and forth as she tried to digest his words. "Oh, Drew, I don't know what to say," she said gently. "It's just so freakish and shocking."

"The tree was half-dead and the night before the accident a storm blew through the area and weakened the trunk. Unfortunately, removing the old oak was already on the city's agenda, but the maintenance men hadn't yet gotten around to the task." His gaze lifted to hers. "For years I was in total shock. Other than work, I could hardly function. Then as more time passed, I got angry at the senselessness of it all. Not to mention I was swamped with guilt."

She stared at him in wonder. "Guilt? Why? You didn't cause the accident."

He grimaced and Josselyn got the impression his wife's death wasn't something he often discussed. Which was understandable. No doubt it raked up a pile of painful memories.

"The morning of the accident it was my turn to drive Dillon to day care. I should've been in the car. Not Evelyn. But I'd gotten an emergency call from the clinic and she'd offered to drive Dillon in order for me to hurry on to work."

"That's only natural. My mom would do the same thing for my dad or vice versa. But all of that is beside the point. Things happen for a reason. Your wife was supposed to be in that car. Not you. And no amount of anger, guilt or grief will change what happened."

He grimaced. "That's the logical way of looking at

it. But that doesn't fix the hole in my life or make up for all that Dillon has missed."

"I suppose not," she said gently. "But it might help you to move forward. To look toward the future."

He looked as though he was about to blurt out another bitter remark, but as she watched his lips slowly yield to a faint smile, she decided something had entered his thoughts to change his mind.

He said, "It must be nice to have your optimism."

The heat emanating from his hand spread through her fingers and rushed all the way to her shoulder. The sizzling sensation reminded her that she'd been touching him all this time. As though she had a right to be close to him.

Embarrassed, she pulled her hand back and quickly hid it beneath the table.

"Now, you're probably thinking I'm too young to know what it's like to lose someone you love—that I can't know how much it hurts. But I do understand."

"How old are you?"

"Twenty-five."

"That's very young," he agreed. "Especially compared to my thirty-three."

She smiled. "You're hardly over the hill," she said wryly.

He didn't reply and an awkward silence began to stretch between them. Josselyn tried to focus on finishing the last of her pie, but as she ate the delicious dessert all she could think about was the man sitting less than an arm's length away from her.

Why had he asked her to join him here at Daisy's? she wondered again. Clearly he wasn't in the market for any kind of romance. He was still in love with his late wife. The fact put a damper on her usually bright spirits.

"You mentioned losing someone you were close to," he finally spoke. "Were you married once?"

Surprised by his question, she glanced over at him. "No. I've never had a steady guy, much less a husband. I was referring to my maternal grandmother. A few days after I'd graduated high school, she died unexpectedly. I was completely devastated. She'd always been more than a grandmother to me. She was my hero and mentor. No one understood me like she did. It was from her that I got my love of books. Now, well, I think she'd be very pleased about my education and my job."

His brown eyes softened and Josselyn felt her heart melting like a snowflake on the tip of her tongue.

"No doubt she would be pleased."

Thankfully, after that he turned the conversation to less personal things. Time flew for Josselyn and before she knew it, she'd emptied her second cup of coffee and finished the last bite of pie on her plate.

"If you're ready, I think we should be going," he finally suggested. "Tomorrow is a school day and I don't want Dillon arguing with my grandparents about waiting up for me."

Nodding, Josselyn reached for her handbag beneath the table. "Of course. I need to be getting home, too."

After taking care of the check, Drew drove them back to the school parking lot, where her little car was parked beneath a streetlight.

By now the night mountain air had turned very cool, and before she climbed into the driver's seat, Drew helped her don the jacket she'd been carrying over her arm.

"There," he murmured, as his hands smoothed the

fabric over the back of her shoulders. "That should keep you warm until your car heater kicks in."

His closeness rattled her, but she tried not to show it as she turned to thank him for the evening.

"I'll be fine," she told him. "It's only a few-minute drive to Sunshine Farm."

"You will drive carefully?"

Even though the lighting was dim she could see his brown eyes were traveling intently over her face. Was he thinking about her safety? Or thinking more about his late wife's accident? *Oh Lord, it shouldn't matter.* But somehow it did.

"Always."

"Well, thank you for joining me for coffee," he said.

Without thinking, she leaned forward and placed a soft kiss on his cheek. "Thank you for asking me, Drew."

Clearly surprised, he stared at her. Then before she could guess his intentions, his hands were on her shoulders, drawing her forward. And then his lips came down on hers in a deep, all-consuming kiss.

The intimate contact momentarily shocked her, and for a split second her senses were so stunned she was incapable of reacting. Until a shower of hot, sweet pleasure shot through her, prompting her to open her lips and kiss him in return.

Josselyn had no idea how long the embrace lasted. As far as her hazy mind was concerned, the time could've been brief seconds, or long minutes. Either way, when he finally lifted his head and gazed down at her, she was totally breathless and aching for more.

"You're welcome, Josselyn," he murmured. "And good night."

Totally bemused, she watched him turn and walk

to his car. Was that all he had to say after that scorching kiss?

Decidedly shaken, she slipped into her own car and with trembling fingers quickly started the motor. As she fastened her seat belt, she noticed he hadn't yet moved his car. Which could only mean he was waiting until he saw her safely leave the parking lot.

He hadn't yet realized that he was the biggest threat to her well-being, Josselyn thought. Especially the condition of her heart.

Chapter Five

The next afternoon, Drew was sitting at his desk attempting to make sense of a patient's chart, but all he could seem to concentrate on was that damned kiss he'd planted on Josselyn's lips.

He still couldn't figure out what had possessed him to do such a thing. Since Evelyn had died, he hadn't touched a woman in a personal way, much less kissed one. And he sure as hell hadn't wanted to.

Releasing a heavy breath, he turned away from the data on the computer screen and raked his fingers through his hair. He should've listened to his gut back in Thunder Canyon and stayed put. From the very first day he'd moved to Rust Creek Falls everything about his life had felt different.

And why should that be upsetting you, Drew? Because for the first time in six years, your life is starting to change? Maybe whatever is in the air or the water here in Rust Creek Falls is pushing you to finally decide to be a man again. A real father to Dillon. What do you want to do? Run from the challenge?

Cursing at the reproachful voice in his head, Drew

left his desk and walked over to a window overlooking South Lodgepole Lane. Two blocks to the west was the elementary school. If he wanted to be honest with himself, he'd admit he wanted to see Josselyn again. Kiss her again.

A faint knock on the door interrupted his agonizing thoughts and he glanced over his shoulder to see Nadine Rutledge, one of the two nurses who assisted him, peering around the door.

"Yes, Nadine. Am I needed?"

The dark-haired woman in her midforties nodded. "You're always needed, Dr. Strickland. That's what you get for being a good doctor. I have Mrs. Peters in room two."

Frowning, he strode toward the nurse. "I don't remember her being scheduled for a visit today."

"She wasn't. She walked in about five minutes ago saying she's not feeling well. Her vitals are okay. Except for her blood pressure. It's far too high."

Drew grabbed his lab coat from a hook by the door and quickly shouldered it on. "Damn. Don't tell me we have another case of toxemia. She's far too early in her pregnancy to induce labor."

Nadine caught him by his sleeve and he paused, one brow arched in question.

She said, "I think you should know she's under a load of stress."

"What kind of stress?" Drew asked. "Family? Work?"

Nadine's lips thinned to a straight line. "Family. Or I should say, lack of one. The baby's father lit out for places unknown. From what I hear, he suddenly decided he didn't want the responsibility of a wife or child."

Sickened by the news, Drew cursed under his breath.

"We can hardly fix that problem for her. But we can try to keep her and the baby physically healthy. Draw blood for a full workup and get it to the lab ASAP."

He started down the hallway with Nadine scurrying ahead of him, and for the next few minutes thoughts of kissing Josselyn were pushed aside.

Later that afternoon, Josselyn was loading a tote bag filled with books onto the back seat of her car when a vehicle wheeled into the space next to her.

At this hour of the day, teachers and staff were leaving the school parking lot, not arriving, she thought, as she turned to see a sleek black car come to a jarring halt.

The vehicle looked vaguely familiar and then it dawned on her that the car belonged to Drew. What was he doing here? He couldn't be picking up Dillon, she decided. School had let out two hours ago.

Her heart tapping out a happy rhythm, she stood near the back fender of her little red car and waited for him to join her.

Smiling, she called to him, "Hello, Drew."

"Hello," he greeted in return. "Looks like I caught you just as you were leaving."

Her gaze slipped furtively over his face. Lines of fatigue were etched around his eyes and lips, but rather than detract from his good looks, they made him appear more human and vulnerable. Qualities that made him even more attractive to Josselyn.

"Yes," she told him. "I was about to head home."

"I just left the clinic and drove by the school on a chance you might still be here."

"You wanted to see me?" After that kiss he'd given her last night, the idea shouldn't have been all that surprising. But it was. She'd gone home telling herself the man was too wrapped up in his past to ever take a second look at her. Perhaps she'd been wrong. The thought made her heart beat even faster.

One corner of his perfectly chiseled lips curled with amusement. "Is that so hard to believe?"

In spite of the cool mountain breeze drifting through the parking lot, her cheeks felt incredibly hot. "To be honest, yes."

She watched the other corner of his lips lift to form a perfect little smile. The result caused her breath to catch in her throat.

He said, "To be honest, it surprises me, too."

Her fingers nervously adjusted the red scarf draped around her neck. "So—uh—are you having a problem with Dillon and his books?"

"No. He seems happy and he's reading. Or, at least, he's pretending to." He moved a step closer. "I wanted to see what you thought about taking Dillon fishing this weekend. Being outdoors might not be your thing, but Dillon would enjoy your company. And so would I."

He wasn't asking her to go on a date, she told herself. Yet it sounded darned close to it and that was enough to send a thrill rushing through her.

"Fishing? Gosh, I used to go fishing with my brothers. But it's been a long time."

"Same here. Maybe we can refresh our fishing skills together. Anyway, it doesn't matter if we catch anything. The outing will be good for Dillon. And for me," he added, as though she needed more persuading.

Even though she was inwardly jumping up and down with joy, she pretended to consider his offer. "When is this fishing trip supposed to happen?"

"Tomorrow is Saturday. If you're free, how about I pick you up about ten? I thought we might drive up the mountain toward the falls. If I remember right, there should be a few trout streams around there. I'll have Claire pack us a picnic basket."

She couldn't contain a cheery smile from spreading across her face. "I'll be ready," she told him, then dared to reach out and touch a finger to the lapel of his lab coat. The white starched garment made him look very professional, not to mention incredibly handsome. "Are you still working?"

He glanced down at himself. "It's been a long day. We just wrapped up a few minutes ago," he said. "I left the clinic in such a hurry I guess I forgot to leave my lab coat behind. But don't worry. I won't be Dr. Strickland tomorrow."

Josselyn was definitely seeing a side of this man that she hadn't seen before. And this new Drew was definitely charming her without even trying.

"Oh, I wouldn't say that," she said impishly. "I might get a fishing lure barb stuck in my hand and need a doctor's attention."

He reached for her hand and lifted the palm up for his inspection. "And such a soft little thing, too. I'll try to make sure that doesn't happen."

His dark brown gaze lifted from her hand to her face and Josselyn could almost feel the warmth of his eyes gliding over the curve of her bottom lip. The sensation very nearly caused her to shiver.

"Uh—do I need to bring anything?" she finally managed to ask.

"Gramps, as Dillon calls him, has all sorts of fishing equipment we can use. I'll bring plenty for the three of us. And I'm supplying our lunch. So all you need to bring is yourself."

"Sounds easy enough."

His gaze continued to delve into hers, while the warmth of his hand was slowly scorching her own. Charged silence settled all around them, until he finally dropped her hand and stepped back.

Clearing his throat, he said, "Great. I'll see you in the morning."

"Yes. In the morning," she repeated.

He took another step backward, which very nearly caused him to bump into the passenger door of his car. But rather than skirt the hood and slide into the driver's seat, he continued to stare at her with a bemused expression.

"Was there something else you wanted to say?" she asked.

"Only about that kiss we shared last night. It was... very nice."

Her heart thumped erratically and she drew in a deep breath, hoping to calm it. "Yes. Very nice," she replied.

"I'd better be going."

He lifted a hand in farewell and Josselyn waved back before she slipped into the driver's seat of her car and started the engine.

It wasn't until she was out of town and driving toward Sunshine Farm that her breathing returned to normal and the smile on her face faded to a dreamy repose.

She was going on an outing with Dr. Drew Strickland. Rust Creek Falls truly was a magical place.

"Dad, what if I don't catch a fish? Miss Weaver will think I'm an awful fisherman."

Drew silently groaned as he steered the car down the country road. At seven years old his son was already concerned about impressing a female. Drew couldn't remember having such thoughts at that age. But then, he supposed males were born with the need for a woman's admiration and attention.

"I wouldn't worry, Dillon. I have a feeling you'll catch a fish. And I think just for today it will be okay for you to call Miss Weaver Josselyn."

In the back seat, Dillon scooted forward until the seat belt strained tight across his chest.

"You really think so?" he asked, his eyes shining with excitement.

"Yes. But at school you'll have to be respectful and go back to calling her Miss Weaver. Can you remember to do that?"

"Oh sure, Dad, I'll remember. But what's respectful? Do I know how to be like that?"

"Sometimes I wonder," Drew murmured under his breath.

"What?"

Drew glanced in the rearview mirror to see a bewildered frown on his son's face.

Hiding a smile, Drew explained, "It means being courteous and minding your manners. I've taught you about manners."

"Yeah. And most of them aren't too fun. Especially being quiet and sitting still. Who likes to do that?"

Drew chuckled and the sound must have caught Dillon's attention because he said, "You're laughing, Dad. You don't ever laugh. You must be feeling good this morning."

Dillon's observation caused Drew to pause with faint

surprise. He did feel good, he realized. In fact, he felt downright close to happy. Something he'd not felt since Evelyn's accident. What did it mean? That he was finally learning to live again? And God help him, would this hopeful feeling last, or die after a few days or weeks?

Determined to shake away the negative thoughts, Drew glanced over his shoulder and smiled at Dillon. "I am feeling good. I'm taking my son fishing."

"And Miss Weaver—I mean, Josselyn—is coming with us! Yippee! We're gonna have fun!"

Fun. By the end of the day, Drew hoped to get reacquainted with the feeling.

The morning had dawned bright and beautiful with only a few wisps of clouds drifting across the sky. Like Wyoming, Josselyn was learning that Montana in September could be cold at night and throughout a portion of the morning. Keeping that in mind, she dressed warmly in jeans and boots and a plaid flannel shirt and topped it with a sheepskin-lined denim jacket.

At five minutes before ten, Josselyn was sitting on the tiny front porch of her little cabin when she spotted a dark green Jeep turning onto the graveled driveway leading into the Sunshine Farm property. It wasn't until the vehicle pulled to a stop in front of her cabin that she realized it was Drew and Dillon.

Her spirits soaring, she gathered up her tote bag and walked out to greet them.

Dillon was the first one out of the Jeep and he raced up to her, his face wreathed with a huge grin.

"Hi, Miss Weaver! Dad says I can call you Josselyn today. Is that okay with you?"

She looked around to see Drew had joined them. As

soon as her gaze connected with his, he gave her a con-spiring wink. The connection warmed her as much as the smile on his face.

"Sure it's okay," she told Dillon. "We're not at school today. We're just friends going fishing. Right?"

"Right!"

He raised his palm for a high five and Josselyn obliged with a quick slap of her hand.

Dillon cast his father a smug grin. "See? She's the best!"

Spotting the uncomfortable look on Drew's face, Josselyn quickly turned the conversation in a different direction. "Would you two like to come in for a warm drink or something before we leave?"

"No thanks. Maybe later," Drew told her. "If you're ready, let's be on our way. Dillon says if the sun gets too high in the sky the fish will quit biting."

"That's what Gramps says," the boy spoke up. "And he knows all about catching trout."

"Well, good news, I have my bag and I'm ready to go," Josselyn informed him.

"I borrowed my grandfather's Jeep today," Drew explained. "Where we're going the roads get a little rough. I hope you don't mind."

She laughed. "Are you kidding? Back in Wyoming, my brothers rattled me all over the mountains in an old pickup truck with a bench seat. The Jeep will be like going in luxury."

Drew helped her into the front passenger seat of the rugged vehicle, then made sure Dillon was safely strapped into the back. Once they were traveling slowly down the graveled drive toward the main road, he glanced over to the three-storied farmhouse and the big yellow barn sitting some distance away from it.

"Looks like the Stocktons have been doing quite a bit of work around here. Last time I was out this way the whole place appeared pretty ragged."

"Yes, from what I understand years went by and the family wasn't even aware that the property still belonged to them. When they discovered the old estate was still in the Stockton name, they decided to make it a home again. Eva told me the main house needed lots of repairs. So did the barn. But the restoration is all slowly and surely coming together."

Peering out the window, Dillon said, "That barn is a funny color. I thought barns were supposed to be red. Like back on Grandpa Jerry's ranch in Thunder Canyon."

"Barns can be any color you want them to be," Drew told him, then grinned over at Josselyn. "Bet you would've never guessed I could be unconventional."

She let out a short laugh. "That's really climbing out of the box, all right."

"Gosh, I've never seen Dad in a box before," Dillon said. "He'd look funny."

Drew cast her a wry glance. "See. I have him fooled."

The fact that he could joke about himself endeared him to Josselyn even more, and as they drove northward into the mountains, she wondered how she was going to get through the day without falling head over heels for the man.

Before they reached the summit of the mountain where the falls were located, Drew turned off on a dim dirt road leading into the forest. From the corner of his eye, he could see Josselyn looking around with interest at the tall pine and fir trees mixed with low underbrush.

"Does this land belong to anyone?" she asked. "I haven't noticed any posted signs."

"I'm not sure who owns this area of the mountain. Gramps assures me that it's always been open to anyone who wants to fish," Drew said as he steered the Jeep over rough patches in the road.

"It's very beautiful," Josselyn commented. "The forests around Laramie aren't nearly this thick."

Drew glanced in her direction. "In the summers, when my brothers and I were teenagers, we'd come to Rust Creek Falls to visit our grandparents. Gramps would bring us up here to fish. By that age, we really wanted to be down on the streets of town, hunting pretty girls to talk to. But for his sake, we fished and pretended we were having a good time."

"You won't have to pretend today, Dad," Dillon spoke up, his face peeking between the two front seats. "You have a pretty girl to talk to while you fish."

Chuckling, Drew reached around and rubbed the top of Dillon's head. "This boy is getting smarter every day," he said to Josselyn.

The roundabout compliment put a warm pink color on her cheek. Drew found himself wanting to stare at her fresh face. Not only was she beautiful, but something about her smiles lifted his spirit and made him feel whole again.

"It's all those books he's reading," she explained.

Drew cast her a wry grin. "Let's hope."

A few minutes later, at the end of the rough trail, they reached an opening in the forest where he and his brothers used to camp with Old Gene. After helping Josselyn and Dillon out of the Jeep, Drew gazed around, remembering lying out in a sleeping bag around the fire, staring up at the stars and wondering if he'd ever grow into a man his father would be proud to call *son*.

"Look at this, Dad!"

Drew glanced over to see Dillon standing near a fire ring built of large rocks. Nearby, a huge fallen log had been hewn with an ax to form a crude picnic table, complete with a pair of smaller logs to serve as benches.

"Someone has been using the old place," Drew commented as Josselyn came to stand beside him. "But other than the fire ring and the picnic table, everything looks just like it did years ago. I wasn't expecting that."

She cast him a gentle smile. "It's nice when good things stay the same. Especially when they're attached to pleasant memories."

"Yes. Very nice," he agreed. "It's also very nice to be making new memories—with you and Dillon."

She didn't say anything, but words were unnecessary as she wrapped her hand around his. As the warmth of her fingers spread through his own, he was quite certain the sky suddenly turned a brighter shade of blue.

Clearing the huskiness from his throat, he said, "Let's go see what Dillon is getting into."

She nodded and hand in hand, they walked over to where Dillon was poking a long stick into the cold ashes inside the fire ring.

"Can we build a fire, Dad?" Dillon asked. "We might need a fire to run off the wild animals. Like coyotes and bears! They might come around to get our food!"

Drew and Josselyn exchanged amused glances.

"I don't think any wild animals will be snooping around in the daylight," Drew informed him. "For now we'll leave the picnic basket in the Jeep. No need to carry it and our fishing gear down to the water. And we'll build a fire later. When we have lunch. Do you two go along with that idea?"

"Yay! I vote for that! Don't you, Josselyn?" Dillon asked, as he hopped back and forth over a small boulder.

"Sounds good to me," Josselyn agreed. "I only wish we had marshmallows to roast."

"You're in luck," Drew told her. "Claire packed a bag of them in the picnic basket."

He walked over to the Jeep and opened the back end. Josselyn followed and helped him unload a tackle box, along with three fishing rods.

"The next time I run into Claire, I'll have to thank her for being so thoughtful to add marshmallows to our picnic," Josselyn said. "Isn't she married to Levi Wyatt?"

"That's right. She's my cousin. She was a Strickland before she married Levi Wyatt. Do you know her?"

"I met her at the back-to-school picnic. Her daughter, Bekka, isn't old enough for kindergarten quite yet, but I think Claire wants to acquaint herself with the teachers before she finally does have to send Bekka off to school. I didn't realize you two were related."

"Her father, Peter, and my father, Jerry, are brothers," he explained. "It's like you said—everyone in Rust Creek Falls is either acquainted or related in some way."

Josselyn laughed. "Good thing I didn't say something bad about the woman."

"That's not likely. There's nothing bad anyone could say about Claire. She's a fine, hardworking woman. Like you," he added as he handed her one of the fishing rods.

The simple compliment appeared to surprise her and then she said jokingly, "You might want to rethink that after you see my fishing skills. I'll probably end up catching more tree limbs than anything."

"We're not going to keep count," he assured her.

Dillon skidded to a stop at Josselyn's side. "I wanta carry my own fishing pole," he told his father. "Gramps lets me."

Drew handed the smallest rod to Dillon. "Okay. Just no running with it or that will be the end," he warned.

"Gee, Dad, what's wrong with running? Isn't that what kids are supposed to do when they're outside?"

Not wanting to ruin Dillon's outing with gory details of injuries and accidents, he answered simply, "At the right time and the right place. This isn't one of them."

Annoyed with his father's explanation, Dillon pushed out his bottom lip. Noticing the boy's reaction, Josselyn patted the top of his head. "What your dad means is that you might seriously hurt yourself and he doesn't want that to happen. Because he loves you."

Drew couldn't decide if Dillon understood the meaning of Josselyn's words or if he was simply happy to hear them from a soft-spoken woman. Either way, she'd managed to put a smile back on his face.

"Okay, Josselyn. No running," he promised, then cast a hopeful eye at his father. "But what about hopping and jumping, Dad?"

Drew cast a hopeless look at Josselyn and he could see she was struggling to contain her laughter. Any other time, Drew would have been losing his patience completely, but with Josselyn's company, he was able to appreciate the humor in his son's antics. How was it that she could make him see both sides of things?

"Once we get to the stream you can hop and jump

all you want," Drew told him. "But just remember all that stomping around will probably scare the fish away."

"Oh, yeah," Dillon said thoughtfully. "I hadn't thought about that."

Drew shut the back of the Jeep and the three of them headed down a hard-packed foot trail through a mixture of evergreens and hardwood trees. Birds chirped among the branches and two squirrels gathered acorns beneath a large oak. Every now and then, bright sunlight managed to break through the forest canopy over their heads, and each time Drew watched the golden shafts sparkle upon Josselyn's blond hair.

Drew had never had an interest in prospecting. And after Evelyn, he'd lost all interest in having a woman in his life. But now, as he watched Josselyn walk casually alongside his son, he realized he'd somehow managed to stumble upon a precious nugget.

It's about time you woke up and realized your good fortune, Drew. What do you intend to do with your golden opportunity? Stand back and let it slip away? Or hold tight and—

"Look! I see deer!"

Dillon's exclamation broke through the taunting voice in Drew's head and he looked ahead, in the direction of his son's pointed finger. A doe was standing with her head up, her nose to the wind. At her side, a fawn was nibbling at a berry bush, unaware of its human audience.

Josselyn lowered her head close to Dillon's ear. "That's a mother and her baby," she said in a hushed voice. "She's watching us to make sure we don't harm her little one."

The fawn continued to nibble for a few more moments before the doe nudged it on to the safety of the forest shadows.

"Aww, there they go!" Dillon watched the animals scurry away, then looked up at Josselyn. "Gosh, I guess fawns are like us kids. They need mommies, too."

She didn't reply. Instead, she simply put her arm around Drew's son's shoulders and urged him forward.

As Drew watched, he wondered if a hand had reached inside his chest. Something was squeezing his heart so tightly that he could scarcely breathe.

Dillon didn't remember having a mother, yet he clearly wanted one now. And it was up to Drew to give him one.

But that didn't mean he should go after Josselyn just to give his son another parent. No, she deserved more than that, Drew thought. She deserved real love from a real man, not an empty shell going through the motions of life. Pretending he could love again.

Chapter Six

The sun was warm on Josselyn's face as she sat on a boulder near the edge of the small stream where the three of them had stopped to fish. During the past couple of hours, she'd tried her hand at catching the rainbow trout swimming about in the clear, cold water. After managing to snag a half dozen and releasing them back into the stream to swim another day, Josselyn had decided to put down her rod and reel and simply enjoy being out in the forest.

A few feet away from her sun-dappled spot, Drew attempted to instruct his son on the finer points of fishing.

"Dillon, you're casting too hard. That's why the lure is landing beyond the stream and into the bushes. Don't cast with your shoulder. Give it a flick of your wrist. Like this."

After watching his father's demonstration, Dillon complained, "I can't do it like that, Dad. Anyway, this is the way Gramps taught me. And that's the way I want to do it."

Drew threw up his hands in a gesture of helpless surrender. "Okay. Do it your way."

Turning away from the boy, Drew walked over to Josselyn and she scooted over to make room for him on the boulder. After he'd taken a seat next to her, he said, "I'm not sure why I bother. It's always 'Gramps this or that.' Or 'Grandpa Jerry has already taught me how to do this.'"

With his shoulder close enough to brush hers, it was a struggle to concentrate on his words. "Grandpa Jerry? Is that what he calls your father?"

Drew nodded, then, with a heavy sigh, glanced in Dillon's direction. "I'm sure you've been hearing it."

"Several times this morning I've noticed him mentioning his grandfathers," she admitted. "Is this something he does often?"

He groaned. "Only about fifty times a day."

"Which makes you feel insignificant."

His grunt was a sound of self-deprecation. "Now you're probably thinking I'm being more childish than Dillon. And you'd be right. It's stupid of me to be envious of my son's relationships with his grandparents."

The frustration etched upon his features told Josselyn just how deeply he wanted his son's admiration. "I don't think you're being childish. More like human. Every father wants his child to look up to him. I know mine does. Probably more so now that his children have grown into adults."

"That's a kind way of putting it," he said, then groaned in afterthought. "I have no right to be envious. It's my own fault that Dillon doesn't respect me in the same way he does his grandfathers."

Josselyn shook her head. "You're wrong. Dillon does respect you."

"Maybe *respect* is the wrong word," he said ruefully. "It's just that our relationship isn't the same strong bond that he has with my father and grandfather. For a while after Evelyn died that fact didn't bother me. It was enough that my son was healthy and safe and that all his needs were being met. I didn't realize that, later on, building a bond with my son would be so hard to do. I'm beginning to think it might even be impossible."

If losing his wife had debilitated him to the point he'd been unable to care for his son, he must have been wildly in love with her. The thought made Josselyn wonder if he was still pining for the woman or if he was making an attempt to forget and find the strength to move forward. Josselyn desperately wanted to believe he was thinking about the future.

"You're being awfully hard on yourself, aren't you?" she asked gently. "I'm willing to bet that you've always been a good father."

He shook his head. "In the sense that I've always provided him with a home and the essentials, that much is true. But there were long blocks of time that I wasn't around when my son needed me."

Her heart ached for him and for Dillon. "Where were you? Lost in your grief?"

"Partly. The rest of the time I was at the clinic, putting in incredibly long hours, hoping the work would ease the tortured thoughts in my head. And all that time, Dillon was growing up and away from me."

Josselyn tried to reason the situation. "But he's here with you now. And I definitely see a father and son. Not just a man babysitting a boy."

His expression pensive, he picked up a tiny pebble and tossed it into the shallow water. "I'll be honest, Josselyn, if it hadn't been for my parents pushing me, I probably wouldn't have made this move to Rust Creek Falls. Obviously, they could see that Dillon and I needed to be together—away from the crutch they provided for the both of us."

The need to reassure him had her reaching over and resting her hand on his forearm. "I believe you made the right move. What do you think?"

He glanced pointedly down at her hand, then back to her face, and suddenly her heart was beating too fast for comfort.

"I'm beginning to believe it's the best move I've made in years," he murmured.

Her gaze locked with his and as she studied the brown depths of his eyes, the warmth of his arm began to seep into her hand and beg her palm to slide upward toward his shoulder. She wanted to move closer. She wanted to say all the things that were racing through her thoughts, even though she knew most of them would probably scare him away.

"Dad, look! I tried—like you told me! And I did it! Watch and I'll show you!"

Dillon's excited yells suddenly broke the momentary spell that had fallen between them.

Stifling her sigh of disappointment, Josselyn removed her hand from Drew's arm and smiled. "See. You're definitely doing something right."

Grinning, he straightened to his full height and walked over to his son. And as Josselyn watched the two of them interact, she wondered if one day she might possibly be the woman who could fill the missing void in their little family. Or was she dreaming the impossible?

You've been existing in a fictional world of books, Josselyn. Otherwise, you could see for yourself that

Drew is never going to make room in his heart for any woman, except his late wife.

There was a chance that the mocking voice in her head could be right, Josselyn thought. But she wasn't going to let herself believe the dismal warning. She was an optimist. A true believer in the impossible coming true.

So what if Drew had been walking along a dark path for these past few years? That didn't mean he'd lost his way completely. He could find his way back to love and happiness. All she had to do was nudge him in the right direction.

With the next day being Sunday, the clinic was closed and Drew had the leisure of hanging around the boardinghouse. Throughout the day, Dillon hung close to his father's side and chattered nonstop about Josselyn and the fishing trip.

Normally, Drew would have grown weary of hearing his son make the same repetitive comments about the same subject. But not now. Not this time. He was beginning to realize just how important it was to listen to his child. And it was thrilling to know that he'd done something right and made a real connection with Dillon.

Later that night, when Dillon climbed into bed, he was still talking about Josselyn, rather than the tooth he'd lost after dinner.

"Dad, you really like Josselyn, don't you?"

Drew finished tucking the cover beneath Dillon's chin before he eased onto the side of the mattress and carefully studied his son's eager face.

"I do. Really like her," Drew told him, while thinking just how very much he meant those words. During the past six years, the idea of enjoying any woman's company had never crossed his mind. But something about Josselyn was eating away at all the protective barriers he'd built around his heart. He was beginning to feel again. Really feel. And the realization was both exhilarating and frightening.

"That's good," Dillon said happily. "'Cause I like her, too. You know what I like the most about her?"

Smiling faintly, Drew reached up and pushed at a hank of hair resting near Dillon's right eye. "Let me guess. That she's pretty and nice and she helps you pick out fun books to read?"

Dillon's wide grin exposed a gap where the tooth was missing. Tonight, after he'd fallen asleep, the tooth fairy would leave a small amount of money beneath his pillow. But so far, he didn't appear to be concerned about the idea of having money to spend. Josselyn seemed to be far more important to him than a visit from the tooth fairy.

Dillon said, "Yeah, all that stuff is nice. But I like her mostly because she makes you smile, Dad. And that makes me happy."

A lump of raw emotion was suddenly choking Drew, making him wonder if he could say a word without his voice breaking. All this time he'd believed his son's feelings for him were mostly indifferent. His assumption had been wrong.

Clearing his throat with a rough cough, Drew said, "You're right, son. Josselyn does make me smile. Until she came along I guess I'd kinda forgotten how to do that."

If possible, Dillon's grin stretched even wider. "Does that mean you're gonna take her on dates and ask her to marry you?"

Drew arched a brow at him. "Whoa, son. You're going way too fast. A guy has to take a woman on lots of dates before he gets around to marrying her. And even if he decides she's the right woman, the woman has to be in agreement."

Dillon thought about that for a moment. "You mean she has to say *yes*?"

"That's one way of putting it."

His expression turning smug, Dillon settled his head deeper into the pillow. "Well, that's no worry, Dad. Josselyn will say *yes*."

"Hmm. You seem awfully certain about that. Remember what you've learned about counting your chickens before they hatch? Sometimes things don't turn out like you think they will."

Dillon's head wagged back and forth against the pillow. "This time they're gonna turn out just right. She's gonna say *yes*. I can tell, 'cause when she looks at you her eyes twinkle."

Deciding for now it was best to let his son have his dreams, and perhaps best for himself, too, he playfully tickled Dillon's ribs. "Silly boy," he teased. "That was just the sun making her eyes sparkle. Now, you go to sleep."

Drew planted a kiss on Dillon's forehead and as he straightened away, the child flung his arms around his neck and held on tight.

"I love you, Daddy."

Emotions pierced Drew's chest and in that moment, Drew realized without a doubt that what he'd told Josselyn yesterday was truer than he'd ever imagined. Moving here to Rust Creek Falls had been the right decision. For him and Dillon.

"I love you, too, son."

After giving him a gentle pat on the cheek, Drew turned out the light and left the small bedroom.

The next day for lunch, Josselyn decided to forgo the school cafeteria and walk the two blocks to the Gold Rush Diner for one of their scrumptious burgers. With September nearing the halfway mark, the weather had been unusually mild and dry. A predicator of a cold wet winter, or so the old-timers around Rust Creek Falls were forecasting. But today the sun was bright, making the gold and red leaves on the trees along the sidewalk look even more vibrant.

Less than a minute away from the eating place, which was tucked a few doors down from the *Rust Creek Falls Gazette* newspaper office, she heard her phone ringing inside her shoulder bag.

Pausing on the quiet sidewalk, she dug out the phone and hurriedly swiped without bothering to check the identity of the caller.

"Hello," she greeted cheerily.

"Josselyn. It's Drew."

Her fingers gripped the phone as she tried to guess why he might be calling her. "Oh, hi, Drew. How are you?"

"I'm good. I was wondering…" He paused, then continued, "It sounds like you're outside. Are you not at work today?"

"As a matter of fact, I just happened to be walking over to the Gold Rush Diner to have lunch."

"Save me a seat," he quickly replied. "I'll be right over to join you."

Before she could say more, the phone went dead.

Josselyn slipped it back into her bag, and though she felt like skipping the remaining distance to the diner, she forced herself to go at a ladylike pace.

Five minutes later, she was seated in a booth, studying the menu lying in front of her, when Drew slid onto the bench seat across from her. Dressed in a blue plaid Western shirt and a pair of jeans and boots, he hardly looked as though he'd spent the morning attending patients at the clinic. But he looked as sexy as all get-out, she decided.

"Hi," she greeted again, her gaze traveling up and down his six-foot-plus frame. "Are you off work today?"

"No." He glanced down at himself. "These are my work clothes. Only no one knows it because they're hidden beneath a lab coat."

"Your patients probably don't know that you were a cowboy long before you became a doctor."

Grunting with amusement, he picked up one of the menus that had been left on the table. "Reckon that would worry them?"

"A few might expect you to pull out a branding iron instead of a stethoscope," she teased, then looked at him curiously. "You haven't explained why you called."

He put down the menu. "I wasn't sure if you were able to leave the school grounds, but I had a bit of a break between patients so I thought I'd give it a try and see if you could join me for lunch."

In spite of her effort to stem it, the smile on her face deepened. How could she not show her feelings around this man? Just being in his presence made her thrilled to be alive.

"What a coincidence," she told him. "I just happened to have a yearning to eat here at the diner today."

He glanced around the long room with its low ceiling and wood plank flooring. Small round tables and chairs filled the inner part of the space, while booths with smooth wooden seats lined the walls. Near the front, a long bar stretched the width of the building, and at the moment, the red swiveled stools in front of it were filled to capacity with diners.

"This place never changes," he said. "Even as a kid I remember it being just as it is today."

"Thank goodness," she replied. "The food is delicious."

She'd hardly gotten the comment out of her mouth when a pretty young waitress with a tangle of dark curls pinned to the top of her head ambled up to their table. After she'd dug out a pad and pencil, her gaze swung furtively back and forth between Drew and Josselyn.

"What can I get you two today? The lunch special is stuffed pork chops and candied yams. The yams are yummy, but the chops are just—" She made a so-so gesture with her hand.

"No matter," Josselyn spoke up. "I want a burger all the way with fries and ice tea."

"The same for me," Drew told her.

"Thanks," she said, with a sidelong glance at Drew. "I'll be right back with your drinks."

Josselyn watched the waitress swish away before casting Drew a coy look. "I think you have an admirer."

His brows lifting, he glanced around the room. "Really?"

She groaned. "The waitress. Don't tell me you didn't notice. She was very pretty."

"So she was. I see pretty women all day long, Josselyn. But I don't see them in *that* way. If I did, I'd be mighty messed up."

Josselyn wished she could kick herself. She sounded like a jealous female. Which was ridiculous. Drew could look at any woman he wanted, in any way he wanted, and it was none of her business. But Lord help her, she wanted it to be.

Her laugh came out more like a croak. "Sorry, Drew. I wasn't thinking. I guess I've never stopped to think about your job. If you don't mind me asking, what is it like anyway, tending to women's medical needs all day long?"

"First of all, it's an honor. When I help a patient get healthy or stay healthy, whichever the case, it's not only for her, but for all those who love her. I see them as mothers and wives and girlfriends, aunts and sisters. It's a family thing. And the babies I help bring into the world make those families even bigger."

"Yes," she said thoughtfully. "I see what you mean."

The waitress returned with their drinks, and after he'd taken a long sip from the tall glass, he looked at Josselyn and smiled. "So have you recuperated from the fishing trip?"

What could she say? That spending the day with him had been the most exciting thing she'd ever done in her life? That she'd spent half the night walking around her cabin, trying to get the scent and the sound and the image of him out of her mind?

"It was a lovely day, Drew. I wasn't tired at all."

A faint dimple appeared in his cheek and Josselyn wondered how it would feel to touch his face at will, to place her lips on his any time she felt the urge. Which was beginning to happen on an all-too-frequent basis.

"Neither was Dillon," he said. "I didn't think he was ever going to fall asleep. By the way, in case you haven't seen him in the library yet today, he lost a tooth last night. A lateral incisor."

She laughed. "You'll have to explain what kind of tooth that is. I didn't make straight As in health."

"That's a bottom tooth. Next to the two middle ones. A child normally loses the two middle ones in the bottom first. Then the two middle at the top, then back to the bottom on the sides. And girls usually go through this development at a younger age than boys. That's your health lesson for today."

"Let me guess—girls lose their teeth earlier because we mature faster," she said with a chuckle. "So did the tooth fairy visit Dillon?"

"Certainly. Although I'm not sure why. Earlier in the evening, Dillon snuck into the kitchen and cut huge hunks out of the pies Claire had baked for the boarders' dinner."

"Oh, your cousin couldn't have been happy about that."

"Dillon was just lucky that his aunt Claire had baked the pies and not his great-grandmother. Melba would've banned him from the kitchen for life."

Josselyn shook her head with amusement. "So did Dillon eat his pie?"

"Every bite. You probably noticed during the fishing trip how much he likes sweets. He would've eaten the whole bag of marshmallows if I'd let him."

"What can I say," she said with a guilty laugh. "I would've eaten the whole bag, too. If I'd let myself."

"Well, it might surprise you to learn that Dillon is a

miser. He's already stuffed the tooth fairy money away in his piggy bank."

"Smart boy. He'll probably grow up to be a financial investor someday." She leveled a pointed look at him. "Or do you want him to be a doctor?"

He shook his head. "I want him to be whatever he wants to be. At the moment that seems to be a match-maker."

Heat tinged her cheeks. "Does that bother you? At the school picnic when we first met you seemed rather upset with him."

His gaze dropped sheepishly to the glass of ice tea sitting in front of him. "I was upset," he admitted. "To have my son telling a stranger that I'm a lonely widower wasn't exactly the way I wanted to spend my afternoon."

Deciding now wasn't the time to be shy, she said, "Frankly, I'm glad that Dillon dragged you over to the punch table. Otherwise, we might not have met."

He grimaced. "No. Probably not. Other than work, I don't get around town much. And I can't remember the last time I introduced myself to a woman. Not since Evelyn died."

Since Evelyn died. Josselyn had already heard him speak those words so many times. It wasn't easy for her to hear them. But she hoped in some small way it was helping Drew purge himself of a grief he'd held on to far too long.

He looked up and her heart did a little skip as she watched a slow grin lift one corner of his lips.

"But I'm glad Dillon noticed you that day. It's nice to have someone to talk to. Someone who will listen to me and not think I'm some sort of disturbed weirdo."

He couldn't know he was turning her heart to helpless mush, she thought. He couldn't see that just being in his company made her incredibly happy. Which was a huge relief. Otherwise he'd be thinking she was the weirdo, or the biggest fool in Rust Creek Falls.

Sliding her hand across the tabletop, she gently touched the tips of her fingers to his. "Why would anyone think you're weird? You're a doctor, for Pete's sake."

He let out a mocking snort. "I'm not exactly a sociable person. And as for me being a doctor, we doctors aren't immune to human frailties. We're just more adept at hiding them."

What was he hiding? Other than an empty hole in his heart. A void that she desperately wanted to fill.

"Now that's a scary thought," she joked. "The next time I go for my annual checkup I'll be wondering if my doctor is really a Jekyll and Hyde."

He laughed and the sound was like a million dollars to Josselyn. She wanted to hear the rich, happy sound again and again.

His fingers slid over her hand, then enfolded it in a tight hold. "That's one of the things I like about you, Josselyn. You make me laugh. And that's a hard thing to do."

Where was all this going? Should she be thinking this impromptu lunch date was special? Or would she be smarter to believe the man was just hungry and didn't want to eat alone?

Thankfully, the questions swirling through her thoughts were interrupted when the waitress suddenly appeared with their food, and the next few minutes passed with them eating and making small talk.

It wasn't until Josselyn's plate was nearly empty and

she was checking her watch that Drew caught her by complete surprise.

"I think we should see each other again." Leaning slightly forward, he added in a husky voice, "On a real date. Without a seven-year-old chaperone. What do you say?"

A real date? She didn't know what constituted a real date for him, but she was already picturing the two of them in some quiet, cozy place with his strong arm around her shoulders, his face temptingly close to hers. Oh, yes, that would be a real date.

"Well, I—I haven't thought that far ahead," she said, hoping not to sound too overeager despite the little voice in the back of her mind yelling, *Liar, liar, you've been dreaming of dating the doctor from the very first moment little Dillon introduced him to you.*

"Then I'm asking you to think on it now," he replied. "We could drive over to Kalispell and have a nice dinner, or go to a movie, or both. Or whatever you'd like."

There was no point in her trying to act coy, Josselyn decided. Not when she was practically squirming with joy over the invitation.

"That's sounds nice, Drew. I'd love to go. When were you thinking to have this date?"

He pushed aside his empty plate and tossed several bills onto the table to take care of the waitress's tip. "What about tomorrow night? I realize the next day will be a workday. But another doctor is scheduled to be on call for me tomorrow evening. So we wouldn't have to worry about our date being interrupted with an emergency. I promise to have you back home by a reasonable hour," he added with a grin.

She'd gladly forgo hours of sleep to spend some private time with this man, but she'd keep that revealing fact to herself. "Then it's a date. Would you like for me to meet you here in town tomorrow evening? It would save you making a trip out to Sunshine Farm to pick me up."

He shook his head. "No. I said I wanted this to be a real date. I'll drive out to the farm about six thirty and collect you. Unless that's too early."

"No, six thirty is fine." Her mouth was suddenly so dry she reached for her tea and gulped down a long drink. "I'd better be going or I'll be late."

"Yes, I need to get back to work, too," he said. "I'll deal with the check. The school is on my way. I'll drop you off."

Later that evening after work, instead of going straight home to Sunshine Farm, Josselyn drove to the corner of Cedar Street and North Broomtail Road and parked her car in front of the only dress shop in town.

The little boutique was one of the first places Josselyn had patronized after she'd moved to Rust Creek Falls, and since then, she'd become friends with the owner. Gilda was a petite blonde in her thirties with an appetite for romance, in spite of a marriage that had ended in divorce court.

A cowbell clanged over the door as Josselyn stepped inside. Thanks to a pair of burning candles, the faint scent of baked apples permeated the air, while at the far back of the room, a radio was twanging out country music. A few feet away, near a circle of newly arrived sweaters, Gilda stood next to a young dark-haired woman Josselyn didn't recognize.

"Oh, hi, Josselyn," Gilda greeted her, then motioned

for her to join them. "Come over here. I want you to meet someone."

When Josselyn reached the two women, Gilda promptly introduced the pretty brunette as Caroline Ruth.

"Caroline has just taken a part-time job with Vivienne Shuster, the wedding planner. I believe you've met Vivienne, haven't you?" Gilda asked.

"Yes. She was at Sunshine Farm, seeing to the details of a barn wedding." Josselyn turned and smiled at Caroline. "From what I see you're going to be very busy. Rust Creek Falls is full of lovebugs, and when a couple gets bitten it seems like a wedding quickly follows."

Caroline smiled back at her. "Perhaps you'll soon be one of our clients," she suggested coyly.

Josselyn brushed away the idea with surprised laughter. "We'll both probably have gray hair by the time that happens."

"Oh, I wouldn't say that," Caroline said cleverly. "Not the way that guy in the Gold Rush was eyeing you."

Gilda was suddenly all ears. "Hmm. I want to hear about this, Josselyn! You were having lunch with a man?"

Rust Creek Falls was a small town, but Josselyn never imagined gossip could circulate this quickly.

She looked at Caroline. "You were at the diner?"

The young woman nodded, then laughed at Josselyn's bemused expression. "Sitting at a table across from you. And to set your mind at ease, I couldn't hear a word that passed between you."

Thank goodness, Josselyn thought. Even though nothing embarrassing had been said, she wouldn't have wanted anyone hearing Drew ask her on a date. That had been a special moment for her, not one she'd wanted broadcasted over the diner.

"Don't keep me waiting. Who was this man?" Gilda interjected the question.

"Dr. Strickland," Josselyn told her. "You might not know him. He only moved here about six weeks ago. He's a widower with a young son."

"Strickland," Gilda repeated thoughtfully, then turning her head, she peered through the front window of the shop. Across the street, the south corner of the four-story lavender-colored building called Strickland's Boarding House could be seen. "Is he related to those Stricklands?"

"Grandson," Josselyn answered.

"Very handsome, too," Caroline chimed in. "You say he's a doctor and single? That's odd, because I think I'm suddenly feeling sick. Very sick."

Josselyn knew the young woman was only teasing; still she felt a prick of jealousy.

"He's an OB-GYN," Josselyn informed her. "Are you having female problems?"

Caroline's laugh was short and sultry. "Only the lack of a good man in my life."

Gilda rolled her eyes. "Caroline is itching to get married. She just can't wait to tie herself to a man. Can you imagine? She's only twenty-three. I've tried to tell her the whole thing is overrated. It's much more fun to play the field."

"Age has nothing to do with wanting to be a wife to a man who loves her," Josselyn stated.

Tossing a smug smile at Gilda, Caroline said to Josselyn, "Like minds. I think we're going to be dear friends."

"I hope so," Josselyn told her.

The young woman started to reply, then paused as a phone inside her handbag rang. "Excuse me," she said, and stepped aside to deal with the call.

Josselyn used the interruption to move across the room to a rack of dresses. Gilda followed close on her heels.

"Looking for something to dazzle the doctor?" she asked.

"Maybe," Josselyn said coyly. "Could be I just had the hankering for a new dress. Not anything fancy, but nice enough to wear for a night out."

Gilda chuckled knowingly. "Like a date with a hunky man?"

Frowning, Josselyn slid the garments back and forth on the rack. Nothing about the dresses caught her eye. "You don't have a clue as to whether Dr. Strickland is hunky," she said to Gilda, then let out a groan of surrender. "Okay, I give up. I do have a date with the man and I want to look—well, appealing."

Gilda's gaze slid up and down Josselyn's slender figure. "Honey, you'd look appealing in hair rollers and a pair of stained sweats."

Josselyn shook her head. "Don't try to flatter me, Gilda. I've stood in front of a mirror. I look like somebody's sister. Or even worse, a librarian."

Gilda lifted her eyes toward the ceiling. "You are a librarian, Josselyn. Does that mean you're supposed to look like a frumpy, ninety-year-old spinster?"

"No. But just for once I'd like to look a little more than nice and neat and—too modest."

Smiling sassily, Gilda crooked a finger at her. "What you want is glamour and you won't find it on this rack. Follow me."

The two of them were moving deeper into the store when Caroline called out, "Duty calls. I have to run. Good luck with your doctor, Josselyn. Viv and I might be planning your wedding soon!"

As the young woman hurried out the door, Josselyn shook her head with dismay. "Has Homer Gilmore been passing out more spiked punch? One date doesn't equal a wedding."

Gilda arched a brow. "No. But it could be one step closer."

That might be true, Josselyn thought, if the date was with any man other than Drew. He wasn't a regular guy looking for marriage. He'd already had a wife, and from what Josselyn could see, the woman was still living in his heart.

Josselyn might be able to make him forget his beloved Evelyn for a few minutes, or even a day. But that was hardly enough time for him to fall in love.

The notion was a dismal one. Still, Josselyn wasn't the type to give up on a cause. Even if it seemed like a lost one. She had to think of this *real* date with Drew as a new beginning for him and for her.

Chapter Seven

The next evening, on the drive to Sunshine Farm, Drew continued to think about his grandparents' reactions when he'd explained that he was going on a date tonight and needed them to watch Dillon.

Melba had eyed her grandson with a sharp look of concern and warned him about jumping into a relationship with a woman before he had time to really get to know her. On the other hand, Old Gene's response had been the exact opposite. He'd slapped Drew on the shoulder and expressed his pleasure at seeing his grandson making an effort to make his life whole again.

Normally Drew's cautious, practical nature would've coincided with his grandmother's response. But not tonight. This time Old Gene had put his finger on Drew's feelings. After all these years of living in a dark, lonely place, he wanted to emerge into the light, to feel more than angry bitterness at the fate he'd been dealt.

This short time he'd known Josselyn had been the brightest days he'd experienced since Evelyn's tragic death had jerked the ground from beneath his feet. And his newfound happiness was apparently making a difference in Dillon's life. Drew could actually feel his son growing closer. Tonight, when he'd learned his father was taking Josselyn on a date, he'd shouted and raced around the room with joyous abandon.

Yet for all the good that was happening since he'd met Josselyn, Drew still couldn't shake away the uneasy feeling that dwelled in the scarred part of his heart. Could this special thing with her really last? Or would something happen to end it all? Would she soon decide that a too-busy doctor and a rambunctious son weren't in the plans she had for herself?

Drew wasn't going to allow his thoughts to languish over those grim possibilities. At least, not tonight. Instead, he was going to give this private time with Josselyn a chance to be special.

A few minutes later while he stood on the porch to Josselyn's cabin, waiting for her to answer the door, he looked around at the adjacent cabins and the big farmhouse in the distance. The Stocktons had endured plenty of heartaches, he thought. But the torn holes in their family appeared to be mending. Especially since Dan and Luke had returned and settled down with their brides.

The sound of the door creaking open had him turning to see Josselyn standing on the threshold. The first thing that caught his attention was the warm smile on her face and then his gaze dipped downward to her figure silhouetted against the lit interior of the cabin.

She was wearing a bottle green blouse that wrapped and tied at the side of her waist. Her knee-length skirt was black and made with a flirty little slit at one side of her leg. Compared to the other clothing he'd seen her wear, this outfit was far saucier. Just looking at her made every male cell in his body hum with attention.

"Hi, Drew."

"Hello, Josselyn. Am I too early?"

"Not at all. Come on in while I finish getting ready. I only need a minute or two."

"No hurry." He followed her into the small rustic apartment. "We still have plenty of time before our dinner reservation."

"Please sit wherever you'd like," she offered. "Would you like anything to drink? Sorry, I don't have anything to make a cocktail, but I do have ginger ale."

He walked over to a butterscotch-colored armchair positioned in a corner of the cozy living room. "Thanks, but I'll wait until later," he told her as he sank onto the soft leather.

Satisfied that he was comfortably settled, she said, "I won't be long."

Drew watched her disappear through an open doorway, then glanced curiously around him. He'd expected the cabin to be furnished with frilly, feminine curtains and furniture that looked nice but felt like a torture chamber. Instead, it was decorated with earthy colors that were easy on the eye. And given her job, he'd thought the room would be filled with shelves of books, but the only reading material he spotted was one paperback lying on the coffee table.

There were probably mounds of books in the bedroom, he decided. She most likely went to sleep with a book wrapped in her arms, rather than a man.

You think? Maybe you need to take a closer look at the woman, Drew.

Like hell, Drew thought, as he resisted the annoying voice in his head. He wasn't ready to make love to another woman. The mere idea made him feel like an adulterer. And yet he couldn't deny that each time he was near Josselyn, each time he looked at her, he felt desire stirring in the pit of his stomach.

Restless now, Drew rose and walked over to a window where a small table held a few knickknacks and one photo in a wooden frame. The snapshot was of a group of people of varying ages gathered outdoors beneath a pair of shade trees. The only person he recognized was Josselyn standing next to another young woman. She was wearing shorts and a T-shirt and her blond hair was pulled into a ponytail. A wide smile was on her face.

"That's my family," she spoke as she reentered the room. "At a Fourth of July get-together. A friend snapped the photo while we were waiting on the homemade ice cream to freeze."

He picked up the framed photo for a closer look. "Is that your sister next to you?" he asked.

She came to stand by his side and Drew was instantly aware of her scent. Sweet gardenia, he decided. Or was it peony? No matter the flower. The fragrance made him want to dip his face against the curve of her neck and breathe in until his head was full of nothing but her.

"Yes. That's Patti. She's three years younger than me and still in college. One of these days I hope I'll see her working as a veterinarian."

"She doesn't look a thing like you."

"No. She's dark haired and dainty and pretty."

His sidelong glance was full of amusement. "So what does that make you?"

Her laugh was self-conscious. "I'm the girl next door. The vanilla cookie."

"Hmm. That's good. Vanilla's probably my favorite flavor."

She cleared her throat and said, "That's my two brothers standing next to me and Patti. Lloyd is on the left and Cameron on the right. Our parents, Velma and Walt, are right behind them. And over in the glider are my paternal grandparents, Otis and Laverne."

"Very nice family, Josselyn." He placed the picture back in its spot on the table, then turned to her. "I'd like to meet them all someday. Do you think they'll ever come visit you here in Rust Creek Falls?"

"I can see my sister and parents coming for a visit. But not my brothers. You can't pry them away from Laramie. And my grandparents are homebodies. What about your family?" she asked curiously. "Do they come to Rust Creek Falls often?"

"Every now and then. It's hard for Dad to leave the ranch, what with all the livestock to be cared for and chores to be done. But once in a while he leaves it up to the hired hands and he and Mom make the drive down. My brother Trey is married to Kayla Dalton and they have a two-and-half year-old son, Gil. Trey manages a riding stable at Thunder Canyon Resort, so he doesn't have much time off. And my other brothers, Ben, LJ, and Billy, are busy with their own lives. Although they do try to see Melba and Old Gene fairly often. Ben is a doctor, too. And Billy and LJ are both ranchers."

"So you have family and roots in Rust Creek Falls and Thunder Canyon," she said. "That must be nice. I purposely moved away from Laramie because I wanted to be independent and out from under my family's wing. But I have to admit that I miss them at times."

"Well, you're making roots of your own. And that's important, I think."

Her eyes met his and Drew was suddenly reminded

that the two of them were completely alone, standing only inches apart. All he had to do was bend his head slightly downward and his forehead would be touching hers, their lips would be oh so close.

She said, "Hmm. My grandmother—the one who passed on—had a saying that a woman wasn't a woman until she was rooted down with a man. Granny was old-fashioned that way."

"Nowadays you women have more progressive ideas than your grandmother." He stated the obvious.

Pink color swept across her cheekbones. "I happen to think a woman can make a home for herself. If that's what she wants," she added.

But what did Josselyn want? She'd once made mention of finding the perfect man for her. But maybe she'd prefer to be independent and not have to answer to any man? Or was she actually dreaming of someday becoming a wife and mother? The questions were on the tip of Drew's tongue when she suddenly turned away and reached for her handbag.

"We should probably be on our way, don't you think?"

She was putting an end to the personal moment and though Drew was a bit disappointed, he figured her decision was the right one. Otherwise, he might be very tempted to draw her into his arms and make them both forget about the dinner reservations in Kalispell.

Fighting the urge, he said, "Yes. Time is ticking. Let me help you with your jacket and we'll be on our way."

The prime rib on Josselyn's plate melted in her mouth, while the cool, dry wine slipped smoothly down her throat and warmed the pit of her stomach. The flickering candlelight on the table and the quiet music playing in the background lent a soft ambience to their private little corner of the opulent hotel restaurant. But compared to the man sitting across from her, all those things faded into the background.

With the candles dappling lights and shadows over his rugged features, she was completely mesmerized by the image he made in his white shirt and brown patterned tie, his dark hair combed back from his forehead.

"Is anything wrong with your food? You're not eating much."

Her knife and fork poised over her plate, she looked at him. "Everything tastes fantastic, Drew. I'm just eating slowly so I can savor my dinner. It's not often that I get prime rib or asparagus. Some evenings I just eat a peanut-butter-and-banana sandwich."

Her eyes focused on his lips as they slanted into a faint smile. She'd never seen him looking so relaxed before, and she wondered if getting out of town and away from the clinic had lifted a bit of stress from his shoulders.

"Nothing wrong with that," he replied. "You're getting protein and other vitamins. I just wouldn't recommend it on a daily basis. You need your vegetables."

"Spoken like a true doctor."

She glanced around at the long dining room filled with elegantly set tables and smartly dressed diners of varying ages. One couple in particular, at a nearby table, caught Josselyn's attention. Looking somewhere in their seventies, they had Josselyn wondering about her own years ahead. By the time she reached that age, would Drew be only a brief memory in her life? She didn't want to think so. She wanted to believe he would always be close.

"I've never been to this restaurant before," he told her. "One of the nurses who assists me at the clinic recommended the place. She and her husband came here for a Valentine's dinner."

She smiled at him and hoped the nerves that were causing her stomach to flutter didn't show on her face. "Wow. I feel special to be treated like this. It's a long time before Valentine's Day."

His dark brown eyes softened to a caramel color. Or was that just the candlelight making them look so warm and dreamy? Either way, the sight of them was causing all sorts of trouble with her breathing.

"You are special, Josselyn," he said. "That's why we're here. That's why I wanted your company."

And what about Evelyn? she wanted to ask. Was the woman sitting next to him right now? At times she felt as though the memory of his late wife was wedging its way between them. But tonight Josselyn wanted to believe his attention was solely on her.

"That's very nice of you to say, Drew." She looked down at her plate and realized he was right. She'd scarcely touched her food. Darn it, ever since she'd walked into her little living room and caught him studying the photo of the Weaver family, something had happened to her. Or him. Or had the change occurred in both of them? The only thing she knew was that once she'd stood close to his side in the quietness of the cabin, everything had altered.

Throughout the drive here to Kalispell she could have sworn electrical currents were zapping around the interior of his plush car. Now the space around their table seemed charged with the same sort of energy.

"I'm not trying to be nice, Josselyn," he said. "I'm trying to be honest."

Her gaze lifted back to his face and her heart lurched as soft, tender feelings pierced her deep inside. And all at once she was wondering where this time spent with Drew was heading. Was she setting herself up for a big letdown? Or even worse, a giant heartache?

It was far too late for her to be worrying about that now, Josselyn decided. She'd leaped into this date with eager abandon and she needed to quit with all the doubts and questions. She needed to simply enjoy being with Drew and let the future take care of itself.

"Okay, then, I'll be honest, too," she murmured the admission. "I wanted to be here with you, too."

Smiling now, he lifted his wineglass toward her. "Let's toast to tonight and being together."

She clinked her glass to his. "Yes. Together," she murmured softly.

For always.

The silent words whispered through her heart.

A half hour later, Drew was finishing the last bite of cherry cheesecake when the sound of a live band in a room next to the dining area had Josselyn looking eagerly around them.

"I hear live music," she stated. "Or did they just dial up the sound of the canned music?"

"I believe that's a real band. If I'm not mistaken, there's a ballroom behind us."

Her green eyes twinkled a challenge. "Can you dance, Dr. Strickland?"

He chuckled. "What's there to know about dancing?

You just shuffle your feet and pretend you know what you're doing."

She put down her fork and extended her hand to him. "Care to show me?"

Grinning, he rose from his chair and helped her to her feet. "As long as you promise not to cry when I step on your toes."

Her soft laugh was like sleigh bells at Christmastime, he thought. It filled his heart with cheer and hope.

"You're a doctor. You can fix my toes."

Feeling almost like a kid again, he took her hand and led her through the dining tables until they reached the ballroom.

Even though the music had just started, there were already several couples moving around the polished hardwood floor.

"Oh, how marvelous!" Josselyn exclaimed as she gazed around at the potted trees and hanging party lights adorning the edge of the dance floor. A small band situated on a disk-shaped platform at one end of the room was playing a song he vaguely recalled hearing his maternal grandmother sing.

She sighed. "I didn't know anyone played Gershwin tunes anymore. Isn't it romantic?"

She could make sitting on a rock in the middle of a desert feel romantic, Drew thought. "I'll take your word for it," he said, then pulled her into the circle of his arms.

At first, she held her body stiffly away from his, but once he guided her onto the dance floor and they merged with the other couples, he could feel her relaxing against him. Her soft, sweet-smelling body very nearly made him forget that music was playing and the two of them were in a public place.

"You do know how to dance," she said after a moment. "And very well, too. Where did you learn these kinds of moves?"

Just to impress her more, he dipped her over one arm, which caused her to release a breathless little laugh.

"My mom," he said. "She's the dancer of the bunch."

"And are your brothers this good at cutting a rug?"

"Hah! All my brothers have two left feet. They'd trip over themselves out here."

"Are you serious?"

"No. They're all pretty graceful guys. When they choose to be," he added impishly.

The song ended, but thankfully the band immediately broke into another. This time a young woman with long dark hair, dressed in a glittery evening gown, walked up to a microphone and began to sing.

"Oh, this is one of my favorite songs," Josselyn said.

She began to hum along to the slow, dreamy tune and soon her cheek was resting against his shoulder. The scent of her hair drifted to his nostrils, while her soft curves seemed to melt into his hard body. Had dancing ever felt like this? Like he was moving across a fluffy cloud rimmed with golden sunshine.

"I think it's becoming my favorite, too," he said in a husky voice.

Her fingers tight around his, she moved her head so that she was looking up at him. The faint smile on her face caused something to stir the darkest parts of him.

He wanted this woman. He wanted to touch her. Kiss her. Make love to her. The realization stunned him and left him feeling as if he'd just woken from years of sleep.

"I'm going to make a guess that you've never heard it before," she said.

His eyes glinted devilishly down at her. "I'm hearing it now. And you know what I've decided?"

"That I'm the one who needs to take dancing lessons?"

"No. I've decided you're much more like your old-fashioned granny than you think. The one who thinks a woman ought to root down with a man."

Her green eyes searched his and Drew suddenly felt so connected to her that he couldn't tear his gaze away. Like two comets crashing together, the explosion had left him addled and incapable of doing anything but staring back at her.

"Maybe," she said. "In some ways."

He tried to draw in a deep breath, but a pressure in his chest hampered the effort.

"Have I told you tonight how beautiful you are?"

Her eyes widened marginally and then her fingers tightened on his shoulder. "It's the dim lighting and the music," she reasoned. "Any woman would look beautiful in these surroundings."

"You're not *any* woman, Josselyn." Bending his head, he whispered against her cheek, "And I want to thank you."

The front of her body pressed closer to his. "For what?"

"Making me feel alive again," he said, his voice thick with emotion.

She seemed to understand that he didn't need any words of response from her, and as she silently nestled her face in the crook of his shoulder, he felt as if he'd finally come home.

Much later that night, when Drew braked the car to a stop in front of her cabin, Josselyn's mind was darting in every direction. Everything inside her, with the exception of one slither of sanity, was screaming at her to invite him inside.

Coffee? TV? A late-night snack? Any reason might do to get him on her couch and into her arms. But the sensible part of her brain that was still working realized she might not be quite ready to make love to the man. And the way she was feeling at the moment, all he needed to do to get her into bed was to ask.

"The evening has been so wonderful, Drew." She unsnapped her seat belt and reached for her coat lying on the back seat. "Thank you for treating me to dinner and dancing."

He shut off the motor and turned toward her, causing Josselyn to unwittingly drop the coat to her lap.

"The pleasure has been all mine, Josselyn."

The nervous beat of her heart was fluttering in her throat. "Well, it's getting late and we both have to be up early. I'd better go in."

"I'll walk you to the door," he said.

"No!" she blurted, then seeing his look of surprise, quickly added, "I mean, there's no need. I left the porch light on. I won't trip between here and there."

A knowing expression came over his face. "And you won't have to ask me in. Is that it?"

She let out a long breath. "Well, sort of," she confessed. "I'd love to invite you in. But I—"

"You're afraid of what it might lead to," he finished for her.

She groaned. "Did you take mind-reading lessons when you studied to be a doctor?"

He leaned toward her, and as his hands settled gently on her shoulders she felt her whole body go mushy.

"Only the mind of a green-eyed blonde with luscious pink lips."

"Drew."

His name was the only sound she could push past her thick throat, and even that response was unnecessary as his mouth was suddenly latched over hers, searing, searching, pushing every capable thought out of her head.

Lost in the delicious taste of him, she rested her hands on his shoulders, then trailed them upward until her fingers were pushing into his hair. Her head tilted to one side as her lips parted and invited him to deepen the kiss.

She heard him groan with need and then his hands were in her hair, cradling the back of her head as he anchored her mouth to his.

Fire licked at the edges of her mind and stabbed splinters of heat over every inch of her skin. There was nothing she could remember ever feeling this good or right. Nothing she had ever imagined could compare to the sensations wrapping around her, swirling her in a blanket of pure pleasure.

It took only moments for their kiss to grow hungry and wild and before she knew it, she was circling her arms tight around his neck, groaning with the need to be closer. At the same time, Drew was moving from behind the steering wheel and drawing her across the low console and onto his lap.

With his mouth moving magically over hers, Josselyn couldn't think, much less resist. Not that she wanted to. That sliver of sanity that she'd been gripping a few minutes earlier had long since dissolved. All she wanted now was to have Drew carry her into the cabin and make slow, sweet love to her.

The desire must have conveyed itself in her kiss because she'd barely had time to process the thought when his hand found its way inside her blouse. And then his fingers were pressing into the soft breast encased in the lacy cup of her bra, eliciting a low moan deep in her throat.

He lifted his mouth from hers and as she gulped for oxygen, he buried his face in the side of her neck.

"As much as I want this to go on, I—I'd better go. Now. Before something happens that we'll both regret."

Regret? No! How could she ever regret making love to this man? She couldn't. But then, he probably wasn't thinking about this in terms of making love. To him this was sex. The reaction of raw, sizzling chemistry and nothing more.

The chilling thought was enough to have her scurrying off his lap and straightening her blouse.

"Uh—yes. You're right, Drew. I'm sure you hadn't planned on this happening. And we don't want to do anything as impulsive as jumping into bed together."

Her face burning with humiliation, she hurriedly fumbled with the door latch.

"I'll see my way to the door. Good night, Drew."

She climbed out of the car only to have him call out to her as she started to shut the door.

"Josselyn, are we going to see each other again?"

She lowered her head enough to enable her to see inside the car. Drew had already situated himself behind the steering wheel. His fingers were on the ignition key, ready to twist the motor to life. Obviously, he had leaving on his mind.

"Well, yes. I mean, if you want to. We could do something safe and simple. Like coffee at Daisy's Donut Shop."

She gave him a little wave, then hurried on to the cabin. It wasn't until she was inside and the door locked behind her that she saw Drew's headlights sweeping across the lawn, then turning in the direction of Rust Creek Falls.

That was where he belonged, Josselyn thought glumly. Back at the boardinghouse with Dillon and his grandparents. Back with his memories of Evelyn and a love that he wouldn't allow to die.

Chapter Eight

Friday evening, after an incredibly hectic week full of emergencies and an overload of patients, Drew entered the boardinghouse in hopes of spending a quiet evening. Instead, the moment he walked into the old-fashioned entrance, Dillon was racing down the staircase, yelling like a banshee was on his tail. But rather than a ghoul chasing his son, it was Robbie wearing a Halloween mask complete with warts and long whiskers.

"Dillon!" Drew caught his son by the shoulder as the child leaped with both feet onto the landing. "You know what I've told you about running. Especially on the stairs!"

"But, Dad, Robbie—I mean Troll Monster—is after me! I gotta get away!"

By now, Robbie had already seen the error of his ways and jerked off the rubber mask. His eyes wide, the child cowered against the bannister as though he expected Drew to throttle him. The idea very nearly broke Drew's heart.

Purposely gentling his voice, Drew said, "It's okay to play, boys. But the both of you could get seriously hurt running down the stairs. Halloween isn't far away. How could you two celebrate if you're hobbling around on crutches?"

"Celebrate?" Robbie tilted his blond head to one side. "What's that?"

Dillon rolled his eyes. "Aw, Robbie, don't be so dumb. You know—it's like having a party. Doing fun stuff and eating things you don't get to eat all the time."

Drew rubbed the top of Dillon's head. "That pretty much explains it."

Robbie's wide-eyed gaze traveled back and forth between Drew and Dillon. "Oh. Will we get to do that here?"

"Will we, Dad?"

"I expect there'll be some sort of Halloween partying going on," Drew answered, then glanced at his watch. "You two better go get washed up for dinner. Melba doesn't want any stragglers."

"Can Dillon eat at the big table with me tonight?" Robbie asked. "I like it better when he's there."

When Drew left the clinic, he'd been dreaming of having a quiet meal upstairs in his private quarters. The last thing he'd planned on doing was joining the rest of the tenants around a boisterous dinner table. But Dillon enjoyed the company. And though, more often than not, Drew was caught up in his own busy life, he had noticed little Robbie. He wasn't sure what had gone on in the boy's life before he and his mother had come to live at the boardinghouse, but it was obvious to Drew that the child needed extra attention.

"Okay, we'll all have dinner together at the big table," Drew told him. "As long as you two promise not to run on the stairs anymore."

Both boys jumped up and down with glee. "We promise!" they shouted in unison.

He was getting as soft as a pat of butter, Drew thought a few minutes later as he washed and changed into a clean shirt. It wasn't his place to try to put a smile on the face of someone else's kid. And before he and Dillon had moved here to Rust Creek Falls, he would've told himself that the emotional well-being of his son's little friend was really none of his business.

But Drew had changed since he'd come to this small mountain town. He wasn't exactly sure when or how it had happened, but he didn't feel like the same man who'd arrived only a few weeks ago. At some point the bitterness that had been gripping his heart for so long had slipped away, and once it had disappeared, everything around him had suddenly come to life. Instead of just seeing patients and studying medical charts, he'd begun to see and understand the needs and wants of his son in a much clearer way. He'd started thinking more of his family and all that his brothers meant to him. Christmas was still a few months away, but Drew was already getting that coming-home feeling of love and togetherness.

You know who and what has made the change in you. You just don't want to recognize how important Josselyn has become to you.

The taunting voice in his head had him taking a stark glance at himself in the dresser mirror.

Josselyn. Three days had passed since their evening together in Kalispell, yet in spite of that and his chaotic schedule, he couldn't get her or their night together out of his brain. Especially the ending.

The depth of the desire he'd felt for Josselyn still left

him stunned. Where had all that hot yearning come from and how had he let it get so out of control?

Even with Evelyn, he'd never experienced such reckless passion. With her it had been all sweet and tender feelings, not an animallike lust to mate.

Dear Lord, if he hadn't put a stop to things when he had, he would have made love to Josselyn right there in the car.

We could do something safe and simple. Like coffee at Daisy's Donut Shop.

The tartly spoken suggestion had made it clear she was frustrated with him, and Drew couldn't blame her. When he'd talked about regret, she'd most likely taken the word personally. But in truth, he'd been thinking more about her feelings than his. Compared to him, she was incredibly young. And she was the type of woman who didn't have sex with a man. She made love to him. If she did ever decide to make love to Drew, he wanted everything in her heart to be certain and settled.

"Dad, did you know tomorrow is Saturday?"

Drew finished snapping the last button on his Western shirt before he glanced over his shoulder to see Dillon standing in the doorway of the bedroom. The boy had made an attempt to tame his hair with an abundance of water and a brush. Some of the dark locks were plastered against his skull while others stuck up in tall spikes. Drew decided that Dillon's effort was all that mattered.

"Yes. I did know that tomorrow is Saturday."

"And you don't have to work on Saturdays," Dillon pointed out. "Unless some woman starts to have a baby. Right?"

"That's right," Drew answered, while wondering

where all this might be going. "Why? Are you thinking it's time for another fishing trip?"

Dillon skipped into the room. "Another fishing trip would be super, Dad. But we can do that some other time. I was thinking it was time you saw Josselyn again. Maybe take her out on a stroll through the woods or a picnic in the park."

Drew kept his amused smile to himself. "Oh, you do, do you? And you think a stroll or a picnic is what a girl likes to do?"

"Sure. That's the kind of stuff I see on TV. And the girls are always laughing so I figure they like it."

"That's only in commercials," Drew informed him.

"Well, I'll bet Josselyn would like going for a walk with you. If you'd hold her hand. And smile at her."

Lord help him, Drew thought. He was definitely going to need it when his son reached his teenage years. "Maybe she would. If no babies suddenly decide to be born tomorrow, I just might ask her."

Grinning broadly, Dillon said, "That's the ticket, Dad. You're getting the hang of things now."

Taking hold of his son's hand, Drew led him out of the bedroom. "Come on. Let's go down to dinner. And, Dillon, whatever you do, don't say any mean things to Robbie. Hear me?"

"Oh, shoot, Dad, I'm never mean to Robbie. Sometimes I have to show him the ropes. 'Cause I know about a lot more things than he does. But he don't mind. That's the way it is with friends. We help each other out."

"And who taught you that philosophy?"

"Why, you did, Dad."

Pride swelled in Drew's chest as he smiled down at

his son. For the first time in years, he was beginning to feel like a real father again.

The next afternoon Josselyn was surprised when Mikayla showed up on her doorstep, minus little Hazel.

"Mikayla, I love that you've come to visit, but I'm very disappointed that you didn't bring the baby," Josselyn told her as the two women sat on opposite ends of the couch. "Is she feeling okay?"

"She's fine. Just a bit fussy. When I finally got her to sleep, Eva practically shoved me out of the house. She thought I needed a break. I've been busy packing."

"Packing? You mean Jensen has finally found a house for the three of you?"

Her eyes sparkling with excitement, Mikayla nodded. "Yes! He's rented one of the Victorians in town. You've probably noticed the houses before. They're over on Falls Street, just north of the river. You know, the ones that Jonah Dalton renovated a couple of years ago."

"Sure. They're beautiful and not far from the elementary school. How nice, Mikayla. So when is moving day?"

"Two days from now. That's why I'm already packing."

"Oh, I'm going to miss you and the baby being close by," Josselyn told her. "But I'm so happy that the three of you will be together."

"I'm not sure how long we'll stay in the Victorian. Jensen has plans to buy land in the area and build a beautiful new home for us."

"Wow. A new baby, a wedding and plans for a dream house. I can't imagine how you must be feeling."

"Like a princess," Mikayla said with a soft laugh.

"Well, Princess Mikayla, just make sure to keep little Hazel bundled during the move. She's going to be the star of your wedding."

Mikayla smiled. "Don't worry. I'm going to make double sure Hazel doesn't have any setbacks. I can hardly wait for our wedding to take place."

"That day will be here before you know it," Josselyn told her. "And by the way, I met Caroline Ruth the other day in Gilda's boutique. And I ran into her again having coffee at Daisy's."

"Caroline Ruth," Mikayla thoughtfully repeated. "I don't think I know her."

"She's taken a part-time job for Vivienne Shuster. So as you start making more wedding plans you'll probably meet her. She's very pretty. Just not too smart. She has this funny idea I'll be next in line for a wedding."

Mikayla chuckled. "What gave her that idea?"

Josselyn grimaced. "She saw Drew and me having lunch at the Gold Rush the other day."

"You haven't told me about any of this."

Josselyn sighed. She hadn't told anyone about her growing relationship with Drew. Not any of the staff she worked with at school, or her family down in Laramie. It was all too new and private. And mostly, too fragile. Why announce something when it was probably going to end as quickly as it had started?

"Well, I haven't had time to talk with you. I haven't even had a chance to tell you about our night in Kalispell."

Mikayla looked at her in surprise. "He asked you out?"

Josselyn nodded, hoping the memory of that night wasn't turning her cheeks pink. After almost four long days she'd expected the memory of being in Drew's arms would've dimmed to a foggy memory. Instead, it was still burning vividly in her brain.

"He did. And we had a very nice time."

Mikayla's eager expression fell flat. "That's all? Just *nice*?"

Josselyn let out a short awkward laugh. "Isn't *nice* enough?"

"Not as far as I'm concerned. I want to hear about fireworks. I want to hear you say you've found the man of your dreams."

There had been fireworks and Drew was everything Josselyn could ever want or hope for. Yet she couldn't get enthused about their relationship. Not after the way their date had ended. She was still feeling the sting of rejection.

Restless now, Josselyn rose to her feet and began to move aimlessly around the small room.

"It's too soon for any of that, Mikayla."

"What about his wife? Or lack of one, I should say."

Josselyn said, "She died in a car accident. It obviously was tragic for him. Dillon was only twelve months old at the time."

"Now that I have Hazel, I can't imagine not having Jensen in our lives. He's my future. My little girl's future. Without him, I'd be…well, so devastated I'm not sure how I could go on. I can't fathom the pain that Dr. Strickland must have gone though."

Sighing, Josselyn paused to look at her. "It clearly hasn't been easy for Drew. His wife has been dead for six years and he's just now starting to have a social life again. But even so… Well, I can see I'm competing with her memory, Mikayla. And as far as I can tell, I'm losing the battle."

Mikayla instantly pushed herself to her feet and crossed the short space to Josselyn. "Honey, you sound miserable. Have you gone and fallen in love with the guy or something?"

"I don't know. It sure feels like it. Even though I know it's hopeless." Her short laugh was mirthless. "My family always said I was the champion of lost causes. Well, they couldn't have been more right."

Mikayla patted her shoulder. "You're putting the cart before the horse. The way I see it, you haven't known Dr. Strickland long enough to know whether things between the two of you are hopeless or just beginning. Besides, you're not a woman who throws in the towel at the first hurdle you come to. You're the kind that fights for what she wants."

Josselyn gave her a sardonic smile. "Let me guess. You were a cheerleader all through high school."

"No. But I believe in having a fighting spirit. And after little Hazel was born, I kept praying that she had a fighting spirit in her, too."

The thought of the thriving baby tilted the corners of Josselyn's lips. "Hazel is a fighter—a survivor. Just like her mom. So I guess you're telling me that I should find my inner strength and put it to use."

"Exactly. And on that happy note, what do you say I go make us some coffee? I'm dying for a cup."

Laughing, Josselyn slipped her arm around the back of Mikayla's waist and urged her toward the kitchen. "You're in luck. I just bought a pound of fresh beans. I'll let you do the grinding."

* * *

The two women had finished their coffee and Mikayla had left to return to the big house when Josselyn's phone rang.

The instant she spotted Drew's number, her heart leaped into her throat. She hadn't heard from him since their date and a part of her had started to wonder if he'd decided to end things without a word or any kind of explanation.

"Hi, Josselyn. Did I catch you at a busy time?"

She swallowed and prayed her voice would come out sounding like a normal woman's instead of a frog with pneumonia. "Um—no. I'm not busy. Just sitting around the cabin."

There was a slight pause and then he asked, "Would you mind if I came out for a while and sat around with you?"

The question very nearly caused her to stagger backward. In fact, she did steady herself by grabbing on to the kitchen table.

She had to make herself breathe. "No. I wouldn't mind. If that's what you'd like."

"I would like."

"Great. I'll see you in about a half hour."

He hung up the phone and Josselyn wilted into the nearest chair.

The night they'd returned from Kalispell, she couldn't have pulled him into this cabin with a log chain and a one-ton truck. Tonight he wanted to come out for a visit. What was going on with the man?

The question whirled through her mind as she forced herself out of the chair and hurried to the bedroom. Yet as she changed into a soft camel-colored skirt and white sweater, she decided she wasn't going to try to analyze Drew's motives. He wanted to see her again. And that was all that mattered.

By the time Drew knocked on the door of the cabin, twilight was settling over Sunshine Farm and with the darkness came a sharp drop in temperature. When she opened the door to let him in, cool air rushed into the room.

"Hi," he said.

The one-word greeting was all it took to put a smile on her face.

"Hello, Drew. Come on in. It's getting cold out."

The scent of fried chicken wafted from a large paper sack resting in the crook of his arm. The aroma drifted across the threshold and her mouth instinctively watered. Although, she wondered if the reaction was more for the taste of him than the food.

"The weather tonight reminds me that winter is coming soon," he said as he stepped inside.

Josselyn closed the door, then turned back to him. And all of a sudden her little living room seemed overloaded with his presence and the vivid memory of being in his arms, kissing his lips.

Seemingly unaware of her rattled nerves, he gestured toward the sack. "I hope you haven't yet eaten. Dillon thought you might like a picnic today. But I had a pair of emergency calls to the clinic this afternoon. The best I could do was bring a meal with me."

He'd been planning to take her on a picnic? The mere thought lifted her spirits. "It smells yummy. And I'm very hungry." She motioned for him to follow her. "Let's take it into the kitchen and I'll make us some drinks."

Inside the small room, he placed the sack on the planked pine table. As she moved over to a short row of cabinets, he looked around at the checkered curtains on the window and the copper pots hanging near a gas range.

"This is homey," he said. "It looks like a real cook lives here."

She laughed. "I am a real cook. I started helping my mom in the kitchen when I was probably seven or eight years old."

"So why do you settle for peanut-butter-and-banana sandwiches?"

Pleased that he remembered such a trivial thing, she smiled. "Cooking for one isn't as much fun. Neither is eating alone."

He moved away from the table and crossed the two steps that separated them. "That's what Dillon says, too. He likes to eat in the dining room with all the other boardinghouse tenants."

"And you?"

His lips twisted to a guilty slant. "Let's just say I'm beginning to appreciate the company."

Her gaze slipped over his face, then downward to the green-and-blue-plaid flannel stretched across his broad shoulders. Even dressed casually in jeans and boots, he managed to look better than any man had a right to.

"That's good."

"Until it gets so loud you can't hear yourself chew."

She chuckled. "That's bad."

Josselyn started to turn toward the cabinets to fetch a pair of glasses for their drinks, but his hand was suddenly on her forearm and she paused, her heart beating wildly.

"No. I'm the one who's been bad, Josselyn. I've been thinking about you and the way things ended the other night. I want you to know that my leaving had nothing to do with you and everything to do with me."

The awkward tension between them caused her gaze to drop to the floor. "It doesn't matter," she said, her voice small and stiff. "You—uh—obviously didn't want to get that close to me."

His fingers tightened ever so slightly on her arm. The reaction caused her gaze to rise back to his face.

"You're wrong," he said. "I did want. Very much."

Her throat was suddenly so thick she could hardly breathe. "But you were overcome with guilt."

He grimaced and then both hands were on her arms, sliding upward until they latched onto both shoulders.

"You're wrong—again. You're very young, Josselyn. And I want—"

She drew in a shaky breath as she waited for him to finish. When he didn't, she decided to do it for him. "You want to keep our relationship platonic. Is that it?"

Amazement paraded across his face and then, without a word, he tugged her forward until the front of her body was pressed against his. "I thought by now that my feelings were obvious. I thought you could see that when I look at you—touch you—nothing feels platonic."

Wondrously, her fingers softly touched his cheek. "Oh, Drew. I've been thinking you probably wanted to end things."

His lips took on a wry slant as his hands slipped down her back. "In a way you're right. I want all these cautious baby steps to end. I want to run and leap right into this fire that's ignited between us. But only if you're sure about me, Josselyn. And about your own feelings."

Josselyn was sure about one thing—she wanted this man with every fiber of her being. And for tonight, that was enough.

The sigh that passed her lips came from the deep yearning in her heart. "I am sure, Drew. So sure."

A warm light was suddenly glowing in his brown eyes. "Do you think we could put off eating for a while?"

Even as he was asking the question, his head was dipping toward hers, and she wasted no time in wrapping her arms around his neck and tilting her face up to his.

"Right now the only thing I'm hungry for is you," she whispered.

Groaning with triumph, he brought his lips down on hers and Josselyn met his kiss with a ferocity that shocked her. In response, his arms tightened around her until her breasts were flattened against his chest and her hips were aligned with his.

Wild, primitive desire took hold of her senses until nothing mattered except having this man make love to her. With the taste of his lips driving her onward, she reached for the snaps on his shirt.

She'd managed to release three of them before he finally tore his mouth from hers. Beneath her hands she could feel his heart pounding and his chest rising and falling with each rapid breath.

"We—uh, need to—"

"Go to my bedroom," she finished in a whispered rush.

"I'm glad one of us can talk."

He murmured the words between a series of tiny kisses pressed upon her cheek. Josselyn grabbed him by the hand and led him out of the kitchen.

The cabin possessed only one bedroom and it was

located on the left side of the structure, directly behind the living room. The small space was dark as the two of them entered and Drew paused on the threshold of the open doorway, while she switched on a small lamp near the head of the bed.

"Sorry about the mess," she said as she straightened away from the lamp and turned back to him. "I pulled out half the closet trying to find something to change into to impress you."

Looking like a man about to set out on an important mission, he walked toward her. "You'd impress me in burlap. But I have a feeling you're going to impress me the most when you're wearing nothing at all."

When he reached her, his hands cupped around both sides of her neck and her heart jigged with wild anticipation.

"You might be disappointed. You see a lot of women without their clothes on."

He shook his head. "Not the way I'm seeing you."

Her arms slipped around his waist as his mouth dipped closer to hers. "How are you seeing me?"

"Like you're mine," he said in a husky voice. "All mine."

"Oh, Drew, I'm so glad you're here. So glad that you want to be with me. Like this."

Her hands tenderly cupped his face as she rose onto the tips of her toes and brought her lips to his.

He drew her so close she could feel his heart beating against hers, feel the bulge of his erection pushing against the juncture of her thighs.

Instinctively, her mouth opened beneath his and his tongue swiftly pushed its way past her teeth. As it teased and tempted, her fingers tightened on the back of his neck.

Using his tongue and his teeth, he kissed her until her knees grew so weak she was forced to grab the front of his shirt to keep from wilting in a pile at his feet.

Tearing her mouth from his, she gulped for oxygen. "Much more of that, Doctor, and you're going to be picking me up from the floor. I hope you're good at resuscitations."

Chuckling, he stepped far enough back to allow himself to grab the hem of her sweater. When he started upward with the fabric, she raised her arms to allow him to pull the garment over her head. Once it was out of the way, he removed her skirt, then tossed her back onto the bed and tugged off her boots.

Resting on her back, wearing nothing but two scraps of pink lace, she watched through lowered lashes as he began to remove his own clothing. Throughout the chore, he didn't pause to touch her, but that hardly cooled her desire. Just looking at his lean, masculine body left her totally aroused and desperate to connect her body to his.

Once he was stripped down to a pair of dark boxers, he joined her on the bed and she rolled toward him. They reached for each other at the same time and the sensation of his bare flesh sliding against hers was enough to send her senses skyrocketing. His body felt so warm and hard against her soft curves. His skin held the mysterious scent of dark forest mixed with the erotic fragrance of a man in his prime. She couldn't touch him enough. Nor could she quench her thirst for the taste of him.

"You're so lovely, Josselyn. So warm and soft beneath my hands." With his mouth nibbling an erotic path down the side of her neck, he reached to the middle of her back and deftly released the clasp on her bra. As soon as the lacy fabric fell away, his fingers went on a slow expedition across her breasts, lingering at the nipples.

Seeming to know what she needed without asking, he dipped his head and lathed one throbbing bud with his tongue. When he finally pulled it fully into his mouth, a white-hot fire swept through her, scattering her senses to the shadowy corners of the room and beyond.

She thrust her fingers into his mussed hair and pressed them tight against his skull, as though she could stop his head from moving and break the incredible spell he was casting over her. But eventually, he raised his head and she opened her eyes to see his dark orbs studying her face.

"You taste sweet. And perfect."

"I'm not perfect," she murmured huskily. "I'm just a woman who wants you. Very much."

"Not any more than I want you. All of you," he added, and with a low groan, he bent his head to the valley between her breasts.

His lips began to mark a blazing trail downward until he was circling her navel, like a hawk readying himself for the main meal. When his hand slipped between her thighs and gently touched her, she whimpered with anticipation.

He lifted his head, and then with a smile on his face that she'd never seen before, he dropped his mouth back to the hollow between her hip bones. Certain the walls of the room were spinning around them, she tried to anchor herself by latching onto his shoulders. It did little to steady her because suddenly his tongue was inside her, teasing, taunting and promising the best was yet to come. Liquid fire shot through her veins, and just when she thought she would shatter into a thousand pieces he pulled back and slipped off the bed.

Confused, she opened her eyes to see he was fishing something from the pocket of his jeans. When she spotted a small packet in his fingers, she realized he'd paused to deal with protection.

"I'm already protected with oral birth control," she said, her voice thick with desire.

His brow arched with wry speculation, causing hot color to sting her cheeks.

"Not because I'm sexually active." She felt the need to explain. "If that's what you're thinking."

Grinning now, he tossed the unopened packet onto the nightstand. "I'm not thinking anything of the sort. I'm actually thinking how fortunate I am that Dillon was brash enough to introduce me to you that day in the park."

A soft laugh eased out of her. "And I'm glad you decided to take your matchmaking son to the school picnic. Otherwise, you might not be here with me. Like this."

He rejoined her on the bed, and as he positioned himself over her, she looked up at him, her eyes full of yearning and her heart brimming over with something that felt dangerously close to love.

"Yes. Like this," he whispered.

With slow, exquisite perfection, he connected his body to hers, and for the next few minutes there was nothing in the world but him and her.

Chapter Nine

Drew had never expected this. He'd never planned on Josselyn feeling so perfectly wonderful in his arms. He hadn't imagined he could feel a passion so hot and wild that he'd totally lost all sense of time and place.

Now as he lay with her warm body tucked into the curve of his, her head nestled on his shoulder, he closed his eyes and tried to digest the soft, protective feelings inside him. Tried to figure where this relationship was going to lead them.

Being with her made him happy. She filled up the empty holes inside him in a way he hadn't thought possible. And he didn't want any of it to end. Plain and simple, he needed Josselyn. He needed to know she would always be around for him. But that wasn't the way life worked.

"The chicken is probably ice-cold now," she murmured.

Opening his eyes, he gently combed his fingers through the damp, tousled hair lying upon her bare shoulder.

"We can always heat it up in the microwave."

"Mmm. Sounds good," she said. "Only I don't want to move. Not yet."

He skimmed his hand over the curve of her hip and down one thigh, all the while thinking her skin was like a piece of heated satin. Just touching its smoothness was an erotic experience.

"I'm glad. Because I don't think I can. Having you here in my arms feels too good to move. I can have food any ole time," he murmured against the crown of her head.

She twisted around so that her face was pressed to the side of his neck and her breasts were brushing his chest. Although he tried to ignore it, desire flickered deep in his belly. How could that be, he wondered, when only moments ago, he'd been certain she'd drained every ounce of energy from his body?

"When you called I didn't have any idea you had this on your mind."

"I didn't," he replied. "I came out to apologize for ending things so abruptly the other night, that's all. Why? Did you think I had this planned?"

"I wouldn't mind if you had. All that matters is that you're here and we're together. Really together." Tilting her head back, she took a slow survey of his face. "Speaking of the other night… I hope you're not having any of those regrets you were talking about."

Smiling gently, he touched his forefinger to the tip of her nose. "No regrets. No guilt."

She reciprocated his smile. "I'm so glad," she murmured, then gently trailed her fingertips across his cheek. "You're good for me, Drew. And I hope I'm good for you."

Her words pricked his heart, and without even knowing it, his hand tightened on her waist. As though his hold on her would always keep her close to him.

"You're wrong, Josselyn. You're better than good for me. You've shown me my life isn't over. And in case you haven't guessed, you've made little Dillon very happy, too. He talks about you all the time. And wonder of wonders, you've managed to make him want to read for the sheer entertainment of it."

"Wow, after saying all those glowing things I'm not about to let you out of my bed. At least, not before midnight," she teased.

"Mmm. We have a few hours before the clock strikes midnight. I'm thinking we better make the most of them. The chicken will keep until later. Much later," he whispered as he lowered his lips toward hers.

Monday morning, when the second-grade class was allowed a morning library break, Dillon was one of the first students to enter the room. Sitting at her desk, Josselyn carefully hid a smile as she watched him struggle to keep from running straight to her.

"Hi, Miss Weaver!" He sidled up to her desk and swiped at the brown hair scattered across his forehead. "Did you know it might snow? That's what Granny Melba says. And she's usually right."

Josselyn glanced toward the windows that overlooked the playground. At the moment, the sky was a bright blue, while orange and yellow leaves tumbled over a span of dormant grass.

"Well, it doesn't look like it might snow at the moment. But I hear Rust Creek Falls gets lots of snow in the winter. I'm sure it will be coming soon. Do you like to make snowmen?"

He nodded with enthusiasm and Josselyn thought how very much he reminded her of Drew. His hair and eyes were the same rich brown as his father's. So was the deep dimple in his left cheek. The big difference between Dillon and Drew was that the child smiled more often than not, whereas Drew's smiles were doled out less frequently. But the man was coming around, she thought. Just thinking of their time together in the cabin was all it took to make her heart beat faster.

Dillon said, "If it snows before Halloween, I'm gonna make a big triple-decker snowman in front of the boardinghouse and put an ugly face on him so it will scare everyone away."

"Why do you want to scare everyone away?"

His giggle was full of mischief. "So me and Robbie will have all the candy to ourselves."

"Who's Robbie?"

"My friend who lives at the boardinghouse with us. He's in second grade, too. But he don't come to the library 'cause he has to go to special reading class."

"I see. Well, hopefully his reading skills will get better soon."

"Yeah. He's doing better. Dad says I need to be extra nice to him. 'Cause Robbie gets kinda sad. I show him my baseball cards and he likes to read those."

"That's nice of you, Dillon."

Her compliment had him throwing back his shoulders in typical male reaction.

"Granny Melba says I'm too mischievous," he told her. "She don't know that I can be nice, too."

Josselyn was trying to stifle a laugh when Rory walked up beside Dillon and shook a forefinger at him.

"Dillon Strickland!" Rory scolded. "You promised to show me a book about ponies. Have you forgotten?"

Dillon rolled his eyes helplessly toward Josselyn. "She's a girl. She can't help it."

Rory grabbed his arm and yanked him away, and as Josselyn watched the pair of children disappear down an aisle of animal-related books, Dillon's words lingered in her thoughts.

She's a girl. She can't help it.

Dillon's observation described Josselyn perfectly. She was a woman and, though it probably wasn't the smartest thing she'd ever done in her life, she'd fallen head over heels for a man.

For the past two days, she'd felt as if she was walking on air. She wanted to sing and shout. She wanted to dance a joyous jig. And most of all she wanted to dream about a cozy little home with children running underfoot and her doctor husband coming home from the clinic every evening to greet her with a kiss.

"Miss Weaver, are you sick?"

The question came from another second grader with bright red pigtails and big blue eyes that would no doubt someday break a boy's heart.

"Why no, Bonnie. Why do you ask?"

"Because you look sorta different today."

She looked like a woman who'd been made love to by a man, Josselyn thought. That was the difference.

Rising from the chair, Josselyn walked around to the little girl. "Would you like for me to help you find something to read?"

"Oh, yes, Miss Weaver. I want to read a fairy tale."

This was the first time since school had started that

a child had asked specifically for a fairy tale, and the request caused her to pause.

"I think we can find one of those," she finally told the girl. "Come along with me to the other side of the room."

As they walked along, Bonnie asked, "You know why I want to read a fairy tale, Miss Weaver?"

The question had been on Josselyn's tongue, but she'd hesitated to press the girl. Over time she'd learned children usually volunteered their thoughts on their own.

"Hmm. I can't guess," Josselyn said. "You'll have to tell me."

Bonnie rubbed the end of her freckled nose, then grimaced. "Because my mommy says a fairy tale is the only place where things are happy. Is that true, Miss Weaver?"

Torn by the hopeless expression on the girl's face, Josselyn paused and bent down to the child's level.

"Oh, no, Bonnie. Happy things are all around us—in real life." She directed the child's attention to the view beyond the window. "See how the sun is shining on the playground. It's warming the little red birds and making them sing happy tunes."

"Well, that's the way it is today. But sometimes it's cold and snowy."

Josselyn gave her a bright smile. "When that happens we can make snow angels and snow ice cream. And that makes lots of people happy."

Bonnie's bottom lip thrust forward. "But sometimes people cry."

Unfortunately, that was true, Josselyn thought. She figured Drew had cried many tears when he'd lost Evelyn. And he'd been sad for far too many years. But Josselyn was determined to change all of that. She aimed to fill his life with smiles and laughter. To prove to him that he could truly love again.

"That's when we have to remember that tears dry and things will always get better."

Bonnie appeared to weigh Josselyn's remarks and then she smiled up at her.

"Miss Weaver, you got me to thinking. I don't think I need to read a fairy tale, after all."

Relieved that she'd managed to make a positive impression on the child, Josselyn gestured to the rows of bookshelves in front of them. "Okay, there's all sorts of stories to pick from. You might like to read about a brave little girl like you who saves a lost kitten. That's a fun book."

Bonnie's eyes twinkled. "Oh, yeah! That would be great!"

Two streets over from the elementary school at Rust Creek Falls Clinic, Drew had finished with his last morning patient and was about to eat a cold sandwich at his desk when his cell phone rang.

Thinking it might be Josselyn, he pulled the phone from the pocket of his shirt to check the ID and was mildly surprised to see the caller was his brother Trey. Given the fact that both of them were extremely busy with their jobs, the brothers rarely called just for a chit-chat. Especially during the middle of the day.

"Hey, big brother," Trey cheerfully greeted. "Can you put down your stethoscope long enough to talk?"

"The only thing in front of me right now is a cold sandwich Claire made for my lunch. And I'm not in the mood to eat it. So tell me what's going on up in Thunder Canyon. Aren't you working today?"

Trey chuckled. "That's a hell of a question. I'm always working. Right now I'm here at the barns, waiting on the farrier to arrive. It's getting cold as heck up here. You'd think folks wouldn't want to visit a dude ranch and ride horses in this kind of weather."

"Been busy, huh?"

With a weary grunt, he said, "Nonstop. Most of the visitors are thinking they're going to see autumn foliage on the equine trails, but they're getting disappointed. Last week a storm with high wind blew through and the trees' limbs are practically bare."

Trey had found his wife, Kayla, right here in Rust Creek Falls. Now the couple was happily married, with a young son, Gil. His brother's good fortune made Drew wonder if there was a bit of magic to this place. Everything had certainly worked out well for Trey's love life. But could Drew expect that same good fortune to land on him? He wanted to think so.

"And you're hearing a bunch of griping," Drew said knowingly as he settled comfortably back in his office chair.

His younger brother chuckled. "It's not that bad. We'll be getting snow soon anyway."

"Will the ranch be closing down the stables? I understand you usually keep things going during the winter months, but the owner could have different plans this year."

Trey let out a short laugh. "Not a chance. With the holidays right around the corner, it's one of the busiest times of the year. The only way we'll shut down is if the snow gets too deep on the trails for the horses to pass through. And that's not likely. The ranch has equipment for clearing the trails. So barring any blizzards it'll be business as usual around here."

"Sounds like you won't be coming down to visit Rust Creek Falls anytime soon," Drew replied.

"Unfortunately, not for a while. Kayla is promising her family she'll be down for Christmas, so I'm going to have to figure out how to get away. For a couple of days, at the least. What about you and Dillon? When are we going to be seeing you back in Thunder Canyon?"

The question brought Drew up short. Sometime in the past few weeks, thoughts of his old hometown had faded into the far distance. Had Josselyn already changed him that much? "You mean for a visit?"

"No. I mean when are you coming back home?"

Home. The word no longer held the same meaning for Drew as it had down in Thunder Canyon. After Evelyn's accident, he'd sold the house they'd called home and moved himself and Dillon back into his parents' ranch house. And until this move to Rust Creek Falls, that's where the two of them had remained. Strickland's Boarding House wasn't Drew's ideal home, but he was beginning to think of it as such. And for some reason this little cowboy town with its quaint shops and quirky characters was making him feel as though he belonged here.

And Josselyn was here, Drew thought. Sweet Josselyn with her soft smiles and even softer lips. Just thinking of her caused his heart to squeeze with longing.

Drawing in a deep breath, he said, "I'm not sure, Trey. After the first of the year a new doctor is supposed to join the staff here at the clinic." He paused a moment. "I guess once that happens I won't be needed here."

Trey snorted. "Doctors are always needed. I'm sure

you could find another job in the area. That is, if you're planning to stick around in Rust Creek Falls."

The sly note he heard in his brother's voice made Drew instantly suspicious. "Okay, Trey, why did you really call me today? And don't tell me it was just to have a brotherly chat."

"Oh hell, Drew, what's the matter with you, anyway? Just because I ask you about coming home you think there's some sort of ulterior motive about my call?"

"There is. But I won't ask. You'll get around to it without me prodding you," Drew said, then changed the subject completely. "I haven't talked to Mom and Dad in a few days. How are they?"

"Missing you and Dillon. I can tell you that much."

"Hmph. They were only too glad to push me out of their hair. And rightly so." He let out a rueful sigh. "Honestly, I don't know how they put up with me for so long. I've pretty much been a jackass these past few years."

Trey coughed loudly. "Excuse me, but am I talking to my brother, Dr. Drew Strickland? I must have a wrong connection."

"It's me all right," Drew quipped. "The real me."

There was a long pause and then Trey asked, "What happened to the jackass?"

A blond-haired, green-eyed goddess had walked into his life, Drew thought. She'd peeled the bitter layers from his eyes and now he was finally seeing his life, and the world around him, in vivid colors.

"He's trying to be human again," Drew answered.

Trey said, "You don't know how relieved I am to hear that. Does this have anything to do with the woman you've been seeing?"

Drew sat straight up in his chair. "I knew you'd called me for a reason. So who's been talking?"

"Dad. Seems that Gramps gave him a call."

"Old Gene has been gossiping? Damn, a man can't trust anyone anymore."

Trey laughed. "So tell me about her. Like how the hell does she put up with you?"

"I haven't figured that out yet. Frankly, Trey, this is all very new for me. I—I'm feeling shaky about the whole thing."

"Well, sure you are, brother. That's only natural. But, Drew, you need to remember that there's some happiness in this world for you, too."

Drew wiped a hand over his face. "That's just it, Trey. Josselyn does makes me happy. And that scares me."

"Because?"

He let out a shaky breath, and though he wished his brother was here with him, he was glad Trey couldn't see him at the moment. He didn't want his brother, or anyone for that matter, to see what a vulnerable man he truly was.

"I'm not sure I'm supposed to feel this way. Or that any of it will last. And then the pain will start all over again."

Trey let out a heavy sigh. "Drew, none of us has any guarantees about tomorrow. You can't live your life in fear. That's not really living."

No. For the past six years Drew hadn't really lived. He'd only gone through the motions. And throughout that time, he'd made a point to keep his feelings wrapped in gauze. Like a wound that had to be carefully protected from the outside world. But like it or not, Josselyn had pulled away the bandages and exposed his heart. There was nothing left for him to do but find the courage to love again.

"You're right, Trey. And I'm working on it."

"I'm proud of you, brother."

His throat thickened and he was wondering how he could push another word out when a knock sounded on the door of his office. Before he could respond, Nadine stepped into the room.

She said, "I'm sorry to interrupt, Dr. Strickland, but there's an emergency. Mr. Anderson just brought his wife in and I think she's in labor. Advanced labor!"

"I'll be right there," he told the nurse. Then he told Trey, "Sorry, brother, we'll have to talk later. I've got an emergency here."

"So I heard. Get to work. And, Drew, be happy."

"Yeah."

Drew cut the connection to his brother, then, dropping the phone back into his shirt pocket, he followed the nurse out the door.

Late the next afternoon, as Josselyn was preparing to leave work for Sunshine Farm, she walked out to the parking lot to see Drew's car parked next to hers. Since she'd only had two short phone calls since he'd spent part of Saturday night at her cabin, she was thrilled that he'd made an effort to stop by the school to see her.

By the time she reached the parked cars, he was standing outside waiting for her and the slanted smile on his lips made her heart thump with excitement.

"Hello, busy lady," he greeted. "I was beginning to wonder if you were going to work until after dark."

He walked forward to meet her and she was mildly surprised when he pressed a kiss on her cheek.

"Wow," she said, darting a glance around the parking lot. "You must not be worried about small-town gossip."

"What's there to gossip about? Doctors and librarians are human, too."

"Very human." She turned a provocative smile on him. "I've missed you, Dr. Strickland. I'm glad you came by."

He smiled back at her and Josselyn was suddenly struck by how much he'd changed since she'd first met him in the park. He'd seemed so tense and sober. Josselyn wanted to think that she might have had something to do with the smile on his face, but there was more going on in his life than meeting a librarian. It could be that he was finally beginning to feel comfortable here in Rust Creek Falls.

"I dropped by with an invitation," he told her.

She chuckled. "You really have a problem with phone conversations, don't you?"

A guilty grin curved his lips. "Okay, I could've picked up the phone and called you rather than drive two blocks over. But this way I get to see you. And invites are always more impressive in person."

"Oh, yes," she said with a teasing smile. "Yours happen to be very impressive. So what do you have on your mind?"

"I wanted to invite you to join Dillon and me for supper this evening at the boardinghouse. And before you say yes or no, I should warn you that it's most often like a three-ring circus around the dining table. But the food is good."

Supper at the boardinghouse? That meant she'd be meeting his grandparents! She tried to tell herself that this wasn't a big deal. But to her it was major. It was stupendous!

"You don't believe in giving a girl much warning, do you?"

A wicked light glinted in his eyes. "Gives you less time to come up with an excuse to turn me down."

Turn him down? The idea was laughable. All he had to do was remember the wanton way she'd made love to him the other night to know it would be a cold day in July before she'd turn down an invitation from him.

"As if I would do that," she murmured, then, clearing the huskiness from her voice, she glanced down at her gray pencil skirt and prim white blouse. "I'm not exactly dressed for an evening with your family and friends."

"You look lovely," he said softly.

The appreciative light in his eyes was the same look he'd given her as she'd lain naked in his arms. The mere memory of that time with him made her want to walk straight into his embrace. But they were standing in an open public area, so the most she could do was give him a tempting smile.

"Then I'd love to join you," she told him.

"Great. Put your things away and we'll drive over to the boardinghouse in my car. We have a few minutes until dinner, so that will give me time to show you where Dillon and I hang our hat and you can say hello to my grandparents."

"It's nearly time for dinner?" She glanced at her watch, then toward the rapidly sinking sun. "I really did almost work until dark, didn't I?"

"Good thing I came by," he teased.

This lighthearted Drew was definitely new to Josselyn and undeniably charming. Yet she had to wonder if this change in his mood was momentary or if he was actually becoming a happy man. She very much wanted to believe the latter.

"Yes, a very good thing," she said.

After situating her work supplies in her car and grabbing her coat, Drew helped her into his car and they began the short drive over to the boardinghouse.

As he steered the vehicle onto North Buckskin Road, he tossed her a sheepish grin. "I apologize, Josselyn, for not calling you earlier about this dinner date. But by the time I finally found a spare moment to pull out my phone, it was time for the clinic to shut the doors."

He couldn't possibly know how happy she was to see him again, to be close to him. Until she'd met Drew, she'd never known how just the sound of a man's voice or the mere scent of him could fill her with such pleasure. "There's no need to apologize, Drew. I like spur-of-the-moment."

He reached across the console and wrapped his hand around hers. "Before I moved here to Rust Creek Falls, I wanted everything on a schedule. And the more work the better," he confessed. "A few weeks ago, I would still be at the clinic, pouring over charts and test results, or the latest medical journal. Unnecessarily, I might add."

She studied his profile, all the while the warmth of his hand spreading through her. "Are you telling me that things are becoming different for you?"

He turned a meaningful glance on her. "Very different. And thank you for that, Josselyn."

"Me?" With a nervous little laugh, she pressed a palm against her chest. "I'd rather think it's this town, Drew. That stuff folks say about Rust Creek Falls having something magical in the air is really true."

"Magic. Hmm. I don't believe in magic. It's nothing more than illusion. But I do believe in fate."

"Like meeting in the park?" she suggested.

"Exactly," he said, then lifted the back of her hand to his lips.

Fate. There were all sorts of connotations attached to the word, Josselyn thought. And not all of them represented a happy ending. But she didn't want to argue that point with Drew tonight.

She'd rather hope that in due time he'd come to believe in the magic of love.

Chapter Ten

Drew wheeled the car to a stop in a small graveled parking area and Josselyn gazed at the back of the four-story lavender structure. Since her move here to Rust Creek Falls she hadn't had any reason to visit Strickland's Boarding House, but she'd often been curious about what it looked like inside.

"Don't get the idea that I'm taking you in the back way to keep you hidden," he told her. "My grandmother is often in her office at this time of the evening and it's located here in the back."

"Front or back doesn't matter," Josselyn assured him. "I've never been inside your grandparents' boarding-house, so I'm anxious to see the place."

Drew helped her out of the car, then, with a hand on her elbow, guided her toward the building.

"I'm not exactly certain when the house was first built. I do know it's been in the Strickland family for many years. The layout is old-fashioned, but Old Gene and Melba have worked hard to keep everything maintained and in good shape. That could be one of the reasons they rarely have vacancies."

"And the fact that your cousin Claire does the cooking is another," Josselyn added. "The chicken and fixings you brought out to the cabin the other night were delicious."

He squeezed her arm. "We had chicken? I don't remember."

She laughed and he joined her.

Their happy mood followed them into the big house, where Drew guided her over to an office. The door leading into the room had a check-in window built into the top half. At the moment the sliding glass was closed tight.

"I don't see anyone inside," Josselyn commented. "Should you ring the bell?"

"No. There's a light on inside. She's probably at her desk and I want to surprise her."

He guided Josselyn around to a side door and knocked. "She keeps everything locked," he explained to Josselyn. Then through the door he called, "Grandma, it's me, Drew."

Melba's muted voice sounded from somewhere inside the room. "Let me guess, Dillon has broken another vase in the parlor. Don't worry about it, Drew. I've started putting out fakes. The thing probably cost a dollar or two."

Drew and Josselyn exchanged amused glances.

"This isn't about Dillon," he spoke to the closed door. "Are you too busy to meet someone?"

Josselyn could hear the faint squeak of a desk chair and then footsteps approached the door.

When the heavy partition swung wide, Melba Strickland, a plump older woman wearing a sensible housedress of printed calico and cushioned black shoes, studied them with surprise.

"Why, Drew, you should have warned me that you had company with you." Frowning, she patted her short graying hair. "I look a mess."

"You look as pretty as ever," he assured his grandmother. "And just to ease your mind, I don't think Dillon has broken anything. At least, not in the past few minutes."

With his arm at the back of Josselyn's waist, Drew urged her slightly forward. "Grandma, this is Josselyn Weaver. She's the school librarian at Rust Creek Falls Elementary. She's the lady who's managed to get Dillon interested in books."

And his father interested in other things. Even though the older woman didn't speak the words, Josselyn could see them parading across her face.

"And, Josselyn," Drew went on with the introduction, "this is my grandmother, Melba. She has roses on her cheeks, but she's actually a woman of steel. Don't let anyone tell you differently."

Melba made a show of swatting away his words before she extended her hand to Josselyn.

"Hello, Miss Weaver. Welcome to Strickland's Boarding House. Call me Melba, if you like. I hope you can stay long enough to take supper with us."

"I'm not about to let her go until she eats some of Claire's spaghetti and meatballs," Drew interjected.

Josselyn smiled at the woman. "It's very nice to meet you, Melba, and please call me Josselyn."

Melba peered over the tops of her reading glasses at her grandson, and Josselyn could see she was totally bemused at this turn of events. Obviously she wasn't accustomed to Drew bringing female company home with him. And so far, Josselyn couldn't tell whether the woman approved of this change in him. Or if she wanted to pull him aside and give him a lecture.

"Well, you might want to show her around the rest of the house, Drew," Melba suggested, then glanced at her watch. "We'll be having supper in fifteen minutes. Will you two be eating in the dining room with the other tenants?"

"That's right," Drew told her. "I want Josselyn to see how we Stricklands live."

Drew nudged her forward, and as they started down a narrow passageway, he said in a hushed voice, "Melba is as old-fashioned as the house and drives folks crazy with some of her strict rules. But she loves her family fiercely."

"And fiercely tries to protect them," Josselyn observed.

"Like a mama grizzly."

At the end of the passageway, they were about to climb a staircase when a door off to their left opened. Josselyn glanced in the direction of the sound and saw an older man with baggy pants and shirt and sparse, graying hair walking toward them.

"Drew, is that you?" the man asked.

His hand resting at the side of her waist, Drew paused at the foot of the stairwell. "That's right, Gramps. I'm glad we ran into you. I want you to meet Josselyn."

The man shuffled over to them, his squinted gaze traveling over Josselyn. "So you're the librarian little Dillon is always talking about. Miss Weaver, isn't it?"

He reached out to shake her hand, and as Josselyn grasped his large bony fingers, she got the impression that the old man was her friend. "That's right. But I hope you'll call me Josselyn."

"Josselyn it is. And you better call me Old Gene. I wouldn't know how to answer to Mr. Strickland." Cracking a grin, he patted the top of Josselyn's hand and cast a pointed look at Drew. "She's a pretty one, boy. You'd better take care of her."

"I intend to, Gramps. Right now we're headed upstairs so I can show her my and Dillon's nook of the house. Do you know where my son is at the moment?"

Old Gene grunted with amusement. "Sure do. He was showing off on his bike in front of some of his friends and fell in a mud puddle. Had dirt and water smeared up to his gills. I sent him upstairs to clean up before Melba caught him dripping on the floors."

Shaking his head in resignation, Drew said, "Don't worry. I'll see that he's dried and presentable before we come back downstairs."

Josselyn and Drew started up the stairs while, behind them, she could hear Old Gene chuckling as he went on his way.

She said, "Your grandfather doesn't seem to have the same strict rules as his wife."

"No. He's crusty on the outside, but he's a marshmallow inside. It's no wonder Dillon wants to spend a big part of his time with him. My son knows just how to work his great-grandfather's soft heart to get what he wants."

Josselyn said, "For what it's worth, when Dillon visits the library, he doesn't talk about Old Gene. He talks about you."

His sidelong glance was full of doubt. "That's to play me up to you."

She laughed. "You know something? It's working."

Laughing along with her, he reached for her hand. "Come on. Let's see if the little matchmaker has managed to clean himself up without destroying the bathroom."

Moments later, when they entered the connecting rooms that Drew called home, Dillon was already cleaned and dressed and sitting dutifully on a small couch situated near a window.

From the look of total surprise on his face, it was clear the child had been unaware that Josselyn was going to be at the boardinghouse this evening. He immediately jumped to his feet and raced straight to her.

Josselyn's heart melted as the boy flung his arms around her waist and hugged her with all his might.

"Josselyn! Yay! Yay! You came to see us!"

Patting his back, she said, "I did come to see you and I'm going to stay for dinner."

Dillon tilted his head back and beamed a wide smile up at her. "This is the best night ever!"

"It might be one of your worst," Drew warned. "On our way upstairs we heard you had a nasty accident."

Dillon stepped back from her and, swiping his damp hair to one side of his forehead, darted a wary glance at his father.

"Oh, shoot, that was nothin'," Dillon assured him. "I'm already clean and dry."

"So I see," Drew said. "But what about the bathroom?"

"Aw, I promise the bathroom is okay, Dad. I picked up all my clothes."

Drew looked at Josselyn. "Since we have to share a bathroom with the tenants down the hall, I need to make sure he didn't leave the place in shambles. I'll be right back. Just make yourself at home."

Drew left the room and Dillon grabbed her hand. "Come on, Josselyn, I'll show you around. Everything is kinda tiny, but it's fun living here." Taking her by the hand, he tugged her into a very small bedroom with one window overlooking the street. "See, I got a little bed in my room and a desk for my homework. But I don't use it much. 'Cause I get my homework done at school."

"Wow, you must be a dutiful student," Josselyn remarked as she glanced around at the sports gear and other playthings lying about.

"Naw. I'm not always good at school. But I make good grades. Betcha I make all As on my first report card this year," he proudly predicted.

"If you do, I'll bake you a giant cake with a smiley face on it."

"With chocolate icing?" he wanted to know.

"Double fudge," she promised with a grin, then gestured to a small framed picture on the desk. "Who are these people?"

"That's my grandma and grandpa down in Thunder Canyon. On some days I kinda want to see them. But we lived with them a long time. It's fun to do something different. And we'll probably go back to Thunder Canyon someday, anyway."

That was a reality that Josselyn tried not to think about. Drew had already explained that his job at the clinic was a temporary position. A new doctor was already scheduled to arrive shortly after the first of the year. The end of September was nearing and January would be here sooner rather than later. Would Drew be ready to go back to his old job at the clinic at Thunder Canyon?

The notion of him and Dillon moving out of her life was becoming unimaginable to Josselyn. And yet she understood it was something she might soon be facing. Unless Drew fell in love with her, she thought. Unless he came to realize he wanted to spend the rest of his life with her. Then it wouldn't matter where they spent their future. As long as they were together.

Pushing those uneasy thoughts from her mind, she wondered why there wasn't a photo of Dillon's mother alongside the one of his grandparents. Did Drew think seeing her picture on a daily basis would be emotionally disturbing for the child? Or would it be more disturbing for Drew, she wondered.

"Hey, you two? Where are you?"

Drew's voice pulled Josselyn out of her deep thoughts and she glanced down to see Dillon grinning up at her.

"We'd better go," the boy said. "Granny Melba's mouth will look like this if we're late to the table."

The boy pressed his lips together in a flat line and Josselyn was trying to contain her laughter when she looked around to see Drew standing in the open doorway. An indulgent smile curved one corner of his lips.

"Is my son telling you knock-knock jokes?"

"No. He's just making funny faces."

"Well, Funny Face, you're in luck for now," Drew told the boy. "The bathroom was dry and neat. But you're not off the hook completely. Later on we're going to talk about this bike accident."

"Okay, Dad," Dillon mumbled, then reached for Josselyn's hand, as though he was quite certain she could save him from the worst of his father's wrath. "But Josselyn doesn't want to hear that kind of stuff tonight. She wants to talk about fun stuff."

Drew gave Josselyn a furtive wink.

"Okay. For tonight it's fun stuff."

Drew had never been an impulsive man. Even as a kid, he'd carefully thought things through before he'd acted. Jerry, his father, had always called Drew his "careful" son, and the description had aptly fit him. Until he'd met Josselyn. Something about her made Drew want to throw caution to the wind and enjoy every precious moment, even if it wasn't planned or wisely thought through.

Now as he sat next to her at the big dining table, listening to her interact with the other tenants, he was more than glad that he'd made the impulsive decision to invite her to the boardinghouse tonight. Dillon was over the moon at having her company. And Drew was… well, he was amazed at how relaxed she made him feel. How much he felt at home each time he looked at her lovely face.

But will all of this last, Drew? Or will something happen to burst this newfound happiness?

The voice whispering in his head was an ugly reminder of all he'd gone through in the past six years. It nagged him at the worst possible times. But tonight he was determined to push it far, far away. Tonight he was going to try his best to believe in the magic Josselyn talked about.

"How do you like living on Sunshine Farm, Miss Weaver?" Thomas, an elderly gentleman who lived on the second floor, asked.

"I like it very much," Josselyn answered. "The Stocktons are a very nice family and the countryside is beautiful. I always wanted to live out of town. So the farm suits me well."

"Where did you live before, Josselyn?"

The question came from Melba, and Drew could only wonder what else his grandmother might ask Josselyn before the night was over. She was well-meaning and she and his grandfather had been an enormous help with Dillon since they'd moved into the boardinghouse. But there were times that Drew wished the woman would remember he was a thirty-three-year-old man with enough sense to keep him from taking a leap off Fall Mountain.

"I lived in Laramie, Wyoming," Josselyn answered. "My family all still live there."

"Hmm. Seems kinda strange, you moving from a city to a little smudge on the map like Rust Creek Falls," Melba remarked.

Old Gene grimaced as he swirled spaghetti around his fork. "Maybe she heard about this place being full of lovebugs. She might've wanted to take her chance on being bitten."

A few chuckles rippled around the table and Josselyn noticed that Melba's lips turned into a flat line of disapproval, just as Dillon had mimicked.

"Oh, what would you know about a lovebug?" the older woman said to her husband. "It's been years since you've done any courting."

"That's true," Old Gene told her. "But a man doesn't forget."

"Well, I hear that Sunshine Farm has gotten a new name," a divorced woman sitting across from Old Gene spoke up. "Word is that folks are now calling it the

Lonelyhearts Ranch. Makes me want to move out there just to see if there's something to it."

Melba frowned, while on the opposite end of the table a younger man, who'd moved into the boardinghouse a few days ago, turned his attention to Robbie's mother.

"Sounds like your kind of place, Mary."

The shy woman hardly glanced up from her plate. "My heart is just fine right where it is, thank you."

Mary's stiff response had Drew glancing at little Robbie. Instead of eating, he'd pressed the side of his face against his mother's arm. From his reaction, the boy didn't want a father. Unlike Dillon, who'd deliberately set out to find himself a mother.

"Actually, the job at the elementary school is what brought me here," Josselyn replied to Melba's comment. "At the time I accepted the position, I didn't have any idea just how charming Rust Creek Falls would be."

"Well, we're all glad that you decided to move here," Old Gene told her. "Isn't that right, Drew?"

Drew reached under the table and found Josselyn's hand lying in her lap. Squeezing it, he said, "Oh, very right, Gramps."

"I'm really glad, Gramps," Dillon spoke up. "'Cause now my dad has a girlfriend. And she makes him act a lot nicer than he used to."

Melba cleared her throat and promptly changed the subject. "Everyone needs to finish up their plates. It's time for dessert."

After rounds of apple cobbler and coffee for the adults, the group began to shuffle out of the dining room.

"What are you gonna do now, Dad?" Dillon asked as he followed alongside Josselyn and Drew.

Drew gave his son a comical look. "Well, I don't know. Maybe we'll go sit in the parlor. Why? Do you want to come along to keep us company?"

"Gosh, no! Me and Robbie are gonna watch TV in his room. Mary said it was okay with her. Is it okay with you, Dad?"

"I suppose so. As long as you behave."

Dillon looked pleased. "Thanks, Dad. And you know what I think? I think you ought to take Josselyn for a walk out back and show her the swing."

Perplexed, Drew frowned. "The swing?"

"Yeah, you know. It hangs down from the tree limb and rocks back and forth. Girls like that sort of stuff. That's what Rory told me."

"Oh, well, Rory ought to know," Drew said, then turned a suggestive grin on Josselyn. "How about it? You think you might like that sort of stuff?"

"It sounds perfect," she told him. "Just let me get my coat."

Short minutes later, as they exited the back of the house, Josselyn looped her arm through his and breathed in the crisp night air.

A security light illuminated the area at the back of the house, but as they strolled across the lawn toward a huge oak, the shadows grew thicker. Drew kept his arm firmly around her waist as he guided her to an old wooden swing hanging from one of the lower branches.

"It's a little chilly out here. Maybe you'd rather not sit," he suggested.

"I'm wearing my coat. I'm not a bit cold. And it's lovely out here," she told him. "The moon is coming up and shining through the branches."

"Okay. As long as you're comfortable we'll sit," he told her.

They eased into the swing, and as he curled his arm around her shoulders, she snuggled close to his side. Drew nudged the ground with the toe of his boot and the slatted-wood seat began to move gently back and forth.

"I'm going to have to thank Dillon for this nice idea," she said.

Chuckling, Drew reached for her hand and enveloped it between both of his. "I don't know how Dillon got to be such a little cupid, but I have to admit he's pretty good at it."

"You mean, he hasn't tried to find you a girlfriend before?"

"Believe me, Josselyn, that day he introduced the two of us at the picnic was the first I'd heard about him wanting to find me a girlfriend, or a wife or anything of that sort. If I looked stunned that day, it's because I was."

"Stunned?" Her short laugh made it clear how amusing she considered that description. "You looked more like you could eat nails before you marched Dillon out of the park."

"I was very annoyed with him," he admitted. "At that time I didn't realize I was meeting a woman who was going to make me laugh again—live again."

His voice grew husky on the last words and the sound filled her with emotions so new and tender that her throat grew tight, making it a struggle to speak.

"I didn't realize I was meeting a man who was going to become so special to me," she managed to say.

He turned toward her, and with the moonlight etched upon his features, she could see doubts and questions flickering across his face.

"Do you really mean that, Josselyn?"

She meant that and so much more. What she wanted to say was how she'd truly and irrevocably fallen in love with him. She wanted to tell him exactly how much he and Dillon had come to mean to her and how very much she wanted the three of them to be a family. Yet the words remained smothered deep inside, held back by the fear that he wasn't ready to hear such things from her. Once he learned she had a forever family on her mind, he might run far and fast.

"Yes," she whispered. "I mean it very much."

"Josselyn."

Her name was the only thing he said before he drew her close against his chest. She tilted her face up to his, and when his lips came down on hers, a thrill of desire rushed through her. Along with something else. Something so sweet and warm that tears stung the back of her eyes.

He kissed her for long moments, and Josselyn hoped her lips conveyed all the hopes and dreams she held deep in her heart.

When he finally lifted his head, she saw a half grin carving dimples in both cheeks. "Dillon was right. I think girls do like this kind of stuff."

Loving the scent of him, the feel of his skin touching hers, she rubbed her cheek against his. "Except for your grandmother," she murmured. "I'm not sure she likes the idea of you and me together."

"She doesn't want me to be hurt. Again."

Easing her head back, she looked into his eyes. "I would never hurt you, Drew. Not intentionally."

"No. I don't believe you would. Not purposely. But things happen."

She cradled his face between her palms. "We're not going to think about *buts*, Drew. Not tonight. Not ever."

A groan sounded deep in his throat, then once again his mouth was slanting over hers. And for a moment, as Josselyn gave herself up to his kiss, she thought she tasted real love on his lips.

Chapter Eleven

The next morning as Josselyn hurried around the cabin, getting ready for work, she paused at the kitchen sink to rinse her coffee cup and was surprised by the sight beyond the window. At the cabin across from hers, a man dressed in jeans and a black T-shirt was in the small front yard doing pull-ups on a bare tree limb. Even at a distance, she could see he was young and in splendid shape.

Who was he? She hadn't even realized anyone had moved into the cabin across the way. Not that she was interested, Josselyn thought as she turned away from the window and grabbed her handbag from the table. The only man in her sights was Drew, and the more she was with him, the more she wanted him.

On her way out of Sunshine Farm, she stopped at the big household to say hello and found Eva in the kitchen scurrying between the refrigerator and the big gas range.

"Are you late for a fire this morning?" Josselyn teased.

Eva groaned as she turned strips of frying bacon. "I was supposed to have this morning off at the donut shop, but the other cook at Daisy's has come down with some sort of virus, so I'm needed. I should have been there thirty minutes ago! But I'm not leaving without fixing Luke's breakfast first." She glanced at Josselyn. "On your way to school?"

Josselyn nodded. "I stopped by to drop off a cookie recipe I thought you might want to try. It's made with coconut, pecans and chocolate chips. Oh, and lots of butter."

"Sounds sinfully delicious. I'll definitely try it," she said with a little laugh. "Thanks. Just lay it anywhere on the counter."

Josselyn placed the envelope with the recipe inside next to a large canister of flour. Eva would never miss seeing it next to a baking ingredient.

"By the way, I just saw a strange man over at the far cabin," Josselyn commented. "Is he a new tenant?"

"He moved in a few days ago. I guess you were probably at school and didn't notice the activity over there. His name is Brendan Tanner. I believe he served in the military, but I'm not sure what branch. Luke says he was originally a cowboy and very good with horses."

"He certainly looks capable of handling a horse," Josselyn remarked. "Did he come here to Sunshine Farm thinking it really is the Lonelyhearts Ranch?"

Eva slanted her an amused glance. "I can't imagine you being romantically interested in Brendan. Not with Dr. Strickland at your beck and call."

Josselyn frowned. "How do you know about Dr. Strickland?"

Rolling her eyes, Eva turned back to the bacon and began forking the pieces onto a plate lined with paper towel. "Josselyn, everyone on Sunshine Farm has seen his vehicle parked in front of your cabin. And none of us figured the good doctor was making a house call. At least not the medical kind," she added slyly.

Josselyn could feel a pink blush blooming on her cheeks. "Okay, we have been seeing each other. And you're right, the only man who interests me romantically is Drew."

Eva broke three eggs into a skillet. "Getting serious?"

Josselyn sighed. "I'm afraid I've gotten very serious. As for Drew…well, I just don't know yet. Sometimes I think I'll always be competing against the memory of his late wife. And then other times I think he might be beginning to care for me."

Eva deftly flipped the eggs, and though Josselyn was proud of her own cooking abilities, she wished she could be as handy in the kitchen as the beautiful blonde. Serving Drew a hunk of homemade pie would probably do more to get his mind on love than handing him a library book.

"To be honest, Josselyn, most everyone around Rust Creek Falls was shocked to discover he had a child, much less that he was a widower. The man obviously kept his private life extremely private."

"Drew would be the first to admit he's not a social person. But I think for a long time it hurt him too much to talk about his late wife or the son he had with her."

Eva dismally shook her head. "How well I understand that. It's taken Luke a long, long time to deal with his family tragedy." She softened her sad words with an encouraging smile. "But don't give up, Josselyn. I'm betting that you're going to win out over that memory of his."

Josselyn had to think so, too. Otherwise, the two of them could never have a future together.

"Oh my, it's getting late!" Josselyn exclaimed as she gave her watch a quick check. "I've got to run!"

"Thanks for the recipe. And good luck with Dr. Strickland," Eva called as Josselyn started toward the door.

"Thanks, Eva. I'm going to need all the luck I can get."

By Friday evening, Drew was desperate to be alone with Josselyn again. Really alone. And the chance to spend extended time with her practically fell into his lap when Dillon explained that Robbie's mother had invited him for a sleepover.

"Are you certain about this, Dillon?" Drew asked as he changed into a clean pair of jeans and a gray-and-brown-plaid Western shirt. "Mary is a busy woman. I'm not sure she has time to entertain two boys."

"She has time," Dillon assured him. "She's gonna make us popcorn balls in the kitchen and we get to help her. And then we're gonna watch a movie. It's a Christmas story about a boy who goes around on his pony delivering gifts."

"Christmas, eh? It's a little early for that, isn't it?"

Dillon shook his head. "Mary says it's never too early for giving gifts from the heart."

Drew paused in the act of reaching for a hairbrush lying on top of the chest of drawers. *Never too early for giving gifts from the heart.* That sounded so much like Evelyn. She'd been a gentle, giving woman, and if she were here today, she'd be teaching Dillon those same values of giving and sharing.

These past few weeks, thoughts of his late wife hadn't entered his mind all that much. A month ago that fact would have left him feeling guilty. For years he'd purposely fought to keep her memory alive and burning inside him, knowing that once he let it slip there would be nothing left of her to hold on to. But now that Josselyn was in his life, he was letting the memory go and letting the guilt follow behind it. He recognized that he was finally moving forward, finally allowing himself to heal. And that had to be a good thing.

"Mary is right about that, son," he said to Dillon. Then he turned to him and asked, "Do you really want to sleep over at Robbie's?"

"Oh, yeah! Will you let me? Will you?"

"Okay. But I'm going to talk to Mary just to make sure everything is all right with her."

"Oh boy! I'm gonna run tell Robbie right now!" Dillon was racing out the door when he suddenly skidded to a stop and looked back at his father. "You're still gonna go see Josselyn tonight, aren't you?"

"That's what I'm planning on. Or would you rather me stay here with you and the two of us do something together?"

Dillon's little face took on a horrified expression and he hurried back into the room to stand in front of Drew. "Oh, no, Dad! You might make Josselyn mad. And if she gets mad she might never want to be my mom."

Emotions pricked the middle of his chest and Drew quickly squatted on his heels and took Dillon gently by the shoulders. "You really want Josselyn to be your mother, don't you?"

He nodded. "I told Owen and Oliver and Rory—my

friends at school—that she was going to be my mom and they all laughed at me."

Drew remembered meeting the three children at the school picnic and their plan to throw pinecones at the first graders. Dillon had been proud to call them friends, and the idea of the three laughing at Dillon over something so important to him left Drew sick inside.

"Why do you think they laughed?" Drew asked gently.

Dillon's bottom lip quivered and Drew wondered why his son hadn't talked to him about this before now.

Is that so hard to figure, Drew? Any time Dillon has brought up the subject of a mother, you've shut him down. You can't see that he needs more than a memory in his life. He needs a real mother to love and nurture him. He wants a real family.

Dillon's expression turned defiant. "Because they don't think Miss Weaver—I mean, Josselyn—wants to marry you. But she does! She will. I know she will, 'cause she loves you!"

Tangled emotions knotted around Drew's heart and tightened until he could scarcely breathe. Did Josselyn love him as Dillon so readily believed? Did Drew want her to love him?

There had been moments in the past week when Drew had thought Josselyn might be falling in love with him. He'd thought he'd felt it in her kiss, her touches, and seen it in the soft light in her eyes whenever she looked at him. He'd kept waiting for her to say the word, or, at least, tell him that he was the one and only man she'd ever want in her life. But she hadn't spoken any of those things.

Had he wanted to hear them? Oh, yes, his heart had

needed to hear that she loved him. That she would always be at his side. Not here one day and gone tomorrow.

Swallowing the thick lump in his throat, Drew gently patted Dillon's cheek. "I wouldn't worry about your three friends at school. If they laugh, just ignore them. They don't understand about you or Josselyn."

"But it makes me mad, Dad. Especially at Oliver. I'd like to jump on him and pound him real good. That would shut his big mouth."

Drew's head swung back and forth. "No fighting, Dillon. That would only get you in trouble with the school principal and with me. Besides, you'd feel awful if you gave Oliver a black eye."

That thought planted a wide grin on Dillon's face. "You really think I could?"

Drew wanted to groan and laugh at the same time. He wasn't about to admit that at Dillon's age he'd gotten in trouble for fighting in the school yard. "Probably. But you're not going to try it. In time Oliver will see that he's wrong."

"Yeah. When he sees Josselyn is really going to be my mom. That'll shut his trap up real good."

This would probably be the best time for Drew to explain to Dillon about love and marriage, he thought. And how it takes time for a couple to figure out if they want to be together for the rest of their lives. He could remind Dillon that a kid can't just choose the mother he wants and expect everyone to magically be happy. But for tonight, he couldn't bring himself to burst Dillon's bubble. Tonight Drew was going to let the boy believe that Josselyn might truly become his mother.

He patted Dillon's cheek again, then straightened to his full height. "You'd better run along now and tell Robbie that you get to sleep over. He's probably out on the stairs waiting for you to show up."

Dillon wrapped his arms around Drew's legs and hugged him tight. "Thanks, Dad."

Josselyn stepped back and studied the little table in her kitchen. Flowers, candles and her best blue-and-white-patterned china were ready and waiting for the meal of pot roast simmering in the oven. The table looked pretty, the cooking food was filling the cabin with delicious aromas, and the soft music playing in the background was the sort that made a girl want to lay her head on her man's shoulder and dance until dawn.

Satisfied that the kitchen was ready for Drew's arrival, she walked into the bedroom and stood before the cheval mirror. The oyster-colored blouse with ruffles at the low neckline gave her skin an iridescent glow, while the green skirt swishing around her calves was flattering without looking overly dressed for an evening at home.

Leaning closer to the mirror, she touched a hand to the hair she'd swept into a messy bun behind one ear. Her hand was trembling slightly and she realized she was nervous about Drew's arrival. Which didn't make sense. From the moment he'd called this morning to say he'd be out to see her tonight, she'd been eagerly waiting for this time to come and anxiously on edge to make their evening together extra special. To show him that they belonged together not for just a few weeks or even a few months, but forever.

His knock suddenly pulled her out of her reverie and she whirled away from the mirror to hurry out to the living room.

When she opened the door and saw him standing on

the threshold, she didn't hesitate. She threw herself into his arms and pressed kisses on both cheeks.

"My, my! What a greeting." He rubbed the tip of his nose to hers. "I should've gotten here sooner."

Laughing, she tugged him into the house and locked the door behind them. "Your timing is perfect," she told him. "Dinner is ready to take out of the oven."

"When you said you'd be cooking I decided to bring wine. It's red." He held up a bottle. "I hope it goes with our meal."

"How thoughtful. You couldn't have chosen better." Looping her arm through his, she urged him toward the kitchen. "Come on. While I take everything from the oven, you can tell me about your day."

While she transferred the pot roast and trimmings onto a serving platter, he placed the wine on the table and collected two long-stemmed glasses from the cabinet.

"My day was good. Just long," he said as he uncorked the wine and tilted the bottle over each glass. "I had three new patients come in today. All of them in the early stages of pregnancy. You know, Josselyn, I'm beginning to think there is something in the water around here. I've never seen so many pregnant women—even in Thunder Canyon, where the population is far larger."

Smiling at his observation, she carried the food over to the table. "I told you—Rust Creek Falls is a magical place."

His short laugh was full of amusement. "Magical, huh? Nadine, one of my nurses, told me the story about Homer Gilmore spiking the wedding punch and the baby boom nine months later. You don't need magic to pour a bottle of spirits into a punch bowl," he said, then his eyes widened with sudden speculation. "Say, you were standing near the punch bowl at the school picnic when Dillon and I came up. Do you suppose someone had spiked it?"

Josselyn laughed. "Drew, think about it. You didn't drink any punch that day."

Clearly disappointed that his theory couldn't be the answer, he said, "You're right. I didn't. Did you?"

"Two cups of it."

Grinning, he snapped his fingers. "That's it! The punch put some kind of spell on you."

She shot him a quizzical glance. "Spell? Why do you say that? Was I behaving strangely or something?"

"No. But there was some sort of aura around you." Snaking an arm around her waist, he pulled her against him. "It made me want to take you in my arms and do this."

Before she could ask him to explain *this*, he promptly showed her by planting his lips over hers.

His kiss never failed to send her senses into orbit. Without even realizing it, she leaned into him and gripped the front of his shirt while her head spun with pleasure.

When he finally eased his mouth from hers, she said, "Mmm. I would've never guessed you had that on your mind."

"I didn't know I had it on my mind, either. Until later."

With a husky chuckle, she eased out of the circle of his arm. "You can show me what else you had on your mind—later," she told him. "Otherwise, my meal is going to get cold and ruined."

"And we can't have that," he said. "Especially when I'm starving. Shall I light the candles for us?"

"Yes, thank you, Dr. Strickland."

While he put a match to the two tall candles, Josselyn pulled a bowl of tossed salad from the refrigerator and placed it on the table with the rest of the food.

"Thank you, Drew."

His gaze locked on hers. "Thank you, Josselyn. For the meal and so many other things."

He was looking at her as though she was something very, very special. As though she was the love of his life. Or was she misinterpreting the tender glow in his eyes?

Don't start questioning his every look or touch, Josselyn. He's here with you now. Make that be enough.

Deciding the voice in her head was giving her the right advice, she shoved the question out of her mind and reached for the platter of food. Offering it to him, she said, "Let's eat. Or the roast really is going to get cold."

"I'm impressed, Josselyn," Drew said after he'd swallowed the last bite of blueberry pie on his plate. "Everything was delicious."

"Thanks, but I have a confession to make." Rising from her chair, she began to gather the leftovers on the table. "I stopped by Daisy's Donut Shop on my way home and picked up one of Eva's pies. No matter how hard I tried, I couldn't top her desserts."

He wagged a forefinger at her. "Naughty girl. That's a punishable crime."

Laughing, she carried the armful of dishes over to the sink. "I had no idea a trip to the bakery was illegal. What's the punishment?"

He slipped up behind her and wrapped his arms around her waist. Nuzzling his nose against the side of her neck, he murmured, "You have to go to bed early."

"Without any TV? Oh, you're really being cruel," she teased, her voice growing huskier with each word that passed her lips.

Placing his hands on her shoulders, he turned her toward him, then slanted his lips over hers. She immediately opened her mouth to invite him inside as she slipped her arms around his neck and pressed the juncture of her thighs to the bulge she now felt beneath the fly of his jeans.

Lifting his head, he looked down to see desire was already fogging her green eyes. "Let's forget about the dishes," he suggested. "We'll do them later. Much later."

She didn't protest as he lifted her into in his arms and, pausing only to blow out the candles, carried her straight to the bedroom.

A tiny night-light was burning in one corner of the room, and this time he could see the small space was neat, with everything in its place. Even the bedclothes were perfectly turned back, as though she'd been sure the two of them would end up sliding beneath them.

At the side of the bed, he swiftly removed her clothing before dealing with his own. Once their garments were lying in a heap on the floor, he laid her on the bed, then stretched out beside her.

When she rolled toward him, he gathered her close and allowed his hands to go on a slow, meandering exploration of her soft curves.

"I've been thinking about this for days, Josselyn. Wanting you. Needing to be inside you," he whispered against her lips.

She said nothing. Instead, she kissed him deeply, her arm tight around his rib cage, her legs wound through his.

The hungry contact of their lips went on and on until

they were finally forced to break for air. While they both restored their lungs with oxygen, she tilted her head back far enough to look into his eyes. By then, Drew figured she could read everything that was going through his mind and his heart. It was a vulnerable feeling, but he was determined not to shy away from it, or the incredible emotions she was evoking from deep within him.

"And this is everything that I've been needing, Drew," she said, her voice thick with desire. "I want you so much. So very much."

For the moment that was all Drew needed to hear. Cradling her face between his hands, he kissed her once more, and with their lips latched together, she rolled to her back and tugged him along with her.

Anchoring his hands on either side of her head, he positioned himself over her. Then, poised and ready, he looked down at her flushed face and the blond waves spilled upon the pillow.

"Oh, Josselyn. Sweetheart. I can't tell you how I feel. It's all too jumbled up inside me. It's all too good. Too precious to describe."

Her head moved slightly back and forth. "You don't have to tell me anything. Just make love to me, Drew. Now. This very second."

Fighting to hold on to his self-restraint, he parted her thighs and entered her with a gentleness that belied the hot desire raging inside him. But as her warm softness enveloped him, his control vanished in a flare of white-hot flames.

The next thing he knew he was driving into her at a frantic pace and she was meeting his every thrust, grinding her hips closer, even as her lips were making a hot foray across his chest and over his flat male nipples.

Too good. Too utterly perfect.

The thoughts were rushing through his head as he felt his body begin the arduous climb to the summit. And though he wanted to pause and catch his breath, to linger along the path and allow his hands and mouth to enjoy the pleasures of her sweet flesh, he couldn't stop the hike to that spot where release awaited him.

It arrived with a sudden burst of stars streaking behind his eyes, while the rest of his body felt as though it was melting and pouring into hers, leaving nothing behind but his beating heart.

Grabbing her shoulders, he gripped her tight against him, and in the back of his spinning senses he registered her soft cry of release.

"Josselyn. My sweet darling."

The words barely had time to slip out of him before she tugged his head down to hers and met his lips.

The kiss was like dessert after a rich feast, and he allowed his lips to linger against hers until the need for oxygen caused him to lift his head and roll to one side of her.

For long moments they lay quietly together, both of them waiting for their breathing to return to normal before either tried to speak.

Finally, Josselyn pillowed her face against his shoulder and slipped her arm across his chest. Drew somehow found the strength to stroke her damp temple and tangled hair.

"Are you ready to wash dishes?" he asked.

She made a grunt of amusement, then snuggled closer to his side. "I'll have plenty of time to do them after you go home. Right now I don't want you to move."

He reached for the sheet and blanket wadded at

their feet and pulled it over them. "I have a surprise for you. I don't have to go home tonight. Dillon is having a sleepover with Robbie. Seems Mary wanted to treat the boys tonight."

Her head reared back as she stared at him, her expression a mixture of awe and delight. "You mean you're going to stay here all night? You're going to have breakfast with me?"

She sounded like a kid opening a Christmas present and the idea humbled him greatly. It took so little to please her, he thought. So little to put that precious smile on her face. The one that filled his heart with warmth and joy.

"That's my plan. Except that breakfast will have to be fairly early. I want to be back at the boardinghouse before Dillon gets up. It might be hard to explain to him that his father has been away all night."

"No problem. I'll wake you up long before sunrise," she promised.

Grinning at the joy on her face, he rubbed his cheek against hers. "I'm sure you will. Or even before," he added coyly.

She chuckled sexily and then her expression took a serious turn. "So does Dillon know you're seeing me tonight?"

Drew sighed. "He does. And he couldn't wait to shoo me out the door. Before I left the boardinghouse this evening we—uh—had a little talk. Seems his friends at school have been teasing him about you."

"Me?" She sat straight up in the bed. "Why me?"

Drew grimaced. "I hadn't planned on telling you. But now…well, I think you deserve to know."

"Know what? If Dillon's friends are saying that I

give him special attention during library visits, then they're wrong. I try to equal my time out between all the children."

Shaking his head, Drew reached over and traced a finger up and down the side of her arm. "It's not that. Dillon has told them that you're going to be his mother. And they've been laughing at him about it."

"Oh, no."

"Oh, yes."

She wiped a hand over her face, then turned a resigned look on him. "I've realized for a long time that Dillon wants a mother. It's not like he tries to hide the fact. Or that he hasn't made it clear that he has his sights set on me. But I never thought he'd be telling his friends about any of this."

"I didn't, either. I thought it was something he only talked about to you and me. When he told me they were laughing at him, it was like a knife stabbed me right in my chest, Josselyn. I think—" Pausing, he shook his head. "I've always loved my son. I just didn't realize how much I loved him until I met you."

"Oh, Drew." Tears filled her eyes as she touched his cheek. "How can that be?"

"I was dead before you, Josselyn. That's the only way I can explain it."

Easing back down, she draped the top half of her body over his torso and rested her chin in the middle of his chest. Drew found himself looking into the depths of her eyes and his heart squeezed as tears pooled in the green orbs and threatened to spill onto her cheeks.

"You can't possibly know how I feel about you," she whispered, her voice choked with emotion. "And Dillon."

Fear of his feelings and the future, their future, was

suddenly trying to swallow him up. Tonight she was here in his arms, warm and giving. But what about tomorrow? What if all of this hope and happiness was suddenly jerked away?

Oh Lord, he couldn't think about that now. He couldn't cower away from all that she was trying to give him.

"Maybe you should tell me, Josselyn."

Chapter Twelve

His hand was on her back, tracing warm circles up and down her spine and across her shoulder blades. How could his touch be exciting and soothing at the same time? It didn't make sense. But then, falling in love in a matter of a few short weeks didn't make a whole lot of sense, either, Josselyn decided. Yet somehow it had happened.

After a long, charged moment passed without her uttering a word, he said, "You don't have to tell me, Josselyn. Not if you don't want to."

She pushed her fingers into his hair, loving the feel of it.

"I do want to." She drew in a long breath and blew it out. "I'm beginning to think of Dillon as my own little boy—my own son. And you—" She stopped long enough to press a kiss to the corner of his lips. "You've settled yourself right smack in the middle of my heart. I love you, Drew."

He stared at her, his expression mainly one of stunned fascination. "That's what Dillon told me. But I took his words as a child's wish."

A wan smile curved her lips. "Apparently Dillon is more observant than you are."

His gaze broke from hers and Josselyn could see he was having a hard time dealing with the confession of her feelings.

"We haven't been together all that long," he reasoned.

"Long enough."

His gaze returned to hers and hope fastened itself to every beat of her heart as she waited breathlessly for him to reply.

"Long enough to be sure about me?" he asked. "About being the mother of a precocious seven-year-old boy?"

Although she hadn't been sure what he was about to say, his questions brought her a huge sigh of relief.

"I'm very sure." She scooted forward, until her lips were planting a row of kisses along his jaw. "You talked about me making you happy, Drew. But you need to know you've done the same for me, and more."

"I don't deserve you, Josselyn. I don't deserve any of this. But I'm going to take it. Every special moment we have together."

Groaning, he rolled her onto her side, and with his mouth warm and searching on hers, he gathered her tight against him.

Josselyn wasn't expecting him to want her again so soon. But he did, and in a matter of moments he was slipping back inside of her, filling her with mindless pleasure.

The morning sky was bright and clear, the way a Montana sky always looked after a night of fast-moving thunderstorms. The sight cheered Drew as he left the breakfast table and headed to the bathroom. He wouldn't have to make a dash to the clinic through a downpour and bolts of lightning.

He was brushing his teeth when, above the sound of the running water, he heard the telephone on the night-stand ring. Damn! The landline never rang unless it was an emergency. And it was his morning to drive Dillon to day care.

Reaching for a towel to wipe his mouth, he spotted Evelyn standing in the doorway of the bathroom.

Yes, the call was an emergency. Drew was needed right away. Don't worry, she told him. She was already dressed and ready to go. She would drive Dillon and he could hurry on to work.

No, he protested. She shouldn't have to sacrifice her time just because he had an emergency.

Smiling smugly, she waggled her fingers at him, then disappeared from the doorway. Drew hurried after her, but she was already headed down the front steps with Dillon in her arms.

See you at dinner, she called cheerfully back at him.

He blew her a kiss, then hurried inside for his jacket and car keys.

At the clinic he found his patient had gone into early labor. He ordered the nurse to start drugs to stop the contractions. Was it too late to help her?

The patient suddenly morphed into Evelyn and he stood beside the gurney, staring at her in frantic disbe-lief. No. This woman wasn't his wife. Dillon had been safely born a year ago. At this very moment, she was taking him to day care.

Then Drew moved away from the clinic, and suddenly he found himself running down a residential street. A half block ahead, at a four-way intersection, a swarm of emergency vehicles and onlookers were blocking the street.

He was a doctor. If someone was injured he might be able to help. He picked up his pace until he reached the chaotic scene, then, panting from the frantic run, he plowed his way through the onlookers until he was standing next to a car partially obscured by a fallen oak. The enormous trunk had crushed the hood and wind-shield, and to his horror, a woman was inside.

He heard someone say the baby was okay, but the woman wasn't so lucky. Was it Evelyn? His wife? Wild with fear, he watched the EMT pull the lifeless body from the wreckage. And then the panic of the moment hit him like a baseball bat to the face.

The woman wasn't Evelyn. It was Josselyn!

"Drew! Drew, wake up! You're having a bad dream."

It took several long moments for him to shake himself away from the clutches of the nightmare, and even then the aftershocks were still reverberating through him.

Eventually he recognized Josselyn's hand was on his shoulder, and she was studying him with great concern.

Relief poured through him. She wasn't gone. The tree hadn't taken her. It had only been a dream. He was here in Josselyn's bed and both of them were warm and safe.

Safe. Like a mocking laugh, the word pierced him and he sat straight up and threw back the tangled covers.

"You were having a nightmare, Drew," Josselyn repeated. "Are you okay?"

No. For as long as he lived, he didn't think he'd ever be okay. Evelyn's death was never going to let him go. Wherever he went it followed him. Even to Josselyn's bed.

"No. I'm not okay! I never will be!"

He scooted to the edge of the mattress and grabbed up his clothing. Scrambling off the mattress, Josselyn stood in front of him and latched her fingers around his arm.

"Drew, please talk to me about this. You were thrashing around like demons were on your heels."

"Demons are always on my heels, Josselyn. Sometimes I'm able to pretend they're not there. But no matter how hard I pretend, they come after me."

Seeing he was in no mood to return to bed just now, she reached for her robe. "I'll go make us some coffee."

"No. No coffee." He stood and swiftly pulled on his jeans. As he snapped his shirt over his chest, he said, "I have to leave, Josselyn."

He dared to glance at her, then winced at what he saw. She looked like he'd just thrown a bucket of ice water in her face.

"Leave? But, Drew, you were planning to stay the night!"

"I was planning on doing lots of things. But I was a fool."

Her wounded gaze caught his and at that moment Drew hated himself for being so weak. And hated fate for dealing him a hand he couldn't discard. Hurting Josselyn was the last thing he wanted to do. But if he didn't leave now, he'd only hurt her worse later.

"Drew, I don't understand. Please tell me what's wrong," she implored.

His jaw set, he jerked on his boots and started out of the bedroom. "That wouldn't fix anything."

She followed him to the door and Drew could hardly bear to look at her face. The sight of her lifeless body in his nightmare was still haunting him, reminding him that no man could control his destiny.

"You're wrong to leave, Drew," she said softly. "So wrong."

The pleading look in her eyes made him feel lower than a bug crawling on the floor. "Don't look at me like that, Josselyn. I'm not the man you think I am. I'm not some sort of hero that saves the lives of women and babies. I'm no good. I can't ever be what you want me to be. I can't even be a good father!"

He stormed out the door and hurried to his car. Thankfully, Josselyn didn't try to follow and stop him. And as he drove back to the boardinghouse, he knew full well he'd just ended the best thing that had ever happened to him.

Josselyn wasn't sure when or how she'd finally fallen asleep after Drew rushed out of the cabin. When she awoke, the sun was already shining brightly and she stared groggily at the golden rays slanting through the bedroom window.

How could the sky look so beautiful when she was so full of pain? Was everything over between them? Just like that?

Nothing made sense about his behavior last night, she thought as she pressed fingertips to her aching temples. Everyone suffered a nightmare from time to time, and she'd be the first to admit it was an unpleasant experience. But Drew had acted as though he'd just learned the world was coming to an end. And the worst part of the whole incident had been his refusal to talk with her about the dream, or his feelings.

Josselyn had exposed her heart by telling him she loved him. Yet he couldn't even tell her about his nightmare. What kind of fool was she for believing such a one-sided relationship between them could ever work?

A lovesick fool, she thought ruefully. Even so, she was determined not to give up on the man.

I'm no good. I can't even be a good father.

She didn't understand why he would think such things about himself. Even if he had allowed his parents to take over Dillon's day-to-day care after Evelyn's death, that didn't make him a bad parent. The way Josselyn saw the situation, he'd been smart enough to realize that he'd needed help raising a baby and he hadn't been too proud to ask for it. In her opinion that was being a much better father than being stubbornly independent and allowing his child to suffer because of it. But apparently Drew didn't see himself as a good father. He didn't view himself as a man worthy of having a family. Somehow, someway, she had to make him see he was wrong.

An hour later, after she'd showered and dressed, Josselyn picked up the phone and rang Drew's cell number. After it went straight to his voice mail, she punched the number again, hoping against hope he'd answer. But when the second try produced the same result, she had to accept that he'd turned off his phone. Most likely to avoid talking with her.

Out in the kitchen she was faced with the dinner mess they'd left stacked in the sink and on the cabinet. The two of them had been so eager to make love they'd only taken time to blow out the candles on the table.

Biting back a sigh, Josselyn filled the sink with soapy water and began to wash the crusty dishes. Yet with each piece she scrubbed, images of Drew and their night together—before the nightmare—paraded in front of her misty eyes.

He hadn't said the words *I love you*. But she'd been certain she'd felt it in his kiss and the way he'd touched her. She'd fallen asleep in his arms believing he wanted to be with her for a lifetime. She had to keep believing that now.

Monday morning, when the second graders entered the library and Dillon headed straight in her direction, Josselyn made sure she put on her cheeriest face, even though the child looked as glum as a cold, rainy day.

"Hi, Miss Weaver. Here are my books. I finished all of them." He placed the stack of books he'd taken home with him for the weekend on the corner of her desk.

Wishing she could gather him in a tight hug, Josselyn compensated by giving him another smile. "That's great, Dillon. I'm very proud of you. You know, the more you read the smarter you'll get."

"Yeah. I guess so," he mumbled.

Without saying more, the boy ambled away from her desk, and the uncharacteristic behavior had Josselyn staring thoughtfully after him.

What was wrong? Had Drew told the child that the chances of her becoming his mother were slim to none? Oh God, surely he wouldn't do something so hurtful.

She started to go after him, but was suddenly bombarded with several more students either asking for her help or returning books. It took several minutes to deal with the children, but Josselyn finally found a break to look for Dillon.

Since fishing was his favorite subject, she thought she'd find him in the sports section. Instead, she was taken aback to find him in the back of the room, standing at the window staring out at the playground. He looked so forlorn Josselyn wanted to gather him in her arms.

"Dillon? Why aren't you looking for a book to read? Library break will be over soon and you won't have any books to take home with you."

"That's all right. I don't want to read now."

Then why had he come to the library? Even though the question was on Josselyn's mind, she kept it to herself.

"Are you feeling okay, Dillon? If not, we might need for your father to come pick you up and take you home."

He frowned. "Dad is at work. He wouldn't come. But I'm not sick anyway."

"Well, if you're not sick then something must be bothering you," she said gently. "Would you like to tell me about it?"

He turned away from the window, then, his eyes cast downward, he scuffed his toe against the hardwood floor. "I've been wondering, Josselyn—I mean, Miss Weaver—did you and Dad have a fight or something? He's been acting really weird."

Weird. That couldn't even begin to describe the way Josselyn had been feeling since Drew had rushed out of her cabin. Two full days and nights had passed since then and she still hadn't heard a word from him. She'd been telling herself that he needed time and space. That after he'd had a chance to think things through, he'd call and say he was ready to see her again. But just how much time and space was he going to need? She was beginning to wonder.

"No. We didn't have a fight, Dillon. What makes you think so?"

"'Cause Dad is acting like he used to. Before he

started dating you. He's back to his old grouchy self. Are you sure you didn't get mad at him?"

Not for anything did Josselyn want little Dillon to get caught in the problems she and Drew were having, so she measured her next words carefully. And though she didn't fib to the child, she did avoid elaborating. "No. I'm not mad. And we didn't have a fight. I think your father is a great guy."

Dillon looked even more perplexed. "Gee, then I don't understand. Why is Dad acting so bad?"

Josselyn's heart was breaking. Not just for herself but also for Dillon. "I'm not sure, Dillon. It could be your father is just working very hard and he's thinking about his patients. He'll get in a better mood soon."

"He might get happier if you would come see him," Dillon suggested.

Well, there wasn't anyone saying Josselyn couldn't go to the boardinghouse and force Drew to see her. But she was hoping it wouldn't come to that. She wanted him to come to her of his own volition.

"I might just do that." She gave Dillon a bright smile to cover up the sadness weighing on her heart. "Now let's go see if we can find a fun book for you to read. I have a new one about a frog who's afraid to jump off his lily pad."

Momentarily forgetting his worries, Dillon asked, "Why is the frog afraid?"

Josselyn took him by the hand and led him away from the window. "Come along and I'll show you."

Later that evening, Josselyn decided to go by Daisy's Donut Shop and have a cup of coffee. Anything would be better than sitting alone in her cabin, wondering if Drew would call or show up.

The bakery was busy, with most of the tables taken. After Josselyn had gotten her order of coffee and an apple fritter, she stood at the edge of the room trying to spot a place to sit. She was about to decide to take her food and drink outside to a bench on the sidewalk when she caught sight of a dark-haired woman waving at her.

Recognizing Caroline Ruth, the wedding-planner assistant, Josselyn made her way across the room to where the young woman was sitting alone at a table for two.

Smiling warmly, Caroline gestured toward the empty seat. "Hi, Josselyn. I was just thinking it would be nice to have a little company and then I spotted you."

Josselyn placed her coffee and fritter on the table and eased into the chair. "And I was standing there thinking it was going to be hopeless to find a place to sit. Thanks for letting me join you."

"My pleasure. You can tell me not to worry about all the calories I'm consuming by eating this piece of cherry pie."

Josselyn forced herself to chuckle, while thinking she was becoming a damned good actress. Any woman who could laugh while tears were flowing inside of her ought to win an Oscar.

"I think we're both in trouble with the calorie count," Josselyn said as she unwrapped the wax paper from her fritter. "But a visit to Daisy's Donut Shop is to be enjoyed. And it's very nice to see you again, Caroline. How's the wedding planning going? Have you and Vivienne been busy?"

"Extremely busy. There really must be something to Rust Creek Falls being the place to fall in love. The weddings seem to be endless. Which is good for me, I suppose. As long as Viv needs help, I have a job."

I'm beginning to think there is something in the water around here. I've never seen so many pregnant women.

Drew's remark that night in the cabin suddenly came back to haunt her. So many times she'd dreamed of being pregnant with Drew's child and giving him a son or daughter to join Dillon. And that night, she'd hoped he might bring up the subject of the two of them having children together. But that never happened.

Josselyn forced herself back to the conversation. "That's nice," she told Caroline, unaware that her voice sounded half-dead. "You have job security and couples are hearing happy wedding bells."

Caroline looked at her. "So how are things going for you? The last time we ran into each other here at Daisy's I forgot to ask if you'd found something sexy at Gilda's to wear for the doctor."

So much had happened since she and Drew had dined at the hotel in Kalispell that it felt like months had passed rather than weeks. "I found something to wear. Whether it was sexy, I couldn't tell you," Josselyn told her. "I never was exactly a femme fatale. Librarians usually aren't."

Caroline laughed. "Oh, Josselyn, you're so funny."

"Really? Wonder why I don't feel like laughing."

The other woman cast her a sober look. "I'm sorry. Is something wrong?"

Straightening her shoulders, Josselyn reached for her coffee. "No. I'm fine," she lied, then asked, "Caroline, did you ever find yourself hanging on to a lost cause?"

The other woman shrugged one shoulder. "If you believe in something strongly enough to hold on, then it's not really a lost cause, is it?"

The woman's philosophy was the perfect balm for Josselyn's wounded spirits. "Thank you, Caroline. That's exactly what I needed to hear this evening. How did you know?"

"Oh, it's just breathing the Rust Creek Falls air, I suppose," she joked, then leaned slightly toward Josselyn. "Tell me about the new tenant out at Sunshine Farm. I've heard he's a real hunk. And single, too."

Smiling wanly, Josselyn shook her head. "You must be talking about Brendan Tanner. I only know what Eva told me. Supposedly he was in the military, but he must be finished with that. Eva and Luke say he's a horseman. I guess with all the ranches around here, he might be thinking about going into the horse business. Eva says he keeps to himself and doesn't talk much, so he's sort of a mystery man around Sunshine Farm."

"Oh, a loner," Caroline said slyly. "Now, there's a challenge for any woman."

How well she knew that, Josselyn thought ruefully. Drew was still wanting to hide from her and from life.

"Are you interested?"

It took Josselyn a moment to realize where Caroline's question was headed. "You mean in Brendan Tanner?"

Caroline nodded.

"Not at all. He's good-looking. At least, what I've seen of him from my kitchen window. But he's not my type."

Caroline grinned as she scooped up the last bite of pie. "That's right. I'm forgetting you like your men in a lab coat."

Josselyn's short laugh held little mirth. "Drew is the only doctor I've ever dated."

And if she had anything to say about it, he was definitely going to be the last.

The next morning, while he waited on Dillon to get ready for school, Drew went through the motions of having toast and coffee in the kitchen. But for all he knew Claire might have served him cardboard spread with jam and he wouldn't have known the difference.

"Drew, I'm sorry, but you've really got to do something about that frown on your face. You're going to have a permanent crease in the middle of your forehead."

He glanced over at Claire, who was standing at the counter doing something to a raw chicken. Why she needed to start cooking dinner this early in the morning he didn't know. But then, Drew had to admit he didn't know much about anything anymore. Especially where Josselyn was concerned.

To think that he'd hurt her, that he was still hurting her by staying away, was literally killing him. She deserved so much better than what he could give her.

"It's a concentration line," Drew told his cousin. "All doctors have them."

"You mean all the good ones?" Claire tossed the question over her shoulder.

Drew stared moodily into his coffee cup. "Don't put me in that category, Claire. I manage to take care of my patients, but I should do better."

"If you did any better, you'd be dead from exhaustion." She walked over to him. "Okay, maybe you should fess up and tell me what's wrong. You haven't been acting yourself lately. Everyone has noticed it. Especially

Dillon. He's been staying here in the kitchen just to avoid you, I think. Did something bad happen at work, or is this about Josselyn?"

"I don't want to talk about Josselyn," he said bluntly. "She's out of the picture."

Rather than looking surprised, Claire grimaced with disgust. "So you're copping out on the best thing that could have happened to you. I should've known. Guess she was making you too happy. And you can't stand that, can you?"

Claire turned back to the chicken on the counter. Drew stared at her in stunned disbelief. It wasn't like his cousin to be so harsh. She was usually the first one to offer him compassion and understanding.

"What's the matter with you?" he asked sharply. "Is it a crime not to smile and laugh all the time?"

"Oh please, Drew. Don't make me start. My patience is too thin for your nonsense. I had hope for you. But it's gone. Totally gone."

Nonsense? She wanted to call his problem nonsense? He'd been through pure hell. He was still going through it.

At that moment, Melba entered the room and made a beeline for the gas range. "What's gone?" the older woman asked.

"Nothing," Claire quickly told her. "I was only saying our good weather will soon be gone."

Spotting Drew at the table, Melba paused to cast him a puzzled glance. "What are you doing here?"

To hell with this, Drew thought crossly. "I live here, Grandma. Surely you haven't forgotten that."

Angered by his tart retort, Melba marched over to the table and leveled a glare at him. "I might be getting older, but I'm not *that* forgetful, smarty britches. I'm talking about here at this moment. I saw Dillon earlier, leaving the house through the front entrance."

"Leaving the house? Why?"

"He said he was going to wait outside on the porch for you. That was fifteen or twenty minutes ago."

"Damn!"

Drew anxiously jumped to his feet and started out of the room, only to have Melba calling after him.

"What's wrong? Where are you going?"

"To take care of my son. That's where!"

Drew practically ran to the front of the building and jerked open the door to the main entrance. But a quick glance outside told him Dillon was nowhere to be seen.

Fearful that his son might've wandered off down the street on his own, Drew turned and took the stairs up two at a time. Once he reached the connecting rooms they called home, Drew yelled out, "Dillon! Are you in here?"

He hurried through the bedrooms and found no sign of the boy. It wasn't until he returned to the sitting room that he spotted a piece of paper on an end table next to the couch.

Recognizing Dillon's large print, he snatched up the small square and read: *Dear Dad, I'm sorry I've made you sad. I think it would be a lot better for you if I went back to Thunder Canyon and stayed with Grandma and Grandpa Jerry. They like me to be on the ranch. And then you and Josselyn could be happy.*

Oh God, what had he done, Drew asked himself. He'd not only ruined everything with Josselyn, he'd also driven his son away.

Tossing down the note, he snatched his phone out of his pocket and quickly dialed Josselyn's number.

Chapter Thirteen

She answered on the second ring and the sound of her sweet voice was like church bells on a cold, clear morning. It touched his heart in a way that very nearly brought tears to his eyes.

"Josselyn, I'm sorry to bother you like this, but I'm worried about Dillon. Have you seen him this morning?"

There was a long pause and then she said, "No. His class doesn't come to the library until the midmorning break."

"Oh. I thought he might have gone on to school without me—to see you before classes started."

"Drew, is something wrong with Dillon?"

Drew felt totally sick inside. Sick and guilty. And very much a huge, oblivious fool. "I hope there's nothing wrong. Could you do me a favor?"

She didn't hesitate. "Of course."

"Could you check and see if Dillon is at school? You see, he took off from the boardinghouse without telling me. I'm afraid he's run away!"

"Oh, Drew, no!" she exclaimed, then added in a rush,

"I'll go to his room right now to see if he's there. Just give me a minute or two and I'll call you back."

"Thank you, Josselyn. I'm grateful for your help."

"Sure."

Drew hung up the phone and after grabbing his keys and Dillon's note, hurried out the back entrance of the boardinghouse to his car. With any luck he might spot Dillon walking along the route they normally took to school.

If something happened to Dillon he'd never forgive himself. The child was everything to him. Everything!

Josselyn is everything to you, too. But you've ignored her. The same way you've been ignoring Dillon. You don't deserve either one of them, Drew. You don't deserve to be a father or husband. The only thing you're good at is feeling sorry for yourself.

The incriminating voice was still droning in his head as he gunned the car out of the parking lot and onto the street. But the dire thoughts were quickly interrupted by the ring of the cell phone he'd tossed onto the passenger seat.

Seeing the caller was Josselyn, he snatched up the phone and punched the accept button as fast as he could, while trying to keep a wave of panic from washing over him.

"Drew, good news," she quickly informed him. "Dillon is in his class safe and sound."

Weak with relief, he sent up a silent prayer of thanks.

"Thank God. He—uh—he doesn't know you were checking on him, does he?"

"No. I went into the room on the pretense that I needed to talk with the teacher."

"Thank you, Josselyn. I am very grateful and relieved."

"You're welcome, Drew. I'm happy I could help." A stretch of awkward silence followed and then she asked, "Uh—is there anything else you need?"

You. I need you, Josselyn. So very much.

The words were on the tip of his tongue, but he held them back. The phone wasn't how he wanted to say all the things he needed to say to her. No. That was going to be done in person. If she still cared enough to give him that chance.

"No. I—uh—have to hang up now. There's something I have to do. Goodbye, Josselyn."

He hung up before she could question him, then, patting his shirt pocket to make sure he still had Dillon's note, he hurried on to the school.

Josselyn stared at the book-order sheet on her desk, but none of the titles or story summaries were making sense.

What was she going to say to Dillon when he came into the library this morning? Should she ask him about leaving the boardinghouse without his father's permission? Should she scold him for walking to school alone?

No. She wasn't his mother. That was Drew's job. But the thought of him running away and putting himself in danger filled Josselyn with so much fear it was all she could do to keep her hands from shaking.

What had happened between yesterday and this morning? she wondered. Had Drew said something to the boy? Something that had caused the little guy so much pain that running away was the only way he could think to deal with it? Something like how Josselyn was never going to be his mother and he needed to forget the idea completely?

The pain in her chest was so great it caused tears to blur her eyes. Fearful that some of her coworkers might walk in and catch her crying, she grabbed a tissue from a box on the corner of her desk.

She was dabbing at the moisture when the sound of the library door swinging open caused her head to swing around and then her mouth to fall open.

Drew!

Feeling sure she was in some sort of trance, Josselyn slowly rose and walked toward him.

He met her in the middle of the room and all she could seem to do was stare at the endearing features of his face.

"What are you doing here?" she finally asked.

A wry slant to his lips, he said, "That's the second time I've been asked that this morning."

"What does that mean?"

"That I'm a hard guy to figure, I suppose."

He took a step closer and Josselyn realized her heart was pumping at the pace of a jackhammer. And every rapid beat was begging her to throw herself into his arms and hang on for dear life.

"That you are, Drew."

"I'm sure you're wondering how I managed to get past security."

"The question has crossed my mind." *That question plus about a hundred more*, she thought.

"I stopped by the office and thankfully the superintendent knows me. She gave me the permission to come back here to the library to see you." He reached inside his brown leather jacket and pulled out a piece of lined paper. "Read this."

Josselyn hastily read the words Dillon had carefully printed, and each one stabbed her in the middle of the chest.

"Oh, Drew. What was he thinking? Why?" She lifted her gaze back to his face. "Did you say something to him about me?"

His expression rueful, he shook his head. "I haven't said much to him at all. Not since I left your cabin Friday night."

"Oh. Well, I think you should know that he believes we had a big row. He's very upset about it."

His brows arched. "He told you that?"

"More or less," she said. "Why haven't you said something to him? He deserves to know that I'm no longer going to be in his life that way. That I'll only see him here at school."

The arch in his brows grew even higher. "That's how you want it to be?"

"That's how you want it." The tone of her voice was brittle, but she couldn't help it. He'd put her through the wringer and she wasn't going to let him off the hook easily.

"No. You're wrong, Josselyn. I want you in my life and in Dillon's life. I need you. He needs you."

His hands closed over her shoulders and Josselyn stumbled toward him. "What are you trying to say?"

"That I've been the biggest kind of fool. And it wasn't until I found Dillon's note that I truly recognized what was really important to me. It's not my work or my past life with Evelyn. All that matters is my love for you, Josselyn. And being the kind of father Dillon deserves."

Her head swung back and forth in disbelief. "Why couldn't you have told me this at the cabin? Do you have any idea what these past few days without you have been like?"

Remorse filled his brown eyes. "That night—I couldn't tell you anything. I was so shaken by what I'd dreamed—"

"That's just it, Drew," she interrupted. "It was only a dream. Not something to run from. Or to make you run from me."

Anguish twisted his features. "You don't understand, Josselyn. I was dreaming about Evelyn's accident. I was on foot, running down the street, trying to reach the crushed car and thinking I could save the driver. When I finally reached it, I realized Evelyn was inside. Then the EMT pulled her free of the wreckage and it wasn't Evelyn. It was you! The accident had taken you from me."

Her groan was full of anguish. "Oh Lord, Drew. If only you'd told me."

He sighed with regret. "Once I felt your hand on my shoulder I realized I'd been having a nightmare. I was so relieved that the horrible images hadn't been real. But then when I looked at you all the fear came rushing back."

She frowned. "I don't understand, Drew. Once you recognized it was all a dream, you should have been comforted."

"Yes, I should have. Instead, I felt the exact opposite. True, it was a dream. But all of a sudden I was struck by the fact that an accident really could happen to you. Just as it did Evelyn. And I knew I couldn't bear that, Josselyn. Not a second time. Not with you. I love you too much."

She stared at him in awe as disbelief and joy battled inside of her. "Love me? But—"

He urged her closer and the cold pain around Josselyn's heart began to melt as she watched his lips curve into a tender smile.

"After the way I've treated you that's probably hard for you to believe."

"Try impossible."

He wrapped his arms around her. "Oh, Josselyn, when I found Dillon's note, it was like somebody had given me a dose of smelling salts. All of a sudden I was wide-awake and it was pretty damned clear I was behaving like my seven-year-old son—running away. These past couple of days—no, make that weeks—I've been running scared, knowing I was falling in love with you. For so long my heart was closed. I wanted to protect it by never letting it feel again. But it's open now, sweetheart. Wide-open. And I'm asking you to step inside, to see for yourself how very much I love you."

Her heart wanted to make an ecstatic leap over the moon, but the lingering doubts in her mind held it back. "Drew, there's always the chance of accidents and illness. Are you going to start worrying again and—"

The shake of his head interrupted her argument. "Accidents and illness are a part of life. I know that. And I'd have to be inhuman not to worry about you and Dillon. But I've come to realize that I have to believe and trust, and accept all the happiness you'll bring me—for as long as that might be."

Tears of pure joy spilled onto her cheeks. "I love you, Drew."

Smiling, he pulled a handkerchief from his pocket

and dabbed away the moisture beneath her eyes. "Then you forgive me?"

"There's nothing to forgive, my darling."

With a sigh of pure contentment, he lowered his lips to hers and Josselyn wondered how a kiss could taste like rainbows and sunshine, full of promises and sealed with trust. But it did. Oh, yes, it did.

They were still locked in the gentle embrace when the bell rang and a group of giggling children rushed into the library and gathered around them.

"See!" A beaming Dillon exclaimed to his friends, "None of you would believe me, but I was right! I told you Miss Weaver loved my dad. And he loves her!"

Oliver and Owen looked at each other in comical disbelief, while Rory giggled and clapped a hand over her mouth.

"Wow, Dillon! Your dad is kissing Miss Weaver like a real prince kisses a princess!" Rory gushed, then sidled closer to Dillon. "When are you going to kiss me like that?"

A look of sheer horror came over Dillon's face before he turned and raced away from Rory and the troop of laughing kids.

"He's running now," Drew said with a chuckle, his arms still firmly planted around Josselyn. "But in a few years he'll be running right back to her. Like his dad has run back to the woman he loves. Will you marry me, Josselyn? Will you be Dillon's mother and give him brothers and sisters? And make our life complete?"

"Yes. Yes. And yes!"

"Did you hear that, children?" Drew's brown eyes twinkled with merriment as he looked at the ogling group of kids. "Miss Weaver has agreed to marry me. Dillon is going to get the mother he wants."

Standing in front of a shelf of fishing books, Dillon heard his father's announcement and grinned with happy satisfaction.

* * * * *

MILLS & BOON

Coming next month

CINDERELLA'S NEW YORK CHRISTMAS
Scarlet Wilson

Leo finished the call. New York. He'd wanted to go back there for days. But somehow he knew when he got there, the chances of getting a flight back to Mont Coeur to spend Christmas with his new family would get slimmer and slimmer.

Here, he'd had the benefit of a little time. Everything in New York was generally about work, even down to the Christmas charity ball he was obligated to attend. As soon as he returned to the States...

His stomach clenched. The Christmas ball. The place he always took a date.

For the first time, the prospect of consulting his little black book suddenly didn't seem so appealing.

'Nearly done.' Anissa smiled as he approached.

'I have to go back to New York.'

Her face fell. 'What?'

She was upset. He hated that. He hated that fleeting look of hurt in her eyes.

'It's business. A particularly tricky deal.'

Anissa pressed her lips tight together and nodded automatically.

The seed of an idea that had partially formed outside burst into full bloom in his head. He hated that flicker of pain he'd seen in her eyes when she'd talked about being in Mont Coeur and being permanently reminded of what she'd lost.

Maybe, just maybe he could change things for her. Put a little sparkle and hope back into her eyes. Something that he ached to feel in his life too.

'Come with me.' The words flew out of his mouth.

Her eyes widened. 'What?'

He nodded, as it all started to make sense in his head. 'You said you've never really had a proper holiday. Come with me. Come and see New York. You'll love it in winter. I can take you sightseeing.'

Anissa's mouth was open. 'But...my job. I have lessons booked. I have chalets to clean.'

He moved closer to her. 'Leave them. See if someone can cover. I have a Christmas ball to attend and I'd love it if you could come with me.' His hands ached to reach for her, but he held himself back. 'I called you Ice Princess before, how do you feel about being Cinderella?'

He could see her hesitation. See her worries.

But her pale blue eyes met his. There was still a little sparkle there. Still a little hope for him.

Her lips turned upwards. 'Okay,' she whispered back as he bent to kiss her.

Continue reading
CINDERELLA'S NEW YORK CHRISTMAS
Scarlet Wilson

Available next month
www.millsandboon.co.uk

COMING SOON!

We really hope you enjoyed reading this book. If you're looking for more romance, be sure to head to the shops when new books are available on

Thursday
6th September

LET'S TALK
Romance

For exclusive extracts, competitions
and special offers, find us online: